W9-AVJ-855

THE NEW DEAD

THE NEW DEAD

A ZOMBIE ANTHOLOGY
EDITED BY CHRISTOPHER GOLDEN

ST. MARTIN'S GRIFFIN
NEW YORK

THE NEW DEAD. Copyright © 2010 by Christopher Golden. All rights reserved. Printed in the United States of America. For information, address St. Martin's Press, 175 Fifth Avenue, New York, N.Y. 10010.

ISBN 978-1-61664-372-0

CONTENTS

CONTENTS

FOREWORD

I have never had any trouble understanding the fascination with vampires. Despite the myriad mythologies that have been invented over the past few decades, the thousand permutations created by authors hoping to present a fresh take on the material, the fundamentals have remained the same. Vampires are both beautiful and terrible (and aren't we always strangely attracted to people with both of those attributes?). The erotic nature of the vampire seduction is unmistakable—the biting, the bleeding, the penetration. And, of course, they live forever. Though we might think better of it once the consequences have been contemplated, who in the world has not wished for immortality, for the chance to cheat death?

But zombies? Not so much. Eating brains, my friends, is not sexy.

And yet in recent years the zombie story has become more and more popular and has evolved from the days of voodoo rituals into big business. The zombie's presence in modern pop culture can probably be attributed largely to George A. Romero, the filmmaker who brought the world *Night of the Living Dead* in 1968. An entire genre seemed to be born with that film, spreading through various media, most especially books and video games.

My good friend, the ever erudite Stephen R. Bissette (who graces us with a story in this volume), could give you a far more thorough history than I of the various elements that contributed to the development of the popular zombie story, not least of which is the biblical tale of Lazarus. What fascinates me, however, is the twenty-first-century surge in popularity that zombies have encountered.

We live in odd times. Strange days, indeed. Times of torture and deceit and celebrity and constant exposure to the worst the world has to offer, thanks to a media that never tires of feeding our hunger for the horrible.

My favorite work of zombie fiction ever is the poem "The March of the Dead" by Robert Service. In a way, it set the tone for this new anthology, though it was published long, long ago. Service wrote of the glorious homecoming of victorious soldiers, celebrated by the townspeople as they paraded through the streets . . . only to be followed by the ravaged, horrible, lumbering dead, the soldiers who did not survive the war.

When I set out to edit this anthology, I sought out a wide variety of perspectives on the modern fascination with zombies. I asked questions. Are we so inured to death that we now find it charming? Or— and this was my suspicion—do we embrace these ideas as an indirect way of processing the horror that we feel at the reality of war and torture and death? The films that have covered the war in Iraq, its foundations and its consequences, have by and large been ignored by audiences, and yet during the height of our horror at the developments there, horror films that dealt with parallel subject matter in a setting and genre divorced from reality were hugely successful.

Something to think about, at any rate.

Now, don't start thinking that what you're going to find within these pages will be war stories or political stories. There are military and political elements to a handful of the tales, but I cast the net much wider than that. What I wanted were, in no uncertain terms, tales of death and resurrection. If, in the process, we were able to examine various facets of pop culture's fascination with zombies, all the better.

That also doesn't mean that there are no traditional zombie stories in here. The beauty of having such a wide variety of contributors is that the tales run the gamut from modern warfare to postapocalyptic futures, from love stories to heartbreaking voodoo horrors, from the Bible to Twitter. Within these pages you will find humor and truly unsettling horror, you will find tales of great brevity, and others of epic sprawl. You will even find one—thanks to the inimitable Joe Lansdale—that answers my questions about death and resurrection in a manner different from all of the others, by eschewing the resurrection element altogether. Lansdale addresses the current zombie fascination with a stay that reminds us that dead is dead. And, interestingly enough, I think that one brings us back full circle to the question, and even back to the vampires.

Why are we fascinated by zombies? Perhaps because nothing is so terrifying as death come calling, in whatever form.

Here, then, *The New Dead*.

Christopher Golden
Bradford, Massachusetts
May 18, 2009

THE NEW DEAD

LAZARUS

BY JOHN CONNOLLY

I

He wakes in darkness, constricted by bonds. There is stone beneath him, and the air he breathes is rank and still. He seems to recall that he heard a voice calling his name, but the voice is calling no longer. He tries to get to his feet, but the bonds around him hinder his movements. There is no feeling in his legs. He cannot see, and he struggles to breathe through the cloth on his face. He begins to panic.

Insects buzz around him. There is a sensation of movement throughout his body, as of small things burrowing into his flesh, yet he feels no pain. His body is bloated with gas and fluids, the liquids forced from his cells and into his body cavity.

There is a sound, stone upon stone. Light breaks, and he shuts his eyes against it as it pierces the cloth. Now there are hands on him, and he is raised to his feet. Fingers gently remove the coverings. He feels tears upon his cheeks, but they are not his own. His sisters are kissing him and speaking his name.

"Lazarus! Lazarus!"

Yes, that is his name.

No, that is not his name.

It was once, but Lazarus is no more, or should be no more. Yet Lazarus is here.

There is a man standing before him, bearded, his robes covered in the dust of many miles. Lazarus recognizes him, beloved of his sisters, beloved of him, but he cannot speak his name. His vocal cords have atrophied in the tomb.

The tomb. He stares down as the last of the grave wrappings are torn from his body and a sheet is thrown over him to hide his nakedness. He looks behind him at the stone that had been removed from the mouth of the cave.

Sickness. He was ill. His sisters mopped his brow, and the physicians shook their heads. In time, they believed him to be dead, so they wrapped him in bandages and laid him in a cave. Yes, a mistake was made, but it has been rectified.

But this is a lie. He knows it even before the thought has fully formed itself. Something terrible has happened. Some great wrong has been committed in the name of pity and love. The one whom he recognized, the beloved, touches him and calls his name. Lazarus's lips move, but no sound comes forth.

What have you done? he tries to say. What have you taken from me, and from what have you taken me?

II

Lazarus sits at the window of his sisters' house, a plate of fruit untouched before him. He has no appetite, but neither can he taste any of the food that has been given to him in the days since his return. The maggots have been ripped from his flesh, and his body has begun to repair itself. He still struggles to walk, even with the aid of a pair of sticks, but where should he walk? This world holds no beauty for him, not in the aftermath of the tomb.

Lazarus does not remember what happened after his eyes closed for the last time. He knows only that he has forgotten something, something very important and beautiful and terrible. It is as though a roomful of memories has been sealed up, and what was once known to him is now forbidden. Or perhaps it is all merely an illusion, just as it seems to him that the world is obscured slightly by gauze, a consequence of the four days spent lying on the stone, for his eyes now have a milky cast to them and are no longer blue, but gray.

His sister Martha comes and takes the plate away. She brushes his hair from his forehead, but she no longer kisses him. His breath smells foul. He cannot taste the decay in his mouth, but he knows that it is there from the expression on her face. Martha smiles at him, and he tries to smile back.

Outside the window, women and children have gathered to gaze upon he who was once dead but is dead no longer. They are amazed and curious and—

Yes, fearful. They are afraid of him.

He leaves the window and staggers to his bed.

III

Lazarus can no longer sleep. He is terrified of the darkness. When he closes his eyes, he smells the air of the tomb and feels the bandages tight around his chest and the cloth blocking his mouth and nostrils.

But Lazarus is never tired. He is never hungry or thirsty. He is never happy or sad or angry or resentful. There is only lethargy and the desire for sleep without the necessity of it.

No, not sleep—oblivion. Oblivion and what lies beyond it.

IV

On the third night, he hears footsteps in the house. A door opens, and a woman appears. It is Rachel, his betrothed. She had been in Jerusalem when he woke, and now she is here. She runs her hands across his brow, his nose, his lips. She lies beside him and whispers his name, anxious not to wake his sisters. She kisses him and recoils at the taste of him. Still, her fingers move down over his chest, his belly, finding him at last, stroking, coaxing, her face slowly creasing in confusion and disappointment.

After a time, she leaves, and she never returns.

V

The priests summon Lazarus. He is brought before their council and made to stand below the dais of the high priest, Caiaphas. Lazarus's voice has returned, but it is an imperfect thing, as though his throat is coated with grit and dirt.

"What do you recall of the tomb?" they ask, and he replies, "Nothing but dust and darkness."

"In the four days that you lay dead, what did you see?"

And he replies, "I do not remember."

There is a murmur of disappointment, of distrust. They believe him to be lying. Voices are raised, questions falling like dead leaves upon his head. They are the priests, and they must know all that he knows.

Only Caiaphas is silent. He regards the young man before him, taking in the discoloration on his skin, the marks of putrefaction that have not yet disappeared. With a wave of his hand, Caiaphas dismisses the rest, so that only he and Lazarus remain. Caiaphas pours wine, but Lazarus does not drink from his cup.

"Tell me," says Caiaphas. "Now that the others have gone, tell me what you saw. Did you see the face of God? Does He exist? Tell me!"

But Lazarus has nothing to offer him, and eventually Caiaphas turns his back on him and tells him to return to his sisters.

It is not the first time that Lazarus has been asked such questions. Even his sisters have tried to find out what lies beyond the grave. But in response, he has been able only to shake his head and tell them what he told the priests:

Nothing. There is nothing, or nothing that I can remember.

But no one believes him. No one wants to believe him.

V I

Caiaphas calls another council, but this time Lazarus is not present.

"Is there no sign of the one who called him from the tomb?" he asks, and the Pharisees reply that the Nazarene has hidden himself away.

Caiaphas is displeased. With each day that goes by, he grows more resentful of Lazarus. The people are unhappy. They have heard that Lazarus can remember nothing of what he experienced after his death, and some have begun to whisper that there is nothing to remember, that perhaps the priests have lied to them.

Caiaphas will not have his power challenged. He orders the stoning of three men who were overheard discussing Lazarus in this manner. They will serve as an example to the others.

VII

Lazarus, lost in himself, seeking buried memories, burns his hand on hot stones as he heats water to bathe himself. He does not notice until he tries to remove his hand and instead leaves a patch of skin behind. There is no pain. Lazarus would find this curious, except Lazarus no longer finds anything curious. The world holds no interest for him. He cannot taste or smell. He does not sleep, and instead he experiences every day as a kind of waking dream. He stares at his raw, bleeding palm, then explores it with his fingers, tentatively at first, then finally tearing at the flesh, ripping it apart until the bones are exposed, desperate to feel anything, anything at all.

VIII

A woman asks Lazarus if he can contact her son, who died in his sleep two years before and with whom she had argued before he went to bed. A man asks him to tell his dead wife that he is sorry for cheating on her. The brother of a man lost at sea asks Lazarus to find out where his brother buried his gold.

Lazarus cannot help them.

And all the time, he is confronted by those who ask him what lies beyond. He cannot answer, and he sees the disappointment in their eyes and their belief that he is lying.

IX

Caiaphas is troubled. He sits in the darkness of the temple and prays for guidance, but no guidance comes.

In the case of Lazarus and the Nazarene, there are only so many possibilities that he can consider.

> i. The Nazarene is, as some whisper, the Son of God. But Caiaphas does not like the Nazarene. On the other hand, Caiaphas loves God. Therefore, if the Nazarene really is the Son of God, then Caiaphas should love him, too. Perhaps the fact that Caiaphas does not love the Nazarene means that the Nazarene is not, in fact, the Son of God, for if he were, then Caiaphas

5

would love him, too. Caiaphas decides that he is comfortable with this reasoning.

ii. If the Nazarene is not the Son of God, then he does not have the power to raise the dead.

iii. If the Nazarene does not have the power to raise the dead, then what of Lazarus? The only conclusion to be drawn is that Lazarus was not dead when he was placed in the tomb; but had he been left there, he most assuredly would be dead by now. Thus, Lazarus *should* be dead, and his continued refusal to accept this fact is an offence against nature and against God.

Caiaphas decides that he is no longer quite as troubled as before, and he goes to his bed.

X

Rachel is released from her obligations to Lazarus and marries another. Lazarus watches from an olive grove as the bride and groom arrive at the wedding feast. He sees Rachel and remembers the night that she came to him. He tries to understand how he should feel at this time and counterfeits envy, grief, lust, and loss, a pantomime of emotions watched only by birds and insects. After a time, he sits in the dirt and puts his head in his hands.

Slowly, he begins to rock.

XI

The Nazarene returns in triumph to Bethany. The people hope that he will give them answers, that he will tell them how he accomplished the miracle of Lazarus and if he is now prepared to do the same for others, for there have been more deaths since last he came to that place, and who is he to say that the grief of Martha and Mary was greater than that of others? A woman whose child has died holds the infant in her arms, its body wrapped in white, the cloth stained with blood and tears and dirt. She raises the corpse up and begs the

Nazarene to bring her child back to her, but there are too many others shouting, and her voice is lost in the babble. She turns away and makes the preparations for her infant's funeral.

The Nazarene goes to the house of Martha and Mary and eats supper with them. Mary bathes his feet with ointment and dries them with her hair while Lazarus looks on, unspeaking. Before the Nazarene leaves, Lazarus begs for a moment with him.

"Why did you bring me back?" he asks.

"Because you were beloved of your sisters and beloved of me."

"I do not want to be here," says Lazarus, but the people have gathered at the door, and the Nazarene's disciples pull him away, concerned that there may be enemies among the crowd.

And then he is gone, and Lazarus is left alone to wonder which is worse—a God who does not care to understand His creation, or a God who thinks that He does.

XII

Lazarus stands at a window listening to the sound of Rachel and her husband making love. A dogs sniffs at him and then licks his damaged palm. It nibbles on his tattered flesh, and he watches it blankly.

Lazarus stares at the night sky. In its blackness, he imagines a door, and behind that door is all that he has lost, all that he left behind. This world is an imperfect facsimile of all that once was and all that should be.

He returns home. His sisters no longer speak to him. Instead, they gaze at him with cold eyes. They wanted their brother back, but all that they loved of him died in the tomb. They wanted fine wine, but all they received was an empty flask.

XIII

The priests come for him again, arriving under cover of darkness. They make much noise—enough, he thinks, to wake the dead, were the dead man in question not already awake—but his sisters do not come to investigate. This time, he is not brought before the council but is taken into the desert, his arms tied behind his back, his mouth stuffed with a rag. They walk until they come at last to the tomb in which

Lazarus had once been laid. They carry him inside, and they place him on the slab. The rag is removed from his mouth, and he sees Caiaphas approach.

"Tell me," Caiaphas whispers. "Tell me, and all will be well."

But Lazarus says nothing, and Caiaphas steps back in disappointment.

"He is an abomination," Caiaphas tells the others, "a thing undead. He does not belong among us."

They bind him once again in bandages, until only his face remains uncovered. A priest steps forward. In his hand he holds a gray stone. He raises it above his head.

Lazarus closes his eyes as the stone descends.

And Lazarus remembers.

WHAT MAISIE KNEW

BY DAVID LISS

There was never a time when keeping Maisie in the apartment felt right to me. It was always a bad deal, right from the get-go, but there were no good deals, and this was the least-bad deal going. I couldn't let her stay out in the world, knowing what she knew, blurting out what she did. It probably would have been fine if I'd left it alone, but I could not live with such a flimsy guarantee. It was the chance that things would not be fine that nagged at me, that kept me awake at night, that made me jump every time the phone rang. I had a wife I loved, and we had a child on the way. I had a *life*, and I wanted to keep it. A person can't live like that, waiting for the other shoe to drop, and so I did the only thing I could do—the only thing I could think of. It was the right call, but it just so happened that it didn't turn out the way I wanted.

It should have been fine. Everything I knew about reanimates told me it should be fine. I'd been around them almost all my life. My parents could barely make car payments, but they rushed out to buy a Series One from General Reanimation when they first came on the market. Kids growing up today can't even imagine what those early models were like—buggy and twitchy, with those ugly uniforms, like weird green tuxedos. I was only five at the time, and the reanimate creeped the hell out of me when it would lumber into my room to check on me at night or when it would babysit while my parents were out. I still remember watching it shamble toward me, a TV dinner clutched hard in its shaky hands. I wasn't phobic the way some people are. I simply didn't like them. Dead people should remain dead. That's one of those things that always made sense, maybe now more than ever.

So I hated going to that apartment where I kept my dead girl, which, on top of everything else, was hard to afford and which I had to hide from my wife, who managed most of the household finances. I'd have rather been anywhere else—at the dentist, the DMV, a tax audit, a prostate exam. But I was there, at the apartment. I opened the front door and walked in, smelled the weird chemical smell that reanimates emitted, and the feeling washed over me that I had no business being there. My name was on the lease, but I felt like an intruder.

It was a crappy apartment on the cusp of the very wrong side of town, cheap, but not too dangerous. The place was a one bedroom—more space than Maisie needed, since she supposedly didn't need any space at all. She wasn't supposed to, but I always wondered. Sometime when I came to check on her, the chairs around the cheap kitchen table would look out of place. I always pushed my chairs in, but these were pulled out at odd angles or even halfway across the floor, as though advertising that they'd been moved. I supposed there was nothing wrong with her taking a seat or moving things around if that was what she wanted to do, but she wasn't *supposed* to want to do it. That's what bothered me.

When I went in that day, she was standing precisely where I last left her, her back to the far wall of the living area, her face to the door, light from the slightly parted curtains streaming over her. I watched the dust motes dance around her eyes, visible through the mask, wide and doll-like and unblinking.

Maisie was a black-market reanimate, but she wore the green-and-white uniform of a licensed General Reanimation unit, and of course she wore that matching green-and-white mask, which made her look, to my eyes, like a Mexican wrestler. Plenty of people, even people who liked having reanimates around, found the mask a bit disconcerting, but they all admitted it was better than the alternative. No one wants to check into a hotel and discover that the reanimate bellboy is one's own dead relative. No one wants to go to a cocktail party and see a dead spouse offering a tray of shrimp pâté on ciabatta.

I hated the uniform—slick and stain resistant, made of some sort of soft plastic. It was oversized and baggy, making it almost impossible to tell that Maisie was female. I hated the full-face mask, but I had her wear it in case there was a fire or the building manager had to send in a repairman to fix something or even if there was a break-in. I didn't want anyone knowing I owned an illegal reanimate. I didn't need that kind of trouble.

I stepped into the apartment and closed the door behind me. "Hello, Maisie. You may take off the mask if you like."

She remained motionless, as still as a mannequin.

"Maisie, please take off the mask."

With her left hand, she reached up and pulled it off but held on to it. I hadn't told her to put it anywhere, and so letting it go would not occur to her dead brain. Underneath the mask, I saw her face, pale and puffy, hanging loose from her skull, but strangely still pretty. She had long, flowing curls of reddish blond hair, her pale blue eyes—I'm sure very arresting in life—dull and cloudy in un-death.

I came to check in on Maisie maybe once a week. I should not have to, of course. I ought to have been able to leave her alone for months, but I knew it was a good idea for reanimates to get some exercise lest they gum up. That was part of it. The other part was that I wanted to be sure she wasn't up to no good. Renanimates weren't supposed to have it in them to be up to no good, but if she hadn't been Maisie, had not acted like herself, she wouldn't be in the apartment to begin with.

"How have you been, Maisie?"

Of course there was no response. What was left of her brain couldn't process so abstract a question. That's what Ryan said, and he seemed to think he knew what he was talking about.

"Maisie, get me a beer from the refrigerator."

I could get my own beer, of course, but I needed to find excuses to make her move. I had to specify one from the refrigerator because otherwise she might get me a warm one from the pantry or she might end up looking for a beer in the medicine cabinet.

Maisie walked off to the kitchen. I followed but only for something to do. I was always bored and uneasy when I came to the apartment. I felt strange, like I was playacting for some invisible audience, like I was a grown-up furtively trying to recapture the magic of childhood toys. Nothing I said to her or did with her felt natural.

Christ, I could talk to a dog and feel less like I was talking to myself. That's why I kept the visits so short. I would drink the beer, order her to do some light cleaning, and then get out of there.

I was thinking about how much I wanted to leave, how much I wanted to get back to my wife, when I walked into the kitchen and saw the fresh-cut flowers on the kitchen table. They were a gaudy assortment of cheap dyed daisies, but they were bright and fresh, very new. They'd been arranged carelessly, and water from the vase puddled on the table. Here's the thing: I had not put the flowers there.

No one else had a key—no one other than the apartment-complex manager or the super. Neither of them had any business in my apartment, and if they did have something important to do, they would have called first. (They had my cell-phone number, since I sure as hell didn't want my wife to know I had an apartment, let alone an apartment where I kept my black-market reanimate.) Even if they had not called first, neither the manager nor the super was about to leave a vase filled with flowers on my kitchen table.

Maisie was now closing the refrigerator and handing me a beer. She did not open the bottle, because I had not asked her to open it. That was how they worked. They did not do anything you did not ask them to do. So where had these flowers come from?

I twisted the cap off the beer and looked at Maisie, who, in the absence of orders, remained perfectly still. "Maisie, where did these flowers come from?"

She stared at me. It was a difficult question for a reanimate, I realized, even as I spoke it. Too abstract. I tried again.

"Maisie, did you put the flowers there?"

It was a yes-or-no question, and she should have been able to answer it, but she said nothing.

"Maisie, answer the question. Did you put those flowers there?"

Again, silence. Dark, looming, unblinking silence. It was like demanding answers from a stuffed animal. No; our genetic, animistic impulses gave speaking to a stuffed animal a sort of logic. This was like demanding answers from a bowl of rice.

I took a long drink from my beer and sighed. This was serious. More than serious. It wasn't just that maybe my reanimate, which wasn't supposed to want anything, somehow wanted flowers. It meant that she had somehow gotten out of the apartment, gone to the store, spent money—money she'd earned from what or stolen from whom? Had she managed to bring it with her from the Pine Box? It meant a whole spiraling vortex of Maisie chaos, and I had to know. I had to.

"Maisie," I said. "Go into the bedroom, remove your clothes, and lie on your back on the bed."

The first thing I need to make clear is that I am not a pervert. I don't have any desire to have sex with reanimates. Given the choice between sex with a reanimate or sex with a real woman, I'll take the real woman every time. Hell, given the choice between sex with a reanimate and no sex, I'd go without sex—at least for a good long while. Like S&M or rubber fetishes or whatever, if you're not into it naturally, it's hard to fake the enthusiasm. If you meet some amazingly hot woman, and she says, "Sure, let's have sex, only I want to tie you up and stick needles in your dick," you're probably going to, with however much regret, take a rain check. Unless you like that sort of thing. Plenty of guys like sex with reanimates. They prefer them to real women. It floats their boat. It does not float mine.

That said, I should point out that in most ways it's kind of like sex with anyone else. It has some unique qualities but also lacks some things that make sex with a living woman enjoyable—for example, that unique sensation of having sex with someone you know is alive. So, if you are looking at it objectively, it's a trade-off. That day, I look at it objectively. I didn't want to have sex with her. I wanted to have sex with my wife and no one else. I *liked* sex with my wife. Sure, I would look at an attractive woman when I saw one on the street, but I wasn't about to make any moves. There had been some parties, some business trips, where I'd felt opportunities opening, but I never pursued them. I was in love with Tori. I was happy and I didn't need complications and problems and guilt and lies.

If you are like most people, there are probably a lot of things you don't know about reanimates. Ryan says you are happier that way. He says the less you have to think about what they are, the easier it is to ignore them, to enjoy the convenience. Ryan says you probably don't know much about their history, for example, because there's no percentage in knowing the history. You also probably don't know much about their nature, and that's a whole other thing. There's a percentage in that one for you. The key thing that I'm getting at is that reanimates have a greater clarity of thought when their feelings are intensified. You can tease out this clarity either with pain or with sex—at least with the females. I'm told it is impossible for the males to have sex, not unless the penis is artificially inflated. There are rumors of male reanimate sex slaves with permanent, surgically crafted boners, but I'm not entirely sure this is true.

Reanimates are totally different creatures during sex. This is a big part of why guys who like to sleep with them get off on it. Also, probably because they are willing and compliant sex slaves whose needs and preferences can be handily dismissed. Then again, some guys just dig the fact that they're dead. But for most of the true enthusiasts, the main thing is that reanimates are hungry for it. They start to feel things, they start to remember themselves, and they—well, I hate to be crass, but the bottom line is that they fuck hungry and hard, and some guys just love it. Not me. It made me feel unclean, like I'd been exposed to something vile and rotting. Even now I don't like thinking about it in too much detail, and the less I say about the particulars, the better.

Adulthood, however, means doing things you don't want to do. So I had sex with Maisie. As soon as I slid into her, it was like a switch flipped inside her soul. She was something else, something vibrant and powerful—something that felt not alive but rather *live*, like a storm of a mass of building electricity. That was how she'd been when I'd had sex with her at the Pine Box. She groaned and moaned and murmured. She thrust her hips up at me with a shocking, awkward violence. I didn't want to be there any longer than I had to, so I waited until she seemed good and worked up, and then I asked, "Maisie, did you get those flowers?"

"Fuck off, you asshole."

I guess saying that she surprised me is an understatement. I leaped off of her in astonishment and fear, and I lost—shall we say—my will to continue. She, in turn, fell back on the bed like a puppet with her strings cut. Just like that, she faded back to her normal, stupefied, lifeless self—still and naked and slightly bloated, not breathing hard like I was, since reanimates did not respirate—looking at nothing, and thinking, I was sure, about nothing.

I began to gather up my clothes. "Maisie, get dressed," I said, "and come sit at the kitchen table."

She complied.

I am a nice guy. I like children and animals. I don't especially like violent movies, so what came next wasn't something I enjoyed. It wasn't something that came naturally to me. It was, however, something I had to do. I thought it over. I looked at all sides of it and tried to find another way, but it just wasn't there.

When Maisie sat at the kitchen table, I told her to place her right arm on the table, on top of a thick bathroom towel. Then I asked her to roll up the sleeve of her uniform. With the puffy, pale flesh of her forearm exposed, I grabbed her wrist in one hand and, with the other, thrust a sharp kitchen knife into her arm, just below the elbow.

I've never stabbed a living person, but I'm pretty sure it feels different. Her flesh offered almost no resistance. It was like stabbing wet dough. I felt the knife nick the bone, but it kept going, all the way through, and I felt the tip of the blade make contact with the towel.

Ryan says that pain works as well as sex, but sex, troubling though it is, bothers me less than torture. Anyone who might begin to think that I was a bad person should keep that in mind. I went for pain only when I had no choice.

Maisie did not scream. She did not stand or pull away or fight. Instead, she looked at me and winced. "You asshole motherfucker."

"Maisie, did you put those flowers there? How did you get them? How did you pay for them?"

Her eyes were now wide and moist, almost clear, almost like a living woman's. The lids fluttered in something like a blink. Her mouth was slightly open, and her usually gray lips were taking on some color.

"Fuck you, Walter," she said without much inflection.

I twisted the knife in the wound. I could feel the flesh pulling and tearing, twisting along with the knife. "Maisie, how did you do it? How did you get the flowers?"

She let out a cry of pain, and then gritted her teeth together in a sick smile. "The more you fuck me, the more you torture me, the more I can think, and all I think about is giving you what you deserve. And it doesn't all go away. Each time I get a little stronger."

I yanked out the knife.

Eight months earlier, I was a different man. I was, at least, not a man who could have imagined he would someday soon be torturing his illegal reanimate just after having sex with her, but life throws you curveballs. That's for sure.

Things were pretty good, and they were getting better. I was married to a woman more wonderful and clever and creative than I ever thought would look twice at me. I swear I'd fallen in love with Tori the first time I saw her at a birthday party for a mutual friend, and I could never quite believe my good fortune that she'd fallen for me.

Tori was a cellist with the local symphony. How's that for cool? She was not, perhaps, the most accomplished musician in the world, which was fine by me. I did not want her perpetually on the road, receiving accolades wherever she went, being adored by men far wealthier, better looking, and more intelligent than I. She'd long since given up on dreams of cello stardom and was now happy to be able to make a living doing something she loved. And Tori was pregnant. We'd only just found out, and it was too early to tell anyone, but we were both excited. I was apprehensive too. I think most men are more uneasy about their first child than they like to admit, but I also thought it would be an adventure. It would be an adventure I went through with Tori, and surely that was good enough for me.

Work was another matter. It was okay, but nothing great. I was an account manager at a fairly large advertising agency, one that dealt exclusively with local businesses. There was nothing creative or even challenging about my job, and the pay was no better than decent. Mostly I tried to get new clients and tried to keep the clients we had happy. It was a grind, trying to convince people to keep spending money on sucky radio advertising they probably didn't need. Most of my coworkers were okay, the atmosphere was congenial enough. My boss was a dick if my numbers slackened, but he stayed off my case if I hit my targets. Mostly I hit my targets, and that was all right. The job paid the bills, so we could get good credit and, consequently, live way beyond our means, just like everyone else. We'd bought a house we could hardly afford, and we had two SUVs that together retailed for about half as much as the house. We usually paid our monthly balance on our credit cards, and if we didn't, we got to it soon enough.

It all changed on a Saturday night. It was the random bullshit of the universe. One of the guys at my office, Joe, was having a bachelor party. He was one of those guys I couldn't stand: He had belonged to a fraternity, called everyone "dude," lived for football season and to tell dirty jokes. I don't think he really wanted me there or at his party, but he'd ended up inviting me, and I'd ended up going. Frankly, I had no desire to drop a bunch of money to get him drunk, but it would have been bad office politics to say no.

It started out in a bar and inevitably moved on to a strip club. We went through the obligatory bullshit of lap dances and stuffing G-strings with bills and drinking too many expensive drinks. I guess it was an okay time, but nothing I couldn't have done without. Hanging out with Joe and his knuckleheaded friends at a strip club or spending an evening in front of the TV with Tori—I'd have taken the night at home in a heartbeat.

Ryan was one of the guys there. I'd never met him before, and I couldn't imagine I would want to meet him again. He was tall and wore his blondish hair a little too long—to look rakishly long, I guess—and had the body of a guy who spends too much time in the gym. He'd grown up with Joe, and the two of them were pretty tight. He was the one that suggested we go to the Pine Box. He said he knew a place that was just *insane*. We wouldn't believe how *insane* it was. We had to check out this *insanity*.

It was a bachelor party, so we were drunk and tired and disoriented from an hour and a half in close proximity to tits. We were all, in other words, out of our right minds, and no one had the will to resist. We drunkenly piled into our car and followed Ryan to his insane place about three amazingly cop-less miles away.

The Pine Box had no markings outside to indicate it was anything, let alone a club. It looked like a warehouse. We parked in the strip-mall parking lot across the street—Ryan said we had to—and then crossed over to the unlit building. Ryan knocked on the door, and when it opened, he spoke in quiet tones to the bouncer. Then we were in.

None of us knew what we were getting into, and in all likelihood, none of us would have agreed if we had, but we were now fired by the spirit of adventure, and so we went into the warehouse, which had been turned into a makeshift club. There were flashing red lights and pounding electronic music and the smell of beer in plastic cups. Tables had been set up all around a trio of ugly, slapped-together stages, and atop them danced strippers. Reanimate strippers.

"Dude, no way!" Joe cried drunkenly but not without pleasure. "This shit is sick." Even while he complained, he forced his way deeper into the crowd. Had anyone else spoken first, had anyone objected, we might have all left. But Joe was in, and so we all were. He found a large table and sat himself down and called over to a waitress. You could tell he was loving it—the pulsing music, the lights, the smell of beer spilled on the concrete floor.

The waitress, I saw after a few seconds, was a reanimate—not as pretty as the strippers but wearing a skimpy cocktail dress and no mask. Somehow I hadn't noticed that the strippers weren't wearing masks, because they were wearing nothing, but this waitress, with its brittle blond hair and dead, puffy face exposed, seemed to me inexpressibly grotesque. It had not been terribly old when it died, but it had been fat. Now it moved in a slow, lumbering gait, like a mummy from an old horror movie. It took our order and served our drinks without eagerness or error.

The music was loud, but not so loud that you couldn't talk, and I had the feeling that was important. People came here to look, but also to make contact with each other. They were reanimate fetishists. I'd never heard of them or knew they existed before that night, but as Ryan told us about his friends, about his Internet groups, about the other underground places in town, I became aware of this entire subculture. There were guys out there who were just into reanimates. Go figure.

Joe seemed drunkenly amused, but Ryan was in heaven. He went up to the stage and put money in their G-strings. He paid for a blocky, jerky reanimate lap dance. He had reanimates shake their reanimated tits in his face.

I thought he was the biggest asshole I'd ever met, and I thought the Pine Box was disgusting. I hated looking at the pale, bloated, strangely rubbery bodies. Even the ones who had been beautiful at the time of death were grotesque now, and many of them bore the scars of the injuries that had taken their lives. One was a patchwork of gashes and rips. One of them, perhaps the one who had been most beautiful in life, had vicious red X-marks on its wrists. It was monstrous and disrespectful and wrong beyond my ability to articulate. I'd never liked dead things, and I knew full well that we only tolerated reanimates because they were hidden behind masks and uniforms that allowed us to forget what they really were.

Ryan saw my mood and tried to get me into the spirit of things. He offered to buy me a lap dance, but I was a bad sport. I wasn't having fun, and I wasn't going to pretend to have fun.

I stared into space and tried not to look at the dancers, though once in a while I would sneak a look just to make sure it was as bad as I thought. It was. But then, out of the corner of my eye, I saw one of the dancers stop. It caused a little commotion, and so I turned to it. A dancer stood on the edge of the stage, its arms slack by its side, slouching and staring out into the audience. Staring, I saw, at me. At least I thought it was me. Its left hand was weirdly angled, and it took a few seconds for me to notice that it was pushing its long fingernails into the soft skin of its palm. Dark and watery reanimate blood dripped onto the stage. A couple of men in jeans and T-shirts came up to it, shouting orders and gesturing violently, but it remained still, its dead, pale eyes locked on mine.

And then I knew it—I knew *her*, knew who she was or who she had been. It was Maisie Harper. Knowing that felt like falling, felt like a plummet toward my doom. I remembered that face, and, more horribly, she remembered mine. She had taken her secret to the grave, but then she had left the grave and brought the secret with her. She stared, and her eyes locked with mine, and I could not turn away. And then she opened her mouth and said one word. Even from a distance I could see what she said: "*You.*" That's when I knew I was in trouble. It was when I knew things would never again be the same.

In the apartment kitchen, I sat staring at that weird, unclotting reanimate black blood drying on the towel. Some of the drops had gotten onto my pants. After I'd stabbed her and Maisie had openly defied me, I'd wrapped up her arm and told her I was done with her. She had gone to stand in the living area, in that spot where she seemed most contented—or whatever passed for contentment with reanimates. Ryan said they couldn't process much information. They had very low brain activity, and their ability to feel or experience from moment to moment was very limited. That was what Ryan said, but I was beginning to get the feeling that Ryan might not know precisely what the fuck he was talking about.

I cleaned up as best I could and went home. It was a Saturday afternoon, and Tori had been out shopping for baby things with a friend, spending more than we could probably afford, which might once have bothered me, but now I had other things on my mind. She'd been long home by the time I got there, and she wanted to know where I'd been. She stood there, still strangely thin despite her advanced pregnancy, looking like a toothpick that had swallowed a grape. She wanted to know what I'd been doing to get blood all over my jeans. I was too uneasy even to lie to her, and so I got angry. I hated to get angry with her, but I was frustrated. I might have told her to fuck off. I was not patient, that much is certain. There was some screaming and crying. She accused me of being insensitive, and I told her she was being irrational because she was pregnant and hormonal. As a rule, pregnant women don't respond well to that sort of thing.

The bottom line is that we didn't usually fight like that. I didn't usually speak to her that way, and it left her confused and angry.

Sunday was no better, and Monday at work was a disaster. I hadn't been sleeping well, and when a client called in with a complaint, I probably wasn't as sympathetic or attentive as is appropriate for a competitive industry like advertising. There was an argument with my boss, who acted like a total asshole, even though he was probably right in this case. Things were falling apart, and I was going to have to figure out what I could do to put them back together.

The Pine Box had a Web site with a password. You got the password for the site at the club, and you got the password for the club at the site. The passwords changed every two weeks or so. It was a clever system designed both to keep the circle of information tight and to insure that regulars kept coming back.

I became a regular. I kept coming back. I had to know just how much Maisie could recall.

Almost every time I went I saw Ryan. It wasn't like we were friends or anything, because I couldn't stand him and thought he was a dick, but he didn't have to know that. Truth was, I needed him or someone like him to guide me though this fucked-up world, and if buying him a few drinks and pretending to laugh at his jokes was what I had to do, then I was willing to take my lumps.

He was into reanimates. That much was probably obvious, but he was into them not just in some weird sexual way. It was the whole package, and he was into them the way some guys are into Hitler or the Civil War. He loved the information most people didn't want. He read books and blogs and articles in scholarly journals. He liked facts and dates and statistics and hidden histories.

We would sit at the bar with nearly naked dead women dancing around us, and Ryan would go on and on about reanimate history. Some of it was stuff I already knew, and other things I'd never heard before.

"Were you old enough to remember when they first began to capture pictures of the soul leaving the body?" he asked me. "You're a few years younger than me, I guess. I was six. It was amazing."

I was too young to remember it, but we'd all seen the pictures, watched documentaries on late-night television. The first pictures were taken by an MIT grad student whose grandfather was dying, and he set up his modified camera in the hospital room. When the pictures first came out, everyone thought it was a hoax, but then they found the process could be repeated every time. Suddenly people knew the soul was a real thing and that it left the body upon death. It changed the way we thought about life, the afterlife, dead bodies— the whole deal. In some way, it changed the nature of humanity. Our mortality defined us, but with that mortality seriously in question, no one was really sure what we were anymore.

"It was all a crock of shit, anyhow," Ryan was saying. "No one knew where the soul went, did they? It could just go up to the clouds and disappear or turn into rain or whatever. Maybe everyone goes on to eternal suffering more horrible than anything we can imagine. No way to tell, but all those assholes imagined they had angels and harps and heavenly choirs sewn up, and that's what opened the door for all this. Soul photography was in 1973, and by 1975 the first-generation reanimates began appearing on the market."

"I always wondered about that," I said. "It only took them two years to figure out how to turn dead people into product."

"That's because they already knew. Here's what they don't teach you in Sunday school: The technique was actually developed by the Nazis during World War II. They were plotting some huge offensive in which they would overwhelm the Allies with an army of the dead, but fortunately the war ended before they had a chance. Americans had the secret for years but knew they could never do anything with it, that the public would flip out. But after the soul photography began, they saw an opening. Christ, do you have any idea how much money the government has made by licensing the procedure? And then there are all the regulations, you know?"

"The regulations," I echoed. "What was that, like the Alabama Accord or something?"

"The Atlanta Convention—a big meeting between industry and government to set the ground rules. When you buy a reanimate from one of the Big Three, they'll warn you never to remove the mask, that it messes up the preservative process, and I think just about everyone obeys. No one wants their reanimate to fall apart on them. And then there are the quarterly servicings. If you miss even one of them, your reanimate becomes unlicensed and can be confiscated by the cops."

Ryan was also very interested in where the reanimates come from. "They pay you, like, what? Seven or eight thousand to sign up, but not a whole lot of people in this country are willing to sell their bodies for eternal slavery, so most of the reanimates come from Africa or Asia. I always thought that was one of the reasons for the masks and the uniforms. I think a lot of white Americans might be more uncomfortable if they had to stare into a black reanimate face. More zombie-ish, I guess."

"So where do these come from?" I asked. Most of the strippers at the club were young white women.

Ryan shrugged. "Some are from Eastern Europe, though those are hard to get because you need ones that spoke English when they were alive. Still, you have any idea how many poor assholes in Latvia are trying to learn English just so they can sell their bodies? But the Americans? They're drug addicts, people with terminal diseases who want something for their families, whatever. A lot of them sell their bodies on the black market. They get less, but there are no taxes. Some young hottie gets pregnant and can't afford an abortion? Maybe she hocks her body, hoping to buy it back. That's the teaser, you know. You can always buy it back. How many reanimates out there do you think were convinced they could get their bodies out of hock before they died? Even the black-market dealers let you do it, because they know people can convince themselves that they'll be able to redeem their bodies. Almost no one ever does."

I wondered if that was what happened to Maisie Harper—some crisis she couldn't tell her parents about, so she pawned her body, sure she would have time to buy it back.

"Bunch of morons," Ryan said. "Convince yourself of anything. It's crazy to think that because some chick believed she would always have more time, you can walk in here and just fucking buy her like you would buy a loaf of bread."

Until that moment, I'd had no idea you could buy a reanimate from the Pine Box. This changed everything. "You mean I could—a person could—buy one of these girls?"

"You thinking about it? Be hard to explain to your wife, but yeah. I mean, it's not like a showroom. You can't just point and say, 'I'll take that one,' but they are sometimes willing to sell if they have extra or if one of them isn't working out." He now waved his fingers at Maisie. "Like that one. I guess you've thought about it."

I turned to him. "What do you mean?"

He grinned. "Oh, I don't know. It seems to have a particular interest in you, and you in it. I've fucked it, you know." He grinned at me again. "It's good stuff. I bet you they would let it go cheap. I mean, if you wanted a messed-up reanimate, that is."

I felt as though I were floating outside my body. Was Ryan hinting that he knew about me and Maisie? How was such a thing possible? But if he did, so what? We were brothers in sick, fucked-up, reanimate enthusiasm, weren't we? And even more importantly, he raised this new thought: They sold reanimates here.

Buying Maisie. It seemed too good to be true. It seemed like all the stars were lining up to make my life easy, or at least to give me an out from unbearable complications. They sold the reanimates, and they might be willing to sell Maisie in particular.

Ryan must have noticed how thoughtful I looked. He laughed. "Before you do something rash like buy, you might want to sample the goods."

"Sample the goods?"

He nodded. "It's only a hundred dollars. They have rooms in the back, and you get a full hour. You can pick any girl you want. If she's on the stage, she's available, but if you are thinking of buying that one, you should check her out first."

I looked over at Maisie. She was dancing around a pole very slowly, and she was looking at me. The idea of having sex with her, with any of them, was utterly repulsive to me. "No way," I said.

"Don't knock it. If you've never had sex with a reanimate, you have no idea what you are missing. They *love* it, man. You wouldn't believe how into it they are. It's like they feel alive when they're doing it. They talk, almost like normal people. Sex and pain do that."

"How do you know about pain?" I asked.

He shrugged. "Different guys have different interests. You meet all sorts of reanimate enthusiasts here. Some are into sex, some are into . . . crazy things."

I was already dismissing this. If people wanted to torture the dead, that was their own business. I was thinking about Maisie and sex. I was thinking about what Ryan had said, that they seemed more human during sex, and they spoke. That meant that Maisie could be telling anyone anything. I really didn't want to try it myself, but I had to know.

I paid my hundred dollars to Yiorgio, one of the Pine Box's owners. He was a good-looking Greek guy with long hair in a ponytail and a linebacker's physique. He looked like someone who would be curt and dismissive, but he was actually very friendly. He spoke with a heavy accent, but he was very gregarious and casual, like paying to have sex with a reanimate was no big deal. He made his customers feel at home, which I supposed made him a good businessman.

The thing with Maisie was awkward. Wearing nothing but a G-string, she came over to stand in front of us. "You want to go with Mr. Walter Molson?" Yiorgio asked her. "He is true gentleman."

I winced when he spoke my name. I didn't want her to know it. She recognized my face, but until that moment, I don't see how she could have known my name. She did not react, and I hoped that maybe the information was lost on her dead brain.

She followed me to the room Yiorgio had given us. I was expecting something unspeakably seedy—a dusty room with cinder-block walls and a stained mattress on the floor—but the space was actually very neat and pleasant, with a bed and some chairs. The room was well lit, the walls newly wallpapered and with paintings—landscapes and fruit and the kind of bland things you see in hotel rooms. The bed looked freshly made. Yiorgio was clearly a class act.

I closed the door, and Maisie stood there looking at me, not blinking. Yiorgio had told me that whenever I spoke to her, I needed to begin the command with her name or she might not listen. I said, "Maisie, sit down on the bed."

She sat.

There I was in that small room with Maisie. She sat on the side of the bed, her face empty and her eyes as unblinking as a doll's. She was all but naked, but totally oblivious. She'd been beautiful when she was alive, I knew, and she was still beautiful in death—if you liked that sort of thing. But even though I felt the surprising heat of her proximity, I had no intention of having sex with her—with it. She was a dead thing, a corpse made active by some mysterious mad science, and that did not get me all worked up. Plus there was the guilt. I didn't want to be the sort of person who would both kill a woman and then fuck her dead body. That wasn't how I saw myself.

"Maisie," I said. "Do you know who I am?"

She did not react.

"Maisie, do you remember ever seeing me before?"

Again, nothing. It was better than getting an answer, but it didn't put my fears to rest. Ryan said it all came out during sex, and I knew I was procrastinating. I was looking for some other way to find out what I wanted to know, but I didn't see it. Taking in a long, deep breath, I told her to take off her G-string and lie on the bed. She did that.

I took off my clothes. I'd been afraid I was not going to be able to perform, but I think her nudity and mine were enough to get things going. Her body was strangely warm, almost hot, but it didn't feel like body heat. It was more like there was a chemical reaction happening just below her skin. And the texture was all wrong. It didn't feel like skin, and her flesh didn't feel like flesh. Lying on top of her felt like lying on top of a water balloon. I didn't want to lick or suck or bite or even run my hands over her. I just wanted to do what I had to do and see what happened.

It was like Ryan had said: She was into it. Really into it. She bucked wildly, grabbed onto me, she grunted, groaned, and murmured. And in the middle, she began to speak. "God damn it," she said, "you killed me. I'm fucking you, and you killed me. Walter Molson, you killed me."

I pushed myself off her and staggered backward to the wall. It was worse than I thought. Far worse. By arranging to have sex with her, by putting her in a position where she could learn my name, I had made it worse. I was going to have to do something about this, and I was going to have to do it soon.

The real beginning of the story was two years before all this. Tori's sister was going through a bad patch with her husband, was maybe thinking of getting divorced, and Tori wanted to go out to California to be with her for a few days. We hadn't been married all that long, and this was going to be my first time alone in the new house. I loved my wife, and I loved living with her, but I was also excited for the solitude, which I missed sometimes. You get to thinking about it and you realize you can't remember the last time you spent more than an hour or two without someone else around.

The first night she was gone I was exhausted from work, and basically fell asleep right away. The second night, a Saturday, was something else. I thought about calling up a couple of friends and going out, but somehow it seemed a waste of an empty house to leave it. I was in it for the quiet, for the privacy, and I didn't want to waste it with socializing. I ordered a pizza, turned on a baseball game, and prepared to enjoy a night of not picking up after myself, of leaving the pizza box on the coffee table until morning.

I took out my bottle of Old Charter, and I swear I only planned to do one shot. Two at the most. I wasn't interested in getting drunk, and I was sure that drinking too much would put me right to sleep. But somehow I didn't stop. The game on TV was exciting, and one shot followed the next with an unremarked ferocity. Come eleven o'clock, I was good and drunk.

Come one o'clock, it seemed to me like a crime against humanity that there was no ice cream in the house, like the UN Office on Desserts was going to come gunning for me if I didn't take care of things. I understood that I was drunk, very drunk, and that driving under those conditions was somewhere between ill-advised and fucking moronic. I also understood that there was a convenience store not half a mile from my house. A straight shot out of my driveway, past four stop signs, and there you are. No need even to turn the wheel. I might have walked. The air would have done me good, but since the idea didn't occur to me, it saved me the trouble of deciding I was too lazy to walk. Something else never occurred to me—turning on my headlights.

That was bad enough, but running that second stop sign was worse. I wasn't fiddling with the radio or distracted by anything. I just didn't see it, and I didn't remember it. With no headlights to reflect against it, the sign was invisible. I had a vague sense that I ought to be slowing down somewhere around there, which was when I felt my car hit something. Sometime thereafter, I knew I had to stop, and after spending a little bit of time trying to find the brake pedal, I did in fact stop. I was a drunk moron, no doubt about it, and I realized I ought to have turned on my headlights before, but I knew enough not to turn on my headlights now.

I grabbed the emergency flashlight from the glove compartment, spent a little while trying to remember how to turn it on, but soon enough everything was under control. I got out of the car and stumbled the hundred or so feet since I hit the thing. My worst fear, I swear it, was that I had hit a garbage can, maybe a dog or cat, but when I approached the stop sign I saw her lying on the side of the road, her eyes open, blood pooling out of her mouth. There was a terrible rattling in her breath, and her upper body twitched violently. And then I saw the damage to her skull. I saw blood and hair and exposed brain. She raised one limp hand in my direction and parted her lips as if to speak. I looked away.

You never know who you are until you are tested. I'd always thought of myself as the guy who does the right thing, but it turned out I wasn't that guy at all. In that moment I understood that I was drunk, I'd been driving without headlights, and this girl was going to die. I could see her brain, and I could hear her death rattle. Nothing I was going to do could save her, and that was a good thing too, because if I'd thought I could save her, I can't say for sure I would have. Even so, I ought to have called 911—I had my cell phone on me—but if I had, my life would have been over. I would have been looking at jail and disgrace. Everything I was and wanted to be would have been done.

All around me it was dark. No lights were on. No dogs barked. No one knew I was there. In an instant both clear and decisive, I got back into the car, turned around, drove past the girl I had broken, and managed to navigate my way into the garage. Amazingly, I could find no sign of damage on the car. I was drunk as hell, and I knew it, which meant I could not trust my judgment, but to my foggy eyes, everything looked good. So with nothing else to think about, I went upstairs, got undressed, made a vague gesture toward brushing my teeth, and went to bed.

In the morning, hungover and panicked, I went out and looked at my car. Nothing. No blood, no scratches, no dents. To be certain, I took my car to an automated car wash. Then I began to relax.

The murder, as they called it, of Maisie Harper was a big story for about a day, but then there was that category-4 hurricane that started heading our way, and no one much cared about Maisie Harper anymore. The hurricane missed us, but it hit about two hundred miles north of here, and that generated enough media attention to keep Maisie's name, if not her body, pretty well buried.

Of course, the cops kept working it, and the story made the paper, though only small stories in the back. At first they had no clue who would kill the twenty-one-year-old college student, home for the summer, out for a late-night stroll because she could not sleep. Then the police began to suspect it was her boyfriend. They arrested him, and it looked like I'd caught a break and this guy would take the fall. I cheered the cops on. I didn't bother to think that he hadn't done it, that he was mourning for this girl he possibly loved and very probably liked. All I could think about was that if they nailed him, I could exhale. But they didn't nail him. They let him go, and they made some noise about pursuing more leads. Every day I would look out the window expecting to see cop cars pulling up, waiting to cart me off in shame. The cars never came. They never suspected me, never came to talk to me. There were no witnesses. No one had seen or heard a thing, and eventually the story blew over. In the process, I learned a very important thing about myself. I could do something terrible and live with it, and when the going got tough, I could keep my cool.

When I was done with my hour, I went to see Yiorgio in his office behind the stages.

"You had good time, my friend?"

"I'd like to buy her," I said.

He laughed. "You did have good time. Ryan, he tells me you have never before been with reanimate girl, yes? Maybe you should try some others before you are so sure."

"I don't want to try others. I like that one. How much?"

"You've been good customer, so I don't want trick you. Maisie is difficult girl. She does not always listen. She becomes maybe a problem for you, and I do not want that you come back and tell me you no longer like so difficult a girl. You maybe tell me you want your money back."

"It won't happen," I said. "No returns. I understand the rules going in."

He shrugged. "So long as you understand. Let me tell you something, though. The reanimates, we give them whatever name we want. This one come, she tell us her name. Would not listen to any other name. Very willful."

I nodded. All of this was making me even more convinced I had to get her out of circulation. She knew who she was. She knew who I was. I didn't know if a reanimate's testimony had any legal standing, but I didn't want to find out.

"I want to buy her," I said.

"Okay, my friend. You are very determined, yes? You may buy her for eight thousand dollars. I hope you know, this is cash, and all up front. But it includes lifetime servicing."

Eight thousand dollars was a good price. An economy reanimate from one of the Big Three would cost at least fifteen thousand dollars. Even so, I did not know how I was going to get that kind of money. We had no real savings, no more than a fifteen-hundred-dollar cushion at any given time. But I had some ideas.

"I'll get you the money," I said. "Soon. Don't sell her to anyone else until I do."

"Who am I to break up true love?" Yiorgio asked.

I blundered my way back to my chair. I hardly noticed Ryan was still sitting there until he started to punch my arm and ask me how I'd liked it.

He was joined by another guy now, a regular named Charlie—older and almost entirely bald but for a strip of white hair and a very white goatee. He was well dressed and spoke very deliberately. He spoke like a rich man.

"This is Walter," Ryan told Charlie. "He and Maisie have that thing."

I was not about to ask what he meant. Better to just be cool, be one of the guys.

We sat around and talked and drank, and then finally, Charlie turned to me. "I'm having a party at my house tomorrow night. Ryan knows about it, but I think it's time you joined our circle. It's the sort of thing a hobbyist like you shouldn't miss."

I was going to have a hard time explaining to Tori where I was going without her. She was about five months pregnant now, starting to show in earnest—not as big as she was going to get, but still new enough to being big to be sensitive about it. You try telling your pregnant wife not to get all worked up about it. You try telling her that she desperately wanted to be pregnant, and now she *was* pregnant, so maybe she should stop complaining about it. Dealing with a touchy pregnant woman who is self-conscious about her appearance makes negotiating with North Korea seem like a pretty sweet deal. There was something about the way Ryan and Charlie spoke that told me that if I skipped the party, they wouldn't quite trust me, wouldn't quite consider me one of them. I didn't know what Ryan might already suspect about me and Maisie, and I didn't want to give him any reason to worry about me.

Tori was furious with me, of course. I was always going out, she said. I was being secretive, she said. I was one of those asshole husbands who cheats on his pregnant wife because she is now fat and ugly. Of course I told her I had never touched another woman, but she didn't believe me, which bothered me. I ended up leaving for Charlie's party with her shouts ringing in my ears and the thin satisfaction of slamming the door.

Charlie lived in a verdant old neighborhood, and his house was massive to the point of being intimidating, probably five thousand square feet and gloriously appointed. Ryan was there, and I recognized quite a few people from the Pine Box, but even so, it was hard at first to shake off the feeling that everyone was judging me for my creepy interests. I drank too much beer too fast, but that made me sociable, and that made things easy. The beer was served by unmasked reanimates in tuxedos. All of them, I soon learned, were black market. And that began to put me at ease. Charlie had illegal reanimates. Why shouldn't I have one?

The party had gone on for a couple of hours, and it seemed like just a regular party to me—people talking and eating, taking hors d'œuvres from trays. Ryan had promised something wild, but I began to think I was missing something. Then, at about ten at night, we all went outside to the fenced-in, private yard. The mood changed at once. It was tense and charged, full of an almost sexual expectation. Everyone spoke in low whispers. A couple of men even giggled nervously. I asked them what was going to happen, but they wouldn't tell me. "Better to be surprised," one said, and then his friend gave him a high five.

There was a big sheet of heavy plastic set out in the middle of the backyard, and Charlie ordered one of his reanimate servants to go stand on it. The thing lumbered onto the plastic and stopped. Charlie told him to turn to face the crowd, and it did so. It looked like it had died when it was in its forties or so. It was a slightly heavyset white man with thinning reddish hair and sad gray eyes.

Charlie turned to his guests.

"Hey, guys," he said, "this is Johnny Boy."

"Hi, Johnny Boy!" the crowd shouted.

"Johnny Boy has been a little slow to obey orders lately," Charlie said. "He's not disobedient, but he's getting a little old."

"Awww!" cried Charlie's guests.

"What do you think? Should we retire him?"

Charlie's guests cheered.

Charlie turned to the animate. "Johnny Boy, would you be so good as to remove your clothes for us?"

With the fumbling and mechanical efficiency of its kind, Johnny Boy began to remove its clothes. Perhaps out of habit or training, it folded each piece of clothing, and it left them piled on the plastic sheet. When it was done, it turned back to us, entirely naked. Johnny Boy looked like it'd been killed in some sort of accident: Its torso was all messed up, not exactly scarred, but exposed and purpled in places. Its belly was distended, its flesh swollen, its penis and testicles so shriveled as to be almost invisible. Charlie's guests raised their drinks and toasted it.

"Johnny Boy," Charlie cried, "be so good as to hold out your arms."

Johnny Boy held out its arms.

Now another reanimate arrived with what looked like an old stained butcher's apron, which he handed to Charlie. After putting it on, Charlie lifted an ax he'd clearly had nearby, though I had not seen it until this moment.

Charlie turned to the crowd, brandishing the ax. "You boys ready to send Johnny Boy off in style?"

The guests made it known that they were ready. I took a step back. I understood now what was happening, the weird grotesqueness of it all. What did it mean? Was it a crime? Was it even cruel? I didn't know, but I didn't *want* to know, I didn't want to see. Yet I knew it would be a mistake to leave or even to show my feelings, to make these guys feel like I thought I was better than they were—which I did, by the way. I stood there and made myself watch.

Charlie, after taking a moment to flash a wolfish grin at his guests, brought the ax up and then swung it down on one of Johnny Boy's outstretched arms. The limb tumbled down to the plastic sheet, continuing to move, and the stump remained outstretched, oozing a slow and steady flow of black, watery liquid. Johnny Boy began to scream. It did not move its legs. It barely moved its head, but it screamed and shrieked and wailed. The guests cheered. People hooted and clapped and drank to its suffering.

"My brakes!" Johnny Boy cried out. "Oh, my god, the truck, the fucking truck!"

The crowd cheered again.

Charlie handed the ax to Ryan, and he cut off the other arm in a quick, clean stroke. Johnny Boy still screamed, sometimes just noise, sometimes about the impending head-on collision with the truck. Its stumps continued to produce their black blood, like a kitchen faucet left running just a little. Then the ax was handed to another friend, and he cut off one leg. The body tumbled over, but this didn't slow the screaming. It seemed not to know or care what was happening now, but the past, its death, was vivid and real and immediate. The crowd loved it.

I stood there feeling nauseated and horrified while the last leg was cut off and the crowd gathered around to laugh and point and cheer on the dismembered torso. I could not have held my breath all that time, but if anyone had asked, I would have sworn I didn't breathe between the time they started hacking up the reanimate until the time they finally put the pieces on the fire and burned them into stillness and silence.

The party began to clear out after that, but it was still too early and I was too shaken to go home. I wanted to make sure Tori was asleep when I got there, so I wouldn't have to deal with her. I went to a bar and drank too much, but I'd learned my lesson. Even though I now drove a car with headlights that went on automatically, I still checked them before driving home at almost 1:00 A.M.

The lights were out, so I thought I was safe, but when I walked through the door, she was waiting for me, sitting in the dark.

"What is going on, Walter?"

"I don't know what you mean," I said. "I wanted to hang out with some friends. Christ, you are the only wife in America that doesn't want to let her husband out of the house once in a while."

"You got a call while you were out," she said.

"A call! Oh, my God, a fucking call! No wonder you are so upset." I stumbled past her.

"I don't know who it was. It was a woman. She sounded, I don't know, retarded or something. I think she was saying your name, but I couldn't understand the rest."

"Jesus Christ, Tori," I shouted. "A wrong number? You are giving me shit about a wrong number? Have you lost your mind?"

I stormed upstairs, and she didn't follow. After fifteen or twenty minutes, I figured she was going to sleep on the couch. Just as well. It gave me time to figure out what the hell I was doing to do with Maisie, who was now calling my house. She must have done it during sex or right after sex or while stabbing herself or something. The point was that someone might have seen her do it. This someone might not have understood this time, but what about the next time or the one after?

Two days later I went to the Pine Box and paid for Maisie. I brought her over to the apartment, and I left her there. Everything was fine for about two months. Then it fell apart.

After the incident with the flowers, I decided I needed to visit more regularly. The next time I went over, she had newer flowers, and on the mantel she'd placed a goldfish bowl with two fish. There was a little tube of fish food next to it. Maisie herself was still and lifeless, as she usually was when I walked in.

"Maisie," I said, "do you want something? Do you need something? Is there anything I can get you that will make you happy?"

She didn't answer.

"I like your fish," I tried.

Nothing.

"Maisie, I order you not to leave this apartment."

Her head moved, just a little. Nothing else, but I knew that deep down she was laughing at me. This dead thing was laughing at me, and she meant to fuck up my life any way she could. Christ, the flowers, the fish—she was toying with me, torturing me. She could ruin me any damn time she wanted to, but she wanted to draw it out. She wanted revenge.

The next day at work was a nightmare. Crap from my boss, fatigue from lack of sleep. As soon as I got out I drove over to Maisie's apartment. Nothing new happened. Maisie seemed like any ordinary reanimate, and I began to think that maybe I had panicked for nothing. Maybe it was a bad patch and now everything had blown over.

Then, on Tuesday, everything changed.

I was halfway through another crappy day when the receptionist rang. "Um, Walter, you need to get out here. There is someone here for you."

"Who is it?"

"Christ, Walter, just get out here."

I went to the reception area, and there was Maisie, uniform on, mask off, her hair and eyes wild. She stood in front of the reception-ist's desk, one palm out, raw and bloodied. The other hand held a piece of glass. She brought the glass down into her palm. Around her were the receptionist, one of the agency creatives, and a guy from the mail room. They were just staring.

"Ahh," she cried. "Walter. Walter Molson. Walter Molson."

Now here was Xander, my boss.

"What the hell is this, Walter?"

"I don't know," I said. "I don't know."

"Get that thing out of here," he said. "I don't know what you're into, but take your perverted, illegal shit somewhere else."

I managed to get her into the elevator—empty, thank God—and into my car. I shoved her in the back and drove her to her apartment. I put her in the bedroom, and I called a locksmith to change the locks to the kind that had to be opened with a key even from the inside. I wasn't supposed to change the locks on these doors, but I didn't give much of a shit at this point. We were into the endgame now. I knew it. I had to get rid of Maisie, and I knew just how to do it.

Once the locks were taken care of, I called Ryan to get the number, and then I called Charlie.

"Hey," I said to him. "How often do you have those little parties?"

I could hear cloth scraping as he shrugged against the phone. "Two or three times a year, I guess."

"The thing is," I said, "I have a unit—" I didn't want to talk about reanimates over the phone. You never knew who might be listening. "I need to get rid of it."

"Maisie, huh?" I could practically hear the grin in his voice. "I wondered if things weren't going to come to this. Now, we don't need a full-blown party to have a good time. Something more casual can be whipped up pretty easily. You bring her over Saturday night; we'll fix things up for you."

I didn't go into work for the rest of the week. I didn't call the office, and the office didn't call me. I guessed that job was done. On Satur-day night I went out, and Tori didn't bother to argue. Things had never been the same since that fight we'd had after Charlie's last party. They would get better, I knew. Things would improve once I'd dealt with Maisie. Everything would be patched up very, very soon.

I picked up Maisie and brought her to Charlie's house. I was expecting just a half dozen guys or less, but there were twenty-five or thirty people there—almost as big as the last party. I brought Maisie out of the car and led her inside.

"Christ," said Charlie. "You sure you want to get rid of it? It's pretty sweet."

"Trust me," I said. "It's gone haywire. You don't want it."

That was good enough for him. We ordered Maisie to stand in the middle of the living room, and we all got beers from a big bucket in the kitchen. A couple of the guys, including Ryan, said they wanted to taste her before the end, and I knew it would be ungracious to refuse. I just nodded and let them take her into the bedroom. There were probably eight guys in all who went with her. I was worried she would speak, but these were not exactly the sort of people who go to the police with their suspicions.

It was maybe eleven before they brought her outside to stand on the plastic sheeting. She was still naked from the antics in the bedroom, and I arranged her so that she was facing the crowd. I knew this was something I had to do, but I didn't feel right about it. I mean, it didn't matter. It shouldn't matter. She'd been stripping long before I stumbled into that club, and she'd been subjected to far more degrading things. I'd subjected her to them myself. What did one more indignity matter to an animated corpse running on some kind of weird biological batteries? But I knew that she wasn't as oblivious as we'd always thought they were. I knew that it would be an indignity, that whatever Maisie was now, I thought she deserved to end this miserable existence with whatever measure of respect I could provide.

Unfortunately, I couldn't provide any. I needed her destroyed, and I didn't have the guts to do it myself. I knew that much. I needed these guys to do my dirty work, and I would give them whatever they wanted, let them take their pleasure with her any way they chose, if only they would get rid of her for me. Anyhow, I knew that Maisie had some kind of will of her own. She could refuse if she wanted to. I wished she would. It would make me feel better, and it would demonstrate to the others why she needed to be destroyed.

Charlie stepped forward with the hatchet, and though I meant to turn away, I could not resist taking one last look at Maisie as she stood naked in the night air. She looked in my direction, but her glassy eyes did not meet mine; they aimed themselves instead at nothingness. In that moment, I felt justified. It really just was some sort of misfiring biological machine. This wasn't murder. It wasn't anything like it. It was a mercy, really.

Then Charlie handed me the ax. "You first," he said.

I shook my head.

He thrust the ax forward again. "No way, bucko. You have to get this party started."

Well, fuck, I thought. I was just standing on ceremony now. I'd already killed her once. There was no point in being squeamish. I told her to hold out her arm, and she did. She didn't look at me, and there was no expression on her face. Maybe she wants this, I thought. Maybe she doesn't want to be a reanimate anymore. I sucked in my breath, and I tried to think about nothing as I swung the ax.

It was like slicing butter. The arm came right off. It was so easy. I probably would have gone for the other arm, but Maisie started screaming, and that distracted me. It wasn't like a normal scream, like a human scream. She opened her mouth wide, impossibly wide, like a snake unhinging its jaws to swallow a rat. Her eyes went wide and wild. There was a pause, only a beat, but it felt long and unnatural, and then she began to let out a long, loud, unnatural scream, not of pain, but of anguish, unimaginable anguish.

With Johnny Boy, the guests had loved the shrieking, but there was something different here, something conscious, and we all knew it. Everyone remained still in a moment of stunned confusion, and then, snapping out of his daze, Charlie took the ax from my hands. He swung with a kind of madness, as though he recognized that Maisie was not a plaything but an abomination, something that had to be destroyed before he was forced to consider what she was, what she meant by her mere existence.

The second arm came off. She had not raised it, and Charlie swung at it as it hung by her side, slicing through just above the elbow and slashing deep into her body.

Maisie screamed again, and Charlie this time swung at her leg. It was a clean cut, and her torso tumbled to the ground, twisting and turning spraying blood in a sickening, black ooze. Still she screamed. She would not stop screaming.

It was my mess, but I could not bear it any longer. I ran to my car, and I drove home and came crashing through the door like a man possessed. I found my bottle of Old Charter and filled half a water glass and drank it down. Only when I was done gagging on its burn did I realize Tori was awake and on the couch. She'd barely noticed my commotion. She was sitting in front of the TV, and she was talking to me.

"I can't believe how sick some people are," she was saying. "I've never heard of anything like it."

And there it was on the TV. The local news anchor was talking, and the words *Reporting Live* flashed over and over again. I saw Charlie's house in the distance behind the reporter, who spoke about shocking scenes of carnage, a twisted sex cult devoted to the rape and mutilation of reanimates. He could barely restrain his disgust as he spoke. In the picture I could see police cars, their lights flashing, and a figure too dim and distant to recognize being pushed into the back.

Would they mention me to the police? I had no idea. I didn't know these guys, not really. They were well and truly fucked, and so maybe they didn't have any reason to betray anyone else. Charlie owned the house, and he would seem like the big fish to the cops. Maybe they wouldn't ask too many questions.

I looked at Tori, so disgusted by the scene before her. She glanced at me, and as saddened as she was by this spectacle of human depravity, something passed between us, some sort of unspoken code, communicated only with our eyes. It said that we were a team, we were alike. People like this were practically of a different species, and they had nothing to do with us.

Maybe I should have confessed everything then. Maybe I should have come clean. I was never one of those guys. Not really. I was drawn in by circumstance. A terrible accident, a split-second decision to do the wrong thing, and then the terrible fallout. But I wasn't one of those monsters. I didn't *like* mutilating or having sex with reanimates. I thought it was sick, beyond sick. So maybe Tori would understand if I controlled the story.

I said nothing, though, because I held on to the belief that there would be no story to control. Maybe the guys at the party would keep their mouths shut and this horrible chapter of my life would finally be closed. In fact, maybe this was the best thing that could happen. Maisie was gone, and the people who knew about me and Maisie were gone. It was perfect.

I went to bed with Tori, and enflamed by this mutual bond of righteousness, she made it clear she wanted to make love. I felt too disgusting to violate her pregnant body. I felt like a polluter. Afterward, however, I was glad we'd done it. One last, sweet memory to hang on to.

The next day when the phone rang, I was sure it was my doom calling. It was, but doom rarely takes the shape we most fear.

"Mr. Molson," said a voice on the other end in tones of practiced official blandness. "This is Detective Mike Gutierrez. I need you to come speak to us, today if you can."

My heart pounded so hard I feared it would burst, but my brain was racing. If they wanted to arrest me, they would not call. Maybe I was safe.

"Regarding what?" I asked.

"Well, it's an unusual matter. I suppose you saw on the TV about the raid on the reanimate mutilators last night?"

"I saw something about that, yes," I said.

"Well, in addition to the arrests, we confiscated the, um, remains of one of their, well, victims, I suppose. Thing was all hacked to bits, but the torso and head were still there. And the thing is, the head is still talking. You see, the damn thing is still alive—or animated or whatever—and it's mentioning a name. Mr. Molson, it's mentioning your name, and you are the only person with that name in this city."

I tried to sound casual. "How odd. What is it saying?"

"I think it's best to discuss that in person. Can you come in today at, say, noon?"

I nodded, but then realizing that he could not hear me, I told him it would be fine. I then hung up the phone and sat very, very still.

This was it, then. They had me. They didn't know it yet, or they would be coming for me instead of asking me to come to them, but it was only a matter of time. Maisie's dismembered body would very likely never testify in a court of law, but the cops would come after me if they could, and at the very least, Tori would leave me and I would be ruined with lawyers' fees. I would become an object of scandal and horror. That was the best-case scenario. The worst—jail, where everyone inside would know what I had done. I would be one of those perverts who would be found murdered after a few months of unimaginable torment.

I could not face any of that. I was ruined, but I did not have to live with the ruin. And why should I? We all knew the soul left the body at death. I'd seen a hundred movies of departing souls. Unlike some cynical people, I didn't think the soul departed only to fade into nothingness. This life was just one part of the journey, and it was time for me to get a move on.

I am not a brave man. I did not own a gun and could not have used it if I had. I did not have the courage or the strength to cut my wrists. Instead, I went back to that bottle of bourbon, and I collected some very strong pain pills Tori had gotten but not really used after she'd broken her wrist last year. I drank all the whiskey and swallowed all the pills. I looked for more pills. I found some muscle relaxers, Ambien, Xanax, and a few others things to throw into the mix. Some probably did nothing, but the whole cocktail ought to be pretty lethal.

It was. I was probably dead within an hour, though time is hard to measure now. Only when I was twinkling out did it occur to me how horribly I'd screwed up. I'd forgotten how I'd raised the money to pay for Maisie in the first place. The offices of General Reanimates had given me almost ten thousand dollars to sign the contract, and that seemed like a good short-term solution. I would buy it back eventually. I didn't see any reason why I couldn't. I had plenty of time. It didn't weigh on me at all, and at the moment when I should have been thinking of nothing else, I was thinking only of escape. Somehow I'd simply forgotten.

I suppose a pill overdose must be a good deal for General Reanimates. No cosmetic work to be done. Not that it much matters. I wear the uniform, and I don't see many living people at all these days. I'm out in the desert, working on an alternative-energy project, setting out solar panels. At least I am making myself useful.

I cannot speak. I cannot will myself even to move, only to follow orders. My mind is mostly still there, though I do not feel entirely like myself. Maybe it is because my soul is gone, and maybe it is because I am dead. I don't know. I don't remember dying, don't remember my soul leaving. I only remember falling asleep and then waking up in the General Reanimates lab. I cannot even wiggle a finger of my own free will. I've given up trying. I cannot imagine how Maisie did it.

There is nothing for me to do but endure my lot and think. It is hot here, and I feel it. We are not insensible. Our uniforms don't breathe, and we cannot sweat. I am miserable and I itch, and every movement is painful. My bones feel like they are scraping together, rubbing, chipping, grinding down. I work twenty-four hours a day. There is no rest and no end. I can do nothing but what I am told, and I have no escape but my memories. I have told my story to myself I don't know how many hundreds of times. I pretend there is an audience, but there is none, and there never will be. Someday, I hope, I will wear out, but for all I know, this torment, with regular servicing, will last a hundred years. A thousand.

Somehow Maisie could break through, if only a little. Maybe it was anger or the sense of being wronged. Maybe if my end were not so fitting, I could find the will, but I doubt it. I have tried. I don't think anyone could try more than I have, but then I suppose we all try. The man right next to me must be trying, too, but he cannot tell me about it. I think it was just that Maisie was exceptional. Maybe in life, certainly in death. She was, and the rest of us are not, and that is what I must endure over the long, unending horizon.

COPPER

BY STEPHEN R. BISSETTE

"I'm home, always home."

Copper stands rock-solid, squints at the noise from across the street.

As usual, the cops didn't show until long after the action was over.

Copper squints and spits over the railing.

"If you need a statement, you know where to find me."

"We won't be needing a statement, sir."

Copper's eyes shift downward, to the young policeman's face. It's the first time he's made eye contact with the kid.

The policeman *is* a kid—hell, even I can tell he's barely out of the academy. I can see that from where I'm looking out, three houses away.

"No questions, nothin' at all?"

Copper spits again, looks from the man in uniform doing nothing, to the men in uniform across the street, also doing nothing.

"This is the sixth house they've gutted in this neighborhood."

"Yes, sir, we appreciate your calling it in."

"I seen it all and I called it in—twenty-six hours ago."

Copper lets that one stand. He tilts his head, cocking his neck, staring the policeman down.

"I've called in every goddamned one of 'em."

I can see the white of the cop's scalp when he looks away from the old man's glare.

The kid clears his throat and looks down, as if there were something of importance in his hand. He already closed his notebook. What can there be to look at? He doesn't even have calluses to gander at.

"City just doesn't care, does it?"

The kid's crew cut is too close, like a fresh military cut. His scalp gleams like a baby's knee. This kid is green, the type that needs a weekly trim and says so, as if that were part and parcel of being a cop, to make up for doing nothing.

"But come tax reassessment time, the city is right at my door."

Of course they send him to talk to Copper.

"I've got one question, officer."

"What's that, Mr. Cyrus?"

"What're you going to do when they come after my house?"

If there is a reply, he doesn't stay long enough to hear it.

The screen door slaps closed without a whisper from the hinges. Copper keeps everything shipshape; no squeaking door on his watch.

It doesn't matter. The cop is on his heel and away, too. His polished shoes are too smart on the tarmac; the crease of his pantlegs are sharp as a paper cut.

He shakes his head and mutters something I can't make out, and his cop cronies make some wisecrack back at him, and they all have a hearty laugh at Copper's expense.

Anything to clear the air of the old man's comment, ignore the truth of it, pretend it wasn't said or heard or didn't matter.

I lay low and watch the old man's porch.

I dream of Mount McKinley.

I dream of fucking, and climbing, and cold, and pain and cold.

I dream of my dick splitting in half.

I wake up on the bare cement floor in the basement of the Baker house.

No pain.

No cold.

I hear Fetus moving around upstairs.

I stand up. Go to the window.

Still have to tell myself I'm home.

Home.

My hometown didn't used to look like this.

It's looking more like the east side of Baghdad every day.

Damn near every house looted, gutted, no electricity, no running water.

I look past the row of shells.

Every house on this street is abandoned but one.

It's the same for blocks.

A neighborhood of shells.

Windows boarded up, sheets of plywood over doorways, broken panes, sagging clapboards, chipping paint, ragged shingles.

All but one.

I see Copper across the way and up the street, sitting on his porch.

Copper sits on his rocker on his porch.

I remember I have something to do.

"So what you want from me?"

Copper sits on his rocker on his porch, still as a stump. One spot-flecked hand over his other wrist.

It's an odd position, and he changes hands to cup the opposite wrist, if you are with him long enough to notice.

Copper later tells me that's how the cold hits him: It stabs his wrists.

His wrists get cold, a deep cold that starts slow before it bites to the marrow and malingers. "Started when I was in my mid-fifties," he later says, "and the damned thing is, it's same as when I was in Korea. Same cold, as if I'd never left it. Like it followed me here."

But that is later.

Today, he sits with one hand over t'other, over the wrist, and gazes at me with those milky blue eyes of his.

"You're here all the time," I say. "I see you keeping watch."

He turns his head and spits without taking his hand off that wrist. Over the rail it goes, a shimmering clam arcing into the perfectly trimmed grass.

"Yep, I'm home, always home. What of it?"

"So, we're looking to start a neighborhood watch."

His eyes don't so much as quiver.

His lips are tight, white, top and bottom.

"Keep an eye on one another's houses, watch out for one another," I offer.

"I'm home."

Another lunger over the rail, into the perfect green grass, somehow without breaking gaze with me.

"Always home."

"Yes, sir."

We let that hang in the air.

We let it hang a while, let it slide to quiet and seep in, like his spit on the blade of grass below is hanging then seeping, though I can't say for sure it is or does, as I'm watching Copper.

Copper doesn't move a notch, and he won't.

Up to me, since I'm the one intruding, to break the silence.

"Since you keep an eye out, it seemed—"

Without breaking the gaze, another lunger, over the rail.

Though his milky blues don't so much as shift, I can tell he's sizing me up—seeing if I break the stare to track his lunger, to see if it's green as the green-green St. Patty's Day grass.

Copper's lawn is perfect, always perfect, the only cut and green lawn on the block, and Copper's lungers won't change that a whit. His eyes stay icy, but I can tell he's a bit amused by all this.

What they say, clear as crystal, is what he won't say.

"—you know, we watch out for one another."

He says it later, just to clear the air.

Later, when we get to know one another a bit, when we are in the basement waiting for T.

Later, when he tells me about how the cold sunk its choppers into his wrists, about Korea, about 'Nam before it was 'Nam, about his wife Becca before she was gone, about his calico cat Hank before T took Hank down into the cellar and did the deed, before all that shit hits all those fans.

He says later what his eyes say now loud and clear, and I hear just fine. He says it later just to make sure there are no hard feelings.

What do I need you for? What do I need you to watch out for me or mine for? What could you possibly offer me that I don't already do or have done or was or am or will be?

I'm home, always home.

Later, he says all that.

Not now, not on the porch.

Not today.

He says, "I remember you, kid."

I look at him.

"You lived over on Spruce and James. Your mom raised you."

Now, he just glares at me, giving up nothing.
"I remember you."
Copper sits on his rocker.
We just stay like this for a long, long time.
From now to now, then to now.
That's when I know Copper's our man.
That's when I know we get along just fine.

It's Fetus who suggests I pay the visit, take in the old man's mettle.
It's Stout who says fuck that, who needs Copper.
Stout grew up around the block from Copper and his wife Becca.
Stout left for boot camp before the cancer took her. I left a week after.
Stout and I were in Baghdad together. Good times. Bad times. OIF 1, the invasion, no food, one MRE per day, nothing too heavy, got to shoot back.
Then Thunderdome.
Ate Alaskan king crab every night for months at FOB Shield. Weird. Mayberry in the shit.
Stout took fire; RPG in the pipeline between Kuwait and Iraq. HMMWV limped away with Stout in it.
Stout lost an arm, part of his chest, but all that's left works. Home he went.
Found him here, back home.
Stout says fuck Copper.
Stout has no use for the old man, never did, but that too changes that night in the basement.
Stout wouldn't brook any ill word about the old lady.
Becca babysat for him and his sister, back when they needed sitting.
He speaks of it, once, only once.
That I remember.
Stout's smile bares his black broken teeth.
It's an occasion whenever Stout smiles.
I remember.
Stout says the army promised him dental. That was before.
The army didn't take care of dental or much else.
The U.S. Army took Stout and took him and his and all he ever

was and never was, all he ever had and all he ever might have been but wasn't and will never be.

The U.S. Army took him and left Stout to Stout and left Stout to us.

Stout says fuck that, who needs the U.S. Army?

Stout says fuck Copper, who needs the old man?

Still, it's Fetus and me who reckon the old man is all right, that we need him.

There's T.

T drives by Copper's house.

I see T drive by Copper's house.

T doesn't turn to look at Copper.

Copper doesn't look at T.

T drives toward the Baker digs.

T looks at the Baker house.

T glares at the Baker house.

I watch T drive away.

I sit in the basement at the Baker house.

I like it here in the basement.

Safe. Like in Baghdad.

We used to sandbag all the windows.

It was dark, except for what light came in through the skylight.

The Baker basement is dark. I like it fine.

I miss the LED lights I used to strap to my head, but otherwise it's the same.

No electricity. Dark. Sleep all day.

Try to remember.

Back in the day.

I remember when Trapper and I signed up.

I remember Trapper—T—I remember T.

I remember T when they took his brother away.

I remember T after that. T said the cops took him and his and all he ever was and never was, all he ever had and all he ever might have been but wasn't and will never be. I remember T says that.

I remember.

I remember T when he grinned at me, after signing up, and I remember the look on the recruiter's face.

Word is T never went over to the shit.

Word is T was shipped right back here.

Word is T got into some shit, and was kept from the shit.

That's before they were taking anyone, anytime, with any record. Miller tells me that's how it is now. Two legs, two arms, two eyes, you in.

Word is T got into some shit, they booted him before he saw sand.

So T made like the Shia did over there—stripped and hauled anything worth anything away.

Makes the neighborhood look like Baghdad East.

Word is T has made a killing on the neighborhood.

Word is T gutted the neighborhood.

Shell by shell, T took all it was and sold it.

That's before I got back, before Fetus came back.

Fetus took three AK-47 rounds three hundred meters from the Alamo; he shouldn't have made it.

He made it.

Came back home.

I remember Fetus before the shit.

Fetus smoked those fucking French Gauloises, cheap tobacco the locals smoked over there.

I remember Fetus before the war took his and him and all he ever was and never was, all he ever had and all he ever might have been but wasn't and will never be.

I don't remember me before.

I don't remember.

I remember T.

I get up.

I look out the basement window, across the street, across the way.

Copper is sitting in his rocker on his porch.

Copper is looking my way.

I don't remember.

Before the shit.

I don't remember much.

I remember T.

* * *

One good thing is Copper has no sense of smell.

Miller says he lit fire to a bag of catshit on Copper's door one Halloween and it was the neighbor who called it in: The old lady was away and Copper didn't smell a thing.

The old man can't smell a damned thing, and that makes a difference.

Meant we can, if we are careful, pick and choose our approach pattern.

I went point, and took it a day at a time.

Copper is watching me now.

Copper's right hand is over his left wrist, and he watches me.

"Your first car was a beat-up Chevy Impala."

I don't remember.

"You rolled it out on Route Four."

I don't remember.

Copper moves his left hand over his right wrist, cupping it.

"Your mother cried all night."

I don't remember.

"I remember you, kid."

I don't remember.

Another good thing is Copper knows this burb like nobody else.

He knows it all, including the backstory of every empty house.

Copper remembers.

I don't remember.

Word is Copper knows the trials and tribs of every occupied house and when who was where and went where and lived it and snuffed it.

I don't remember. Once, I knew some of it, but no more.

Stout remembers.

Fetus remembers.

Word is that Copper and Becca settled here after Korea.

Word is that young Copper had been in just about every one of these houses, those left standing.

Word is that Copper and Becca had been in and out of these doors, on and off these front and back porches, and grilled and drank and spat in these backyards for longer than I've been on this mudball, before or after the day.

Word is that middle-aged Copper had done some handiwork in just about every house within six blocks, at one time or another.

Word is that old man Copper has kept watch every day of his life, especially since Becca was planted.

Old man Copper watches me now.

I wave.

Old man Copper watches and doesn't move.

I sit.

Old man Copper sits.

What Copper built, T takes.

House by house, shell by shell.

What Copper knew, T sells.

T takes it all.

T and his crew work fast, under cover of night.

In through a cellar window, case the joint.

T goes in. Always T.

T cases his own shells.

T through the window, in and out, rally the boys and clean it out, fast.

Tally, score.

The amateurs start with the laundry room and boiler, maybe the radiators if they can get them out.

T has it down to a science.

Tools, not by hand.

Professionals.

Out with the plumbing and gas fixtures—hot-water cylinder, the copper pipes, the spouting, the pumps.

Cut the gas line when needed; whatever.

One house blew and burned on Orvis Street; not T's worry.

That is the amateurs.

T never blows a house.

Might be more to take.

Easy yield of three to five hundred or more per property on copper alone.

The rest is gravy.

Sweet.

House by house, street by street, block by block, up the ante.

Air-conditioner handlers and compressors.

House in good shape, T and company snag kitchen cabinets, toilets, French doors, windows.

Bathroom vanities, especially when they're choice.

T takes it all.

There's T.

T drives by Copper's house.

I see T drive by Copper's house.

T doesn't turn to look at Copper.

Copper doesn't look at T.

Copper is sitting.

I am sitting on Copper's porch step.

"Have you thought about it?"

Copper spits.

"I appreciate the offer, kid."

Copper looks at me.

"I don't need anybody, kid."

I look at Copper.

"I've got mine, and I don't need anybody."

I look at Copper.

"Besides, I'm home, always home."

I look at Copper.

"Nobody's going to be breaking into my place."

Copper looks away.

"Appreciate the offer, though."

I look away.

"You're OK, kid. I remember you."

I don't remember.

"But I don't know your buddies, and I don't want them around here."

I sit on Copper's porch steps.

I look over at the shell across the street.

There's T.

T drives by Copper's house.

I see T drive by Copper's house.

T doesn't turn to look at Copper.

Copper doesn't look at T.

T turns to look at me.

T waves at me.

I lift my hand and wave back.

I watch T drive away.

Copper spits.

"For that matter, I reckon I don't want you coming around for a while."

I look away.

I get up.

I walk.

I walk.

Fetus and I walk.

Nobody notices.

Nobody cares.

Fetus and I walk two days, two nights.

Fetus and I find new shells.

Fetus and I hunker down.

Fetus and I feed in the shells.

Fetus and I meet Croak and Shimmy.

Croak was with the Tenth Mountain Division, ended up in Afghanistan with the Eighty-second Airborne. Shimmy was in Uruzgan Province. Talk talk talk.

We talk shit.

Croak and Shimmy show us new shells. They call one their FOB.

Croak and Shimmy invite us in.

Shimmy shows off two assault rifles he's stashed in the FOB, and his walking armory.

Wears an assault vest, jammed with four loaded AK-47 magazines, thirty rounds in each mag. I ask what he needs it for.

Shimmy laughs.

Croak and Shimmy and Fetus and me cherry-pick a strip gang in the FOB.

Croak and Shimmy and Fetus and me dig in.

Croak and Shimmy and Fetus and me have a fine time.

* * *

Croak and Fetus are shouting.

Fetus grabs Croak's left ear. Comes right off.

Shimmy breaks it up.

Fetus licks his fingers clean, right there in front of Croak.

Croak is shouting again.

Shimmy slams the door.

We are so out of the FOB.

Fetus and I are walking.

Fetus and me walk.

We walk.

We walk.

Fetus and me walk more.

Fetus and me hook up with Snake.

Snake tells me Stout is looking for me.

Snake tells me Stout has news.

Roger that.

Word is there are ambulances outside of Copper's house.

Word is Copper had a heart attack.

Word is Copper managed to dial 911.

Word is the medics showed up two days before the cops did.

Word is Copper is in the hospital for two days.

Word is Copper is released two days later.

Fetus and me walk.

Fetus and me walk for two days, two nights.

Nobody notices.

Nobody stops to pick us up.

Nobody honks their horns.

Nobody cares.

Fetus and me walk.

Word is Stout is still looking for me.

I see Stout up ahead.

Stout meets us.

Stout tells Fetus and me about Copper.

Word is Copper is released after two days in the hospital.

Word is Copper finds his house stripped.

Out with the plumbing and gas fixtures—hot-water cylinder, the copper pipes, the spouting, the pumps.

T doesn't cut gas lines.
T took the lines and the tanks.
T never blows a house.
Word is T left the upstairs wiring alone.
Word is T and his gang demolished the basement and main floor.
Word is Copper is up shit's creek without a paddle.
I walk.
I walk.
I walk.

Copper sits in his rocker on his porch.
I walk to Copper's porch.
"Mind if I join you?"
"Suit yourself, kid."
Copper's right hand is wrapped around his left wrist.
Copper's right arm crosses over his buttoned-up shirt.
I see white gauze between the buttons, where Copper's shirt is open a wee bit.
Copper is pale, his eyes filmy and pained.
"Word is you've been away."
"Two days."
Copper sits.
I sit on the porch steps.
Copper sits.
I sit.
"Word is you—"
"I should have listened to you, kid."
We sit on Copper's porch.
"I've got to replace everything. Plumbing, wiring, hot-water heater—all of it."
Copper looks away.
"I haven't seen you in a while, kid."
"Went away."
"Been gone a while."
"Went with Fetus."
"You guys, you served together?"
"Roger that."
Copper sits.

"I could use another pair of eyes, kid."

Copper looks at me.

"Yes, sir."

Copper slowly releases his left wrist. I can see the white impressions of his fingers.

Copper holds out his right hand.

I reach up and take Copper's hand.

He shakes my hand.

Copper places his right hand back on his left wrist.

Copper looks at me.

"You OK, kid?

Copper looks at me, odd-like.

"And I thought my hands were cold."

I look at Copper.

I hear a car coming.

There's T.

T drives by Copper's house.

I see T drive by Copper's house.

T doesn't turn to look at Copper.

Copper doesn't look at T.

Copper sits.

"You stay here on the porch, kid, while I go get some groceries?"

"Yes, sir."

Copper groans.

Copper gets up.

It takes a few minutes.

"Wait for me here, will you?"

"Yes, sir."

Copper goes into his house.

I hear him walk, old man steps, into the house.

I sit.

I sit.

I hear Copper's garage door open.

I hear Copper's car start up.

I see Copper's car pulling out of the driveway.

I see Copper looking at me.

Copper waves.

I wave at Copper.

* * *

I stand behind Copper's car.

Copper pops the trunk.

Copper is talking about somebody I don't remember.

Hank.

I don't remember any "Hank."

Something upsets Copper.

It is Hank.

No, it's T.

It's what T and his crew do to Hank that breaks Copper.

"A cat." He shook his head. "Who would do that to a cat?"

I lift the bags of groceries out of Copper's car trunk.

Copper walks ahead of me, old man steps, slow and deliberate.

Copper opens the back door and lets me in.

I've been here before.

I can't remember.

Kitchen, all neat.

Copper sets down his bag of groceries.

Shelves, pantry, cupboards.

All neat, nice.

Copper keeps it nice.

In the kitchen window, a ceramic sign:

WHOEVER DIES WITH THE MOST THINGS, WINS.

I set the groceries on Copper's oak table.

I see Copper flinch as he passes the cellar door by the pantry.

What the hell?

Copper doesn't flinch; here he is, flinching.

I offer to put away the groceries.

Copper nods and motions for me to bring a bag to the pantry.

I offer to pass them to him, it'll go quicker, just to see what he'll say.

Copper shakes his head and motions for me to carry the bag to the pantry.

I press the point.

"Something wrong with that cellar door, Copper?"

Copper shoots me a pained look.

His milky blues go flat, watery.

I press the point.

"They took Hank downstairs," he whispers, and his voice splinters.

I'm sorry.
"I'm sorry."
"I found him down there . . ."
Copper sags and sighs, his voice almost inaudible.
"I don't go there no more."
I'm sorry.
I'm sorry.
I'm sorry.

I look down the hallway, toward the living room.
Copper points to the hallway wall.
"That quilt, she made it."
The quilt is hung on the wall, like a tapestry.
"My Becca made that."
The quilt is made of a street made of cloth.
The quilt is made of houses made of cloth.
The quilt is the neighborhood.
"She was quite the quilter," Copper sighs.
The quilt is the neighborhood, as it was.
Cloth people are in front of their cloth houses.
Cloth Copper is on his cloth rocker on his cloth front porch.
I touch cloth Copper.
I leave a wet stain on cloth Copper.
"I better go."
I look back at the cloth houses and the cloth Copper and the cloth neighborhood.
I look at Copper.
He doesn't see the stain.
He doesn't smell me.
I'm sorry.
"I'm sorry."
I go.

I have the dream of Mount McKinley.
I screw twenty virgins on my way to the top, crest the ridge with a raging boner.
I find my uniform across the lobby, and my dick is completely exposed.

Damn, it's fucking cold.

I pop my helmet over my cock, the way I did when there was incoming, but I'm too late. It's cold on McKinley.

The subzero temps kiss my dick; the wet bead of blood and jizz on the tip deep-freezes into an instant Santa's cap.

My joint blues and splits with a sudden *snap*, like a log in a splitter.

I'm pushing my helmet between my legs to cover my nuts, keep them warm, careful not to hit my bleeding rod, but my nuts are in full retreat, my sac hard and taut and wrinkled like a walnut and my cojones seeking warmth up in my fucking lungs, a height from which they will never drop ever again.

I wake up.

It's how I wake up every time I sleep the sleep of the dead, which isn't sleep at all, it's reruns.

I grope around down there to see if anything's wet.

Hand to crotch.

Dry as a bone.

Dry reruns.

I am standing by T's car.

You'd think he could smell me.

Maybe he can; T won't let me in his car.

I must be getting rank; I can't tell.

I am outside T's car.

T is quiet.

It's the first time I've been near T's car since I came back.

I can't remember coming back.

T's just chilling, waiting.

T's watching Copper, a block away.

I'm not watching Copper.

I am looking down at the sidewalk.

Among the tags on what's left of the sidewalk, six faded spray-painted letters, now soft as chalk:

RAPIST

Two yellow-orange letters intrude, the colors still vibrant:

TRAPpIST

That's the best Trapper could muster ten years ago.

T sees me seeing looking at the sidewalk.

T clears his throat.

"Shit, man, leaving a bigger mark now."

T won't look at me.

T glares at the Baker house.

"You gut something, you leave a mark."

"Where's everyone?" I ask.

T looks away.

"I only see you around here."

T smiles.

"Me and that old fucker," T says.

"Copper."

"That his name?"

"What about Jeph?"

"J? Shit. Don't ask."

"I'm asking."

T puts his long fingers to his face, pinches his eyes.

There's a ring on every finger.

"J and C. Shit."

"C?"

"Connie, man. You remember."

I don't remember.

T remembers.

"They got each other through high school and through all kinds of neighborhood shit."

"That's a lot of shit, T."

"That shit killed a lot of folks, y'know?"

"Killed me."

I remember dying, in the Baker House basement.

I remember the needle, the cold, the slow draining, the cold.

T laughs.

T thinks I'm joking.

T keeps his eyes closed.

"Jeph just about got to graduation, and Connie was honor roll her freshman and sophomore year. But she was two years younger than Jeph, and her father hated his bones; like, sicko shit, man. Made no sense."

T's a talker. Always was.

I let him.

I keep mum.

T leans in close. He stinks of anger.

"No sooner J turned eighteen to the second than her pop had the state on his ass for statutory rape."

T pointed to the Baker digs.

"Right fucking there, man. The cops crashed his birthday party and took him out in handcuffs."

He shuts up, still working his bile.

"I remember."

I do remember.

T, just a kid, crying.

J in the cop car.

Connie crying.

I remember.

"Turns out her pop had been prepping for this for over a year; had witnesses lined up and everything."

"Set up."

"The sick fuck joke of it all is Jeph and Connie had never done the deed."

T glares at the Baker house.

"She was still a virgin, saving herself for when she turned eighteen and they could marry. That meant they'd done everything but the mission—you name it, anything to bring her pleasure but keep her pure, crazy-ass abstinence-only shit, all short of the deed."

"Huh."

"She was still cherry, but Connie's dad got the medical examination barred from testimony. And J got four years in the pen."

I remember.

"Connie gave up. She banged every swinging dick in the senior class and ditched home base before her seventeenth. She was gone baby gone; stopped writing J after he told her what was happening to him after lights out."

T's eyes are slits, cold blades.

"He fought, but Jeph wasn't packing muscle; he was a skinny kid. Lost it all on his eighteenth birthday, all for loving that bitch and being a stand-up beau."

"You?"

"I'm hard long before Iraq."

I think, T, you were never there.

I say, "Yep."

"I'm hard from the second I saw them cram his head down into the backseat of the cruiser. I see that move—man's hand on his head, pushing him down—every time I thought of what J had to do to survive in the pen."

T bites something back, spits.

"That lovey-dovey true-love shit hit the wind forever. Fuck that, fuck family, fuck this whole fucking shit-hole. Jeph believed all that, lived all that, and it got him sucking sap with his ass spread, shooting shit to shut it all out."

"You and Uncle Sam?"

"I fucked every girl I could before the end of my seventeenth year and signed up and off to boot the day of my eighteenth birthday. Nine-eleven was my ticket out."

T grinned at the Baker digs.

"Just wish I coulda torched Connie's home into the fucking cellar before I was on the bus."

"Now?"

"Shit, ain't you been listening?"

T leans in close and hisses at me.

"I'm gonna strip and torch every shell in this shit-hole—every stick—and I'm gonna fuck and fuck up every cat, every dog, every four-legged or two-legged or one-legged motherfucker I find here."

T taps my ring.

"And I'm going to get fucking rich doin' it."

I've got nothing to say.

T wants, T waits, but I've got nothing.

"Man, get your stinky shit offa my car. You gotta fucking shower," T snarls.

I grunt.

"You got no pride? Man can't carry his shit in his drawers."

T turns on me.

"Get away from my car, you fuck! You ain't gonna stain my honeybucket!"

I step away from T's car.

"I leave you alone, you leave me alone—deal? For old time's sake," T snarls.

I'm standing on the T and the R in TRAPpIST.

"Clean yourself up, man! Got no more pride?"

I look down.

T drives away.

I stand on the sidewalk and look up.

Copper sits on his porch.

Copper watches.

Copper sits on his porch.

I sit on Copper's step.

"I see you and your buddies."

Good thing he can't smell.

"T is no buddy of mine," I stammer.

Copper spits.

"Not him. The others."

Copper looks at me.

"I see you in that basement where you don't belong."

T drives by.

Copper watches T drive by but acts like he doesn't.

T doesn't look at Copper.

T drives out of sight.

"I see you with that boy too."

"Trapper. T."

"I remember his family."

I can't remember.

"Good family."

Now I remember.

"You remember his brother?" I ask.

Copper looks over at the Baker house.

"Yes," he whispers. "I remember."

"T hates this place."

Copper spits.

"T. He hates this place."

"You can't blame a whole town for what one damned fool does."

I don't remember this place, before.

63

I remember T, before.

I remember T smiling at me, after he signed up.

"This was a good place, once."

Copper looks at me.

"I don't remember."

We sit on Copper's porch.

"We live in the basements."

Copper spits.

"We."

"We."

"I see uniforms."

I rattle off our names, ranks, branches, service records.

Don't even have to think about it.

I remember.

"We stay in the basements. Feels safe down there."

Copper looks at me.

"All of you?"

"All but McFay—McFadyen. We all signed up after nine-eleven."

Copper looks hard at me.

I rattle off where we were out of, where we were stationed, where we came back to.

When we were back.

I stop there.

"You did your country proud, kid."

"Bullshit."

"No need for language, kid."

I remember dying in the Baker-house basement.

"Nobody cares, nobody."

Copper shifts in his rocker.

"Didn't I just say I do?"

"Nobody knows we're here."

Copper looks over at the Baker house.

"You got the short end of the stick, kid."

I remember draining into the floor of the Baker basement.

I remember the cold.

I remember.

Copper spits.

"They didn't treat us like that back in the day."

Copper's voice is hard, cutting.

"I stayed on. Joined the Guard afterward. The service treated me and mine good. Still do."

I remember dying in the basement, over there.

I look down.

"You've got no pride."

"We don't bother anybody."

"Squatters."

I tipped my chin toward what was left of the neighborhood.

"These houses, they're empty."

"You're empty."

"Old man, you don't know the half of it."

Copper spits.

"So tell me."

Copper sits on his rocker.

I hunker down on the top stair, drop my voice.

I tell him about dying in the Baker basement.

I remember, and I tell him.

I don't tell him how much it hurt to die.

I do tell him it doesn't hurt anymore.

Copper looks at me, close, real close.

"You're not lying," he whispers.

I look at Copper.

Copper looks at me.

Sizing me up.

Copper looks at me.

I look at Copper.

A long time.

"Why doesn't anyone—"

"We're everywhere. Nobody sees us."

Copper looks away.

"There's empty houses everywhere. Every town."

Copper coughs.

"We move from town to town, city to city. There's empty houses everywhere."

"Like here."

"Like here."

I tip my head back to look at Copper.

"I had to come back here. Don't know why."

"It's home."

"Home."

The old man looks at me.

"Shells. They're everywhere. We move in. We move out. We move around."

"What about your vet benefits? How do you—"

A dry rasp. My laugh.

"There was nothing to count on when I was still ticking."

I laugh.

"Sure ain't shit now. They don't even know I'm dead."

Copper sits on his porch.

"Waited nine months to see a shrink. Never saw him."

"What happened to you over there, kid?"

I remember.

I tap my forehead.

"TBI. Took a hit from below—IED. Blew me right out of the HMMWV."

I remember.

"Shipped me back. Took care of me till I was stateside."

I remember.

"Then all I could do was self-medicate. Not a good idea. Released me—honorable discharge—for drunk and disorderly."

I remember.

"Couldn't get treatment. Couldn't get help. Couldn't get the time of day."

I remember.

"Couldn't get out of my own way."

I remember dying.

"Waited nine months."

I remember the smell of the basement floor.

"Nobody ever saw me."

I remember dying in the Baker house basement.

"Found my own way to deal with the headaches."

I remember the basement floor, draining out onto it, into it.

"Nobody sees us."

I remember.

"Nobody cares. We bother nobody."

Copper spits.

"You're bothering me, kid."

"We gravitate to our hometowns, if they're big enough."

Copper spits again and turns to me.

"How do you live?"

"Live?"

I let that hang.

I let that hang a long time.

"What do you live on, kid?"

"There's plenty to live on."

Copper spits.

"What?"

I spit.

"They just come to us."

"Who?"

"Kids. Gangs. Shell strippers."

Copper sits on his porch.

"They come to us in the shells."

Copper sits on his porch.

"We take them."

Copper sits on his rocker.

I sit on his porch step.

The sun is behind the trees.

The crickets sing, quiet at first, then louder.

Copper sits on his porch.

I sit on his porch step.

"So, what's this got to do with me?"

"There's nothing left here but you and us and strippers like T."

"I'm not in your army, kid."

"It isn't an army."

Copper spits.

"Never was."

His lunger shimmers a light green on the brown lawn.

"You're the same as that kid I see you with. T."

"We haven't taken anything."

"Suit yourself."

"It's been left for us."

"You take them."

"They come to us. They take, we take."

Copper spits.

"I didn't sign up for this."

"Shit, none of us did."

"No need for language, kid."

"We'll clear out for now."

Copper turns away.

"For the best."

I look up the street.

"T?"

"What about T?"

"We watch out for you, old man."

"I've got nothing left to take."

I remember T saying what he said.

"He'll leave me be."

I remember Copper flinching by the basement door.

I remember dying in the Baker basement.

I don't remember what I had before I lost it.

"Your call, old man."

Copper sighs, won't look at me.

"Dead meat, no use to anyone."

Copper looks over his porch railing to the boarded-up windows of 272 Gilmore.

"You're no use to me at all."

Copper moves his left hand over his right wrist.

"Getting colder."

"Don't matter."

Copper looks at me with those baby blues, clouded with age and loss and pain and the coming cold and the sure knowledge of how cold it's going to get.

"We don't feel it, old man."

Copper looks at me for a long, long time.

"We don't feel nothing."

I look up at Copper.

"No cold."

Copper gets up and goes inside.

Maybe he does know.

I walk down Gilmore to Spruce and turn right.

Stout winks at me from the basement window of Ratboy's old digs.

Fetus and Shiner meet me in front of the old Baker home, and we go inside.

It is our last night in the Baker digs.

Stout stays behind while Fetus, Shiner, and me hook up with the two amputees and McFay to squat in a new basement on the other end of town.

We pull down four of the strip gangs over the next two months.

McFay is skank enough to keep tabs on the latest discards, and we move from shell to shell, lingering on the upper floors until Shiner brings some action our way.

Shiner is fresh enough to mingle and spread the word among the lifers that there's cherry-pickings in the new shells.

We sit tight for a time until the action arrives.

Let them go to work on the plumbing and wiring downstairs, letting the noise cover our formation.

Take them out, one by one, then dig in.

We tie on the feed bag and sit tight for more.

Usually can get one, two strip teams before it's time to move on.

More come.

It's a big town.

It's a big state.

There's a lot of shells.

There's a lot of strip gangs.

It's a long winter.

Word is Copper lost his nest egg on the repairs after T stripped Copper's house.

Word is the repairs sucked up over twenty grand.

Word is no sooner did Copper replace the gutted plumbing and wiring than the insurance inspectors showed up and demanded further repairs on the roof and clapboards, on threat of cancellation of policy.

Word is Copper had to refinance to make those repairs, and on his lonesome signed away the farm without even knowing it.

Word is a zombie bank ate Copper's bankroll.

A zombie fucking bank.

Zombie bank?

What a world.

Word is even with his veteran benefits, Copper thought he was broke.

Wouldn't have happened with Becca.

She would have kept the paperwork straight.

Copper was never any good with all that.

Word is he thought he was so high and dry by St. Patty's Day that he stopped paying some bills.

Word is the power company shut him off, the last house on Gilmore with juice dark at last.

Word is the juice was off when the cold snap hit, nights of ten below.

Word is Copper is still there.

I enter through the kitchen door.

I've been here before.

I remember.

Kitchen all neat.

Shelves, pantry, cupboards.

All neat, nice.

Copper keeps it nice.

In the kitchen window, a ceramic sign.

It's dark, I can't read it.

I remember, though:

WHOEVER DIES WITH THE MOST THINGS, WINS.

I rest my fingers on Copper's oak table.

I pass the cellar door by the pantry.

I walk down the hallway.

The quilt is not on the wall.

I touch the wall.

I leave a little stain on the wall.

I walk down the hallway.

I find Copper in the living room.

I find Copper in the front room, on his chair.

There are six blankets over him, all askew.

There are six blankets and a quilt over Copper.

Becca's quilt is bundled close to his neck.

Cloth houses on the cloth street, bundled around Copper's neck.

Cloth Copper on his cloth rocker on his cloth porch.

Cloth Copper with a stain on his cloth clothes.

I put that stain there.

There's a fresh stain over mine.

A stain from Copper's mouth.

A reddish, ruddy stain.

Copper sits in his chair.

Copper, wrapped in the cloth houses and cloth street and cloth neighbors and cloth Copper in his cloth rocker on his cloth porch.

Six blankets and the cloth neighborhood didn't keep him warm.

Six blankets and a quilt, but how to cover oneself when you can't feel your fingers?

Six blankets and a quilt, but it's not enough, and it doesn't quite do the trick.

Six blankets and a quilt, but one leg is bare between the top of the sock and edge of the pant leg, its crease gone.

The bare skin is blue-white.

Copper is blue-white, his skin the color of his eyes.

Under the blankets, his right hand is wrapped over his left wrist, his left hand clutching his right wrist, his fingers locked over wrists like dead crow feet.

The cold bit deep this time, deeper than deep.

Copper's face is waxed, his jaw fixed cocked to the side, his lower gums bared, mouth slightly open.

A light frost bristles on his lips, spiking from his unshaven chin, whiter than the paraffin-white of his skin.

The frost continues down onto the cloth Copper on his cloth rocker on his cloth porch.

Copper's spider-leg eyebrows crook upward over his nose, frozen in surprise.

I remember dying in the Baker basement.

It was cold.

Copper hates the cold.

Copper hates the cold, but it still took him by surprise, a slow, steely revelation of how bad it really had become, could be, was, is.

It took Copper hard.

It hurt.

It took a long fucking time, and it fucking hurt; it hurt bad.

The cold took him and his and all he still had and all he'd been.

Took it hard.

I sit and watch.

I sit and watch Copper.

I watch him until he's watching me.

I watch his eyes trade one glaze for another, just like when I watched Fetus when his eyes did the same thing.

When was that?

I can't remember.

I watch Copper's brow furrow, his milky blues go from watching nothing to watching something to eventually taking me in.

"It hurt, didn't it?"

Copper straightens his jaw.

His jaw pops, and he works it back and forth.

"The cold, I mean."

He closes his mouth and purses his lips, testing them, like an infant.

"It really fucking hurt, didn't it, old man?"

Copper glares at me.

"No need for language, kid."

Turns out Fetus and I were right.

Turns out Copper is just what we need:

A commanding officer.

Copper takes command.

Copper knows the neighborhood.

Turns out Copper knows more than this neighborhood.

Copper knows more than this burb.

Turns out Copper knows most of the city.

Turns out Copper has maps and charts and floor plans.

"How do you remember all this?" I ask.

"Worked in just about every nook and cranny at some point, kid."

Copper winks at me when he says it.

"What I didn't work, my brother-in-law did."

Copper reprimands us for thinking small.

Copper has plans.

Copper has plans and makes plans.

Copper is in command.

Copper sets up his command outpost in his own basement.

Copper doesn't flinch at the basement door.

Copper leads us all downstairs.

Basement is clean, neat, tidy. Like the whole house.

Copper spreads out the floor plans and the street plans, and Copper looks and makes marks and asks questions and looks some more.

Copper calls Fetus and Stout and Shiner and McFay and those two amputees and me in for a powwow.

He lays it all out and we drink it all in and we sit real quiet for a long time and think about it, and we sit real quiet.

Copper calls Shiner and Fetus in with state maps.

Copper has big plans.

I stop dreaming about Mount McKinley.

I can't remember Mount McKinley anymore.

I wake up on the cot Copper provides and I make my bed.

I fold the corners the way I was taught in—

I can't remember.

Copper reminds me.

I remember dying in the Baker house basement.

Now I'm in Copper's basement.

It's nice.

Copper brings us LED lights.

Copper brings in stuff to read.

It's nice.

I don't remember the cold.

I remember how to make my bed.

I don't remember Mount McKinley.

Copper stays put on his porch, day after day, and watches.

Copper watches the cops drive by when they bother to drive by at all, and they don't wave, and Copper doesn't wave.

Copper doesn't cup his wrists in his hands anymore, because Copper doesn't feel the cold anymore.

Nobody knows Copper doesn't feel the cold, no more than anyone knows how badly he felt it over his long, slow passing back in March, except for me.

Copper watches, and nobody knows any better.

Nobody is watching.

Nobody cares.

Copper is watching.

Copper cares.

Copper sees T drive by.

Copper watches T drive by.

T doesn't turn his head.

Copper doesn't wave.

Copper and Shiner go away for—

I don't remember.

I remember how to make my bed.

I sit on Copper's porch but never in his rocker.

I look out the Baker house basement window.

I remember Copper.

Copper and Shiner come back in a pickup truck with two other men.

Copper and Shiner meet with the men for I don't know how long.

Copper and Shiner put away the state maps and the map of the United States and call me and Stout and McFay in.

"Pack your gear, we're moving out next week, kid."

"I'll miss you."

"No, no, you're coming too."

Copper winks.

"New detail. New plans."

Copper talks about the big plan.

Lots of towns, lots of houses.

Lots of states.

"Will we come back?" I ask.

"Back?"

"Home?"

"Wherever we are, kid, it'll be home."

Home.

"This country is our home."

Home.

"We'll make it our home."

Plans.

"This country owes you that much, kid."

Plans.

Homes.

Cities.

States.

A whole big country, full of grunts like us.

Nobody sees us.

Nobody cares.

Nobody cares about our plans.

Lots of plans.

"We move out next week."

Copper winks at me.

"We've got a job to finish."

Copper lays out the floor plans and points to the street plan and hands his pickup keys to McFay.

McFay and Shiner drive off and come back.

Stout and me stack the copper piping just as we were told to—half in and half out of Copper's basement window.

Stout leaves two coils of wire in Copper's driveway, one leaning against the basement-window casing.

Shiner is boarding up the other windows.

Shiner leaves only one window open—the one with the pipes half in, half out.

Copper sits on his porch, watching.

Copper and I sit on this porch.

Copper sits on his porch.

Copper sees T drive by.

Copper watches T drive by.

T doesn't turn his head.

Copper waves.

Copper sits in his basement.

Copper looks at an old stain on the wall.

Fetus and Shiner and McFay sit on the bench by the furnace, which hasn't fired up in months.

I sit by the two amputees in the far corner.

Copper sits in his basement with us.

We hear the crunch of gravel outside, footsteps on the driveway.

Copper sits in his basement.

The piping in the window moves.

Copper sits in his basement.

The piping shifts and then slowly slides out of the window frame, into the night.

Copper sits in the basement.

Fetus and Shiner and I sit tight.

McFay sits still.

A flashlight beam cuts in from the open window.

Copper sits in the basement, satisfied with his plan.

We're positioned just so.

The flashlight beam can't reach us.

The beam alights on lengths of copper pipes and coils of wiring.

T's head appears at the window.

Copper cocks his head slightly, listening.

There's only the sound of T, moving with all the stealth he can muster.

It isn't much.

T is alone.

Copper sits in the basement.

T leans his head in farther, craning for a better look-see.

Copper gives the order.

Copper's hands are on T, his fingers locked around the kid's head, one thumb deep in his left eye socket.

T shrieks like a girl and tries to lash out, but I've got his right arm and Fetus is on the other and he's our wishbone.

We pull as one and something gives and something splashes black from the windowsill and something deeper than shadow pools across the floor, and T's screams grow louder as we pull him in.

Fetus bends to drink from the floor in a rectangle of moonlight.

I see Stout's smile.

His teeth are black and violet in the dim light, his chin is wet, dimples deep.

Before he is out of eyeshot, he gulps like a newborn, stopping only once to tip his head back and gurgle with joy.

Window becomes mouth, cellar becomes throat; broken glass teeth slip through T.

T spills inside, and we take him and his and all he ever was and never was, all he ever had and all he ever might have been but wasn't and will never be.

I help Copper pull T's wiring and strip his plumbing.

T's song is sweet, shrill, short. Copper is humming to himself.

Dark, tough laces of T cat-cradle between us, ropes of him spill, stretch, and break. The cement is baptized with beads of him and puddles of him and steaming streams and rivers and oceans of him.

We spread him; he is bread, water, wine.

We dig in.

Blood becomes rust, bone becomes sliver; flesh becomes fire, death becomes home.

Home.

Always home.

IN THE DUST

BY TIM LEBBON

We should have known that one day they'd refuse to let us leave.

I'd already seen the fresh smoke rising from the cremation pits, and a sensation of cold dread had settled in my stomach. But I chose not to mention it to the others. Jamie's bluff and bluster would only piss me off, and I feared it would send Bindy over the edge. If in the end events drove her to madness or suicide, I didn't want to be the catalyst.

So it wasn't until we reached the old stone river bridge that the truth began to dawn.

"What the fuck?" Jamie said.

"Toby . . ." Bindy let go of the cart and grabbed my hand. Before the plague, we'd only known each other in passing, and there was nothing sexual here, but contact helped her cope. As for me . . . it only made me think of the past.

"They've blocked the bridge," I said.

"And they're burning something in the pits." Jamie jogged off ahead of us, approaching the barrier of roughly laid concrete block and barbed wire they'd built while we'd been searching.

"Toby . . . ?" Bindy said again, her hand squeezing hard.

"It's okay," I said, squeezing back. Though I knew it was not.

I looked down at the cart we'd been pushing. The body of a small child stared back at me. She had died during the initial outbreak and had been motionless since the Purge three weeks earlier, but her eyes still held a glimmer of something resembling life. That was always the worst thing for me—not that they'd moved when they were dead or were mindless or craved the gristly hearts of the living, but that in their eyes they looked so alive.

The girl stared back at me, unseeing. I looked away.

"Hey!" Jamie shouted. "Come and see!"

"Toby, I don't want to go up there," Bindy said.

"Then stay with her," I said, letting go and walking after Jamie. I heard Bindy's sharp intake of breath and knew that I could be cruel. But she was weak, and sometimes I lost patience with her.

I reached the block wall and climbed, joining Jamie where he looked through the swirls of razor wire topping it. I could still smell the rich, warm odor of wet cement.

"Something's happened," he said. For once, his understatement was surprising.

There had been an army camp on the other side of the bridge. For three weeks, the three of us had been bringing bodies out of Usk, back over the bridge and delivering them into the hands of the scientists. We each had different reasons for doing so, and all of them involved dead people. We had found Jamie's sister on day one, torn apart in a pond in their garden, her chest opened and heart ripped out. There had been a squirrel feeding on her eyes, and I'd been shocked, because I never knew a squirrel would eat meat. Bindy's parents were two of the infected killed during the Purge, and we'd brought them both out during the second week. Her mother had been covered with dried blood, and in her father's hand was the remains of something meaty. They'd had those same staring, glittering eyes, wet and knowing, even in true death.

My own dear Fiona eluded me still.

Now the camp was abandoned. There were still a few of the prefab huts they'd used, and a tent flapped in the lonely breeze. The field was churned up, and the old cottage they'd requisitioned as a command post was empty. Its windows and door had been left open, and that just seemed so careless. *The rain will get in*, I thought. I laughed softly.

"What is it?" Jamie asked.

"Nothing."

"So where the fuck have they gone?"

I shrugged, but my eyes were drawn to the smoke still rising from the pyres, the fires and pits hidden beyond a thick copse of trees. After we brought the bodies out and they'd done their tests, that was where they disposed of them. Someone was burning now. The smoke was black and greasy, the smell sickly and mouthwatering.

"Moved back," I said. "Pulled the perimeter out away from the village."

"Why?" he asked, but I could see him looking at the smoke as well. "Fuckers," he said softly.

I turned and looked back down the curve of the bridge at Bindy. She'd stepped in front of the trailer so she did not have to look at the little dead girl, and she was staring up at us, eyes wide and hands clasped between her breasts. When she saw my expression, she looked at the road surface.

"They should tell us what they found, shouldn't they?" Jamie asked.

"So ask them."

"What do you mean?"

I nodded across at the torn-up field. Birds were flocking across it, exploring for worms where the soil had been recently turned. "You don't think they'd leave us alone, do you? We could climb the wall, swim the river. Walk out of Usk." I was scanning the landscape as I spoke, searching for movement, or the telltale glint of sunlight on binoculars or rifle scopes. I could see nothing, but that didn't mean they were not there. "They'll be there to make sure we don't."

"Well, I'm going to try," Jamie said.

"Don't be a fool."

"Fool?" He turned to me, eyes wide and glaring, and the fear beneath his constant outrage was patent. "You've been treating me like a kid ever since we started this, and I'm a lot younger than you, so I can take that. But I'm not a fucking fool."

"Fair enough."

He turned back to the view, scanning the hedgerows and hillside beyond, as I had.

"They'll let us out, Toby, won't they?" Bindy said behind us.

"No," I said. It was so quiet that she didn't hear, but Jamie did. He glanced at me again as he jumped down from the wall.

"Later," he said. "I'm going to swim the river and get out of this shit-hole later."

I followed him back down to the street.

"What do we do with that?" he said, pointing at the girl's body.

For a second, I was at a loss. By discovering the corpse splayed on a tomb slab in the churchyard, we had effectively taken ownership of it, and the thought of simply dumping her somewhere felt terrible. She was somebody's daughter, someone's little girl, and she deserved more than that.

"Well, chuck her down a drain somewhere for all I care," Jamie said, when neither of us answered. He walked off along the street. "I'm going to the Queen's. I'll be in the bar."

Bindy turned to me.

"Let's put her back where we found her," I said, and she seemed to find that acceptable. She almost smiled.

Jamie was on the way to drunk by the time Bindy and I arrived at the Queen's Hotel. He was sitting at a table in the bar, and we arrived in time to see him stagger across, lift the bar flap, pour himself a single whiskey, and then sway back to his seat. By the time he sat down again, he'd almost finished his drink, but perhaps there was something comforting in the process.

"Whadidya do with her?" he asked.

"Back in the churchyard," Bindy said.

Jamie snorted, but I wasn't sure what that meant.

"I'll get food," I said. "Then we should talk about what to do."

"Talk?" Jamie shouted. He looked ready to rage, and I tensed. Then the glass slipped from his hand and dropped to the table, landing upright without spilling a drop, and he put one hand to his forehead. He sobbed, once, then looked up at us again, putting on his hard face again.

"Jamie—" Bindy began.

"Fuck it!" he said. "There's nothing to do but get out. I've done nothing . . . nothing wrong. Nor you." He pointed at us, and I wondered how many people he saw. "It's wrong, them keepin' us in, and . . . I'll get out."

"I'm getting food," I said. I sensed Jamie about to break—it had been coming for days—and I had no wish to see that. I went through behind the bar and into the big kitchen, glancing at the huge walk-in freezer door we hadn't dared open since the power had gone off. There was still enough food in the larder—tinned stuff, packets, dehydrated fruit and vegetables. At lunchtimes over the past few days, we'd almost laughed about how disgusting it was, but knowing we were now trapped here with no chance of escape, laughter was distant.

I knocked together something quick to eat, because there were more important things to do. I carried it back through to the bar and was amazed to see that Jamie had calmed down. He was still drinking steadily, and Bindy sat at the table opposite him with an open bottle of wine and two glasses in front of her. As I sat down she poured me a glass. Jamie stayed on the whiskey.

"That fire," she said. "We haven't taken a body out for two days. Could it be that one?"

I remembered the body she meant—a huge, fat woman, naked, her breasts pawed and scratched and teeth clotted with rotting meat. And those eyes, so falsely alive.

"They burnt that one the day we took her out," I said.

"Right," Jamie agreed.

"So there's been another outbreak," Bindy said. She was staring into the deep violet depths of her glass. The drink had already stained her lips, an effect that I had always found unbearably sexy in women drinking red wine. Not in Bindy, though.

"Not necessarily," I said. "If there had been, why trap us in here?"

"It's in the dust," Jamie said. "I've told you, haven't I? I've been saying it all along." He ran one finger around the inside of his glass, smearing whiskey and touching his finger to his tongue. From day one, Jamie had been suggesting that the plague—virus, bacteria, nobody yet seemed to know exactly what caused it—could be alive in the dust of the deserted town. He'd seen dust settled on the eyes of the bodies we'd found, filtering the light that entered their dead eyes, and I think perhaps it had driven him slightly mad. We were all allowed our own madness.

We drank some more but didn't really come up with anything like a plan. Jamie was drunk and bitter and scared; Bindy was too distant; and I really had no need of a plan at all. My aim had always been to find Fiona's corpse, wherever it might be, and only one thing really kept me going—the hope that she had been killed and eaten by what people had started to call zombies.

The alternative was that she had become one herself, and the thought of looking into her dead eyes knowing that was just too terrible to bear.

We took three en-suite rooms next to each other. Bindy and I carried Jamie to bed, trying to ignore his rantings and tears, and then back in the corridor I bid her goodnight.

"Toby," she said, and her voice sounded different. "I know what you think of me, but I'm trying. I'm really trying." She slurred slightly, but she was more in control than I had ever seen her. She'd once served me breakfast at a café in town—maybe four years ago—and I'd flirted with her. "I keep thinking tomorrow will be another day, but it won't. It'll always be today." She turned to go to bed, and I reached out and held her arm. She touched my hand and smiled sadly.

"Maybe they've just upped and left." It was fucking stupid, and I knew that, but I couldn't think of anything else to say.

"They built a wall," she said. "And Jamie's right: None of us has done anything wrong." She went to bed then, and so did I.

I lay there for some time trying to sleep. The town lay around me, its geography altered completely by what had happened. The town square, its attractive clock tower bedecked with flower troughs, its cobble paving slippery in light summer rain, was now the place where I had found six dead zombies with the remains of several small children they had been fighting over when the Purge came. Where the old castle once stood, I could now only recall seeing the family that had fled there to die—father, mother, and two children, surrounded by their mingled blood vented by the knife in the man's hand. Streets where I had walked with Fiona, pubs we had drunk in, restaurants where we had eaten and laughed and talked quietly of the possibility of children, all now tainted in some way by what had happened. Some taints were simply the silence; others, blood and rot and death.

I was trapped in my hometown, but I had never been in a place so strange.

As I drifted to sleep I wondered yet again what had happened to the rest of Usk's residents. Most of them had fled after the first few attacks, but they were soon rounded up and kept in confinement in the old military base in Glascoed. The majority of those who stayed behind were killed or infected, and then came the Purge, where the whole town was sprayed hourly for three days with what the military had called an "antidote" when Bindy, Jamie, and I walked out of town across the stone river bridge; the only reason we weren't shot is that their solution hadn't killed us.

They'd let us stay, suggesting that we help appropriate zombie corpses for the scientists to study. Every day they let us out to sleep in comfortable quarantine, and each morning, I expected it to be the day they no longer let us out. I didn't care, because Fiona had remained behind and had not yet been found.

Faces of old friends and people I knew from the town appeared to me as I dropped into an uneasy slumber. Some of them smiled, some were slack in death.

Some of them raged.

The sound of helicopters woke me up. I went to the window and saw a military chopper buzzing the town. At first I thought they were spraying again, but then I noticed the cameras mounted under its nose.

"Please come out into the street where we can see you," an electronic voice said. "Stand at the road junction, and make yourselves known."

Make yourselves known! I thought. We'd been dragging corpses from the dead town for three weeks for these bastards, and they couldn't even use our names.

I met Bindy out in the corridor, and we knocked on Jamie's door. *He's dead*, I thought, *veins slashed, heart given up, brain popped with the pressure.* But then he opened the door, squinting in the dawn light. He had a hangover. I chuckled.

"Fuck's wrong with you?" he growled.

"Nothing. Come on, let's find out what's going on."

Bindy and I waited at the road junction outside the hotel for several minutes before Jamie joined us. In that time the chopper swept past three times, the cameras seeming to turn slightly as it went. It was warm already this morning, but the rotors caused a storm in the street that blew waves of dust against smashed shop windows.

Jamie coughed and spluttered, washing dust from his mouth with a swig from the whiskey bottle he carried.

"You're kidding me," I said.

"Hey, it's a free country!" He giggled maniacally and took another drink.

The chopper came in again and hovered a hundred feet along the street. We could barely see against the dust and grit, and the sound was tremendous. The speakers were even louder.

"For your own safety, you will remain in quarantine within the town limits for the next forty-eight hours."

This is unfair, I thought. *We can't ask them anything.*

"During that time, certain work will be undertaken. You must not attempt to impede or interfere in any way. You must not attempt to escape."

"Try and fuckin' stop me, you bastards!" Jamie shouted. I realized that he was still drunk.

"Any escape attempt will result in the use of deadly force."

The sound seemed to decrease, and the three of us were trapped in a surreal bubble of shock. *They'll shoot us*, I thought, and their military-speak suddenly annoyed the hell out of me. Why couldn't they just say what they meant?

I glanced past Bindy at Jamie. He caught my eye, smiled, and shrugged. Bravado.

"Toby Parsons, please proceed alone to the road crossing outside the primary school. There you'll be given more instructions, and any questions will be answered."

I hated the sound of that voice, distorted by technology. The speaker could have been laughing or crying, and we'd never know.

The chopper lifted away quickly and disappeared over the rooftops, and Jamie gave it the finger.

"What does all that mean?" Bindy said. "What work are they going to do?"

"Hopefully I'll find out," I said.

"Why just you?" Jamie said. "Why the hell is it you who—"

"Jamie," I said softly, quietly, and he listened. Maybe I'd never spoken to him in this tone of voice before, but it was about fucking time. "Stay here. Drink coffee. Have a wash. I'll go and find out what's happening."

I glanced at Bindy, and though she was frowning, I could see that she seemed comforted somehow with me taking charge. Not that I wanted to. Last thing I wanted was these two hanging on my back.

The only thing I wanted . . .

But we'd been looking for three weeks, and if Fiona had been a victim rather than a zombie, I was sure I'd have found her by then. I knew all the places she knew. I'd checked all the places we'd been together. And if I really thought about it, I didn't really want to keep looking at all.

I started along the street. It took me five minutes to reach the school, and all the while I could hear that chopper somewhere in the distance. It was the first time I'd been alone out on the streets since the Purge: Every other time, one or both of the others had been with me. I thought I'd be scared, or at least nervous, but I found it quite settling. Most things had changed, but liking my own company was not one of them.

As I reached the zebra crossing by the school, I looked along the curving road at the roadblock. It had been there since the first plague outbreak in the town, and I'd seen it a couple of times in the past few days when we went looking for bodies in the school. But now it looked different—larger, for a start, and it had also been added to. Whereas before it had been constructed of a couple of cars turned on their sides and piles of sandbags, now there were several heavy, dark metallic structures behind that. Tall fences stretched away on either side, the one on the left disappearing behind a house and heading uphill, the one leading right forming a straight line across the school's playing field, merging with the woodland beyond.

On either side of the road stood tall posts topped with cameras. They both turned slightly, and I imagined them as eyes observing my approach. Fifty feet away, an amplified voice said, "Remain where you are."

I stopped, sighed. Everyone was shouting at me today.

A man appeared atop the roadblock, obviously standing on a raised section on the other side. He looked across the town behind me before focusing on my face. He appeared nervous.

"Toby Parson?"

"That's me."

"I'm Peter O'Driscoll. I'm a doctor assigned to the research team looking into—"

"You're one of the scientists that have been cutting up the bodies I've been hauling out of here."

"Yes, if you like." He did not seem at all perturbed by my comment.

"So what have you found out?"

He paused, but only for a second. "I'm afraid that's classified."

I laughed. It was the first real laughter I'd uttered since the plague and since losing touch with Fiona. We'd been half a mile apart when the first attacks came, by my reckoning. Close enough to hear each other screaming.

"You're joking!" I said. "What movie do you think you're in?" I laughed some more.

"Your help has been appreciated," O'Driscoll said.

"Got a medal for me?"

"No, no medal."

"So what do you want? Is there another infection? Has it spread?"

"It's still contained," O'Driscoll said. "But there's been a recurrence, yes."

A recurrence. My blood ran cold. The Purge was supposed to have been the end solution, the final cleansing of what had happened in Usk. Blame went everywhere from the moment it struck, the media filling the channels with political and religious pundits, ex-military personnel and any C-list celebrity who had a fucking opinion. When the military had issued assurances that the Purge would end the slaughter, such assurances were taken as an admission of guilt. How could they know how to stop it if they claimed not to know how it began?

"Where?" I asked. And then a greater chill ran through me, and I couldn't prevent myself from spinning around. The chopper, the cameras . . . "In the town?"

"No, Mr. Parsons. Usk is clear . . . or so we believe. The recurrence was in one of the corpses you brought out."

"So the infection is still here."

"We hope not. We hope it was an isolated case, and we're looking into it. But . . ." He glanced down at something in his hand.

"Okay," I said. "So you're watching us, just in case."

O'Driscoll nodded, lips pursed. "Just in case."

"And if we're still fine a week from now? Two weeks?"

He went to leave.

"Hey!" I called. "You can't just go!"

He paused, squatting down ready to jump away from the road-block. He seemed to have nothing else to say.

"You can't just leave us in here like this. We've haven't done anything wrong!"

"But you might," he said, and dropped back into his world.

I was left staring at the roadblock while the cameras stared back. I gave them the finger. It felt childish, but it made me feel better.

Turning to walk back into town, I felt watched every step of the way. As I passed the school, I looked at the low brick building, infant-class windows splashed with colorful drawings. Self-portraits with big round pink faces, bright blue eyes, and smears of yellow or brown hair. If I went closer I'd probably see the names, but I had no wish to do that. I might end up seeing the cartoon face of the little girl we'd left back in the churchyard.

The chopper drifted in again, skimming low over the trees beyond the school and disappearing from view. I jogged along the street, eager to see what they were doing, and as I passed the burned-out fire station, I saw through a gap between buildings. The chopper was hovering above the four-story block of flats—one of the tallest buildings in Usk—and two men were rappelling down a rope to the rooftop.

"What the hell . . ." I muttered.

Maybe they wanted us. They'd confine us somewhere, send in their teams of doctors and scientists like O'Driscoll with their syringes and knives, and slice us open one by one to see if they could find out what was happening. Because even if they'd known at the beginning, I had the feeling that they were lost now. The plague had progressed—evolved, perhaps—and with a recurrence somewhere beyond the town's perimeter, their understanding of whatever caused the plague had lessened considerably. Desperate times called for desperate measures, I knew that. But suddenly I was very, very afraid.

We're expendable, I thought. *At least we know the town, the streets, know the places to hide.* . . . But that was just foolish. If they sent in forces to find us, we would be found.

But the two men on the roof did not look like they had been here for long. They were setting up a large tripod topped with a box, weighing down the feet, clipping some sort of cover over the box. The chopper had drifted away, but it was merely performing a circuit of the town.

More cameras.

Even as I realized that, the helicopter came in low and lowered a rope ladder, and the two men climbed back up.

I could just see the smooth movement as the camera turned this way and that. Someone back at control was testing it. I waved.

Walking back to the Queen's Hotel, I heard and saw several more choppers coming in. They chose the tallest buildings.

"What are they doing?" Bindy asked as I arrived back. She was sitting on one of the hotel's wide stone windowsills, waiting for me. For a moment I was irritated at her question, but then I sighed softly and sat beside her.

"Setting up cameras to try and keep track of us," I said.

"Why?"

"There's been a recurrence in one of the bodies we took out. I guess they want to watch in case we're infected too."

Bindy nodded grimly. "So that's it then," she said, and I couldn't bring myself to answer. I didn't want to admit the end of anything.

"Where's Jamie?"

"Went inside. I expect he's in the bar."

"Right. I need to tell him what's going on."

Bindy stayed where she was, which surprised me a little. I thought she'd latch on to me again like a lost puppy, her eyes wide and expectant. Maybe somewhere she'd found her own strength.

"Bindy," I said from the main doorway. She glanced at me. "We'll get out. When they've sorted it all, when they know exactly what's happening."

"Thanks, Toby," she said. Then she looked away again.

I went inside to find Jamie.

The first plague victim I had seen was an old man who used to run an optician's office on the main street. He was in the early, raging phase, and he stalked the street, smashing shopwindows with his own hands and head, picking up big shards of glass, and slashing at passersby. This was still early on, and though most people knew that *something* was wrong with Usk, few knew exactly what. People screamed, the old man shouted and growled, and then he pinned a woman down and started cutting her up. He was completely insane.

A teenager smashed him over the head with a golf club, five times.

He fell on the bleeding woman and died in the street, and seconds later he hauled himself slowly upright again. The rage was gone now, and he started digging into the woman beneath him for her heart.

When I entered the bar, Jamie was raging.

My heart stuttered; my balls tingled with fear. I stood back against the wall and watched.

Jamie was overturning tables and chairs, smashing bottles, kicking out at the bar, spitting and shouting. *This is it*, I thought; *it's all over for us now.* And suddenly, facing that, I found my purpose again: I could not die here, because I had to find Fiona.

As I was backing away, Jamie saw me. He stopped and fell to his knees, crying.

"It's not fair," he said. "None of it's fair."

I let out a breath, sagging against the wall. *Just drunk. Christ.*

"You heard what I told Bindy."

"Through the window." He lay down among smashed glass on the whiskey-stained carpet, and I left him there. There was little I could do, and for a moment he'd scared the hell out of me. I wondered what they'd do if they saw him raging like that.

I went back outside, but Bindy had gone. So I went to look for Fiona.

We'd lived in one of eight flats in an old renovated church in the town square, and the building had been gutted the day of the outbreak. Fiona was gone by then, and since the Purge I'd been back into the church three times looking for her body. So I went there again, climbing the warped metal staircase. However hard I tried to avoid touching any surfaces, by the time I reached the first floor, my hands were black with soot. It was as if the air itself was stained.

Our flat was at the rear of the church, and I had to pass two others to get there. They were both ruins, and were empty of bodies or bones.

I reached the place we had shared and loved, and I was thankful that it looked nothing like home. That would have been hard to take. I felt no hint of nostalgia, because the place was black and burnt and there was little to recognize. The layout was familiar, but even that had changed where walls had burned through and ceilings had fallen. In what had been our bathroom, the floor was gone, and I could see the shattered remains of our bathroom suite in the flat below. In the bedroom, the bed was a charred mound, and none of the wardrobes had survived.

I'd done it before, but I sifted again, moving ash and blackened wood around with my feet. Clouds of dust rose up, and soon I knew my vision would be blurred, so I worked quickly. Bedroom, living room, kitchen—there was nothing to suggest that Fiona had been here when the fire broke out.

I loved her, but right then I so wanted to find her bones.

Leaving the church, I realized that I would never go home again. There was no need, because it was no longer there. So I walked the town once more, looking in places where I had already searched, glancing into gardens which were already becoming overgrown, amazed at the silence of this place. That was something I could not grow used to. Never a particularly busy town, nevertheless there had always been an atmosphere of bustle. The main street was where most of the shops were, and it was forever frequented by the town's retired contingent going for coffee or their morning papers, and at lunchtime office workers would visit the several restaurants and pubs. In the evenings too it was a lively place, though rarely any more than that. Now, even though the place was not completely silent, it was devoid of the chatter of people.

Birds seemed to have taken over. Perhaps their songs had always been there, subsumed beneath the constant rattle of traffic, but now they were given free rein. They lined the rooftops and windowsills, pecked around on the roads, and flitted overhead in manic celebration.

It wouldn't be long, I knew, before Usk began to take on a wild appearance. Always proud of their town, most of the residents had gone to great lengths to make sure their gardens were well planted. Those plants would no longer have to fear the shears or clippers of artifice.

"Toby!" The shout came from far away, the direction confused by echoes.

"Bindy?"

"Toby, the river!"

I ran. Past the old law courts, across the parking lot, through an alleyway, and out onto the main street. I was gasping already and cursing the middle-aged spread that I'd willingly let settle. *Something for me to hold on to*, Fiona had said once as we made love. As I pelted along the road, the river bridge came into view around a curve in the main street. Bindy was standing on it, not far from the block wall, leaning over the stone parapet and looking down.

"What is it?" I called as I ran.

She glanced up and pointed. "Jamie!"

I heard his voice then, more drunken shouting and rambling, and if he'd been close to me, I'd have gleefully punched him. He was a tiresome idiot. *Am I really trapped here with him for however long?*

I ran up beside her and looked over the stone parapet. Jamie was down at the river's edge, and he had something slung over his shoulder. His things?

"Don't be an asshole!" I shouted. "You get over, they'll shoot you before—"

"Fuck off," he said wearily.

"He won't listen," Bindy said. "And he's not going to swim."

I realized what he had over his shoulder then—the little dead girl from the churchyard.

I climbed onto the parapet and judged the drop. Maybe twelve feet. *And if I break my leg?* I thought. *I'm stuck in Usk with a waitress and a loser, and I'll end up dying in bed.*

"Jamie, what are you doing?" It was a stupid question, because I could already guess. As ever, he was trying to be defiant, because that was the only way he could hide his fear.

"Helping her escape," he said, giggling. "See how far she'll get."

"They're trying to keep this thing contained," I said, and I blinked, confused. Did I *agree* with what they were doing? I hadn't really given myself time to consider that, not yet.

"You're a pompous shit, Toby. Y'know that? You should listen to yourself sometimes, look at yourself." Jamie stepped down the riverbank onto some mud flats. The river rushed by several feet from him.

I almost jumped. If I had, perhaps I would have stopped him. But the real reason that kept me up on the bridge was the idea that the trees across the river could be home to snipers. I didn't want to be close to Jamie when they started shooting.

But there was no gunfire as he approached the river, and none as he shrugged the girl off his shoulder and into the mud. Her limbs were still loose, eyes clear. *There's been a recurrence.*

"Jamie, do you want other people to go through what you're going through?" Bindy asked.

"Yes," Jamie said. He pushed the child into the water. I winced, expecting gunfire, and as we watched her float away, I realized that I had failed. I was a coward. A jump, a punch, and I could have stopped him.

"Fuck," I said.

"Yes, 'cause if I have to go through it, why shouldn't other people?" There wasn't an ounce of regret in his voice. In fact, I thought I heard an element of glee as he giggled again, took a half bottle of whiskey from a pocket in his cargo pants, and started drinking.

"You're a fucking idiot, Jamie," Bindy said, "and you'll get us all killed." She was watching the little girl carried out by the river.

The water flow was quite fast here after being channeled through the bridge's three arches, and the body started to turn as it moved downriver, spinning clockwise with arms and legs splayed, hair billowing out around it. *The dust will be washed from her eyes now*, I thought. A tree overhanging the river snagged her clothing for a beat, but then she moved on, and soon she was out of sight around a bend.

I realized that Jamie had already walked back up the bank and skirted around the old tollhouse at the bridge's end. He was heading back along the main street, bottle clasped loose in one hand, and he swayed slightly as he walked. Still drunk. Jamie would always be drunk, and I wondered how much worse he'd be sober.

"What do we do now?" Bindy asked. She had moved closer to me, and she reached out as she spoke. I took her hand.

"Just carry on," I said. "I'm still looking."

"But if you *do* find her—"

"I'm still looking." I let go of Bindy and started following Jamie.

"You're not, in case you were wondering," she said, as she followed on behind.

"Not what?"

"A pompous shit."

I shrugged as if I didn't care.

Jamie was sitting on the curb close to the post office, a stupid grin on his face. Waiting for us. Waiting to gloat.

"What?" Bindy said. I cursed her silently for encouraging him.

"Showed them," he said. He laughed, but I detected an uncertainty in him. The laughter was there to cover that, perhaps for himself.

"Yes, you really showed them, Jamie," I said. "They're sure to buck up their ideas and let us leave now. Prick."

He went to stand, swayed, and I saw violence cloud his face. I didn't want to fight him, because I'd never been a fighter. But I realized it was something else that would come between him and his uncertainty, and he was set on the course now.

He threw his empty bottle away and took a step toward me, and then the chopper came.

"What do they want now?" Jamie said. He sounded scared.

"Stay where you are," that mechanical voice instructed.

"Lecture," I said. "We're their pets, and they're going to give us a good talking-to."

I was right. But they didn't say another word. Instead, as the chopper hovered just above the buildings fifty yards along the street from us, a man leaned out with something in his hand. *Camera and microphone*, I thought, and then Jamie flipped back onto the pavement, blood spewing from his throat just below his Adam's apple. His eyes were wide, hands waving like separate animals as they tried to find the wound, and before they could, a second shot rang out. This one was right on target, and the top and back of his head splashed across the post office's front steps.

The helicopter left. Bindy had turned away, but I couldn't help but look. I'd seen a lot of death, but there was something worse about this one. For a few seconds, as blood dripped, his left foot twitched, and his eyes slowly turned up in his head. I couldn't work out what it was.

"And then there were two!" Bindy said, verging on hysteria.

And that was it. Because inside I knew we'd be in here for a very long time, and prick though he was, Jamie was company. And prick though I was, distant and aloof, I knew I could never hope to survive this on my own.

I went to Bindy and held her, and this time it was me taking comfort from the contact as well. She felt warm and alive, and I held on to that with everything I had.

That night, Bindy moved into my room at the hotel. I did not object, and she didn't ask. She simply dropped her small bag of belongings next to mine, stripped to her underwear, and climbed into bed. I put my arm around her shoulders, and she rested her head on my chest, and soon she was asleep. There was nothing sexual at all. I smelled her, felt her heat, felt her heavy breasts pressed against my side, but I didn't stir. This was pure survival instinct, and though we didn't need each other's bodily warmth, there was so much more to share.

The next day we went about burying Jamie. I tied a bag around his head so that we didn't have to look at where wildlife had been picking at him. Bindy broke into a hardware and do-it-yourself store to find a shovel and pick. We carried him together across the main street and through a small alley that led to a pub garden. There were rose beds here, so the ground was still quite soft even in the summer heat, and I saw no reason to carry him all the way to the church.

We took turns digging. While Bindy dug, I squatted and watched her. There had never been any attraction—and the thought of betraying Fiona's memory was terrible to me—but for the first time I realized what a striking young woman she was. Perhaps fear took this away from her, but now, digging in shorts and a vest top, sweating in the morning sun, mud streaked up her legs, she was quite beautiful. I enjoyed watching her, and that enjoyment ceased only when I saw movement from Jamie's body.

I gasped, stood upright, and saw sparrows flitter away from his bloodied chest. *Only them*, I thought; *it was only them.* But when it was my turn to dig again, I used the pick and made sure we planted him deep.

It took a couple of hours, and halfway through, Bindy went to the shop and came back with a couple of bottles of water. The shop stank now—so much stuff in there had rotted, its stink was rank and stale—but there was enough canned and bottled goods to see us through for a long time.

"Are we going to be here forever?" she asked, as I shoveled dirt in on top of Jamie.

I paused, panting and sweating hard, and leaned on the shovel.

She doesn't seem so scared now, I thought. And there *was* something changed about her. Maybe it was because Jamie had gone, or perhaps it was the simple fact that we'd slept comforting each other, holding the nightmares at bay.

"Maybe," I said. "Or at least until they know exactly what happened here." Past her head I could see one of the camera tripods on a building's rooftop. Soon, it wouldn't be long before they could watch us almost anywhere if we were outside.

Bindy nodded, then looked down at Jamie's grave. "We'll be okay," she said, and she sounded so certain that I wondered if she'd been stronger than me all along.

The helicopter overflew the town all day, turning a tight circle several times if it saw us in the street. It dropped those two men down a few times, letting them set up other cameras before lifting them away again. I supposed we could have gone to those buildings and smashed up the cameras, but maybe there would be a punishment for that. These people seemed keen to keep their own special lab rats under control.

Bindy helped me look for Fiona. I couldn't find it in me to say I wanted to do it on my own. Then after we stopped for lunch, I realized that I *wanted* her with me. She was good company; she seemed to have taken her fear under control; and I found myself stealing more glances at her as we walked. *I really am a pompous shit*, I thought, because I'd never given myself a chance to know this woman at all.

We started going into houses we hadn't had a chance to explore before, and we found the remains of eight people. None of them were zombies, that we could tell: Rot had taken them all, and some of them were badly mauled and chewed, their bones and remains strewn around. None of them was Fiona. I went to great pains to sift through the remains, gagging, puking several times when the smell became too much, and I never found anything of her I recognized. No jewelry, no hair, no clothing. It was a continuation of the most terrible thing I had ever done—we'd been shifting and hauling bodies for three weeks—but I had to make sure.

Bindy came with me every time, but she always stayed outside those rooms. I could not blame her at all, though as time went on that day, I found myself missing her company more and more, as I moved splintered bones and stinking things aside.

By early evening we were exhausted, and we went back to the hotel. They'd been there while we were away and installed cameras in the upper corners of the hallway, bar, kitchen, pantry, and the corridor upstairs outside our room. Greasy footprints marked their route up and down the stair carpet, and I was outraged at them for not removing their boots.

"They're really interested in what happens to us," she said, as if truly realizing our predicament for the first time.

I nodded, not wanting to speak. *They're watching us right now. Maybe O'Driscoll is with them, drinking good coffee, eating a doughnut, and they'll be looking for signs of infection or madness or rage.* I had no wish to say anything to them, so I motioned for Bindy to come into our room.

I spent some time looking around for cameras and microphones. Would they really have any respect for our privacy? There were no bootprints on our light room carpet, but maybe that was just them being sly. I could find nothing—no cameras, whose presence would have been obvious, and no microphones either. I actually caught Bindy smiling as I looked inside the lamp shades and behind the mirror, and I smiled back, remembering what I'd said to O'Driscoll. *What movie do you think you're in?*

We ate downstairs in the bar, sharing a bottle of wine, and it was the most relaxed meal we'd had since being thrown together by this. Jamie's agitated presence had always been a pressure, but something about Bindy had changed. I thought that Jamie being gone perhaps allowed her to assess her panics and fears without his own stoking them.

We slept in the same bed again that night, sharing comfort, relishing contact. Though I was aware of the heat of her more than before, and the feel of her molded to me, still there was no tension at all. I appreciated that, and I fell asleep dreaming of Fiona planting roses in our garden, laughing, and wiping dust out of her eyes with delicate thumbs.

The helicopter didn't come the next day. As we continued our search through the deserted town and the sun reached its zenith, I saw a column of smoke rising far in the distance.

"Is that another cremation pit?" Bindy asked.

"I don't think so. Something about it's different."

"How do you mean?" She came closer and held my hand.

"It's a long way away."

She squeezed. The implications of that did not need stating. It was a wide column, and high, and if it was several miles distant, the fire must be huge.

When I said that I was going to the edge of town to see what I could see, she shook her head and backed away from me.

"I don't want to see," she said. "I don't want to know."

"Bindy, the chopper hasn't been around this morning."

She nodded, looking away from me.

"And you've noticed the cameras?"

"Yeah." They weren't turning to follow our progress. I'd been keeping a wary eye on them since I noticed that, first thing in the morning, but I hadn't wanted to mention it to her.

"We have to know."

She was shaking her head, but there were no tears. She was far from the Bindy she'd been just a couple of days before. Now I saw calculation and consideration in her eyes, not blind panic.

"*I* have to know." I went to her and held her, and she was hot, her skin already tacky with sweat. It was the hottest day I could remember, and I felt a rush of affection for her then. I kissed the side of her head, she kissed my shoulder, and we both hugged tighter.

"I'm going to keep looking," she said, nodding toward the street we'd been searching. They were big houses, and there were five left on this row.

"You're sure?"

She touched the claw hammer she carried in her belt. We'd both agreed that it would be handy for breaking the locks out of doors, but it didn't need saying that it was also a weapon.

"I won't be long," I said, but that turned out to be a lie. It would be evening before I saw Bindy again, and by then our whole world had changed once more.

I went back toward the roadblock by the school. I stood there shouting for a while, waving at the cameras, trying to get their attention. Stepping left and right across the road, the cameras did not follow my progress.

"I need to speak with O'Driscoll!" I shouted. Silence was my answer.

In the distance to the south, beyond a range of hills, the column of smoke still rose. It could have been Cwmbran several miles away, or maybe Newport, several miles farther. Whichever it was, I judged its fiery base to be miles wide.

Waving at the cameras was stupid. There was no one there to see.

So I climbed the roadblock and started walking along the road. To begin with, I cursed myself with every step, knowing how foolish I was being, wincing at the expectation of a high-powered rifle shot. *I'll be hit before I even hear the shot*, I thought, and that was no comfort at all. But there was no gunfire, no helicopters, and no loud mechanical voices exhorting me to "Please don't attempt escape." Right then there was nothing I wanted to hear more.

The road ran for a mile before splitting and filtering down onto a dual highway heading north and south. It was deserted and quiet, save for the wildlife that was becoming braver day by day: I saw a fox watching me from a large house's garden, and a buzzard sat on the road eating something it had just caught, not even glancing up at me as I passed within fifteen feet of it. I tried to identify what it was eating, but I could not. There was no fur.

I saw them from far away. I knew what they were. And I gave thanks to gods I had never believed in that the military had seen fit to erect a second line of protection.

The fence spanned the road just before it split to curve down to the highway. It was high, heavy-duty, and I could track its route across fields and in front of a distant copse of trees, curving around the north end of the town. In the other direction it was soon lost to view, but I hoped it was just as long, and just as strong.

I sat down in the road and watched them pressing against it.

Most of them wore army uniforms, those who weren't in underwear or naked. Many bore terrible wounds, and the blood still flowed. Dead blood must have been different, though, because its stench did not attract their brethren. A zombie's heart, it seemed, did not taste so sweet.

There were maybe fifty of them. Most were clumped against the section of fence built across the road, but I saw a few down in the fields as well. One of those still seemed to be carrying a rifle across his back, though now I hoped he no longer remembered how to use it.

They were making very little noise. A few moans and groans, but none of the raging growls that had marked the first phase of infection. All these were past that now. They'd gone mad and killed and died, and now they were back again, and all they saw when they looked at me was my succulent still-beating heart.

There's been a recurrence, O'Driscoll had said. Smug prick. I looked for him but didn't see him. I hoped he'd been killed and torn apart, found true death, because however much I hated him, I'd had contact with him, and he was a human being like me. He was only doing what he thought was right, and this was no way to end up.

I tried to make out exactly what this meant. The Purge had worked in Usk, for a while at least, and now that there had been an outbreak beyond the town, surely the military would launch another Purge . . . ? But there was no sound of vehicles anywhere, neither ground nor air, and I could see no plane trails in the sky.

And there was that burning city.

I sat and watched them for a while, trying not to appreciate the stark truth of things—that this plague had gone farther, and perhaps was still traveling.

Then I knew what I had to do before returning to Bindy, because I couldn't go back to her with half-truths and suppositions. I had to make sure that we were safe and that our prison had become our refuge.

I walked north first of all, following the fence all around the town until it reached the river. I looked into the town at the stone bridge, and from here I could just see the clumsy block barrier that they'd built at its center. The fence extended right across the river and continued on the other side, obviously encompassing what had been their encampment.

I followed the fence back around the town, crossing the road where most of them were still gathered. They pushed and shoved, but the fence was solid, and they had no real strength.

A mile to the south of town I saw O'Driscoll. He was naked, and his entire front was a mass of dried blood. I couldn't make out whether or not it was his own, and I gave him a wide berth. He leaned against the metal upright, banging his head rhythmically against it as he watched me pass.

The fence reached the river on that side too and crossed over, and I knew I had to swim over to make sure. I half-swam, half-walked, and on the other side, where their encampment had been, I found that the fence only enclosed a small part of it. Gates were built in at two points, both of them padlocked and chained. I'd found no breaches and no areas where any of them could climb over. The military had been very thorough and determined to keep us in, and as I forded the river again and walked back into town, I thanked them for that. It was a good thing they'd realized how dangerous we could be.

Bindy was in the hotel bar, sipping nervously from a glass of wine. When I entered she jumped up and ran to me, cursing and crying and wrapping her arms around my neck.

"Where the fucking hell have you been?"

"I'm sorry," I said, "I'm sorry."

"You're all I've got, Toby; you're all that's left. Don't you dare scare me like that again, *ever!*" She pulled back and held my face, staring into my eyes, and I realized something both striking and comforting then: In her own quiet way, Bindy was in charge.

"I won't," I said. She held me tightly again, and I hugged her back. "You're all I've got too, Bindy."

She pulled away, stalked back to the bar, poured some drinks. She wouldn't catch my eye.

"It's spread outside," I said.

"I know. I guessed. I walked and saw the fence, and some of . . . them."

"That big fire's still burning."

"Yeah."

"Maybe they'll starve."

We sat down together and drank, shoulder to shoulder on a leather sofa, the contact so important. There was so much more that needed to be said, but I knew it could wait. We both realized the truth—that our entrapment had become the only freedom left.

Later, just before midnight, I asked her what she'd found as she continued searching the big houses on that street. Her hesitation was just too long for me to ignore, and she would not meet my eyes. But when she said "Nothing," I nodded and let it stand. For then, at least.

That night in bed, we began our future together. It was beautiful and intense, and I think the passion came more from our continuing freedom than anything else. I should have felt guilt, but there was none, because the past was now so far away and obscure that it felt like someone else's memories. Maybe in the daylight things would be different, but then it felt so right.

Afterward, lying in the dark listening to a silence that would become the norm, she told me.

"I found her," she said.

"I know."

"In the last house. I nailed the doors shut."

"Good."

"So . . . ?"

"Tomorrow, yes. We'll go and set a fire."

I did not sleep at all that night. The fear was there that we had left it too late, and I listened every second for sounds that did not come—the creaking of footsteps on the stairs, the low grumbling of my wife come to berate me and regain my heart.

Even though she said nothing, I knew that Bindy remained awake as well. She was looking after me.

Dawn brought the smell of burning from afar, and we went out together to finish cleansing our town.

LIFE SENTENCE

BY KELLEY ARMSTRONG

Daniel Boyd had overcome many obstacles in his life, and mortality was simply the latest challenge. He'd been born into an illustrious family of sorcerers, owners of a multinational corporation. Money and magical powers. The proverbial silver spoon . . . or it would be, if your father hadn't screwed the company over and gotten himself—and his sons—disinherited. But Daniel had surmounted that barrier, and so he would with this one.

"We're heading down to the laboratory," Shana said, her voice coming through his computer speaker. "It's underground, so let's hope we don't lose the connection."

They'd better not, considering how much Daniel had paid for the equipment. He leaned back and watched the screen bob as Shana descended the steps, the camera affixed to her hand.

The doctor had given him the death sentence two weeks ago. Inoperable cancer. Six months to live. Daniel didn't accept it. He had money, he had power, he had connections; he would find a way to commute this sentence. So he'd begun his search, delving in the black market of the supernatural world.

Shana finally reached the underground Peruvian laboratory. As much as Daniel wanted this cure, he wasn't flitting across the world to get it. There was no need to when he had Shana.

She was, as he'd always said, the perfect assistant. Loyal enough to follow orders without question. Astute enough to anticipate his every need. Attractive enough to make everyone presume he was bedding her, and smart enough never to correct that presumption.

She'd been with him for six years, and he didn't know what he'd do without her. Luckily, he didn't need to worry about that.

"Still there, sir?" Shana asked.

"I am. Audio and visual working fine."

A man's face filled the screen, coffee-stained teeth flashing. "*Hola*, Mr. Boyd! I'm delighted that you've taken an interest in my studies. May I be the first to welcome you to—"

"I have a meeting in twenty minutes."

"Of course. You're a busy man. I mustn't keep you—"

"No, you mustn't," Shana said. "Now, this is the lab, I take it?"

The camera panned a gleaming, high-tech laboratory. Dr. Gonzales was funded by a European Cabal that wouldn't appreciate him double-dipping with another client, but he'd been unable to resist Daniel's offer.

Gonzales walked to a table full of beakers and tubes and started explaining how he'd distilled the genetic component.

"Not interested," Daniel said. "I only care about the end result."

"You can send the results to me," Shana said. "So our scientists can check your procedures."

"Yes, of course. Well, then, on to the subjects."

The screen dimmed as they returned to the hallway. Daniel answered three e-mails while they walked and talked about the cure. It wasn't a cure for cancer; Daniel had realized early that was a Band-Aid solution to avoid tackling the underlying problem of mortality.

Vampirism seemed the best solution. Semi-immortality plus invulnerability. But as it turned out, the process of becoming one was far more convoluted than he'd expected and promised only a 20 percent chance of success . . . and an 80 percent risk of complete annihilation of life and soul.

Most vampires, though, were hereditary, and therein he believed lay the answer. After some digging, he finally found a lead on Gonzales, a shaman who claimed to have isolated and distilled the genetic component that would make anyone a vampire, for the right price.

"Sir?" Shana murmured.

He glanced at the screen to see what looked like a hospital ward. He counted eight subjects, varying ages, all on their backs, unconscious, hooked up to banks of monitors.

"We began clinical trials five years ago, starting with rhesus monkeys—"

"Could you tell us about these subjects, please," Shana cut in.

"Have they completed the trial? How much attrition did you experience? Have you managed to induce invulnerability as well as semi-immortality?"

"They've all completed the procedure. We had two subjects whose bodies rejected the infusion. One survived. One did not. As for invulnerability, naturally, that is part of the package—"

Gonzales stopped as Shana stepped up to a sleeping subject.

"—though it hasn't been perfected yet," he hurried on. "It will be, though."

Shana wrote something on her tablet notebook. Sweat trickled down Gonzales's cheek.

"Why are they unconscious?" she asked, still writing.

"We had some difficulty finding willing subjects, and while I'm sure they'll be pleased with the results, we thought it best to . . ."

"Ease them into the reality of their new life."

His head bobbed. "Yes. Exactly. Thank you."

"Wake one up."

Gonzales stared at her. Then he looked into the camera.

"When Ms. Bergin speaks, she is speaking for me," Daniel said.

Gonzales blathered on about the danger of reversing an induced coma. Shana set the camera down so he could speak directly to Daniel, then she walked away, as if giving them privacy. She walked behind Gonzales, quietly opened a medical cabinet, took out a syringe, and scanned the bottles before choosing one. Daniel smiled. The perfect assistant. Always resourceful. Always anticipating his needs.

As Gonzales continued, Shana filled the syringe, stepped up to the nearest subject, and plunged it in.

The man bolted upright, gasping and wild-eyed. Not unexpected, under the circumstances. The screams were. Unearthly shrieks filled the lab as the man grabbed at his skin, fingers and nails digging in, ripping, blood splattering the white bed, the white walls. Gonzales radioed for help as he ran to the medicine cabinet.

Shana walked over to the camera, then glanced back at the subject, still screaming and rending his flesh as if acid flowed through his veins.

"Well, now we know why they were sedated," she said, and turned off the camera.

* * *

One didn't reach Daniel's position in life by giving up easily. Yet neither did one get there by clinging to hope past all reasonable bounds. He spent another month researching promises of vampire life, then gave up on that particular cure.

"They've been making huge strides in zombification lately," Wendell said, between bites of his Kobe burger. Wendell was Daniel's second cousin, a VP in the family Cabal. Relations with his family had greatly improved a decade ago, coinciding with his own company's appearance on the NYSE. An independently successful Boyd could be useful to the Cabal, and Daniel felt the same about them.

Wendell swiped the linen napkin across his mouth. "Did you hear what I said?"

"I heard. I'm ignoring it, having no overwhelming desire to spend my eternity in a state of decomposition."

"Oh, you don't rot forever. Eventually the flesh is gone and you're a walking skeleton." He leaned over to thump Daniel's shoulder. "I'm kidding. Well, not about the rotting part, but for years, scientists have been working on curing that little drawback. We had our own R & D department working on it for a while, before we decided it was simpler to monitor the independent guys, wait until they're done, then buy the research."

"For zombies?" Daniel's lip curled with distaste. The server—thinking he didn't like his meal—rushed over, but he waved her away.

"Sure. Think of the applications. We've got a lawyer on his deathbed right now. Guy's been with us almost fifty years. A wealth of information is about to disappear. We could change that."

"Huh." Daniel tore off a chunk of bread and chewed it slowly. "You have any names?"

"Not on hand. I can get them. If this works, though?" Wendell smiled. "Biggest favor ever."

Biggest favor ever was right. Savvy businessman that he was, Wendell had known exactly how much his information was worth. If it worked, he wanted a new job—with Daniel's corporation. That was fine. Wendell would make a good addition to the firm. Besides, if he had a stake in Daniel's continued survival, he'd make damned sure he gave him every contact the Boyd Cabal had. Plus, if it worked, he'd be able to swoop in and snatch up the research from under the Cabal's nose, in which case, Wendell wouldn't have a job anyway . . . and might be in need of the immortality solution himself.

Wendell got Daniel the names, and Shana started making the appointments. The first was with a whiz-kid half-demon who'd recently parted ways with a renowned researcher and had accidentally walked out with the man's work, which he'd refined and was now prepared to sell.

Daniel sat in the boardroom as the kid gave his spiel, Shana hurrying him along with reminders that Mr. Boyd was a very busy man.

"Your time is valuable," the kid said. "Especially now, huh?"

He grinned. Daniel and Shana remained stone-faced.

"I believe you brought a test subject?" Shana said. "One you have successfully transformed into a zombie."

"Right. Yes. He's in the . . . Just hold on."

The kid hurried from the room and returned with another college-age kid. He walked a little slowly, and his face was paler than Daniel liked, but at this point, he wasn't being fussy.

"How long has it been since you turned him?" Shana asked.

"Three months."

"Any side effects?"

"His reflexes are a little slow, but we're working on that."

Shana motioned for the subject to turn. He did a 180.

"He's breathing," she said.

The whiz kid smiled. "Yep. Breathing, got a pulse, eats, drinks, just like a living person."

"Impressive."

"Does he talk?" Daniel asked.

"Sure," the zombie said. "What do you want me to say?"

"Recite the multiplication tables, starting at six."

As the zombie performed, Shana eased behind them and removed a gun from her purse. She hesitated, just a second, but at a look from Daniel she nodded and shot the zombie in the back. He fell, gasping and clutching his chest. The whiz kid stared, then dropped to his knees beside his subject, who was bleeding out on the floor, eyes glazing over.

"Not a zombie," Daniel said. "Next time, Shana?"

"I'll ask for a demonstration of resurrection."

"Thank you."

"Is the lighting adequate, sir?" Shana asked.

She swept the camera around the dark cemetery. The image jittered as she shivered. November really wasn't the best time for such things, but she hadn't complained, of course.

"Doctor Albright is—" she began.

The shower turned on in his hotel suite's adjoining bathroom, drowning her out. Daniel glowered, then scooped up the portable screen and moved into the sitting room. The girl in the bathroom called out, asking if he wanted to join her. He closed the door and settled onto the sofa, then asked Shana to repeat herself.

"Doctor Albright is setting up at the gravesite. I'm heading there now."

A yelp, as she tripped over a half-buried gravestone.

"Careful, Shana. That equipment is very expensive."

"Y-yes, sir," she said through chattering teeth.

"Get yourself a stiff drink when you finish," he said. "That'll warm you up. Bill the company."

"Thank you, sir."

He smiled. Little things, but crucial in employee relations. Even watching the screen made him chilly. He reached over and jacked up the heat on the gas fireplace, then poured himself a brandy.

He turned up the sound as the girl in the bathroom yelled for the shampoo. He supposed she had a name, but he couldn't remember it. Not as if he planned to. Just another young woman in a bar, who'd assessed the cut of his suit and spread her legs, a Pavlovian response to the smell of money.

Shana finally found Albright. Along with two assistants, he'd begun digging up a recent grave. It was long, cold work, and partway through, Daniel had to turn off the screen and bid farewell to the girl. Apparently, she'd expected to stay the night and complained bitterly about being sent out with wet hair, so he'd handed her the suite's blow-dryer and hurried her out the door with a couple hundred bucks "for the taxi."

By then they'd dug down to the casket and were waiting for him, all shivering now, breath steaming in the air.

"I've resurrected the corpse inside," Albright announced, talking loudly to be heard over the muffled bangs and cries.

"Mr. Boyd can hear that," Shana said. "Now, the ritual you used is supposed to return the body to its original form, free of any aftereffects of death, correct?"

"Absolutely, as you will see in a moment."

The assistants opened the casket. The man inside jerked, all limbs flailing, then sat up, gulping breaths of air before frowning, as if only just realizing he didn't need those breaths. He squinted up at the people surrounding his casket.

"Wh-what's going on?" he asked.

"You've been resurrected, Mr. Lang. Congratulations."

The man's frown deepened as he seemed to consider this. Then he nodded and tried to stand. Shana motioned to Albright, who stopped him. Shana ran her tests, confirming he did, indeed, appear to be dead. Or undead, as it were.

She took out a folder and consulted a list.

"And you are James Lang, who died in an automobile accident on February twentieth?"

He nodded.

"You're sure?"

"Course I'm sure."

She plucked out a sheet of paper and showed it to him. "Because you don't look like Mr. Lang. And I noticed, Dr. Albright, that you began digging before I arrived, contrary to our agreement."

"I knew it would take a while and it's a cold night—"

"I appreciate your consideration. I do not appreciate your duplicity. You started because you wanted to disguise any indication of recent digging; perhaps to lay a fresh zombie in Mr. Lang's grave."

"I didn't—"

"Then you won't mind me returning Mr. Lang to our offices, where he can be monitored for signs of decomposition." She turned to the zombie. "Don't worry. Having skipped the embalming phase, it shouldn't take long."

* * *

As expected, the zombie rotted and, in the meantime, Daniel knocked three more names off the list Wendell had provided, grumbling each time he did so, well aware that his cousin seemed to be getting the best of this deal. If Daniel succeeded, Wendell got a cushy new job. If he failed, Wendell could go to the Cabal board of directors and tell them he'd used Daniel to cull their list of zombification experts.

Of the five rejected so far, only the whiz kid seemed to be a career con man. The rest were serious researchers, seriously researching the subject but years from selling a perfected cure. So, like all scientists—desperate for that big windfall that would let them continue their work—they tried to trick him into funding their work. He understood, though that didn't mean they hadn't paid dearly for the mistake.

Two more researchers came and went, and Daniel was nearing the end of the list, when one at the bottom, perhaps hearing rumors, took it upon himself to make the initial contact. He came; he requested an audience; he was refused; he stayed. When Daniel left work, the man was still there. When he returned the next morning, he was still there. Daniel decided he could find a few minutes to hear the man out. And a few minutes was all it took, because the man followed Shana into Daniel's office and announced, "I don't have the cure you're looking for."

Shana sighed and started ushering him out, murmuring apologies to Daniel, but the man stood his ground and said, "I don't have it, but I can get it. I'm just missing one crucial ingredient."

"Money," Daniel said, leaning back. "Lots and lots of money."

The man gave a strange little smile, almost patronizing. "No, Mr. Boyd. I have many investors. What I lack are test subjects. Seems there aren't a lot of people willing to die in hopes of being reborn in a rotting corpse."

When Daniel didn't respond, the man took that as encouragement and stepped forward, opening his briefcase on Daniel's desk. He took out a folder the size of *War and Peace.*

"My project to date. I'm asking you to take this and have your scientists go through it. My work, I believe, will speak for itself. All I need is someone to provide me with an unlimited supply of test subjects."

"Unlimited?" Shana said.

"My projections suggest I need between ten and fifty, depending on the number of stages required to perfect the serum. That is, however, an estimate at this point. More may be needed."

"More than fifty?" Shana caught Daniel's look and dropped her gaze, an apology on her lips. She stepped back.

Daniel took the file. He leafed through it. For show, of course. In high school, he'd blackmailed a fellow student to get him passing grades in science.

"Leave your card with Ms. Bergin. I'll get back to you."

Two days later, Daniel had Shana call and tell the man—Dr. Boros—that he'd get his test subjects, with a cap of fifty. Not that Daniel really intended to cut him off at fifty, but one had to set limits. And it placated Shana, which was, admittedly, important. He couldn't afford to lose her now.

Within a week, Boros had the first subjects ready for Daniel's inspection.

"They aren't nearly at the stage you need," Boros said into the camera. "But I want complete transparency, Mister Boyd. You can see how far I've progressed and how far I need to go. No charlatans' tricks. I believe you've had enough of those?"

"I have."

Boros clearly wasn't putting his money into his laboratory—a shabby set of basement rooms. It was clean and the equipment was top-notch but hardly the high-tech, gleaming lab such experiments should have.

Boros also lacked assistants. Again, not for want of funds, but in this case, apparently, because of understandable paranoia. He trusted only one young man, a fellow scientist and fellow necromancer. Daniel understood the sentiment: He felt the same about Shana. But more staff would mean faster results, and at this stage, with only three months to go, Daniel desperately needed fast.

Boros's assistant brought in the first subject . . . strapped down on a gurney. Shana's sigh whispered across the audio connection.

"At least he's conscious," she murmured to Daniel.

"This subject has been zombified for a week, and if Ms. Bergin would care to examine him, she'll see no signs of decomposition. However, we have another problem."

Shana waved at the restraints. "He's unstable?"

"In a manner of speaking."

The assistant undid the restraints. The man lay there, blinking at the ceiling.

"Rise," Boros said.

The man didn't move. He should have: Zombies had to obey the necromancer who resurrected them.

"Well, you've cured the control aspect," Daniel said. "Thankfully."

"Actually, I haven't. On examining his brain activity, it seems he would respond, if he could. In attempting to remove the necromancer's control, it seems he has lost all control."

As if in response, a wet spot spread across the subject's pants.

"That's a problem," Daniel said.

A small smile. "I suspected you'd say that." Boros waved, and his assistant brought in the second subject. To Daniel's relief, this one was walking. He was also leaving a trail of decomposing flesh, falling like dandruff in his wake.

"That too is a problem," Daniel said.

"Agreed."

Boros turned to the subject. "Clap three times."

The man only looked at him.

"Touch your toes."

"Why?" the man asked.

Boros stepped between the two subjects. "In one, I've stopped decomposition at the expense of bodily control. In the other, I've freed him of the necromancer's control while accelerating decomp. Which problem would you like me to solve first? I know you'd like me to work on both, but my resources here—"

"You're not working there anymore. Your study is coming here. I'm clearing my laboratory and putting my specialists under your control."

"I'd really rather not—"

"You will. Or you don't have a client. Now, if you'll excuse me—"

"Sir?" Shana cut in. "The . . ." She paused and motioned for the assistant to remove the test subjects. When they were gone, she turned to Boros. "Can they be saved?"

Boros shook his head. "One will remain in a permanent state of complete paralysis. The other will continue to rapidly decompose."

"So they'll be terminated? Humanely?"

"Not so fast," Daniel said. "If there's still something to be learned from them, keep them."

"But—" Shana began.

"Bring them to the lab. There's a storage room we can use. We'll keep them there."

He flicked off the screen.

Within two months, Boros was getting so close to a cure that Daniel started postponing his visits to the doctor. Cancer wasn't going to be a death sentence, not for him. Even if it ravaged his body tomorrow, Boros was far enough along that Daniel could take the temporary cure and then wait out the final one.

He didn't know how many subjects they'd gone through. Shana kept him updated every week, when Boros put in his requisition, but he paid no attention. It was during one of those weekly updates that she said, "We can't keep this up, sir. He's demanding ten more in the next week. There's a limit to how many transients can disappear from a city before someone starts investigating—"

"Then send the team to another city."

"We're doing that. But it's a slow process. He needs healthy, clean subjects. Do you have any idea how hard it is to find them among that population? We test them, but he still rejects a third of the ones—"

"Then we need to come up with an alternative."

A soft sigh of relief. "Thank you, sir. Now, I've done the calculations, and if you were to take his cure in its present form, we could slow the testing, meaning we could cut back the number of subjects significantly and—"

"I'm not taking a substandard cure unless it's an absolute last resort."

"I understand, sir, but we *are* reaching that stage—"

"No, we aren't. I want you to comb through the employee files. Find anyone with a terminal illness. Offer two years' salary to their families in return for their participation. Emphasize the benefits of the procedure and minimize the side effects."

When she didn't answer, he looked up from his computer golf game. She was staring at him.

"Employees, sir?"

"That's what I said. If we don't have enough with a terminal ill-ness, make it a general offer and increase it to triple salary."

She continued to stare.

"How's Lindsey, Shana?"

She blanched. When Shana came into his employ, her eleven-year-old daughter had been suffering from a rare liver disease, on a trans-plant list and failing fast. As her signing bonus, Shana got that liver for her daughter and all the care she'd needed to make a full recovery. And Daniel got the perfect assistant—one indebted to him for life.

"I-I think we can fill this latest requisition with transients," she said. "I'll split the team and send them farther afield."

He smiled. "Thank you, Shana."

She started to leave. He called her back and handed her a check for ten thousand dollars.

"A bonus. Buy something special for yourself and Lindsey."

She stared at it, and, for just a second, he thought she was going to hand it back. After only that brief hesitation, though, she murmured, "Thank you, sir," pocketed it, and left.

Finally, the day came. And not a moment too soon, as Daniel strug-gled to get into work every day, ignoring his wife's nervous clucking, ignoring the little voice inside himself that said, "Take the cure as it is, before it's too late." Boros was close, though, and Daniel willed himself to hang on. The pain and exhaustion were simply more ob-stacles to overcome.

And then it was ready.

Daniel made Boros go through the final stage twice—two batches with four subjects each time. When he was assured of the results, he ordered six of those subjects killed, the other two left alive and stored for long-term monitoring and potential future tests. He wasn't sure what Shana objected to more—killing successful subjects or holding the other two captive. He had assured her, though, that once he'd been treated, all the failures could be terminated and sent on to their afterlives. That satisfied her.

Killing the successful subjects and keeping two for testing was but one of the precautions he took. He knew he was heading into the most dangerous phase of the testing. He was about to die and put his rebirth in the hands of others. It would be the final test of loyalty for his assistant, and while he trusted her more than anyone in his life, he took precautions with that too, guaranteeing she wouldn't decide at the last moment that he could stay dead.

Then he let Boros kill him by lethal injection. Not pleasant but, according to his research, the quickest and most reliable method. The next thing he saw was Shana's face, floating above his, her pretty features drawn with concern, worrying that the cure might have failed. While he'd like to think she was worried for his sake, he knew better.

"Sir?" she said, when he opened his eyes.

He blinked hard. "Yes?" He had to say it twice. When he spoke, the relief on her face . . . there was a moment there when he wished it was for him.

He tried to sit up. She helped him. She gave him a glass of water. She wiped his face, made him feel more himself, and he was grateful.

Daniel had undergone surgery a couple of times in his youth, and this reminded him of that, coming out of the anesthetic, slow and groggy. Boros bustled around, administering tests, checking his reflexes and responses to visual and audio stimuli. Shana kept him comfortable.

At last, Boros declared the conversion a success. He had Daniel get up and move around, do a few tasks on his laptop, make sure his physical and mental capacities were normal.

"All right, then," Boros said. "Go back to bed."

Daniel didn't want to go back to bed. He felt fine and he needed to relocate to the safe room in the basement, where he'd remain for a few days, presumably "on vacation" until he was fully recovered.

When he tried opening his mouth to refuse, though, he couldn't. Instead, he found himself walking back to the bed. And, as he lay down, he realized with no small amount of horror that he'd been tricked.

Boros walked over. "Did you really think I'd give up the chance to have a man like yourself as my personal puppet?"

Daniel started to sit up.

"Lie down."

He did.

Boros smiled. "Yes, I know, you checked and rechecked, making sure I gave you the right formulation. And I did. You can ask Ms. Bergin. Unfortunately, it appears there is no way to remove the control a necromancer has over his zombies."

"But—"

"I know, I demonstrated it to you. With subjects raised by my assistant, meaning they would have no reason to obey *me*."

Daniel tried to look at Shana, but she'd disappeared behind Boros.

"Don't bother appealing to her. She's been paid well for her cooperation. Yes, you're holding a chit on her, but considering that you're under my control, that's a problem easily remedied. So let's start there. Please release—"

The muffled hiss of a silenced gunshot cut him short. Boros slumped forward, a small-caliber bullet through the back of his head. Shana was behind him with a gun. As Boros lay on the floor, blood oozing down his balding scalp, Daniel sat up, slowly, eyes on the barrel. She lowered it to her side.

"I trust you'll make that call now, sir?" she said.

He did, having her daughter released, then giving the phone to Shana. Out of Daniel's earshot she spoke to her daughter.

"You'll be well compensated—" he began when she returned, and for the first time since they'd met, she interrupted him.

"I know. I'll be very well compensated. And, as soon as I've set you up in the safe room, my employment is at an end."

He understood and said as much. She called a pair of guards to come for Boros's body and to detain his assistant. Then she called in two shamans who'd been part of the research team and, as such, knew Daniel's secret and would be tending to him during his recovery. The four of them set off for the room that would be his temporary home.

"There's one last thing I'll ask," Shana said, as they took the elevator to the basement. "You promised to release the other subjects—"

"Excluding the two successes. I may still need them."

She nodded. "The others, though . . ."

". . . can have their souls released immediately. And there won't be any more. I presume that's why you killed Boros?"

She nodded, and he felt a small prickle of disappointment. Had he really thought she'd done it to protect him?

She handed him a form authorizing the subjects' release. He

arched his brows, surprised at the formality, but she met his gaze
with a level stare. She didn't trust him, and he'd earned that mistrust,
so there was nothing to do now but make a clean break of it. When
they reached the basement lab, she faxed the signed forms to the records department.

Outside the safe room, Shana slid her card through the reader,
coupled with a retinal scan. The electronic door *whooshed* open.
Daniel walked in and looked around. He hadn't seen the work they'd
done to prepare it. He hadn't even told Shana what he'd wanted. But
it was exactly as he'd expected—a storage room converted into a
luxury hotel suite.

The shamans hurried in to help him sit, then retreated behind
Shana. She hadn't said a word since the elevator. He supposed he
couldn't expect more, under the circumstances, so he made a call,
wiring a million dollars into her account, and she waited in silence
until she received confirmation on her cell phone. Then, with the shamans flanking her, she closed the door.

Daniel was just settling onto the bed when the speaker overhead
clicked on. It was Shana.

"The records department has received the fax on releasing the
zombies. I'm going to do that now, before I go."

Daniel smiled. There was no need to tell him that, but it was obvious she couldn't bring herself to walk away. As angry as she was, she
had a good job, and she'd hoped—expected—he'd try to convince
her to stay.

"How much, Shana?" he asked.

"Sir?"

"To stay. What do you want? More money? A bigger office?" He
chuckled. "An assistant of your own?"

"No, sir. I was simply calling to confirm that it's all right for me to
release the zombies."

He sighed. She was going to be difficult. "Yes, yes. Release them.
Now about—"

A *whoosh* cut him short. He glanced at the door. It was still shut.

"You!" snarled a voice behind him.

He wheeled to see that a section of the wall had opened. One of
the zombie subjects stood in the opening, squinting at him with its
good eye, the other shriveled.

"You did this to me," the zombie said, struggling to speak through rotting lips.

"No," Daniel said slowly, carefully. "A scientist—"

"You don't even remember me, do you? But I remember you. Sitting there, barely paying attention, busy talking on your cell phone as you sentenced me to this." He waved at his rotting body.

Daniel looked up at the speaker. "If this is your idea of a lesson, Shana—"

"No sir," her voice crackled. "*This* is my idea of a lesson."

Another zombie appeared behind the first. Then a third, crawling on stubs of arms. A fourth slithered past him. They crowded into the doorway, grumbling and grunting, all glowering at Daniel. Then the first stepped aside, and they rushed forward, zombie after zombie, running, lurching, dragging themselves toward him.

Daniel ran to the door. Pounded on it. Screamed.

"Don't worry, sir," Shana said. "Your procedure was a success. No matter what they do, you can't die."

A click, and the speaker went silent as the zombies swarmed over him.

DELICE

BY HOLLY NEWSTEIN

The grinding sound of stone on stone was muffled by the hot, still air. Moments later a heavy stench so foul as to be almost visible filled the night like an exhalation. A white-clad figure leaned into the opened tomb and pulled something bundled in a stained sheet out into the moonlight. It slid to the brick pavement with a thud.

The white wraith closed the tomb with a groan of effort. It bent over the bundle and gently pulled the sheet aside.

"*Ah, me, cette petite. Quelle dommage.*" It lifted the bundle from the bricks and carried it away, until they were both swallowed up in the inky shadows.

A sickly yellow flash of lightning illuminated the "dead-houses" in the cemetery. Thunder sounded a rolling boom in the distance.

The first thing Delice heard was the storm. Fat raindrops thrummed on the tin roof, but it would bring no relief to the stifling August night. "*Ce pauve, ce pauve,*" crooned a strange, soft alto voice. Skirts rustled as the voice's owner moved about the room.

The voice and the rain and the whisper of fabric were very soothing to her. She had not had many peaceful moments in her short life, so she lay quite still, taking small breaths. She did not want the spell broken nor the moment lost.

A warm hand touched her cheek.

"*Ma pauve,* wake up now."

Delice opened her eyes.

A tall, turbaned woman smiled down at her. She was slender, with café-au-lait skin and slanting black eyes. Deftly she slipped a necklace over Delice's head, placing the cloth amulet on her chest.

"Some *gris-gris* for you. To help Ava Ani. Now we bathe you."

Delice felt a strange pulsing heat fill her chest. She watched as the woman filled a basin with warm water. Then she took little ceramic jars from a shelf and began adding things to the water—powders and dried leaves. Fragrance filled the room—a sweet green smell, different from the earthy, mildewy, rotten-meat odor that clung to the inside of Delice's nostrils. While Ava Ani steeped the leaves in the basin of water, she chanted softly in a language Delice did not quite understand. It was French, to be sure, but it was from the islands—Hispaniola, perhaps. Not the dialect Delice was used to here in New Orleans. The one Madame and Monsieur spoke.

The woman found a clean white cloth and brought it and the basin over to where Delice lay motionless on the table. Ava Ani turned Delice over onto her belly. She gasped as she looked at Delice's back. Delice had never seen her own back, but she knew it was crisscrossed with scars from the whippings Madame had administered over the fourteen years of Delice's life. Madame had a temper, oh, yes. Ava Ani traced each scar with a smooth fingertip.

"Each tells a story, no, *ma pauve?* But this one will have a happy ending. Oh, yes, Ava Ani will help make it so. And you will help also."

Ava Ani began washing Delice's thin backside with the scented water. Such tenderness! Delice could not remember ever being touched like that. No, she had only been touched to hurt, or worse.

A tiny shudder went down her spine. Ava Ani must have felt it.

"Good, good," she murmured. "The spirits fill you."

When Ava Ani finished bathing Delice, she combed rose oil through her hair, making her matted woolly locks become smooth waves and ringlets. Then she helped Delice sit up and dressed her in a red silk dress that fit her perfectly, even over the chest, where Delice's womanness was beginning to show. Delice had never owned such a fine dress.

"*Ne pas ce pauve. Maintenant, elle est belle!*" Ava Ani grinned at Delice, showing straight, white teeth. "Now I need a ribbon, a red silk ribbon." As Ava Ani looked for the ribbon, Delice glanced around.

She was in a one-room cottage, sitting on a table. There was a bed in one corner and a fireplace in the other. Everything was clean and neat, down to the mysterious bottles and boxes arranged on a shelf over the bed. Hanging down from the shelf was a cloth, embroidered with an intricate, multicolored design. A *veve*.

Delice realized that she was in the house of a *mambo*, a priest of the *voudou*. But how did she get here? Last night she had been home, at the Maison DuPlessis. And something had happened. Something bad. And was it last night? It seemed longer, somehow.

Suddenly it was hard to remember. Hard to think. Madame always called her stupid. Jeannette always said *Madame* must be stupid to think such a thing, but perhaps Madame was correct. Right now Delice felt like her head was full of wet cotton.

Ava Ani was back, tying up Delice's new curls with a ribbon. "*Non, non, non!*" she exclaimed. "Madame, she is the stupid one. I know, and soon we shall tell Erzulie too. Erzulie is a powerful *djabo*, and she will help. Madame will learn, and Monsieur too. No need to look so surprised, *ma petite*. Oui, Ava Ani knows all." She helped Delice down from the table and placed her in a chair in the corner.

"Now, *petite fille*, you sit and rest. Wait until the evening comes."

Delice did as she was told, closing her eyes. She listened to the sounds of the Vieux Carré coming alive as the rain stopped and the clouds gave way to a hot, red, fiery dawn. The fragrance of the bougainvillea hung sweet and heavy in the air.

In front of the Maison DuPlessis, a crowd was gathered. Ava Ani joined them, listening to their conversations and waiting for a glimpse of Monsieur or Madame. The house was still, the shutters tightly closed over the windows as if in shame.

Shame, *vraiment*, thought Ava Ani. She knew the story, perhaps better than anyone in New Orleans. The DuPlessis were a prominent family in society, wealthy and handsome. But their neighbors whispered to each other about the strange sounds that came from the house late at night—screams and inhuman moans, like animals in pain. Finally the neighbors' curiosity was at last satisfied.

Last week, Delphine DuPlessis had chased her maid all through the house until the terrified slave girl had sought refuge on the roof. Madame DuPlessis had followed her onto the roof, and somehow the girl had fallen from the roof to her death.

A cursory investigation had been made, and the DuPlessis were charged a fine for maltreatment. That was the end of that. But a few hours later, someone had set the kitchen on fire, and when the fire department arrived, they made a grisly discovery.

On the third floor, Denis DuPlessis had a private, locked chamber. When the door was opened, the officials discovered four young slave girls chained to the wall. Whips, ropes, iron pokers, and other grisly implements were found. All of the girls had had their tongues cut out so that they could not tell what had happened to them in the room, and one had her eyes sewn shut as well. They were horribly scarred and filthy, faces and limbs deformed from unspeakable abuses.

Delphine had known of her husband's peculiarities and not only tolerated them but acted as a procuress for him. The girl who fell to her death had been selected by Delphine for the chamber but had escaped before she was bound and chained.

A shutter flicked open an inch or so, then closed. A barely perceptible movement, but Ava Ani saw. That meant Monsieur and Madame DuPlessis were still there. They would not be for long, Ava Ani knew. No, no, with their money and their position, they would make their escape from New Orleans. Back to France, perhaps.

Time is short, thought Ava Ani. *Very well. Ce soir.*

Her hands closed tightly into fists, fingernails digging red crescents into her palms.

While Ava Ani was gone, Delice tried to remember how she got here. She found that her mind worked slowly, so slowly. It took her most of the day to piece it together.

She remembered that Madame had summoned her quite late to Madame's fine, high-ceilinged bedchamber. Madame was thin and pale, with eyes like ice. Madame had looked her up and down. Her eyes lingered on Delice's chest and the spot where her legs joined her body. Delice wondered if Madame could see through her threadbare calico dress and see the sprouting of soft dark hair that was growing there. Before Jeannette left, she had told her that the hairs meant you could have a baby now. Delice missed Jeannette terribly and wished with all her heart that Madame had not sold her last year.

"It is time." Madame sighed. "Go wash, Delice, and then come back."

"Yes, Madame," Delice had replied. She quickly returned to Madame's chamber, face and hands clean.

"Denis wants you," Madame had said, and then laughed queerly. "Come, we will go upstairs."

Madame's laugh frightened Delice. But she dared not show it lest she be whipped. Maybe she would be whipped anyway; Madame was so strange tonight. She timidly approached the third-floor room, her hands twisting in the pockets of her dress. Madame followed her at a distance, her shoes tapping lightly on the floor.

Monsieur opened the door to the room with a big smile and put out a hand to welcome Delice. But then a puff of wind had opened the door wide. The smell of excrement and infection and pure raw fear had filled Delice's nostrils. She saw the bodies of the girls, chained in dumb misery, limbs smeared with feces and blood. One had lifted her head and met Delice's gaze, her eyes vacant under a mat of blood-crusted hair.

"Jeannette!" Delice breathed, recognizing her girlhood friend. Jeannette had not been sold. Jeannette had been here, for almost a year.

Delice wasted no breath screaming. Her muscles jumped to life. She pushed back Monsieur's fat white hand and turned, moving with catlike speed. She shoved Madame to the floor and ran to the hall door. She tugged frantically at the knob, but it would not open. Madame and Monsieur were running after her, the shoes tapping out a frantic beat now.

Delice spun around and ran into one of the guest bedchambers. At the far end, a window opened onto the second-floor roof. She would climb down somehow, she thought. She flung the shutters open and crawled out onto the roof. She pressed herself into the shadows, her heart pounding.

She heard Madame say, "Give it to me, Denis, you fool." Then the rustling of Madame's silken skirts, like a snake's hiss, as she too made her way onto the roof.

Delice tried to make herself small, to inch her way along the sloping, slippery tiles without being seen. Madame's pale eyes were sharp, though, and cut through the darkness like a lantern.

"Delice!" she called, and out of habit Delice looked up.

The clouds parted, and the moon shone down on Madame. She stood not ten paces' distance. Her dark hair was tumbled and wild, her face ghostly white in the silver light.

In her hand was a pistol.

"Delice, get back inside. Now!" Madame commanded. She raised the pistol, pointing it at her.

Delice had stared at the pistol. Madame would surely kill her. But to go back inside . . . that was worse than death. Suddenly Delice was no longer afraid.

If I am to die, then I will die. But I choose.

She rose up and began to run. She heard a pop, and then a ball sang past her ear. She felt the hot rush of air against her cheek. She ran and ran, and suddenly she was flying. Flying . . .

And then there was nothing. Nothing until she had awakened here, at Ava Ani's.

That night, two slender figures moved slowly and silently through the black-velvet darkness that enshrouded the city. They disappeared down an alley that ran behind the Maison DuPlessis and slipped over the fence that enclosed the rear yard. Ava Ani paused as two shiny blue eyes watched her from under the boxwood hedge.

"*Venez ici,*" she whispered, staring back at the eyes. Delice watched as Madame's white Persian cat came out from under the shrubs and approached Ava Ani. It moved slowly and deliberately, like a child's pull toy, straight toward her. Delice watched, fascinated. She hated Henri. She had been bitten and scratched countless times by that ill-tempered cat.

As Henri reached Ava Ani, she reached down and picked him up by the scruff of his neck. A blade flashed, and in a moment Henri was dead, his belly opened. Ava Ani dusted fine powder around him in intricate patterns and began to chant softly in a strange dialect.

The chant grew louder and louder, until the sound seemed to come from inside Delice's head. Her ears pounded. Her body no longer felt heavy and clumsy. She felt light and quick—and a fever began boiling in her veins. She rose up on her toes, threw her head back, and opened her mouth.

A cool wind, light as a zephyr, sprang up. It circled around the cat, ruffling the blood-caked fur, barely disturbing the *veves* Ava Ani had designed around the sacrifice. It rustled through Delice's red silk skirts. Suddenly Delice's mouth snapped shut, and her body shuddered convulsively. Then she was still and slowly turned her head toward Ava Ani, who bowed her head in fearful respect before the powerful *djabo*. A fierce, terrible beauty suffused Delice's narrow face.

Delice spoke. "This cat pleases me. I will do as you ask. It will be my pleasure, oh, yes, indeed." Delice laughed, a merry sound in the darkness, and with a swirl of red skirts she was gone.

Ava Ani fled.

The rustle of silk was the only sound in the Maison DuPlessis that night. Something moved through the house like an avenging angel. When the sun came up, the Vieux Carré pulsed with screams, as more grotesque discoveries were made at the Maison DuPlessis.

Next to the well behind the house lay the bloody, disemboweled carcass of the DuPlessis' cat. Fine flour had been carefully sprinkled around the body. In the ominous red early-morning light, flies were already thick and buzzing on the cat's exposed organs and its sightless china-blue eyes.

Denis DuPlessis was found in his bed. His throat was slashed, his eyeballs cut out and placed neatly, side by side, on his tongue, which had been pulled from his mouth and down over his chin. His hands had been cleanly amputated at the wrists and lay on the gore-soaked coverlet, palms up as if in supplication.

Madame DuPlessis was also in bed with her throat cut, her nightgown pulled up around her waist, and the murder weapon sheathed to the hilt between her legs. It was a long, exquisitely sharp knife, of the kind used to cut sugarcane. Blood had spattered and splashed all over the walls and the ceiling, making glistening black rivulets as the drops rolled toward the floor.

No one in the house had heard anything except the faint sibilance of silk on the parquet tiles and the oriental carpet. But under the stench of the house, the smell of hot pennies and vomit and sulfur, was the sweet fragrance of rose oil.

Ava Ani had been waiting. Delice arrived just at dawn, her dress stiff with blood, her eyes gleaming, her hands caked with gore. She had smiled broadly at Ava Ani.

"It was pleasant indeed, *mambo*. Now I return the girl to you." Delice's eyes rolled back, and she fell to the floor, a small, limp bundle.

Ava Ani picked her up and carried her to the fireplace. Even though the morning was stifling hot, a fire burned. In front of the fireplace there was a tub filled with the same scented water she had washed Delice with the night before. Ava Ani pulled off Delice's red silk dress and threw it in the fire, where it smoldered then suddenly blazed with a bright blue-and-white flame.

Delice's eyes opened again, and she found herself once more at Ava Ani's. How had she gotten here from the DuPlessises'? The fire caught her eye. Delice thought the flames looked clean and pure, not smudgy and orange like usual. Then she saw the remnants of her dress burning in the fire. Why was Ava Ani burning her new dress?

It was a shame to burn that pretty red dress, but Delice could not find the words to protest.

Ava Ani bathed Delice again, and the water turned red as it ran down her thin body.

"You see, *ma fille*. Erzulie came when Ava Ani called. Erzulie liked Madame's fine Persian *chat* enough to ride you to justice. Yes, yes. It says in the Hebrew Bible, 'Justice, justice shalt thou pursue.'" She poured clean water over Delice's head as she stood in the tub.

Delice blinked. She remembered nothing of a woman named Erzulie. And what was this about liking Henri? She opened her mouth to ask, but no sound came out. Her voice was gone.

Ava Ani saw Delice's mouth open and close, like a fish's. "You cannot speak. But I think you wish to know what has happened. The DuPlessises, *ils est mort*. Erzulie killed them in their beds as they slept the sleep of the damned. And you, *ma fille*, you made a fine *cheval* for her. She used your feet, your hands, to do what needed to be done." Ava Ani helped Delice step out of the tub and wrapped her in a length of white linen. She took Delice's face in her hands and looked into her eyes.

"You remember, do you not? Madame chased you onto the roof. She had a pistol, no? She pointed it at you, her hair all tumbling and looking like a devil from hell."

Delice nodded. She was trembling. Her mind was so slow, her body so heavy. Her hands throbbed as though she had worked them very hard. Ava Ani's eyes searched her face.

"You ran, *petite fille*. You ran right off the roof and fell. Fell onto the stones in the courtyard. Fell hard."

Delice finally understood. She was a *zombi*. Ava Ani had brought her back to life in order to avenge her own death. Her dark eyes widened in terror.

Now she was enslaved forever, mute and stupid. Ava Ani had stolen the blessed release of death that she had chosen for herself—the one thing she had been able to choose, denied her for eternity.

Delice tried to scream, but all she could do was breathe out a rusty croak. She tried to pull away from Ava Ani, but the *mambo* tightened her grip on Delice's face and shook her head.

"Your work is done here, *ma pauve*. I have no more need for you. Soon you will sing again. This time, with the angels." She began to chant low, swaying with the rhythm of the song. Delice swayed with her, her hands curled around Ava Ani's wrists, her eyes shut. A white fog filled her mind, and she thought she heard singing.

"*Mambo* Ava Ani?"

Ava Ani whirled, her white skirts flashing in the darkness. "Who wants to know?" she replied, hiding her fear under anger.

"Philippe LaPlace," came the response. "Why are you here? Did the . . . information I gave you not serve?" Philippe came forth from behind a tomb.

"It served me very well," Ava Ani replied, her teeth clenched. She did not like this *bokor*-man of the Cochon Gris. But she could not be rude. She had come to him, filled with rage and grief for the victims of the DuPlessis. He had helped her in her plan to rid New Orleans of them and taught her the powerful dark *voudou* she would need to know. She knew Philippe was powerful, and he frightened her. Still, she did not care to be spied on. She turned away from him in order to place a linen-wrapped bundle into the tomb she had just opened.

"So I heard," he said. A low chuckle echoed in the deep indigo shadows. "Erzulie is a creative one, is she not?"

Ava Ani shuddered. Philippe came forward and stood next to her. He ran his hand along the open edge of the tomb. "You sent the little girl back then?" he asked. "Pity."

"Delice did all that was needed. I have no need for a *zombi* to do my bidding. She spent her life enslaved. No need for her to spend her death there too." Ava Ani rolled a length of red ribbon, scented with rose oil, into a small tight coil. She slipped it into the *gris-gris* bag she wore around her neck.

"You are too soft, Ava Ani," scoffed Philippe. "Join with us in the Cochon Gris and find your true power."

"*Non, merci,*" she replied, a bit tartly. Ava Ani leaned her weight against the stone slab. She pushed with every ounce of strength she had, and slowly the slab slid back into place, sealing the tomb. Delice again shared a dead-house with the corpses of the other DuPlessis slaves.

Ava Ani straightened up, wiping the sweat from her forehead. In the faint starlight she saw Philippe scowling at her. Her almond eyes narrowed, but she forced a smile.

"Erzulie liked the fancy white *chat* I fixed for her," Ava Ani said sweetly. "*Mais oui,* she liked it very much. She said to me that she had never had such a fine gift." She watched Philippe's shadowed face. A moment passed—and then a flash of white teeth answered her.

"Very well, *mambo*. I see you made a friend of Erzulie. You go back to your little magic and I will go back to mine."

"*C'est bon,*" Ava Ani said, but he was already gone. She turned back to the dead-house.

"No more *voudou, ma fille*. Now only angel songs." She got down on her knees and fumbled around her neck. Under the *gris-gris* bag that hung between her breasts she found her rosary. She pulled the cross out from the neck of her dress and let her fingers slide along the warm, smooth ebony beads. "Now I pray to the Catholic gods for your eternal rest, *ma petite*." She knelt in front of the dead-house and crossed herself.

"Hail *Marie*, full of grace, the Lord is with thee. . . ."

THE WIND CRIES MARY

BY BRIAN KEENE

Even in death, she returns to visit me every night.

If time mattered anymore, you'd be able to set your watch by her arrival. Mary shows up shortly after the sun goes down. She lumbers up our long, winding driveway, dragging her shattered right leg behind her like it's a dog. I often wonder how she can still walk.

Of course, all the dead walk these days, but in Mary's case, a shard of bone protrudes from her leg, just below the knee. The flesh around it is shiny and swollen—the color of lunch meat. The wound doesn't even leak anymore. I keep expecting her to fall over, for the bone to burst through the rest of the way, for her leg to come completely off. But it never happens.

Her abdomen has swollen, too. We were never able to have children, but death has provided her with a cruel pantomime of what pregnancy must be like. I dread what will happen when those gases trapped inside of her finally reach the breaking point. Her breasts have sunken, as have her cheekbones and eyes. Her summer dress hangs off her frame in tatters. It was one of my favorites—white cotton with a blue floral print. Simple yet elegant, just like Mary. Now it is anything but. Her long hair is no longer clean or brushed, and instead of smelling like honeysuckle shampoo, it now smells of leaves and dirt and is rife with insects. Her fingernails are filthy and cracked. She used to take so much pride in them. Her hands and face are caked with a dried brown substance. I tell myself that it is mud, but I know in my heart that it's blood.

None of this matters to me. Her body may be changing, but Mary is still the woman I fell in love with. She is still the most beautiful woman I have ever known. She is still my wife, and I still love her. Death hasn't taken that away. It has only made it stronger.

We had fifteen good years together. Death does not overcome those times. Her body may be rotting, but those memories do not decay. I am sure of this. Why else would she return here, night after night, and stare at the house, fumbling at the door and searching for a way in? It can't be to feed. If it were, she would have given up by now, moved on to the new housing development a few miles up the road, where I am sure there are still plenty of families barricaded inside their homes, too scared or stupid to stay quiet for long. Easy pickings. I don't know what she does during the day. Certainly it isn't sleep. The dead never sleep. I assume she eats. Wanders, perhaps. But the question remains, Why does she return here night after night? Mary doesn't know I'm in here. Of this, I am certain. Although she paws at the door and the boarded-up windows, she can't see inside of our house. She can't see me or hear me. So why does she return?

The answer is simple: She remembers. Maybe not in the way the living remember things, but somewhere, rooted deeply in whatever is left of her brain, there is some rudimentary attachment to this place. Perhaps she recognizes it as home. Maybe she just knows that this was a place where she was happy. A place where she once lived.

Mary hated me the first time we met. It was at a college party. She was an art major. I was studying business. I was a drunken frat boy, a young Republican in training, the next-generation spawn of the Reagan revolution. Mary was a liberal Democrat, involved in a number of volunteer social programs. When she walked into the party, a blonde and a brunette were feeding me a forty-ounce of Mickey's through a makeshift beer bong. She glanced in our direction then turned away. I was instantly infatuated. Not love at first sight, but certainly lust. Love came later.

I got her number from a mutual acquaintance. It took me two months to get a date with her. I was on my best behavior. The date lasted all night. We saw *Pulp Fiction* (I loved it; she hated it). We went to Denny's (I had steak and eggs; she had a salad). We went back to her place. We talked all night. Kissed a little, but mostly we just talked. And it was wonderful. When the sun came up, I asked for a second date and got it.

We dated for years and broke up a half-dozen times before we finally got engaged. It wasn't that we fought. We were just very different people. Sure, we shared some similar interests. We both liked to read. We both enjoyed playing Scrabble. We both liked Springsteen. But these were small, superficial similarities. At our core, we were different from one another. There are two kinds of people in this world—my kind and Mary's kind. But we made it work. We had love. And we were happy.

Until Hamelin's Revenge. That's the name the media gave it, because the disease started with the rats. Hamelin was the village where the Pied Piper cured the rat problem once and for all. Except that in real life, the rats came back, infected with a disease that turned the dead into rotting, shambling eating machines. Some television pundit called them "land sharks." I thought that was funny at the time. I don't any longer. The disease jumped from the rats to other species, including humans. It jumped oceans too. It showed up first in New York, but by the end of the week, it spread to London, Mumbai, Paris, Tel Aviv, Moscow, Hafr Al-Batin, and elsewhere. Armies couldn't fight it. You could shoot the dead, but you couldn't shoot the disease. Global chaos ensued. Major metropolitan areas fell first. Then the smaller cities. Then the rural areas.

Mary and I stayed inside. We barricaded the house. We had enough food and water to last us a while. We had weapons to defend ourselves. We waited for the crisis to pass. Waited for someone—anyone—to sound the all clear and restore order. But that someone never came.

Mary died a week ago. She'd gone outside just for a second to dump the bucket we'd been using as a toilet. A dead crow pecked her neck. Panicked, Mary beat it aside and ran back into the house. The wound was just a scratch. It didn't even bleed.

But it was enough.

She died that night. I knew what had to be done. The only way to keep the dead from coming back is to destroy their brains. I put the gun to her head while she lay still, but I didn't have the courage to pull the trigger. I couldn't do that to her, not to the woman I loved. Instead, I cracked the door open and placed her body outside.

The next morning, she was gone.

That was when I put the gun to my own head and did to myself what I could not do to my wife. That should have been it.

But I came back anyway—not as a shuffling corpse. No, I am a different kind of dead. My body is decomposing on the kitchen floor, but I am not in it. All I can do is watch as it slowly rots away. I can't leave this place. There is no light. No voices from beyond. No deceased loved ones to greet me from the other side.

There is only me . . . and Mary.

I cannot touch her. Cannot follow. I've tried to talk to her, tried to let her know that I am still here, but my voice is just the wind, and she does not notice. Each night, I cry for us both, but I have no tears, so my sobs are just the breeze.

There used to be two kinds of people in this world. Now, in the aftermath of Hamelin's Revenge, there are two kinds of dead—my kind and Mary's kind.

We made it work once before.

I wonder if we can make it work once again?

FAMILY BUSINESS

BY JONATHAN MABERRY

I

Benny Imura couldn't hold a job, so he took to killing.

It was the family business. He barely liked his family—and by family, that meant his older brother Tom—and he definitely didn't like the idea of "business." Or work. The only part of the deal that sounded like it might be fun was the actual killing.

He'd never done it before. Sure, he'd gone through a hundred simulations in gym class and in the Scouts, but they never let kids do any real killing. Not before they hit fifteen.

"Why not?" he once asked his Scoutmaster, a fat guy named Feeney, who used to be a TV weatherman back in the day.

"Because killing's the sort of thing you should learn from your folks," said Feeney.

"I don't have any folks," Benny countered. "My mom and dad died on First Night."

"Oh, hell," said Feeney, then quickly amended that. "Oh, heck. Sorry, Benny—I didn't know that. Point is, you *got* family of some kind, right?"

"I guess. I got 'I'm Mr. Freaking Perfect Tom Imura' for a brother, and I don't want to learn *anything* from him."

Feeney had stared at him. "Wow. I didn't know you were related to him. Your brother, huh? Well, there's your answer, kid. Nobody better to teach you the art of killing than a professional killer like Tom Imura." Feeney paused and licked his lips nervously. "I guess, being his brother and all, you've seen a lot of killing."

"No," Benny said, with huge annoyance. "He never lets me watch!"

"Ask him when you turn thirteen. A lot of kids get to watch when they hit their teens."

Benny had asked, and Tom had said no. Again. It wasn't a discussion. Just, "No."

That was two years ago, and now Benny was six weeks past his fifteenth birthday. He had four more weeks' grace to find a paying job before county ordinance cut his rations by half. Benny hated being in that position, and if one more person gave him the "Fifteen and Free" speech, he was going to scream. He hated that as much as when people saw someone doing hard work and they said crap like, "Damn, he's going at that like he's fifteen and out of food."

Like it was something to be happy about. Something to be proud of. Working your butt off for the rest of your life. Benny didn't see where the fun was in that.

His buddy, Chong, said it was a sign of the growing cultural oppression that was driving humanity toward acceptance of a slave state. Benny had no freaking idea what Chong meant, or if there was even meaning in anything he said. But he nodded in agreement because the look on Chong's face always made it seem like he knew exactly what was what.

At home, before he even finished eating his birthday cake, Tom had said, "If I want to talk about you joining the family business, are you going to chew my head off?"

Benny stared venomous death at Tom and said, very clearly and distinctly, "I. Don't. Want. To. Work. In. The. Family. Business."

"I'll take that as a no, then."

"Don't you think it's a little late now to try and get me all excited about it? I asked you a zillion times to—"

"You asked me to take you out on kills."

"Right! And every time I did you—"

"There's a lot more to what I do, Benny."

"Yeah, there probably is, and maybe I would have thought the rest was something I could deal with, but you never let me see the cool stuff."

"There's nothing 'cool' about killing," Tom said sharply.

"There is when you're talking about killing zoms!" Benny fired back.

That stalled the conversation. Tom stalked out of the room and banged around in the kitchen for a while, and Benny threw himself down on the couch.

Tom and Benny never talked about zombies. They had every reason to, but they never did. Benny couldn't understand it. He hated zoms. Everyone hated them, though with Benny it was a white-hot, consuming hatred that went back to his very first memory—a nightmare image that was there every night when he closed his eyes. It was an image that was seared into him, even though it was something he had seen as a tiny child.

Dad and Mom.

Mom screaming, running toward Tom, shoving a squirming Benny—all of eighteen months—into Tom's arms. Screaming and screaming. Telling him to run.

While the *thing* that had been Dad pushed its way through the bedroom door, which Mom had tried to block with a chair and lamps and anything else she could find.

Benny remembered his mom screaming words, but the memory was so old and he had been so young that he didn't remember what any of them were. Maybe there were no words. Maybe it was just her screaming.

Benny remembered the wet heat on his face as Tom's tears fell on him when he climbed out of the bedroom window. They had lived in a ranch-style house. One story. The window emptied out into a yard that was pulsing with red and blue police lights. There were more shouts and screams. The neighbors. The cops. Maybe the army. Benny thought it was the army. And the constant popping sounds of gunfire, near and far away.

But of all of it, Benny remembered a single, last image. As Tom clutched him to his chest, Benny looked over his brother's shoulder at the bedroom window. Mom leaned out of the window screaming at them as Dad's pale hands reached out of the shadows of the room and dragged her back out of sight.

That was Benny's oldest memory. If there had been older memories, then that image had burned them away. Benny remembered the hammering sound that was Tom's panicked heartbeat vibrating against his own chest, and the long wail that was his own inarticulate cry for his mom and his dad.

He hated Tom for running away. He hated that Tom hadn't stayed and helped Mom. He hated what their Dad had become on that First Night all those years ago. And he hated what Dad had turned Mom into.

In his mind they were no longer Mom and Dad. They were the *things* that had killed them. Zoms. And he hated them with an intensity that made the sun feel cold and small.

A few years ago, when he found out that Tom was a zombie hunter, Benny hadn't been proud of his brother. As far as he was concerned, if Tom really had what it took to be a zombie hunter, he'd have had the guts to help Mom. Instead, Tom had run away and left Mom to die. To become one of *them*.

Tom came back into the living room, looked at the remains of Benny's birthday cake on the table, then looked at Benny on the couch.

"The offer still stands," he said. "If you want to do what I do, then I'll take you on as an apprentice. I'll sign the papers so you can still get full rations."

Benny gave him a long, withering stare.

"I'd rather be eaten by zoms than have you as my boss," Benny said.

Tom sighed, turned, and trudged upstairs. After that they didn't talk to each other for days.

11

The following weekend Benny and Lou Chong had picked up the Saturday edition of the *Town Pump* because it had the biggest help-wanted section, and over the next several weeks, they applied for anything that sounded easy.

Benny and Chong clipped out a bunch of want ads and tackled them one at a time, having first categorized them by "most possible money," "coolness," and "I don't know what it is but it sounds okay." They passed on anything that sounded bad right from the get-go.

The first on their list was "Locksmith Apprentice."

That sounded okay, but it turned out to be humping a couple of heavy toolboxes from house to house at the crack of frigging dawn while an old German guy who could barely speak English repaired fence locks and installed dial combinations on both sides of bedroom doors and installed bars and wire grilles.

It was kind of funny watching the old guy explain to his customers how to use the combination locks. Benny and Chong began making bets on how many times per conversation a customer would say "What? Could you repeat that?" or "Beg pardon?"

The work was important, though. Everyone had to lock themselves in their rooms at night and then use a combination to get out. Or a key; some people still locked with keys. That way, if they died in their sleep, they wouldn't be able to get out of the room and attack the rest of the family. There had been whole settlements wiped out because someone's grandfather popped off in the middle of the night and then started chowing down on the kids and grandkids.

Zoms can't work a combination lock. They can't work keys either. The German guy installed double-sided locks, so that the doors could be opened from the other side in a real, nonzombie emergency; or if the town security guys had to come in and do a cleanup on a new zom.

Somehow, Benny and Chong had gotten it into their heads that locksmiths got to see this stuff, but the old guy said that he hadn't seen a single living dead that was in any way connected to his job. Boring.

To make it worse, the German guy paid them a little more than pocket lint and said that it would take three years to learn the actual trade. That meant that Benny wouldn't even pick up a screwdriver for six months and wouldn't do anything but carry stuff for a year. Screw that.

"I thought you didn't want to actually work," said Chong, as they walked away from the German with no intention of returning in the morning.

"I don't. But I don't want to be bored out of my freaking mind either."

Next on their list was "Fence Tester."

That was a little more interesting because there were actual zoms on the other side of the fence. Benny wanted to get close to one. He'd never been closer than a hundred yards from an active zom before. The older kids said that if you looked into a zom's eyes, your reflection would show you how you'd look as one of the living dead. That sounded very cool, but he never got the chance for a close-up look, because there was always a guy with a shotgun dogging him all through the shift.

The shotgun guy got to ride a horse. Benny and Chong had to walk the fence line and stop every six or ten feet, grip the chain links, and shake the fence to make sure there were no breaks or rusted weak spots. That was okay for the first mile, but after that the noise attracted the zoms, and by the middle of the third mile he had to grab, shake, and release pretty damn fast to keep his fingers from getting bitten. He wanted a close-up look, but he didn't want to lose a finger over it. If he got bit, the shotgun guy would blast him on the spot. Depending, a zom bite could turn someone from healthy to living dead in anything from a few hours to a few minutes, and in orientation, they told everyone that there was a zero-tolerance policy on infections.

"If the gun bulls even *think* you got nipped, they'll blow you all to hell and gone," said the trainer, "so be careful!"

They quit at lunch.

Next morning they went to the far side of town and applied as "Fence Technicians."

The fence ran for hundreds of miles and encircled the town and the harvested fields, so this meant a lot of walking, mostly carrying yet another grumpy old guy's toolbox. In the first three hours they got chased by a zom who had squeezed through a break in the fence.

"Why don't they just shoot all the zoms who come up to the fence?" Benny asked their supervisor.

" 'Cause folks would get upset," said the man, a scruffy-looking guy with bushy eyebrows and a tic at the corner of his mouth. "Some of them zoms are relatives of folks in town, and those folks have rights regarding their kin. Been all sorts of trouble about it, so we keep the fence in good shape, and every once in a while one of the townsfolk will suck up enough intestinal fortitude to grant permission for the fence guards to do what's necessary."

"That's stupid," said Benny.

"That's people," said the supervisor.

That afternoon Benny and Chong were sure they'd walked a million miles, had been peed on by a horse, stalked by a horde of zoms—Benny couldn't see anything at all in their dusty eyes—and yelled at by nearly everyone.

At the end of the day, as they trudged home on aching feet, Chong said, "That was about as much fun as getting beaten up in recess."

He thought about it for a moment. "No . . . getting beaten up is more fun."

Benny didn't have the energy to argue.

There was only one opening for the next job—"Carpet-Coat Salesman"—which was okay because Chong wanted to stay home and rest his feet. Chong hated walking. So Benny showed up neatly dressed in his best jeans and a clean T-shirt and with his hair as combed as it would ever get without glue.

There wasn't much danger in selling carpet coats, but Benny wasn't slick enough to get the patter down. Benny was surprised that they'd be hard to sell, because everybody had a carpet coat or two. Best thing in the world to have on if some zoms were around and feeling bitey. What he discovered, though, was that everyone who could thread a needle was selling them, so the competition was fierce and sales were few and far between. The door-to-door guys worked on straight commission, too.

The lead salesman, a greasy joker named Chick, would have Benny wear a long-sleeved carpet coat—low knap for summer, shag for winter—and then would use a device on him that was supposed to simulate the full-strength bite of an adult male zom. This metal "biter" couldn't break the skin through the coat—and here Chick rolled into his spiel about human bite strength, throwing around terms like *PSI, avulsion,* and *post-decay dental-ligament strength*— but it pinched really hard, and the coat was so hot the sweat ran down inside Benny's clothes. When he went home that night, he weighed himself to see how many pounds he'd sweated off. Just one, but Benny didn't have a lot of pounds to spare.

"This one looks good," said Chong over breakfast the next morning.

Benny read, "'Pit Thrower.' What's that?"

"I don't know," Chong said, with a mouthful of toast. "I think it has something to do with barbecuing."

It didn't. Pit Throwers worked in teams to drag dead zoms off the back of carts and toss them into the constant blaze at the bottom of Brinkers Quarry. Most of the zoms on the carts were in pieces. The woman who ran orientation kept talking about "parts" and went on and on about the risk of secondary infection; then she pasted on the fakest smile Benny had ever seen and tried to sell the applicants on the physical-fitness benefits that came from constant lifting, turning, and throwing. She even pulled up her sleeve and flexed her biceps. She had pale skin with freckles that looked like liver spots, and the sudden pop of her biceps looked like a swollen tumor.

Chong faked vomiting into his lunch bag.

The other jobs offered by the quarry included "Ash Soaker"— "Because we don't want zom smoke drifting over the town, now do we?" asked the freckly muscle freak. And "Pit Raker," which was exactly what it sounded like.

Benny and Chong didn't make it through orientation. They snuck out during the slide show of smiling Pit Throwers handling gray limbs and heads.

"Spotter" was next, and that proved to be a good choice, but only for one of them. Benny's eyesight was too poor to spot zoms at the right distance. Chong was like an eagle, and they offered him a job as soon as he finished reading numbers off a chart. Benny couldn't even tell they were numbers.

Chong took the job, and Benny walked away alone, throwing dispirited looks back at his friend sitting next to his trainer in a high tower.

Later, Chong told Benny that he loved the job. He sat there all day staring out over the valleys into the Rot and Ruin that stretched from California all the way to the Atlantic. Chong said that he could see twenty miles on a clear day, especially if there were no winds coming his way from the quarry. Just him up there, alone with his thoughts. Benny missed his friend, but privately he thought that the job sounded more boring than words could express.

Benny liked the sound of "Bottler" because he figured it for a factory job filling soda bottles. Benny loved soda, but it was sometimes hard to come by. But as he walked up the road, he met an older teenager— his pal Morgie Mitchell's cousin Bert—who worked at the plant.

When Benny fell into step with Bert, he almost gagged. Bert smelled awful, like something found dead behind the baseboards. Worse. He smelled like a zom.

Bert caught his look and shrugged. "Well, what do you expect me to smell like? I bottle this stuff eight hours a day."

"What stuff?"

"Cadaverine. I work a press to get the oils from the rotting meat."

Benny's heart sank. Cadaverine was a nasty-smelling molecule produced by protein hydrolysis during putrefaction of animal tissue. Benny remembered that from science class, but he didn't know that it was made from actual rotting flesh. Hunters and trackers dabbed it on their clothes to keep the zoms from coming after them, because the dead were not attracted to rotting flesh.

Benny asked Bert what *kind* of flesh was used to produce the product, but Bert hemmed and hawed and finally changed the subject. Just as Bert was reaching for the door to the plant, Benny spun around and walked back to town.

There was one job Benny already knew about—"Erosion Artist." He'd seen erosion portraits tacked up all over town, and there were thousands of them on every wall of each of the town's fence outposts.

This job had some promise because Benny was a pretty fair artist. People wanted to know what their relatives might look like if they were zoms, so Erosion Artists took family photos and zombified them. Benny had seen dozens of these portraits in Tom's office. A couple of times he wondered if he should take the picture of his parents to an artist and have them redrawn. He'd never actually done it, though. Thinking about his parents as zoms made him sick and angry.

But Sacchetto, the supervising artist, told him to try a picture of a relative first. He said it provided better insight into what the clients would be feeling. So, as part of his audition, Benny took the picture of his folks out of his wallet and tried it.

Sacchetto frowned and shook his head. "You're making them look too mean and scary."

He tried it again with several photos of strangers the artist had on file.

"Still mean and scary," said Sacchetto, with pursed lips and a disapproving shake of his head.

"They *are* mean and scary," Benny insisted.

"Not to customers, they're not," said Sacchetto.

Benny almost argued with him about it, saying that if he could accept that his own folks would be flesh-eating zombies—and that there was nothing warm and fuzzy about that—then why couldn't everyone else get it through their heads.

"How old were you when your parents passed?" Sacchetto asked.

"Eighteen months."

"So you never really knew them."

Benny hesitated, and that old image flashed once more in his head. Mom screaming. The pale and inhuman face that should have been Dad's smiling face. And then the darkness as Tom carried him away.

"No," he said bitterly. "But I know what they looked like. I know *about* them. I know that they're zoms. Or maybe they're dead now, but I mean—zoms are zoms. Right?"

After the audition, he hadn't been offered the job.

| | |

September was ten days away, and Benny still hadn't found a job. He wasn't good enough with a rifle to be a Fence Guard, he wasn't patient enough for farming, and he wasn't strong enough to work as Hitter or Cutter. Not that smashing in zombie heads with a sledgehammer or cutting them up for the quarry wagons was much of a draw for him, even with his strong hatred for the monsters. Yes, it was killing, but it also looked like hard work, and Benny wasn't all that interested in something described in the papers as "demanding physical labor." Was that supposed to attract applicants?

So, after soul-searching for a week, during which Chong lectured him pretty endlessly about detaching himself from preconceived notions and allowing himself to become part of the co-creative process of the universe or something like that, Benny asked Tom to take him on as an apprentice.

At first Tom studied him with narrowed, suspicious eyes.

Then his eyes widened in shock when he realized Benny wasn't playing a joke.

As the reality sank in, Tom looked like he wanted to cry. He tried to hug Benny, but that wasn't going to happen in this life, so Tom and he shook hands on it.

Benny left a smiling Tom and went upstairs to take a nap before dinner. He sat down and stared out the window as if he could see tomorrow, and the tomorrow after that, and the one after that. Just him and Tom.

"This is really going to suck," he said.

I V

That evening they sat on the front steps and watched the sun set over the mountains.

"Why do you do this stuff?" Benny asked.

Tom sipped his coffee and was a long time answering. "Tell me, kiddo, what is it you think I do?"

"Duh! You kill zoms."

"Really? That's all that I do? I just walk up to any zombie I see and *pow!*"

"Uh . . . *yeah*."

"Uh . . . *no*." Tom shook his head. "How can you live in this house and not know what I do, what my job involves?"

"What's it matter? Everybody I know has a brother, sister, father, mother, haggy old grandmother who's killed zoms. What's the big?" He wanted to say that he thought Tom probably used a high-powered rifle with a scope and killed them from a safe distance; not like Charlie and Hammer, who had the stones to do it *mano a mano*.

"Killing the living dead is a part of what I do, Benny. But do you know why I do it? And for whom?"

"For fun?" Benny suggested, hoping Tom would be at least *that* cool.

"Try again."

"Okay . . . then for money . . . and for whoever's gonna pay you."

"Are you pretending to be a dope, or do you really not understand?"

"What, you think I don't know you're a bounty hunter? Everybody knows that. Zak Matthias's uncle Charlie is one, too. I heard him tell stories about going deep into the Ruin to hunt zoms."

Tom paused with his coffee cup halfway to his lips. "Charlie—? You know Charlie Pink-Eye?"

"He gets mad if people call him that."

"Charlie Pink-Eye shouldn't be *around* people."

"Why not?" demanded Benny. "He tells the best stories. He's funny."

"He's a killer."

"So are you."

Tom's smile was gone. "God, I'm an idiot. I have to be the worst brother in the history of the world if I let you think that I'm the same as Charlie Pink-Eye."

"Well, you're not exactly like Charlie."

"Oh, that's something then."

"Charlie's cool."

"'Cool,'" murmured Tom. He sat back and rubbed his eyes. "Good God."

He threw the last of his coffee into the bushes beside the porch and stood up.

"Tell you what, Benny . . . tomorrow we're going to start early and head out into the Rot and Ruin. We'll go deep, like Charlie does. I want you to see firsthand what he does and what I do, and then you can make your own decisions."

"Decisions about what?"

"About a lot of things, kiddo."

And with that, Tom went in and to bed.

V

They left at dawn and headed down to the southeastern gate. The gatekeeper had Tom sign the usual waiver that absolved the town and the gatekeeping staff of all liability if anything untoward happened once they crossed into the Ruin. A vendor sold Tom a dozen bottles of cadaverine—which they sprinkled on their clothing—and a jar of peppermint goo, which they dabbed on their upper lips to kill their own sense of smell.

They were dressed for a long hike. Tom had instructed Benny to wear good walking shoes, jeans, a durable shirt, and a hat to keep the sun from boiling his brains.

"If it's not already too late," Tom said.

Benny made a rude gesture when Tom wasn't looking.

Despite the heat, Tom wore a lightweight jacket with lots of pockets. He had an old army gun-belt around his narrow waist and a pistol snugged into a worn leather holster. Benny wasn't allowed to have a gun yet, though Tom stowed an extra one in a pack. The last thing Tom strapped on was a sword. Benny watched with interest as Tom slung a long strap diagonally across his body from left shoulder to right hip, with the hilt standing above his shoulder so that he could reach up and over for a fast right-handed draw.

The sword was a *katana*, a Japanese long sword, which Benny had seen Tom practice with every day for as long as he could remember. That sword was the only thing about his brother that Benny thought was cool. Benny's Mom—who was Tom's adopted mother—was Irish, but their father had been Japanese. Tom once told Benny that the Imura family went all the way back to the Samurai days of ancient Japan. He showed Benny picture books of fierce-looking Japanese men in armor. Samurai warriors.

"Are you a samurai?" Benny had asked when he was nine.

"There are no samurai anymore," Tom said, but even back then Benny thought that Tom had a funny look on his face when he said that. Like maybe there was more to say on the subject but he didn't want to say it right then. When Benny brought the subject up a couple of times since, the answer was always the same.

Even so, Tom was pretty damn good with the sword. He could draw fast as lightning, and Benny had seen him do a trick—when Tom thought no one else was looking—where he threw a handful of grapes into the air, then drew his sword and cut five of them in half before they fell to the grass. The blade was a blur. Later, after Tom had gone off to a store, Benny came down and counted the grapes. Tom had thrown six into the air. He'd only missed one.

That was cool.

Of course, Benny would rather be burned at the stake than tell Tom how cool he thought that was.

"Why are you bringing that?" he asked, as Tom adjusted the lay of the strap.

"It's quiet," Tom said.

Benny understood that. Noise attracted zoms. A sword was quieter than a gun, but it also meant getting closer. Benny didn't think that was a very smart idea. He said as much, and Tom just shrugged.

"Then why bring the gun?" persisted Benny.

" 'Cause sometimes quiet doesn't matter." Tom patted his pockets to do a quick inventory to make sure he had everything he needed. "Okay," he said, "let's go. We're burning daylight."

Tom tipped a couple of Fence Runners to bang on drums six hundred yards north, and as soon as that drew away the wandering zoms, Tom and Benny slipped out into the great Rot and Ruin and headed for the treeline.

Chong waved to them from the corner tower.

"We need to move fast for the first half mile," cautioned Tom, and he broke into a jog-trot that was fast enough to get them out of scent range but slow enough for Benny to match.

A few of the zombies staggered after them, but the Fence Guards banged on the drums again, and the zombies, incapable of holding on to more than one reaction at a time, turned back toward the noise. The Imura brothers vanished into the shadows under the trees.

When they finally slowed to a walk, Benny was sweating. It was a hot start to what would be a scorcher of a day. The air was thick with mosquitoes and flies, and the trees were alive with the sound of chattering birds. Far above them the sun was a white hole in the sky.

"How far are we going?" Benny asked.

"Far. But don't worry, there are way stations where we can crash if we don't make it back tonight."

Benny looked at him as if he'd just suggested they set themselves on fire and go swimming in gasoline. "Wait—you're saying we could be out all night?"

"Sure. You know I'm out here for days at a time. You're going to have to do what I do. Besides, except for some wanderers, most of the dead in this area have long since been cleaned out. Every week I have to go farther away."

"Don't they just come to you?"

Tom shook his head. "There are wanderers—what the Fence Guards call 'noms,' short for nomadic zombies—but most don't travel. You'll see."

The forest was old but surprisingly lush in the mid-September heat. Tom found fruit trees, and they ate their fill of sweet pears as they walked. Benny began filling his pockets with them, but Tom shook his head.

"They're heavy and they'll slow you. Besides, I picked a route that'll take us through what used to be farm country. Lots of fruit growing wild."

Benny looked at the lush pears in his hand, sighed, and let them fall.

"How come nobody comes out here to farm this stuff?" he asked.

"People are scared."

"Why? There's got to be forty guys working the fence."

"No, it's not the dead that scare them. People in town don't trust anything out here. They think there's a disease infesting everything. Food, the livestock that have run wild over the last fourteen years—everything."

"Yeah . . ." Benny said diffidently. He'd heard that talk. "So, it's not true?"

"You ate those pears without a thought."

"You handed them to me."

Tom smiled. "Oh, so you trust me now?"

"You're a dork, but I don't think you want to turn me into a zom."

"Wouldn't have to get on you about cleaning your room, so let's not rule it out."

"You're so funny I almost peed my pants," Benny said without expression.

Tom walked a bit before he said, "There's town and then there's the Rot and Ruin. Most of the time they aren't in the same world, you know?" When it was clear that Benny wasn't following, Tom said, "Think about it and we'll talk later."

He stopped and stared ahead with narrowed eyes. Benny couldn't see anything, but then Tom grabbed his arm and pulled him quickly off the road. He led him in a wide circle through the groves of trees. Benny peered between the hundreds of tree trunks and finally caught a glimpse of three zoms shuffling slowly along the road.

He opened his mouth and almost asked Tom how he knew, but Tom made a shushing gesture and continued on, moving soundlessly through the soft summer grass.

When they were well clear, Tom took them back up to the road.

"I didn't even see them!" Benny gasped, turning to look back.

"Neither did I."

"Then how—?"

"You get a feel for this sort of thing."

Benny held his ground, still looking back. "I don't get it. There were only three of them. Couldn't you have . . . you know . . ."

"What?"

"Killed them," said Benny flatly. "Charlie Matthias said he'll go out of his way to chop a zom or two. He doesn't run from anything."

"Is that what he says?" Tom murmured, then continued down the road.

Benny shrugged and followed.

VI

Twice more Tom pulled Benny off the road so they could circle around wandering zombies. After the second time, once they were clear of the creatures' olfactory range, Benny grabbed Tom's arm and demanded, "Whyn't you just pop a cap in them?"

Tom gently pulled his arm free. He shook his head and didn't answer.

"What, are you afraid of them?" Benny yelled.

"Keep your voice down."

"Why? You afraid a zom will come after you? Big, tough zombie killer who's afraid to kill a zombie."

"Benny," said Tom with thin patience, "sometimes you say some truly stupid things."

"Whatever," Benny said, and pushed past him.

"Do you know where you're going?" Tom said, when Benny was a dozen paces along the road.

"This way."

"I'm not," said Tom, and he began climbing the slope of a hill that rose gently from the left-hand side of the road. Benny stood in the middle of the road and seethed for a full minute. He was muttering the worst words he knew the whole time he climbed after Tom up the hill.

There was a smaller road at the top of the hill, and they followed that in silence. By ten o'clock they'd entered a series of steeper hills and valleys that were shaded by massive oak trees with cool green leaves. Tom cautioned Benny to be quiet as they climbed to the top of a ridge that overlooked a small country lane. At the curve of the road was a small cottage with a fenced yard and an elm tree so gnarled and ancient that it looked like the world had grown up around it. Two figures stood in the yard, but they were too small to see. Tom flattened out on the top of the ridge and motioned for Benny to join him.

Tom pulled his field glasses from a belt holster and studied the figures for a long minute.

"What do you think they are?" He handed the binoculars to Benny, who snatched them with more force than was necessary. Benny peered through the lenses in the direction Tom pointed.

"They're zoms," Benny said.

"No kidding, boy genius. But what *are* they?"

"Dead people."

"Ah."

"Ah . . . what?"

"You just said it. They're dead *people*. They were once living people."

"So what? Everybody dies."

"True," admitted Tom. "How many dead people have you seen?"

"What kind of dead? Living dead like them or dead dead like Aunt Cathy?"

"Either. Both."

"I don't know. The zombies at the fence . . . and a couple people in town, I guess. Aunt Cathy was the first person I ever knew who died. I was, like, six when she died. I remember the funeral and all." Benny continued to watch the zombies. One was a tall man, the other a young woman or teenage girl. "And . . . Morgie Mitchell's dad died after that scaffolding collapsed. I went to his funeral, too."

"Did you see either of them quieted?"

Quieted was the acceptable term for the necessary act of inserting a metal spike at the base of the skull to sever the brain stem. Since First Night, anyone who died would reanimate as a zombie. Bites made it happen, too, but really any recently deceased person would come back. Every adult in town carried at least one spike, though Benny had never seen one used.

"No," he said. "You wouldn't let me stay in the room when Aunt

Cathy died. And I wasn't there when Morgie's dad died. I just went to the funerals."

"What were the funerals like? For you, I mean."

"I dunno. Kind of quick. Kind of sad. And then everyone went to a party at someone's house and ate a lot of food. Morgie's mom got totally shitfaced—"

"Language."

"Morgie's mom got drunk," Benny said, in way that suggested correcting his language was as difficult as having his teeth pulled. "Morgie's uncle sat in the corner singing Irish songs and crying with the guys from the farm."

"That was a year, year and a half ago, right? Spring planting?"

"Yeah. They were building a corn silo, and Mr. Mitchell was using the rope hoist to send some tools up to the crew working on the silo roof. One of the scaffolding pipes broke, and a whole bunch of stuff came crashing down on him."

"It was an accident."

"Well, yeah, sure."

"How'd Morgie take it?"

"How do you think he took it? He was fu— He was screwed up." Benny handed back the glasses. "He's still a little screwed up."

"How's he screwed up?"

"I don't know. He misses his dad. They used to hang out a lot. Mr. Mitchell was pretty cool, I guess."

"Do you miss Aunt Cathy?"

"Sure, but I was little. I don't remember that much. I remember she smiled a lot. She was pretty. I remember she used to sneak me extra ice cream from the store where she worked. Half an extra ration."

Tom nodded. "Do you remember what she looked like?"

"Like Mom," said Benny. "She looked a lot like Mom."

"You were too little to remember Mom."

"I remember her," Benny said, with an edge in his voice. He took out his wallet and showed Tom the image behind the glassine cover. "Maybe I don't remember her really well, but I think about her. All the time. Dad too."

Tom nodded again. "I didn't know you carried this." His smile was small and sad. "I remember Mom. She was more of a mother to me than my mom ever was. I was so happy when Dad married her. I can remember every line on her face. The color of her hair. Her smile. Cathy was a year younger, but they could have been twins."

Benny sat up and wrapped his arms around his knees. His brain felt twisted around. There were so many emotions wired into memories, old and new. He glanced at his brother. "You were older than I am now when—y'know—*it* happened."

"I turned twenty a few days before First Night. I was in the police academy. Dad married your mom when I was sixteen."

"You got to know them. I never did. I wish I . . ." He left the rest unsaid.

Tom nodded. "Me too, kiddo."

They sat in the shade of their private memories.

"Tell me something, Benny," said Tom. "What would you have done if one of your friends—say, Chong or Morgie—had come to Aunt Cathy's funeral and pissed in her coffin?"

Benny was so startled by the question that his answer was unguarded. "I'd have jacked them up. I mean *jacked* them up."

Tom nodded.

Benny stared at him. "What kind of question is that, though?"

"Indulge me. Why would you have freaked out on your friends?"

"Because they dissed Aunt Cathy. Why do you think?"

"But she's dead."

"What the hell does that matter? Pissing in her coffin? I would *so* kick their asses."

"But why? Aunt Cathy was beyond caring."

"It was her funeral! Maybe she was still . . . I don't know . . . *there* in some way. Like Pastor Kellogg always says."

"What does he say?"

"That the spirits of those we love are always with us."

"Okay. What if you didn't believe that? What if you believed that Aunt Cathy was only a body in a box? And your friends pissed on her?"

"What do you think?" Benny snapped. "I'd still kick their asses."

"I believe you. But why?"

"Because," Benny began, but then hesitated, unsure of how to express what he was feeling. "Because Aunt Cathy was mine, you know? She was my aunt. My family. They don't have any right to disrespect my family."

"No more than you'd go take a crap on Morgie Mitchell's father's grave. Or dig him up and pour garbage on his bones. You wouldn't do anything like that?"

Benny was appalled. "What's your damage, man? Where do you come up with this crap? Of course I wouldn't do anything sick like that! God, who do you think I am?"

"Shhh . . . keep your voice down," cautioned Tom. "So, you wouldn't disrespect Morgie's dad . . . alive or dead?"

"Hell no."

"Language."

Benny said it slower and with more emphasis. "Hell. No."

"Glad to hear it." Tom held out the field glasses. "Take a look at the two dead people down there. Tell me what you see."

"So we're back to business now?" Benny gave him a look. "You're weird, man. Deeply weird."

"Just look."

Benny sighed and grabbed the binoculars out of Tom's hand, put them to his eyes. Stared. Sighed.

"Yep. Two zoms. Same two zoms."

"Be specific."

"Okay. Okay—two zoms. One man, one woman. Standing in the same place as before. Big yawn."

Tom said, "Those dead people . . ."

"What about them?"

"They used to be somebody's family," said Tom quietly. "The male looks old enough to have been a dad, more likely a granddad. He had a family, friends. A name. He was somebody."

Benny lowered the glasses and started to speak.

"No," said Tom. "Keep looking. Look at the woman. She was, what? Eighteen years old when she died? Might have been pretty. Those rags she's wearing might have been a waitress's uniform once. She could have worked at a diner right next to Aunt Cathy. She had people at home who loved her. . . ."

"Don't, man—"

"People who worried when she was late getting home. People who wanted her to grow up happy. People—a mom and a dad. Maybe brothers and sisters. Maybe grandparents. People who believed that girl had a life in front of her. That old man might be her granddad."

"But she's one of them, man. She's dead," Benny said defensively.

"Sure. Almost everyone who ever lived is dead. More than six billion people are dead. And every last one of them had family once. Every last one of them *were* family once. At one time there was someone like you who would have kicked the ass of anyone—stranger or best friend—who harmed or disrespected that girl. Or the old man."

Benny was shaking his head. "No, no, no. It's not the same. These are zoms, man. They kill people. They eat people."

"They used to *be* people."

"But they died!"

"Sure. Like Aunt Cathy and Mr. Mitchell."

"No, Aunt Cathy got cancer. Mr. Mitchell died in an accident."

"Sure, but if someone in town hadn't quieted them, they'd have become living dead, too. Don't even pretend you don't know that. Don't pretend you haven't thought about that happening to Aunt Cathy." He nodded down the hill. "These two down there caught a disease."

Benny nodded. He'd learned about it in school, though no one knew for sure what had actually happened. Some sources said it was a virus that was mutated by radiation from a returning space probe. Others said it was a new type of flu that came over from China. Chong believed it was something that got out of a lab somewhere. The only thing everyone agreed on was that it was a disease of some kind.

Tom said, "That guy down there was probably a farmer. The girl was a waitress. I'm pretty sure neither of them was involved in the space program. Or worked in some lab where they researched viruses. What happened to them was an accident. They got sick, Benny, and they died."

Benny said nothing.

"How do you think Mom and Dad died?"

No answer.

"Benny—? How do you think—?"

"They died on First Night," Benny said irritably.

"They did. But how?"

Benny said nothing.

"How?"

"You let them die!" Benny said in a savage whisper. Words tumbled out of him in a disjointed sputter. "Dad got sick and . . . and . . . then Mom tried to . . . and you . . . you just ran away!"

Tom said nothing, but sadness darkened his eyes, and he shook head slowly.

"I remember it," Benny hissed. "I remember you running away."

"You were a baby."

"I remember it."

"You should have told me, Benny."

"Why? So you could make up a lie about why you just ran away and left my mom like that?"

The words *my mom* hung in the air between them. Tom flinched.

"You think I just ran away?" he said.

"I don't *think* it, Tom—I remember it."

"Do you remember why I ran?"

"Yeah, 'cause you're a freaking coward, is why!"

"Jesus," Tom whispered. He adjusted the strap that held the sword in place and sighed again. "Benny . . . this isn't the time or place for this, but someday soon we're going to have a serious talk about the way things were back then, and the way things are now."

"There's nothing you can say that's going to change the truth."

"No. The truth is the truth. What changes is what we know about it and what we're willing to believe."

"Yeah, yeah, whatever."

"If you ever want to know my side of things," said Tom, "I'll tell you. There's a lot you were too young to know then, and maybe you're still too young now."

Silence washed back and forth between them.

"For right now, Benny, I want you to understand that when Mom and Dad died, it was from the same thing that killed those two down there."

Benny said nothing.

Tom plucked a stalk of sweet grass and put it between his teeth. "You didn't *really* know Mom and Dad, but let me ask you this: If someone was to piss on them, or abuse them—even now, even considering what they had to have become during First Night—would it be okay with you?"

"Screw you."

"Tell me."

"No. Okay? No it wouldn't freaking be okay with me? You happy now?"

"Why not, Benny?"

"Because."

"Why not? They're only zoms."

Benny abruptly got up and walked down the hill, away from the farm and away from Tom. He stood looking back along the road they'd traveled as if he could still see the fence line. Tom waited a long time before he got up and joined him.

"I know this is hard, kiddo," he said gently, "but we live in a pretty hard world. We struggle to live. We're always on our guard, and we have to toughen ourselves just to get through each day. And each night."

"I freaking hate you."

"Maybe. I doubt it, but it doesn't matter right now." He gestured toward the path that led back home. "Everybody west of here has lost someone. Maybe someone close, or maybe a distant cousin three times removed. But everybody has lost someone."

Benny said nothing.

"I don't believe that you would disrespect anyone in our town or in the whole west. I also don't believe—I don't want to believe—that you'd disrespect the mothers and fathers, sons and daughters, sisters and brothers who live out here in the great Rot and Ruin."

He put his hands on Benny's shoulders and turned him around. Benny resisted, but Tom Imura was strong. When they were both facing east, Tom said, "Every dead person out there deserves respect. Even in death. Even when we fear them. Even when we have to kill them. They aren't just 'zoms,' Benny. That's a side effect of a disease or from some kind of radiation or something else that we don't understand. I'm no scientist, Benny. I'm a simple man doing a job."

"Yeah? You're trying to sound all noble, but you *kill* them." Benny had tears in his eyes.

"Yes," Tom said softly, "I do. I've killed hundreds of them. If I'm smart and careful—and lucky—I'll kill hundreds more."

Benny shoved him with both hands. It only pushed Tom back a half step. "I don't understand!"

"No, you don't. I hope you will, though."

"You talk about respect for the dead, and yet you kill them."

"This isn't about the killing. It isn't and never should be about the killing."

"Then what?" Benny sneered. "The money?"

"Are we rich?"

"No."

"Then it's obviously not about the money."

"Then *what*?"

"It's about the *why* of the killing. For the living . . . for the dead," Tom said. "It's about closure."

Benny shook his head.

"Come with me, kiddo. It's time you understood how the world works. It's time you learned what the family business is all about."

VII

They walked for miles under the hot sun. The peppermint gel ran off with their sweat and had to be reapplied hourly. Benny was quiet for most of the trip, but as his feet got sore and his stomach started to rumble, he turned cranky.

"Are we there yet?"

"No."

"How far is it?"

"A bit."

"I'm hungry."

"We'll stop soon."

"What's for lunch?"

"Beans and jerky."

"I hate jerky."

"You bring anything else?" Tom asked.

"No."

"Jerky it is, then."

The roads Tom picked were narrow and often turned from asphalt to gravel to dirt.

"We haven't seen a zom in a couple of hours," Benny said. "How come?"

"Unless they hear or smell something that draws them, they tend to stick close to home."

"Home?"

"Well . . . to the places they used to live or work."

"Why?"

Tom took a couple of minutes on that. "There are lots of theories, but that's all we have. Just theories. Some folks say that the dead lack the intelligence to think that there's anywhere other than where they're standing. If nothing attracts them or draws them, they'll just stay right where they are."

"But they need to hunt, don't they?"

"*Need* is a tricky word. Most experts agree that the dead will attack and kill, but it's not been established that they actually hunt. Hunting implies need, and we don't know that the dead *need* to do anything."

"I don't understand."

They crested a hill and looked down a dirt road to where an old gas station sat beneath a weeping willow.

"Have you ever heard of one of them just wasting away and dying of hunger?"

"No, but—"

"The people in town think that the dead survive by eating the living, right?"

"Well, sure, but—"

"What 'living' do you think they're eating?"

"Huh?"

"Think about it. There're more than three hundred million living dead in America alone. Throw in another thirty-odd million in Canada and a hundred and ten million in Mexico, and you have something like four hundred and fifty million living dead. First Night happened fourteen years ago. So—what are they eating to stay alive?"

Benny thought about it. "Mr. Feeney says they eat each other."

"They don't," said Tom. "Once a body has started to cool, they stop feeding on it. That's why there are so many partially eaten living dead. They won't attack or eat each other even if you locked them in the same house for years on end. People have done it."

"What happens to them?"

"The trapped ones? Nothing."

"Nothing? They don't rot away and die?"

"They're already dead, Benny." A shadow passed over the valley and momentarily darkened Tom's face. "But that's one of the mysteries.

They don't rot. Not completely. They decay to a certain point, and then they just stop rotting. No one knows why."

"What do you mean? How can something just stop rotting? That's stupid."

"It's not stupid, kiddo. It's a mystery. It's as much a mystery as why the dead rise in the first place. Why they attack humans. Why they don't attack each other. All mysteries."

"Maybe they eat . . . like . . . cows and stuff."

Tom shrugged. "Some do, if they can catch them. A lot of people don't know that, by the way, but it's true. They'll eat anything alive that they can catch. Dogs, cats, birds, even bugs."

"Well, then, that explains—"

"No," Tom said. "Most animals are too fast. Ever try to catch a cat who doesn't want to be caught? Now imagine doing that if you're only able to shuffle along slowly and can't strategize. If a bunch of the dead came upon cows in a pen or fenced field, they might be able to kill them and eat them, but all the penned animals have either long-since escaped or they died off in the first few months. No . . . the dead don't need to feed at all. They just exist."

They reached the gas station. Tom stopped by the old pump and knocked on the metal casing three times, then twice, and then four more times.

"What are you doing?"

"Saying hello."

"Hello to . . . ?"

There was a low moan, and Benny turned to see a gray-skinned man come shuffling slowly around the corner of the building. He wore ancient coveralls that were stained with dark blotches, but incongruously around his neck was a garland of fresh flowers. Marigolds and honeysuckle. The man's face was in shade for a few steps, but then he crossed into the sunlight and Benny nearly screamed. The man's eyes were missing, and the sockets gaped emptily. The moaning mouth was toothless, the lips and cheeks, sunken in. Worst of all, as the zombie raised its hands toward them, Benny saw that all of its fingers had been clipped off at the primary knuckles.

Benny gagged and stepped back, his muscles tensed to turn and run, but Tom put a hand on his shoulder and gave him a reassuring squeeze.

"Wait," said Tom.

A moment later the door to the gas station opened, and a pair of sleepy-eyed young women came outside followed by a slightly older man with a long brown beard. The were all thin and dressed in tunics that looked like they had been made from old bedsheets. Each wore a thick garland of flowers. The trio looked at Benny and Tom and then at the zombie.

"Leave him be!" cried the youngest woman as she ran across the dirt to the dead man and stood between him and the Imura brothers, her feet planted, her arms spread to shield the zombie.

Tom raised a hand and took his hat off so they could see his face.

"Peace, little sister," he said. "No one's here to do harm."

The bearded man fished eyeglasses from a pocket beneath his tunic and squinted through dirty lenses.

"Tom . . . ?" he said. "Tom Imura?"

"Hey, Brother David." He put his hand on Benny's shoulder. "This is my brother, Benjamin."

"What are you doing here?"

"Passing through," said Tom. "But I wanted to pay my respects. And to teach Benny the ways of *this* world. He's never been outside of the fence before."

Benny caught the way Tom put emphasis on the word *this*.

Brother David walked over, scratching his beard. Up close he was older than he looked—maybe forty, with deep brown eyes and a few missing teeth. His clothing was clean but threadbare. He smelled of flowers, garlic, and mint. The man studied Benny for a long moment, during which Tom did nothing and Benny fidgeted.

"He's not a believer," said Brother David.

"Belief is tough to come by in these times," said Tom.

"You believe."

"Seeing is believing."

Benny thought that their exchange had the cadence of a church litany, as if it was something the two of them had said before and would say again.

Brother David bent toward Benny. "Tell me, young brother, do you come here bringing hurt and harm to the Children of God?"

"Um . . . no?"

"Do you bring hurt and harm to the Children of Lazarus?"

"I don't know who they are, mister, but I'm just here with my brother."

Brother David turned toward the women, who were using gentle pushes to steer the zombie back around the far side of the building. "Old Roger there is one of Lazarus's Children."

"What? You mean he's not a zom—"

Tom made a noise to stop him.

A tolerant smile flickered over Brother David's face. "We don't use that word, little brother."

Benny didn't know how to answer that, so Tom came to his rescue.

"The name comes from Lazarus of Bethany, a man who was raised from the dead by Jesus."

"Yeah, I remember hearing about that in church."

The mention of church brightened Brother David's smile. "You believe in God?" he asked hopefully.

"I guess. . . ."

"In these times," said Brother David, "that's better than most." He threw a covert wink at Tom.

Benny looked past him to where the girls had taken the zombie. "I'm like totally confused here. That guy was a . . . you know. He's dead, right?"

"Living dead," corrected Brother David.

"Right. Why wasn't he trying to . . . you know." He mimed grabbing and biting.

"He doesn't have teeth," said Tom. "And you saw his hands."

Benny nodded. "Did you guys do that?" he asked Brother David.

"No, little brother," Brother David said with a grimace. "No, other people did that to Old Roger."

"Who?" demanded Benny.

"Don't you mean 'Why'?"

"No, *who*. Who'd do something like that?"

Brother David said, "Old Roger is only one of the Children who have been tortured like that. All over this county you can see them. Men and women with their eyes cut out, their teeth pulled, or jaws shot away. Most of them missing fingers or whole hands. And I won't talk about some of the others things I've seen done. Stuff you're too young to know about, little brother."

"I'm fifteen," said Benny.

"You're too young. I can remember when fifteen meant you were still a child." Brother David turned and watched the two young women return without the old zombie.

"He's in the shed," said the blonde.

"But he's agitated," said the redhead.

"He'll quiet down after a spell," said Brother David.

The women stood by the pump and eyed Tom, though Tom seemed to suddenly find something fascinating about the movement of the clouds. Benny's usual inclination would have been to make a joke at Tom's expense, but he didn't feel like it. He turned back to the bearded man.

"Who's doing all this stuff you're talking about? To that old man. To those . . . others you mentioned. What kind of dirtbags are out here doing that stuff?"

"Bounty hunters," said the redhead.

"Killers," said the blonde.

"Why?"

"If I had an answer to that," said Brother David, "I'd be a saint instead of a way-station monk."

Benny turned to Tom. "I don't get it . . . *you're* a bounty hunter."

"I guess to some people that's what I am."

"Do you do this kind of stuff?"

"What do you think?"

But Benny was already shaking his head.

Tom said, "What do you even know about bounty hunters?"

"They kill zombies," Benny said, then flinched as he saw the looks of distaste on the faces of Brother David and the two women. "Well, they do! That's what bounty hunters are there for. They come out here into the Rot and Ruin and they hunt the, um, you know . . . the living dead."

"Why?" asked Tom.

"For money."

"Who pays them?" asked Brother David.

"People in town. People in other towns," said Benny. "I heard the government pays them sometimes."

"Who'd you hear that from?" asked Tom.

"Charlie Matthias."

Brother David turned a questioning face to Tom, who said, "Charlie Pink-Eye."

The faces of the monk and the two women fell into sickness. Brother David closed his eyes and shook his head slowly from side to side.

"What's wrong?" asked Benny.

"You can stay to dinner," Brother David said stiffly, eyes still closed. "God requires mercy and sharing from all of His Children. But . . . once you've eaten I'd like you to leave."

Tom put his hand on the monk's shoulder. "We're moving on now."

The redhead stepped toward Tom. "It was a lovely day until you came."

"No," said Brother David sharply, then repeated it more gently. "No, Sarah . . . Tom's our friend, and we're being rude." He opened his eyes, and Benny thought that the man now looked seventy. "I'm sorry, Tom. Please forgive Sister Sarah, and please forgive me for—"

"No," said Tom. "It's okay. She's right. It was a lovely day, and saying that man's name here was wrong of me. I apologize to you, to her, to Sister Claire, and to Old Roger. This is Benny's first time out here in the Ruin. He met . . . that man . . . and had heard a lot of stories. Stories of hunting out here. He's a boy and he doesn't understand. I brought him out here to let him know how things are. How things fall out." He paused. "He's never been to Sunset Hollow. You understand?"

The three Children of God studied him for a while, and then one by one they nodded.

"What's Sunset Hollow?" Benny asked, but Tom didn't answer.

"And I thank you for your offer of a meal," said Tom, "but we've got miles to go, and I think Benny's going to have a lot of questions to ask. Some of them are better asked elsewhere."

Sister Sarah reached up and touched Tom's face. "I'm sorry for my words."

"You've got nothing to be sorry about."

She smiled at him and caressed his cheek; then she turned and placed her hands on either side of Benny's face. "May God protect your heart out here in the world." With that she kissed him on the forehead and walked away. The blonde smiled at the brothers and followed.

Benny turned to Tom. "Did I miss something?"

"Probably," said Tom. "Come on, kiddo, let's roll."

Brother David shifted to stand in Tom's path. "Brother," he said, "I'll ask once and then be done with it."

"Ask away."

"Are you sure about what you're doing?"

"Sure? No. But I'm set on doing it." He fished in his pocket and brought out three vials of cadaverine. "Here, Brother. May it help you in your work."

Brother David nodded his thanks. "God go with you and before you and within you."

They shook hands, and Tom stepped back onto the dirt road. Benny, however, lingered for a moment longer.

"Look, mister," he began slowly, "I don't know what I said or did that was wrong, but I'm sorry, you know? Tom brought me out here, and he's a bit crazy, and I don't know what . . ." He trailed off. There was no road map in his head to guide him through this conversation.

Brother David offered his hand and gave him the same blessing.

"Yeah," said Benny. "You, too. Okay?"

He hurried to catch up to Tom, who was fifty yards down the road. When he looked back, the monk was standing in the road. He lifted his hand, but whether it was some kind of blessing or a gesture of farewell, Benny didn't know. Either way it creeped him out.

VIII

When they were far down the road, Benny said, "What was that all about? Why'd that guy get so jacked about me mentioning Charlie?"

"Not everyone thinks Charlie's 'cool,' kiddo."

"You jealous?"

Tom laughed. "God! The day I'm jealous of someone like Charlie Pink-Eye is the day I'll cover myself in steak sauce and walk out into a crowd of the dead."

"Hilarious," said Benny sourly. "What's with all that Children of God, Children of Lazarus stuff? What are they doing out here?"

"They're all over the Ruin. I've met travelers who've seen them as far east as Pennsylvania, and all the way down to Mexico City. I first saw them about a year after First Night. A whole bunch of them heading across the country in an old school bus with scripture passages painted all over it. Not sure how they got started or who chose the name. Even Brother David doesn't know. To him it's like they always were."

"Is he nuts?"

"I think the expression used to be 'touched by God.'"

"So . . . that would be a yes."

"If he's nuts, then at least his heart's in the right place. The Children don't believe in violence of any kind."

"But they're okay with you, even though you kill zoms?"

Tom shook his head. "No, they don't like what I do. But they accept my explanation for why I do it, and Brother David and a few others have seen *how* I do it, and whereas they don't approve, they don't condemn me for it. They think I'm misguided but well-intentioned."

"And Charlie? What do they think of him? Can't be anything good."

"They believe Charlie Pink-Eye to be an evil man. Him and his jackass buddy the Motor City Hammer and a bunch of others. They think most of the bounty hunters are evil, in fact, and I can't fault them for those beliefs."

Benny said nothing. He still thought Charlie Matthias was cool as all hell.

"So . . . these Children, what do they actually *do*?"

"Not much. They tend to the dead. If they find a town, they'll go through the houses and look for photos of the people who lived there, and then they try and round up those people if they're still wandering around the town. They put them in their houses, seal the doors, write some prayers on the walls, and then move on. Most of them keep moving. Brother David's been here for a year or so, but I expect he'll move on, too."

"How do they round up zoms? Especially in a town full of them?"

"They wear carpet coats and they know the tricks of moving quietly and using cadaverine to mask their living smells. Sometimes one or another of the Children will come to town to buy some, but more often guys like me bring some out to them."

"Don't they ever get attacked?"

Tom nodded. "All the time, sad to say. I know of at least fifty dead in this part of the country who used to be Children. I've even heard stories that some of the Children give themselves to the dead."

Benny stared at him. *"Why?"*

"Brother David says that some of the Children believe that the dead are the 'meek' who were meant to inherit the earth, and that all things under heaven are there to sustain them. They think that allowing the dead to feed on them is fulfilling God's will."

"That's sick."

Tom shrugged.

"It's stupid," Benny said.

"It is what it is. I think a lot of the Children are people who didn't survive First Night. Oh, sure, their bodies did, but I think some fundamental part of them was broken by what happened. I was there, I can relate."

"You're not crazy."

"I have my moments, kiddo, believe me."

Benny gave him a strange look.

That's when they heard the gunshots.

I X

When the first one cracked through the air, Benny dropped to a huddle, but Tom stood straight and looked away to the northeast. When he heard the second shot, he turned his head slightly more to the north.

"Handgun," he said. "Heavy caliber. Three miles."

Benny looked up at him through the arms he'd wrapped over his head. "Bullets can go three miles, can't they?"

"Not usually," said Tom. "Even so, they aren't shooting at us."

Benny straightened cautiously. "You can tell? How?"

"Echoes," he said. "Those bullets didn't travel far. They're shooting at something close and hitting it."

"Um . . . it's cool that you know that. A little freaky, but cool."

"Yeah, this whole thing is about me showing you how cool I am."

"Oh. Sarcasm," said Benny dryly. "I get it."

"Shut up," said Tom with a grin.

"No, you shut up."

They smiled at each other for the first time all day.

"C'mon," said Tom, "let's go see what they're shooting at." He set off in the direction of the gunshot echoes.

Benny stood watching him for a moment. "Um . . . wait . . . we're going *toward* the shooting?"

Benny shook his head and followed as quickly as he could. Tom picked up the pace, and Benny tried to keep up. They followed a stream down to the lowlands, but Benny noticed that Tom never went closer than a thousand yards to the running water. He asked Tom about this.

Tom asked, "Can you hear the water?"

Benny strained to hear. "No."

"There's your answer. Flowing water is constant noise. It masks other sounds. We'll only go near it to cross it or to fill our canteens; otherwise quiet is better for listening. Always remember that if we can hear something, then it can probably hear us. And if we can't hear something, then it might still be able to hear us and we won't know about it until it's too late."

However, as they followed the gunshot echoes, their path angled toward the stream. Tom stopped for a moment and then shook his head in disapproval. "Not bright," he said, but didn't explain his comment. They ran on.

As they moved, Benny practiced being quiet. It was harder than he thought, and for a while it sounded—to his ears—as if he was making a terrible racket. Twigs broke like firecrackers under his feet; his breath sounded like a wheezing dragon; the legs of his jeans whisked together like a crosscut saw. Tom told him to focus on quieting one thing at a time.

"Don't try to learn too many skills at once. Take a new skill and learn it by using it. Go from there."

By the time they were close to where they'd heard the gunshots, Benny was moving more quietly and found that he enjoyed the challenge. It was like playing ghost tag with Chong and Morgie.

Tom stopped and cocked his head to listen. He put a finger to his lips and gestured for Benny to remain still. They were in a field of tall grass that led to a dense stand of birch trees. From beyond the trees they could hear the sound of men laughing and shouting and the occasional hollow crack of a pistol shot.

"Stay here," Tom whispered, and then he moved as quickly and quietly as a sudden breeze, vanishing into the tall grass. Benny lost track of him almost at once. More gunshots popped in the dry air.

A full minute passed, and Benny felt a burning constriction in his chest and realized that he was holding his breath. He let it out and gulped in another.

Where was Tom?

Another minute. More laughter and shouts. A few scattered gunshots. A third minute. A fourth.

And then something large and dark rose up in the tall grass a few feet away.

"Tom!" Benny almost screamed the name, but Tom shushed him. His brother stepped close and bent to whisper.

"Benny, listen to me. On the other side of those trees is something you need to see. If you're going to understand how things really are, you need to see."

"What is it?"

"Bounty hunters. Three of them. I've seen these three before, but never this close to town. I want you to come with me. Very quietly. I want you to watch, but don't say or do anything."

"But—"

"This will be ugly. Are you ready?"

"I—"

"Yes or no? We can head southeast and continue on our way. Or we can go home."

Benny shook his head. "No, I'm ready."

Tom smiled and squeezed his arm. "If things get serious, I want you to run and hide. Understand?"

"Yes," Benny said, but the word was like a thorn caught in his throat. Running and hiding. Was that the only strategy Tom knew?

"Promise?"

"I promise."

"Good. Now . . . follow me. When I move, you move. When I stop, you stop. Step only where I step. Got it? Good."

Tom led the way through the tall grass, moving slowly, shifting his position in time with the fluctuations of the wind. When Benny realized this, it became easier to match his brother step for step. They entered the trees, and Benny could more easily hear the laughter of the three men. They sounded drunk. Then he heard the whinny of a horse.

A horse?

The trees thinned, and Tom hunkered down and pulled Benny

down with him. The scene before them was something out of a nightmare. Even as Benny took it in, a part of his mind was whispering to him that he would never forget what he was seeing. He could feel every detail being burned into his brain.

Beyond the trees was a clearing bordered on two sides by switchbacks of the deep stream. The stream vanished around a sheer sandstone cliff that rose thirty feet above the treeline and reappeared on the opposite side of the clearing. Only a narrow dirt path led from the trees in which the Imura brothers crouched to the spit of land framed by stream and cliff. It was a natural clearing that gave the men a clear view of the approaches on all sides. A wagon with two big horses stood in the shade thrown by the birch trees. The back of the wagon was piled high with zombies, who squirmed and writhed in a hopeless attempt to flee or attack. Hopeless, because beside the wagon was a growing pile of severed arms and legs. The zombies in the wagon were limbless cripples.

A dozen other zombies milled around by the sandstone wall, and every time one of them would lumber after one of the men, it was driven back by a vicious kick. It was clear to Benny that two of the men knew some kind of martial art, because they used elaborate jumping and spinning kicks. The more dynamic the kick, the more the others laughed and applauded. When Benny listened, he realized that as one stepped up to confront a zombie, the other two men would name a kick. The men shouted bets at each other and then rated the kicks for points. The two kick-fighters took turns while the third man kept score by drawing numbers in the dirt with a stick.

The zombies had little hope of any effective attack. They were clustered on a narrow and almost water-locked section of the clearing; but far worse than that—each and every one of them was blind. Their eyes were pits of torn flesh and almost colorless blood. Benny looked at the zombies on the cart and saw that they were all blind as well.

He gagged but clamped a hand to his mouth to keep the sound from escaping.

The standing zombies were all battered hulks, barely able to stand, and it was clear that this game had been going on for a while. Benny knew that the zombies were already dead, that they couldn't feel pain or know humiliation, but what he saw seared a mark on his soul.

"That one's 'bout totally messed up," yelled a black man with an eye patch. "Load him up."

The man who apparently didn't know the fancy kicks bent and picked up a sword with a heavy, curved blade. Benny had seen pictures of one in an *Arabian Nights* book. A scimitar.

"Okay," said the swordsman, "what're the numbers?"

"Denny did his in four cuts at three-point-one seconds," said Eyepatch.

"Oh, hell . . . I got that beat. Time me."

Eyepatch dug a stopwatch out of his pocket. "Ready . . . steady . . . *Go!*"

The swordsman rushed toward the closest zombies—a teenage boy who looked like he'd been about Benny's age when he died. The blade swept upward in a glittering line that sheared through the zombie's right arm at the shoulder, and then he checked his swing and chopped down to take the other arm. Instantly he pivoted, swung the sword laterally, and chopped through both legs an inch below the groin. The zombie toppled to the ground, and one leg, against all odds, remained upright.

The three men burst out laughing.

"Time!" yelled Eyepatch, and read the stopwatch. "Holy crap, Stosh. That's two-point-nine-nine seconds!"

"And three cuts," yelled Stosh. "I did it in three cuts!"

They howled with laughter, and the third man, called Denny, squatted down, wrapped his burly arms around the limbless zombie's torso, picked it up with a grunt, and carried it over to the wagon. Eyepatch tossed him the limbs—one, two, three, four—and Denny added them to the pile.

The kicking game started up again. Stosh drew a pistol and shot one of the remaining zombies in the chest. The bullet did no harm, but the creature turned toward the impact and began lumbering in that direction. Denny yelled, "Jump-spinning back kick!"

Eyepatch leaped into the air, twisted, and drove a savage kick into the zombie's stomach, knocking it backward into the others. They all fell, and the men laughed and handed around a bottle, while the zombies clambered awkwardly to their feet.

Tom leaned close to Benny and whispered, "Time to go."

He moved away, but Benny caught up to him and grabbed his sleeve. "What the hell are you doing? Where are you going?"

"Away from these clowns," said Tom.

"You have to *do* something!"

Tom turned to face him. "What is it you expect me to do?"

"Stop them!" Benny said in an urgent whisper.

"Why?"

"Because they're . . . because . . ." Benny sputtered.

"You want me to save the zombies, Benny? Is that it?"

Benny, caught in the fires of his own frustration, glared at him.

"They're bounty hunters, Benny," said Tom. "They get a bounty on every zombie they kill. Want to know why they don't just cut the heads off? Because they have to prove that it was they who killed the zombies and didn't just collect heads from someone else's kill. So they bring the torsos back to town and do the killing in front of a bounty judge, who then pays them a half day's rations for every kill. Looks like they have enough there for each of them to get almost five full days' rations. They'll probably swap some of the rations for goods and services with people in town. Especially with women in town. Single moms will do a lot to get enough food for their kids. You following me?"

"I don't believe you!" snarled Benny.

"Keep your voice down," Tom hissed. "And, yes, you do believe me. I can see it in your eyes. I can tell you're thinking about that—and then about what that dirtbag Charlie Pink-Eye told you and the other boys. I'll bet he's told you about all the women he's screwed. How do you think an ugly ape like him *gets* women? Even *he* wouldn't risk rape—not with the death penalty on that—and the only hookers in town are uglier than the zombies. No, Charlie and his buddies buy it with food rations from women who will do *anything* to feed their kids. And as far as I'm concerned, that's not a lot better than rape."

Blotches of fiery red had blossomed on Tom's face as he said this in a fierce whisper. He stopped, took a few breaths, let the fury pass. When he spoke again his face was calmer but his words had as many jagged edges.

"The game these guys are playing? That's ugly, right? It got you so upset that you wanted me to step in and do something. Am I right?"

Benny said nothing. His fists were balled into knuckly knots at his sides.

"Well, as bad as that is . . . I've seen worse. A whole lot worse. I'm talking pit fights where they put some dumb-ass kid—maybe someone your age—in a hole dug in the ground and then push in a zom. Maybe they give the kid a knife or a sharpened stick or a baseball bat. Sometimes the kid wins, sometimes he doesn't, but the odds-makers haul in a fortune either way. And where do the kids come from? They *volunteer* for it."

"That's bull. . . ."

"No, it's not. If I wasn't around and you lived with Aunt Cathy when she was sick with cancer, what would you have done, how much would you have risked to make sure she got enough food and medicine?"

Benny shook his head, but Tom's face was stone.

"Are you going to tell me that you wouldn't take a shot at winning maybe a month's worth of rations—or a whole box of meds—for ninety seconds in a zom pit?"

"That doesn't happen."

"No?"

"I never heard about anything like that."

Tom snorted. "If you did something like that, would you tell anyone? Would you even tell Chong and Morgie?"

Benny didn't answer.

Tom pointed. "I can go back there and maybe stop those guys. Maybe even do it without killing them or getting killed myself, but what good would it do? You think they're the only ones doing this sort of thing? This is the great Rot and Ruin, Benny. There's no law out here, not since First Night. Killing zoms is what people do out here."

"That's not killing them! It's sick."

"Yes it is," Tom said softly. "Yes it is, and I can't tell you how relieved and happy I am to hear you say it. To know that you believe it."

There were more shouts and laughter from behind them. And another gunshot.

"I can stop them if you want me to. But it won't stop what's happening out here."

Tears burned in Benny's eyes, and he punched Tom hard in the chest. "But *you* do this stuff! You kill zombies."

Tom grabbed Benny and pulled him close. Benny struggled, but Tom pulled his brother to his chest and held him. "No," he whispered. "No. Come on, I'll show you what I do."

He released Benny, placed a gentle hand on his brother's back, and guided him back through the trees to the tall grass.

X

They didn't speak for over a mile. Benny kept looking back, but even he didn't know if he was checking to see if they were being followed or if he was regretting that they'd done nothing about what was happening. His jaw ached from clenching it.

They reached the crest of the hill that separated the field of tall grass from an upslope that wound around the base of a huge mountain. There was a road there, a two-lane blacktop that was cracked and choked with weeds. The road spun off toward a chain of mountains that marched into the distance and vanished into heat haze far to the southeast. There were old bones among the weeds, and Benny kept stopping to look at them.

"I don't want to do this anymore," said Benny.

Tom kept walking.

"I don't want to do what you do. Not if it means doing . . . that sort of stuff."

"I already told you. I don't do that sort of stuff."

"But you're around it. You see it. It's part of your life." Benny kicked a rock and sent it skittering off the road and into the grass. Crows scolded him as they leaped into the air, leaving behind a rabbit carcass on which they'd been feeding.

Tom stopped and looked back. "If we turn back now, you'll only know part of the truth."

"I don't care about the truth."

"Too late for that now. You've seen some of it. If you don't see the rest, it'll leave you—"

"Leave me what? Unbalanced? You can stick that Zen crap up your—"

"Language."

Benny bent and snatched up a shinbone that had been polished white by scavengers and weather. He threw it at Tom, who side-stepped to let it pass.

"Screw you and your truth and all of this stuff!" screamed Benny. "You're just like those guys back there! You come out here all noble and wise and with all that bull, but you're no different. You're a killer. Everyone in town says so!"

Tom stalked over to him and grabbed a fistful of Benny's shirt and lifted him to his toes. "Shut up!" he snarled. "You just shut your damn mouth!"

Benny was shocked to silence.

"You don't know who I am or what I am," Tom growled, giving him a shake. "You don't know what I've done. You don't know the things I've had to do to keep you safe. To keep us safe. You don't know what I—"

He broke off and flung Benny away from him. Benny staggered backward and fell hard on his ass, legs splayed among the weeds and old bones. His eyes bugged with shock, and Tom stood above him, different expressions warring on his face. Anger, shock at his own actions, burning frustration. Even love.

"Benny . . ."

Benny got to his feet and dusted off his pants. Once more he looked back the way they'd come and then stepped up to Tom, staring up at his big brother with an expression that was equally mixed and conflicted.

"I'm sorry," they both said.

They stared at each other.

Benny smiled first.

Tom's smile was slower in coming, though.

"You're a total pain in my butt, little brother."

"You're a big dork."

The hot breeze blew past them. Tom said, "If you want to go back, then we'll go back."

Benny shook his head. "No."

"Why not?"

"Do I have to have an answer?"

"Right now? No. Eventually? Probably."

"Yeah," said Benny. "That's okay, I guess. Just tell me one thing. I know you said it already, but I really need to know. Really, Tom."

Tom nodded.

"You're *not* like them. Right? Swear on something." He pulled out his wallet and held up the picture. "Swear on Mom and Dad."

Tom nodded. "Okay, Benny. I swear."

"On Mom and Dad."

"On Mom and Dad." Tom touched the picture and nodded.

"Then let's go."

The afternoon burned on, and they followed the two-lane road around the base of the mountain. Neither spoke for almost an hour, and then Tom said, "This isn't just a walk we're taking, kiddo. I'm out here on a job."

Benny shot him a look. "You're here to kill a zom?"

Tom shrugged. "It's not the way I like to phrase it, but yes, that's the bottom line."

They walked another half mile.

"How does this work? The . . . job, I mean."

"You saw part of it when you applied to be an Erosion Artist," said Tom. He dug into a jacket pocket and removed an envelope, opened it, and removed a piece of paper, which he unfolded and handed to Benny. There was a small color photograph clipped to one corner that showed a smiling man of about thirty with sandy hair and a sparse beard. The paper it was clipped to was a large portrait of the same man as he might be now if he were a zombie. The name *Harold* was handwritten in one corner.

"*This* is what people do with those pictures?"

"Not always, but a lot of the time. People have the pictures done of wives, husbands, children—anyone they loved, someone they lost. Sometimes they can even remember what a person was wearing on First Night, and that makes it easier for me, because as I said, the dead seldom move far from where they lived or worked. Guys like me find them."

"And kill them?"

Tom answered that with a shrug. They rounded a bend in the road and saw the first few houses of a small town built onto the side of the mountain. Even from a quarter mile away, Benny could see zombies standing in yards or on the sidewalks. One stood in the middle of the road with his face tilted toward the sun.

Nothing moved.

Tom folded the erosion portrait and put it in his pocket, then he took out the vial of cadaverine and sprinkled some on his clothes. He handed it to Benny and then gave him the mint gel after he dabbed some on his upper lip.

"You ready?"

"Not even a little bit," said Benny.

Tom drew his pistol and led the way. Benny shook his head, unsure of how exactly the day had brought him to this moment, and then he followed.

X I

"Won't they attack us?" Benny whispered.

"Not if we're smart and careful. The trick is to move slowly. They respond to quick movements. Smell, too, but we have that covered."

"Can't they hear us?"

"Yes, they can," Tom said. "So once we're in the town, don't talk unless I do, and even then, less is more and quieter is better than loud. I found that speaking slowly helps. A lot of the dead moan, so they're used to slow, quiet sounds."

"This is like the Scouts," Benny said. "Mr. Feeney told us that when we're in nature we should act like we're part of nature."

"For better or worse, Benny, this is part of nature, too."

"That doesn't make me feel good, Tom."

"This is the Rot and Ruin, kiddo. Nobody feels good out here. Now hush and keep your eyes open."

They slowed their pace as they neared the first houses. Tom stopped and spent a few minutes studying the town. The main street ran upward to where they stood, so they had a good view of the whole town. Moving very slowly, Tom removed the envelope from his pocket and unfolded the erosion portrait.

"My client said that it was the sixth house along the main street," Tom murmured. "Red front door and white fence. See it? There, past the old mail truck."

"Uh-huh," Benny said, without moving his lips. He was terrified of the zombies who stood in their yards not more than twenty paces away.

"We're looking for a man named Harold Simmons. There's nobody in the yard, so we may have to go inside."

"Inside?" Benny asked, his voice quavering.

"Come on." Tom began moving slowly, barely lifting his feet. He did not exactly imitate the slow, shuffling gait of the zombies, but his movements were unobtrusive. Benny did his best to mimic everything he did. They passed two houses at which zombies stood in the yard. The first, on their left, had three zombies on the other side of a hip-high chain-link fence—two little girls and an older woman. Their clothes were tatters that blew like holiday streamers in the hot breeze. As Tom and Benny passed by them, the old woman turned in their direction. Tom stopped and waited, his pistol ready, but the woman's dead eyes swept past them without lingering. A few paces along, they passed a yard on their right in which a man in a bathrobe stood staring at the corner of the house as if he expected something to happen. He stood among wild weeds, and creeper vines had wrapped themselves around his calves. It looked like he had stood there for years, and with a sinking feeling of horror, Benny realized that he probably had.

Benny wanted to turn and run. His mouth was as dry as paste, and sweat ran down his back and into his underwear.

They moved steadily down the street, always slowly. The sun was heading toward the western part of the sky, and it would be dark in four or five hours. Benny knew that they could never make it home by nightfall. He wondered if Tom would take them back to the gas station, or if he was crazy enough to claim an empty house in this ghost town for the night. If he had to sleep in a zombie's house, even if there was no zombie there, then Benny was sure he'd go completely mad-cow crazy.

"There he is," murmured Tom, and Benny looked at the house with the red door. A man stood looking out of the big bay window. He had sandy hair and a sparse beard, but now the hair and beard were nearly gone and the skin of his face had shriveled to a leather tightness.

Tom stopped outside of the paint-peeling white picket fence. He looked from the erosion portrait to the man in the window and back again.

"Benny?" he said under his breath. "You think that's him?"

"Mm-hm," Benny said with a low squeak.

The zombie in the window seemed to be looking at them. Benny was sure of it. The withered face and the dead pale eyes were pointed directly at the fence, as if he had been waiting there all these years for a visitor to come to his garden gate.

Tom nudged the gate with his toe. It was locked.

Moving very slowly, Tom leaned over and undid the latch. The process took over two minutes. Nervous sweat ran down Benny's face, and he couldn't take his eyes off of the zombie.

Tom pushed on the gate with his knee, and it opened now.

"Very, very slowly," he said. "Red light, green light, all the way to the door."

Benny knew the game, though in truth he had never seen a working stoplight. They entered the yard. The old woman in the first garden suddenly turned toward them. So did the zombie in the bathrobe.

"Stop," hissed Tom. He held the pistol close to his chest, his finger lying straight along the trigger guard. "If we have to make a run for it, head into the house. We can lock ourselves in and wait until they calm down."

The old lady and the man in the bathrobe faced them but did not advance.

The tableau held for a minute that seemed an hour long.

"I'm scared," said Benny.

"It's okay to be scared," said Tom. "Scared means you're smart. Just don't panic. That'll get you killed."

Benny almost nodded, but he caught himself.

Tom took a slow step. Then a second. It was uneven, his body swaying as if his knees were stiff. The bathrobe zombie turned away and looked at the shadow of a cloud moving up the valley; but the old lady still watched. Her mouth opened and closed as if she was slowly chewing on something.

But then she, too, turned away to watch the moving shadow.

Tom took another step and another, and eventually Benny followed. The process was excruciatingly slow, but to Benny it felt as if they were moving too fast. No matter how slowly they went, he thought that it was all wrong, that the zombies—all of them up and down the street—would suddenly turn toward them and moan with their dry and dusty voices, and then a great mass of the hungry dead would surround them.

Tom reached the door and turned the handle.

The knob turned in his hand, and the lock clicked open. Tom gently pushed it open and stepped into the gloom of the house. Benny cast a quick look at the window to make sure the zombie was still there.

Only he wasn't.

"Tom!" Benny cried. "Look out!"

A dark shape lunged at Tom out of the shadows of the entrance hallway. It clawed for him with wax-white fingers and moaned with an unspeakable hunger. Benny screamed.

Then something happened that Benny could not understand. Tom was there and then he wasn't. His brother's body became a blur of movement, as he pivoted to the outside of the zombie's right arm, ducked low, grabbed the zombie's shins from behind, and drove his shoulder into the former Harold Simmons's back. The zombie instantly fell forward onto his face, knocking clouds of dust from the carpet. Tom leaped onto the zombie's back and used his knees to pin both shoulders to the floor.

"Close the door!" Tom barked, as he pulled a spool of thin silk cord from his jacket pocket. He whipped the cord around the zombie's wrists and shimmied down to be able to bring both of the zombie's hands together and tie them behind the creature's back. He looked up. "The door, Benny—*now!*"

Benny came out of his daze and realized that there was movement in his peripheral vision. He turned to see the old lady, the two little girls and the zombie in his bathrobe lumbering up the garden path. Benny slammed the door and shot the bolt, then leaned against it, panting as if he had been the one to wrestle a zombie to the ground and hog-tie it. With a sinking feeling, he realized that it had probably been his own shouted warning that had attracted the other zombies.

Tom flicked out a spring-blade knife and cut the silk cord. He kept his weight on the struggling zombie while he fashioned a large loop like a noose. The zombie kept trying to turn its head to bite him, but Tom didn't seem to care. The biting teeth were nowhere near him—though Benny was still terrified of those gray, rotted teeth.

With a deft twist of the wrist, Tom looped the noose over the zombie's head, catching it below the chin, and then he jerked the slack so that the closing loop forced the creature's jaws shut with a *clack*. Tom wound silk cord around the zombie's head so that the line passed under the jaw and over the crown. When he had three full turns in place, he tied it tight. He shimmied farther down the zombie's body and pinned its legs and then tied its ankles together.

Then Tom stood up, stuffed the cord into his pocket, and closed his knife. He slapped dust from his clothes as he turned back to Benny.

"Thanks for the warning, kiddo, but I had it."

"Um . . . holy sh—!"

"Language," Tom interrupted quietly.

Tom went to the window and looked out. "Eight of 'em out there."

"Do-do we . . . I mean, *shouldn't* we board up the windows?"

Tom laughed. "You've listened to too many campfire tales. If we started hammering nails into boards, the sound would call every living dead person in the whole town. We'd be under siege."

"But we're trapped."

Tom looked at him. "*Trapped* is a relative term," he said. "We can't go out the front. I expect there's a back door. We'll finish our business here and then we'll sneak out nice and quiet and head on our way."

Benny stared at him and then at the struggling zombie, who was on the carpet.

"You-you just . . ."

"Practice, Benny. I've done this before. C'mon, help me get him up."

They knelt on opposite sides of the zombie, but Benny didn't want to touch it. He'd never touched a corpse of any kind before, and he didn't want to start with one that had tried to bite his brother.

"Benny," Tom said, "he can't hurt you now. He's helpless."

The word *helpless* hit Benny hard. It brought back the image of Old Roger—with no eyes, no teeth, and no fingers—and the two young women who tended to him. And the limbless torsos in the wagon.

"Helpless," he murmured. "God . . ."

"Come on," Tom said gently.

Together they lifted the zombie. He was light—far lighter than Benny expected—and they half carried, half dragged him into the dining room. Away from the living-room window. Sunlight fell in dusty slants through the moth-eaten curtains. The ruins of a meal had long since decayed to dust on the table. They put him in a chair, and Tom produced the spool of cord and bound him in place. The zombie continued to struggle, but Benny understood. The zombie was actually helpless.

Helpless.

The word hung in the air. Ugly and full of dreadful new meaning.

Tom removed the envelope from his pocket. Apart from the folded erosion portrait, there was also a piece of cream-colored stationery on which were several handwritten lines. Tom read through them silently, sighed, and then turned to his brother.

"Restraining the dead is difficult, Benny, but it isn't the hardest part." He held out the letter. "This is."

Benny took the letter.

"My clients—the people who hire me to come out here—they usually want something said. Things they would like to say themselves, but can't. Things they need said so that they can have closure. Do you understand?"

Benny read the letter. His breath caught in his throat and he nodded as the first tears fell down his cheeks.

His brother took the letter back. "I need to read it aloud, Benny. You understand?"

Benny nodded again.

Tom angled the letter into the dusty light and read:

My dear Harold. I love you and miss you. I've missed you so desperately for all these years. I still dream about you every night, and each morning I pray that you've found peace. I forgive you for what you tried to do to me. I forgive you for what you did to the children. I hated you for a long time, but I understand now that it wasn't you. It was this *thing* that happened. I want you to know that I took care of our children when they turned. They are at peace, and I put flowers on their graves every Sunday. I know you would like that. I have asked

Tom Imura to find you. He's a good man, and I know that he will be gentle with you. I love you, Harold. May God grant you His peace. I know that when my time comes, you will be waiting for me, waiting with Bethy and little Stephen, and that we will all be together again in a better world. Please forgive me for not having the courage to help you sooner. I will always love you. Yours forever, Claire.

Benny was weeping when Tom finished. He turned away and covered his face with his hands and sobbed. Tom came and hugged him and kissed his head.

Then Tom stepped away, took a breath, and opened his knife again. Benny didn't think he would be able to watch, but he raised his head and saw Tom as he placed the letter on the table in front of Harold Simmons and smoothed it out. Then he moved behind the zombie and gently pushed its head forward so that he could place the tip of his knife against the hollow at the base of the skull.

"You can look away if you want to, Benny," he said.

Benny did not want to look, but he didn't turn away.

Tom nodded. He took another breath and then thrust the blade into the back of the zombie's neck. The blade slid in with almost no effort in the gap between spine and skull, and the razor-sharp edge sliced completely through the brain stem.

Harold Simmons stopped struggling. His body didn't twitch; there was no death spasm. He just sagged forward against the silken cords and was still. Whatever force had been active in him, whatever pathogen or radiation or whatever had taken the man away and left behind a zombie, was gone.

Tom cut the cords that held Simmons's arms and raised each hand and placed it on the table so that the dead man's palms held the letter in place.

"Be at peace, brother," said Tom Imura.

He wiped and folded his knife and stepped back. He looked at Benny, who was openly sobbing.

"This is what I do, Benny."

XII

They left by the back door, and there were no problems. Benny's tears slowed and stopped, but it took a while. They walked in silence, side by side, heading southeast. Miles fell away behind them. They passed another gas station, where Tom greeted another monk. They didn't linger, though. The day was burning away.

"We'll be back in an hour," Tom said to the monk after gifting him with vials of cadaverine and a wrapped package of jerky. "We'll need to stay the night."

"You're always welcome, brother," said the monk.

They walked on for another fifteen minutes, through a grove of trees that were heavy with late season oranges. Tom picked a few, and they peeled and ate them and said almost nothing until they reached the wrought-iron gate of a community that was embowered by a high red-brick wall. A sign over the gate read SUNSET HOLLOW.

Outside of the gate there were trash and old bones and a few burned shells of cars. The outer walls were pocked with bullet scars. To the right of the gate someone had used white paint to write *THIS AREA CLEARED. KEEP GATES CLOSED. KEEP OUT.* Below that were the initials T. I.

Benny pointed. "You wrote that?" It was the first time he'd spoken a full sentence since leaving the house of Harold Simmons.

"Years ago," Tom said.

The gates were closed, and a thick chain had been threaded through the bars and locked with a heavy padlock. The chain and the lock looked new and gleamed with oil.

"What is this place?" Benny asked.

Tom tucked his hands into his back pockets and looked up at the sign. "This is what they used to call a gated community. The gates were supposed to keep unwanted people out and keep the people inside safe."

"Did it work? I mean . . . during First Night?"

"No."

"Did all the people die?"

"Most of them. A few got away."

"Why is it locked?"

"For the same reason as always," Tom said. He blew out his

cheeks and dug into his right front jeans pocket for a key. He showed it to Benny and then opened the lock, pushed the gates open, restrung the chain, and clicked the lock closed with the keyhole on the inside now.

They walked along the road. The houses were all weather damaged, and the streets were pasted with the dusty remnants of fifteen years of falling leaves. Every garden was overgrown, but there were no zombies in them. Some of the doors had crosses nailed to them, around which hung withered garlands of flowers.

"Your other job's here?" Benny asked.

"Yes," said Tom. His voice was soft and distant.

"Is it like the other one?"

"Sort of."

"That was . . . hard," said Benny.

"Yes it was."

"Doing this over and over again would drive me crazy. How do you do it?"

Tom turned to him as if that was the question he'd been waiting for all day. "It keeps me sane," he said. "Do you understand?"

Benny thought about it for a long moment. Birds sang in the trees and the cicadas buzzed continually. "Is it because you knew what the world was before?"

Tom nodded.

"Is it because if you didn't do it . . . then maybe no one would?"

Tom nodded again.

"It must be lonely."

"It is." Tom glanced at him. "But I always hoped you'd want to join me. To help me do what I do."

"I . . . don't know if I can."

"That's always going to be your choice. If you can, you can. If you can't, then believe me, I'll understand. It takes a lot out of you to do this. And it takes a lot out of you to know that the bounty hunters are out there doing what they do."

"How come none of them ever came here?"

"They did. Once."

"What happened."

Tom shrugged.

"What happened?" Benny asked again.

"I was here when they came. Pure chance."

"What happened?"

"Maybe it's better that I don't tell you."

Benny looked at him. "You killed them," he said. "Didn't you?"

Tom walked a dozen steps before he said, "Not all of them." A half dozen steps later he added, "I let two of them go."

"Why?"

"To spread the word," Tom said. "To let the other bounty hunters know that this place was off-limits."

"And they listened? The bounty hunters?"

Tom smiled. It wasn't boastful or malicious. It was a thin, cold knife-blade of a smile that was there and gone. "Sometimes you have to go to some pretty extreme lengths to make a point and to make it stick. Otherwise you find yourself having to make the same point over and over again."

Benny stared at him. "How many were there?"

"Ten."

"And you let two go."

"Yes."

"And you killed eight of them?"

"Yes." The late-afternoon sunlight slanting through the trees threw dappled light on the road and painted the sides of all of the houses to their left with purple shadows. A red fox and three kits scampered across the street ahead of them.

Benny opened his mouth to say something to Tom but didn't. Tom stopped in the middle of the street.

"Benny, I don't really want to talk about that day. Not now, not here, and maybe not ever. I did what I thought I had to do, but I'm not proud of it. Telling you the details would feel like bragging, and I think that would make me sick. It's already been a long day."

"I won't ask, Tom," said Benny.

They stood there, taking each other's measure perhaps for the very first time. Taking each other's measure and getting the right values.

Tom pointed, and Benny turned toward the front door of a house with peach trees growing wild in the yard. "This is it."

"There's a zombie in there?"

"Yes," Tom said. "There are two."

"We have to tie them up?"

"No. That's already been done. Years ago. Nearly every house here has a dead person in it. Some have already been released, the rest wait for family members to reach out and want it done."

"I know this sounds gross, but why don't you just go house to house and do it to every one of them? You know . . . *release* them."

"Because most of the people here have family living in our town. It takes a while, but people usually get to the point where they want someone to go and do this the way I do it. With respect, with words read to their dead family. Closure isn't closure until someone's ready to close the door. Do you understand what I mean?"

Benny nodded.

"Do you have a picture of the . . . um . . . people in there? So we know who they are? So we can make sure."

"There are pictures inside. Besides, I know the names of everyone in Sunset Hollow. I come here a lot. I was the one who went house to house and tied the dead up. Some monks helped, but I knew everyone here." Tom walked to the front door. "Are you ready?"

Benny looked at Tom and then at the door.

"You want me to do this, don't you?"

Tom looked sad. "Yes. I guess I do."

"If I do, then I'll be like you. I'll be doing this kind of thing."

"Yes."

"Forever?"

"I don't know, Benny. I hope not. But for a while? Yeah."

"What if I can't?"

"I told you. If you can't, then you can't, and we go to the way station for tonight and head home in the morning."

"Tom, why don't people from town come out to places like this and just take them back? We're so much stronger than the zoms. Why don't we take everything back?"

Tom shook his head. "I don't know. I ask myself that every day. The people on the other side of the fence—for the most part they don't even want to admit to themselves that the rest of the world exists. They feel safe over there."

"That's stupid."

"Yes," Tom said, "it surely is."

He turned the doorknob and opened the door. "Are you coming?"
Benny came as far as the front step. "It's not safe in there, is it?"
"It's not safe anywhere, Benny."
They were both aware in that moment that they were having a different discussion than the words they exchanged.
The brothers went into the house.
Tom led the way down a hall and into a spacious living room that had once been light and airy. Now it was pale and filled with dust. The wallpaper had faded, and there were animal tracks on the floor. There was a cold fireplace and a mantel filled with picture frames. The pictures were of a family. Mother and father. A smiling son in a uniform. A baby in a blue blanket. Brothers and cousins and grandparents. Two sisters who looked like they might have been twins but weren't. Everyone was smiling. Benny stood looking at the pictures for a long time and then reached up and took one down. A wedding picture.
"Where are they?" he asked softly.
"In here," said Tom.
Still holding the picture, Benny followed Tom through a dining room and into a kitchen. The windows were open and the yard was filled with trees. Two straight-backed chairs sat in front of the window, and in the chairs were two withered zombies. Both of them turned their heads toward the sound of footsteps. Their jaws were tied shut with silken cord. The man was dressed in the tatters of an old blue uniform; the woman wore a tailored suit and frilly white blouse. Benny came around front and looked from them to the wedding picture and back again.
"It's hard to tell."
"Not when you get used to it," said Tom. "The shape of the ears, the height of the cheekbones, the angle of the jaw, the distance between the nose and upper lip. Those things won't change even after years."
"I don't know if I can do this," Benny said again.
"That's up to you." Tom took his knife from his pocket and opened it. "I'll do one, and you can do the other. If you're ready. If you can."
Tom went to stand behind the man. He gently pushed the zombie's head forward and placed the tip of the knife in place, doing everything slowly, reminding Benny of how it had to be done.

"Aren't you going to say anything?" said Benny.

"I've already said it," said Tom. "A thousand times. I waited because I knew that you might want to say something."

"I didn't know them," said Benny.

A tear fell from Tom's eye onto the back of the struggling zombie's neck.

He plunged the blade and the struggles stopped. Just like that.

Tom hung his head for a moment as a sob broke in his chest. "I'm sorry," he said, and then, "Be at peace."

He sniffed and held the knife out to Benny.

"I can't!" Benny said, backing away. "Jesus fucking Christ, I can't!"

Tom stood there, tears rolling down his cheeks, holding the knife out. He didn't say a word.

"God . . . please don't make me do this," said Benny.

Tom shook his head.

"Please, Tom."

Tom lowered the knife.

The female zombie threw her weight against the cords and uttered a shrill moan that was like a dagger in Benny's mind. He covered his ears and turned away. He dropped into a crouch, face tucked into the corner between the back door and the wall, shaking his head.

Tom stood where he was.

It took Benny a long, long time. He stopped shaking his head and leaned his forehead against the wood. The zombie in the chair kept moaning. Benny turned and dropped onto his knees. He dragged a forearm under his nose and sniffed.

"She'll be like that forever, won't she?"

Tom said nothing.

"Yes," said Benny, answering his own question. "Yes."

He climbed slowly to his feet.

"Okay," he said, and held out his hand. His hand and arm trembled. Tom's trembled, too, as he handed over the knife.

Benny stood behind the zombie, and it took six or seven tries before he could bring himself to touch her. Eventually he managed it. Tom guided him, touching the spot where the knife had to go. Benny put the tip of the knife in place.

"When you do it," said Tom, "do it quick."

"Can they feel pain?"

"I don't know. But you can. I can. Do it quick."

Benny took a ragged breath and said, "I love you, Mom."

He did it quickly.

And it was over.

He dropped the knife, and Tom gathered him up, and they sank down to their knees together on the kitchen floor, crying so loud that it threatened to break the world. In the chairs, the two dead people sat slumped, their heads tilted toward one another, their withered mouths silent.

The sun was tumbling behind the edge of the mountain by the time they left the house. Together they'd dug graves in the backyard. Tom locked up the house and then relocked the chain on the front gate. Side by side they walked back the way they had come. The knife was in Benny's pocket. He had asked Tom if he could keep it.

"Why?" his brother asked.

Benny's eyes were puffy from crying but they were dry. "I guess I'll need it," he said.

Tom studied him for a long time. His smile was sad but his eyes were filled with love. And with pride.

"Come on," he said. "Let's head back."

Benny Imura looked back at the wrought-iron gates and at the words painted outside. He nodded to himself.

Together they walked through the gathering twilight back to the way station.

THE ZOMBIE WHO FELL FROM THE SKY

BY M. B. HOMLER

In Jesus-like effigy, the body hung impaled upon the spire atop the tallest building in town—city hall. It rested with arms sagging back, legs dangling down, torso firmly rooted in place. When the body landed, there had been a loud *shuck* and townsfolk in the street felt a fan of light rain—a rain not in the forecast—sprinkle down on top of them. Bespattered with red, they had to admit it was a gruesome landing, maybe a perfect ten in gruesomeness. Slivers of dried flesh floated like confetti in the streets. On a random street corner, an eyeball stared upward. No one got to see it except for a passing Chihuahua, who gobbled it down—with minimal choking and hacking—before his owner could surmise what happened. Most in this small town, unknown for providing entertainment beyond small-time gossip and the occasional affair, were transfixed by the sudden and illogical impaling.

Response on the scene was quick. Cop cars and firetrucks roared to siren-wailing stops in front of city hall. Due to the graphic nature of the incident, they closed every nearby street to keep bystanders back. Firemen raised the fire ladder out as far as it would go and swung it over to the body, smacking the corpse and sending guts flying. Several firemen went up the ladder and stepped off onto the roof. They looked up at the spire. Walkie-talkies to their mouths, they reported what they saw in detached journalistic fashion. Desiccated body . . . mouth stripped of flesh . . . gums fully exposed . . . lips missing . . . yellow-green teeth filed down . . . a mass of bloody innards, guts and pus oozing . . . freely . . .

When the corpse on the pole twitched, everybody jumped.

They never did get it down. Oh they tried: They pulled and pushed and moved the body up and down the spire—an image reminiscent of firefighters running back and forth with a safety net trying to catch a threatening jumper—but they could not get it off. After putting in a great many hours, they gave up, let the corpse slide back down, and left it there. *Thump*. Their attitude was fuck it. The mayor's attitude was fuck it. Let rigor mortis and the flesh-eating maggots and buzzards of the world take care of it!

So that's what they did, and though many townsfolk claimed to have seen the body twitching, as if the crows were taking to it—their wish fulfilled—this unfortunately was not the case. The crows would go nowhere near it. They remained far away and aloof on a telephone wire.

Scared? They might have been.

Danny McDanielson worked as a short-order cook in the diner down the street from city hall. Being a short-order cook meant that no one took him seriously, and while he tried to pretend it didn't bother him, it did. A young poet, not bad looking, with Johnny Depp hair that he was always peeking out from under, he struggled to keep his burgeoning feelings of inadequacy to himself. When the corpse had fallen from the sky, Danny was one of the few people unable to rush out and gawk. His girlfriend of the last three years, Jennifer Bugles, the same one that fawned over his morbid poetry and tousled his scarecrow mane of hair to no end, had been in the process of breaking up with him. She didn't know why; it seemed like the right thing to do.

"Hey, Danny. You know that screen that appears at the end of Ms. Pac Man when you die?"

"Yeah."

"It's Game Over for us."

"Why?"

"If you have to ask, I can't tell you."

"What?"

"Are you trying to make this difficult?"

"Huh?"

"Oh gee, right, Danny. You know what? Screw you. I'm out of here."

Hurt, stunned, Danny didn't know what to say. But there was not much he could say when Jennifer came back into the diner minutes later with her new beau, Trevor Moses, a dude who had patches of facial hair, piercings, and tattoos. Danny could hardly stomach the image of Jennifer standing there slightly bent at the hips while this man thumbed the G-string poking out of her jeans shorts. He would never forget the smug grin on Trevor's face either. It was as if a gold tooth were glinting at him. "What are you looking at, geekazoid?" Danny withdrew to the kitchen and tried to let it all fade to black.

The diner was empty this early evening. Danny was feeling tired. It was hot in the kitchen and hot outside. Perspiration dripped from his face, horseshoed the pits under his T-shirt and at the small of his back. With Charlene Guttersnipe, his demanding boss, out on an errand, he decided to take a break. Normally he would go out the back door and sit on the stoop wishing that he were a smoker, but he wasn't. Instead he took his notepad and pencil outside. He often used this notepad to draw pictures and work on turns of phrases, however unlikely they might be.

He sat on the stoop trying to think, but nothing came to him. He had heard some of the talk about the body that landed on the spire, and now that hours had passed and everyone had forgotten about it—that was how this town was—this was his opportunity to go see it. He was curious. With his apron still on, he walked the several blocks to city hall. There, he squinted up at the spire. The glare of the sun sawed his eyes. He couldn't see. He needed to get closer.

Using the emergency stairs inside city hall, he walked to the roof. When he first came through the door, his hand went to his mouth and he muttered, "For shit sakes!" Once the initial shock passed, he took it in, drank it down like cold water. It was an amazing sight. On his notepad, he began to sketch the head, with words percolating in his own: *The creature*, not a person, *limbs shambling and pale*. The more he stared at it, the more entranced he grew. And for some ugly reason he kept seeing Jennifer's face appear in front of him. Could he not escape this girl? Even in the presence of this hideous sight, he still found himself thinking of her.

When he realized how late it was, the trance wore off. He had taken too long of a break and strayed far from the diner. He hurried, thoughts racing with his legs, and as he was departing, taking that first couple of steps, he swore he saw the body twitch. Unsure, he looked back, stared, and nothing. The wind picked up. He shook his head. It couldn't have been. Just a creepy thought.

On his hurried return, he wondered why the town seemed okay with this body up there. It didn't strike him as normal, as practical, as something everyone should be okay with. Even for them.

Charlene, a tomato-bottomed woman who often walked around with her hands on her hips, was waiting for him when he got back. Her lacquered nails tip-tapped on her hip as her tongue clucked at the top of her mouth. The frown she wore on her face was orgasm by expression but lacking all pleasure.

"Where have you been? I've got customers here trying to eat and no cook to make the food!"

"Sorry . . . I went for a walk."

"Would that be a walk of leisure or away from your job? Next time you decide to pitter-patter off, do so on your own time. This is a business I run, not a support center for retards that can cook."

She turned to the customers, the two people that were seated there, apologized to them for the lateness of the food, and declared that the food would be free, meaning that it would be paid for out of Danny's salary.

Danny went back into the kitchen and picked up the orders. Though he was supposed to be cooking, he couldn't get his mind off the body sitting atop city hall. Something was nagging at him, and it wasn't Charlene. . . .

When he returned home that evening, all he wanted to do was relax, sit on the couch, veg out, consider the frat-house-party-mess his life had become. Sitting there, eating sardines out of a can, staring at his barely reception-worthy TV, he could think of nothing more than how angry Jennifer had made him. He thought if he could get even with her, it would make him feel better, but really, he just wanted her back.

The local news was advertising top stories to come. The redheaded newscaster Terra Gerstner gave the highlights: "Bear Mauls Teens Having Sex" and "Toupee Injures Construction Worker in Rare Scalping" and "Man Cooking Weiner-Dogs at County Fair Burns His Britches" and "Airplanes Disappear in New Bermuda Triangle."

Danny's notepad lay on the coffee table. And while watching TV like this was supposed to be the life, he spent the time pissed off. Fortuitously, his brooding abruptly ended when the doorbell rang. He didn't get visitors, didn't have friends, and there wasn't a chance that Jennifer could have dropped by—or was there? He went to the door and looked out the peephole. No one was there. Was it someone playing a game? The doorbell rang again. He looked again. No one.

"Who is it?"

He heard something in response but wasn't sure what it was. Some kind of moan or grunt. Frustrated, annoyed, he grabbed the knob and flung the door open. To his shock and surprise, Jennifer stood before him.

"Jennifer?" he said, with a sneer of disgust but also maybe a hint of hurt. "Why are you here?"

She didn't say anything. He turned his back and went inside and left the door open. Hadn't everything been bad enough? Now he had to deal with this. Her here. Here to talk. Talk about what?

When he realized that she hadn't said anything, he turned back around. She still stood in the doorway.

"Well. Aren't you going to come in?"

For the first time, under the porch light, he noticed something was off.

"Are you okay—?"

"*The plague . . . has come.*" She said this almost as if she were a lizard, hissing it out.

"What the—?"

She was stooped and haggard looking in a way he had never seen her. Sure, sometimes he thought she wasn't as pretty without the makeup, but good God, was that her upper lip curled into a rictus snarl? And her hair was standing on end as if electrified. Her face bore a gray hue to it that seemed to be darkening the closer she got. He looked at her breasts. What the hell had happened to her breasts? They had shrunk and were poking through her T-shirt like tree branches and not mounds of flesh.

"*It has . . .*"

She didn't finish the thought, and Danny could see why when part of her brain slid out of her nose.

She came at him moaning. He tried to reason with her, but she rammed him against the arm of the couch. He noticed the eyes—yellow, evil looking, disturbed. And teeth—crooked, filed down to slivers. She scratched at his face. She tried to bite him. He grabbed a glass off the kitchen table and smashed it against her head. He winced, fearing that he had hurt her. She gave no reaction, came after him again. He grabbed a pen—the only thing near at hand—and made for the door, but she grabbed his foot, pulled him toward her. She lifted him into the air and held him up by his ankle. Where did she get the strength? He couldn't believe this was happening. When he glanced up her nose, he saw what looked to be vermicules crawling around inside and lost his shit. He brandished the pen, swung his body up, and drove the pen into the side of her eye with such force that it popped out through the socket of the other eye, sending the two eyeballs toppling to the floor.[1]

She dropped him on his head.

Then she staggered back, screeched like a Poe raven, and blood jetted, spraying indecipherable graffiti around his apartment. He started to see words in the splatterings . . . until he came to his senses and realized that he was lucky to escape with his life. Then reality hit him. He had killed his ex-girlfriend.

He threw up on the carpet.

Before the menace fell from the sky and landed in the center of town, far away in an undisclosed location worked a scientist named Dr. Parkingapp. He was part of an elite team of scientists perfecting the supersoldier serum for the United States government, codenamed Project Captain America. He believed, after years of research and thousands of hours of tests—measured out in the lives of a billion mice, along with perpetual graphing and calculating at the expense of tax-payer dollars—that he had finally discovered what would make it work. This so-called working serum he had poured into a single test tube, and now he looked upon it with glee. The government, however, didn't share in his glee and was talking about cutting his funding so that they could build a rumored weapon, the Earth

---

[1] The biblical implications were not lost on him. See the collected notebooks of Danny McDanielson for "Shades of Exodus 21:23–27," the incomplete poem.

bomb, which no one would talk about at length except to say that it was a destroyer of worlds and could one day be used against the threat of alien invasion, in case aliens were real.

Not wanting to lose his funding, Dr. Parkingapp was eager to test the formula. But since he had no more mice to destroy—he had tested the mice that had been injected with his formulas by seeing if they could withstand conditions of extreme heat, and if they could, that meant that the formula worked[2]—it was time for him to use it on himself.

With his stereo cranked to full, he stood with his legs spread and pointed to an imaginary crowd while holding a liquid-filled test tube in hand. Springsteen's "Born in the USA" rocked his loudspeakers. He sang along in a punched-testicle falsetto, using the test tube as a microphone. When he broke into a dance step, he accidentally tripped and spilled a drop of serum on the tip of his shoe. It was more acidic than he thought. It ate through his shoe and into his foot.

"Ah, shit. I fucked up. Oh, my god, I fucked up. Holy crap it burns!"

His screams of agony were drowned out by the music.

Danny grabbed his notepad and ran from the house, leaving the door wide open. He ran down the street in a state of panic. He had killed the only woman he had ever loved. It was awful, horrendous. He felt hideous.

After a while he stopped running to catch his breath and try to get hold of his emotions, which seemed to be overpowering him with grief. Despite the obvious signs that Jennifer had contracted some terrible sickness, he was convinced it was his fault. He looked around town and saw the street where they had walked hand in hand for the first time. There was part of a fuselage on the sidewalk. He didn't notice that. It was unfortunate that he focused only on his own grief, because if he had stopped to turn around before running off, he would have seen Jennifer sit back up on the floor of his home and grumble, "Rreor."

Exhausted, Danny found a light pole on a street corner to rest against. From this vantage point, he surveyed the downtown area. It

---

[2] He used microwave ovens to do this.

seemed normal, at first glance. Then he spotted the plane wing sitting in the road. There was an alarm going off at the local bank. Screams of terror. People running. The cops were on the scene, only they didn't seem to be doing anything. They were standing around. Danny didn't know what to do. Cops? What if they were looking for him? He was a murderer now. He was trying to save his life, but was it worth it? Maybe he should have let her kill him; maybe he deserved that, but . . . what was going on? This scene didn't seem right. He moved in closer, finding some of his energy coming back to him. He looked at the back of a plane engine lying in the street. There were feet sticking out from under it.

Oh, my god!

One of the officers was swaying back and forth as if he were a leaf being pushed by the wind. When Danny got two steps closer, all of that changed. The officer turned around. He looked as if he had been buried underground for the past nine weeks and had somehow come unearthed. He let out a sound somewhere between a murmur and a roar. Danny looked past the man-thing and saw that the screaming inside the bank was no longer going on and that there were more of these moaning and groaning man-things coming out of the bank. He backed up, shaking his head in disbelief.

A bony hand fell on his shoulder, and an inhuman voice hissed in his ear: "I likey . . . fresh . . . meeeeat."

Danny jumped, pulled at the arm, and felt it give. Next thing he knew he was running down the street with someone's arm in his hand, the body that it belonged to far behind him. He ducked around a corner and winged the arm on the ground in disgust. When he saw it move, he stomped on it and booted it away. He was breathing hard. It wasn't just Jennifer anymore. It was the entire town.

"Jesus Christ."

He looked toward city hall, where the impaled body hung, roasting in the sinking sun. He thought he saw it twitch.

Did he? Yup. He did.

"Jesus Christ!"

Dr. Parkingapp was no longer coherent. Placed in a straitjacket, he was bounding up and down and cackling like a madman, swinging his shoulders into the soldiers that had been brought in to restrain him. General Deaconheinz, a tall swarthy man with a handlebar mustache, stood there grinning wildly. His unit commander was at his side, fussing with his nose, attempting not to appear as if he was picking it, although that was exactly what he was doing.

"This is the greatest day in our nation's history."

"Sir, I don't understand, the supersoldier serum was a failure."

"No, it wasn't a failure. It just wasn't a supersoldier serum."

"Sir?"

"It's classified. But let me put it to you this way: He wasn't working on a supersoldier serum. That's a load of hokum from the comic books. You'd have to be pretty stupid to believe he was working on that. That's the brilliant thing about these genius scientist types. They're smart enough to make discoveries but dumb enough to misunderstand what they're discovering. Soldier, he was developing a very dangerous biological weapon."

"Shit from Shinola, sir. That's positively brilliant."

"I know. I'm the one that thought of it. Now let's get him aboard the plane and get the hell out of here."

It wasn't safe to stay, Danny knew that, but what he would do he did not know. It was just that he had to leave. First, he had to get back to the diner and warn everyone. While he didn't like the patrons of the diner, they were still people, and he was still freaking out about Jennifer. If Charlene was good for anything, it was setting him straight. He had to hurry, and then he'd flee for good. He went in through the back entrance. He wanted to get a few things from his locker. He undid the lock and took out some money and a knapsack that had water, spare clothes, and protein bars. He filled it frantically with more food from the kitchen and then slung it on his back. He walked out through the kitchen and into the diner's main room. What he beheld looked normal. The customers were seated in their booths, and Charlene was at the front of the diner looking out the window, perched on the ledge.

The television on the counter was on. The broadcast made Danny halt. Newscaster Terra Gerstner, in bobbing red curls, was giving a stunning report. She looked different from the last time he'd seen her on TV.

"Two planes heading due north appear to have disappeared over a small town. Now there is word that the planes might have been involved in a fatal midair collision that has caused the quarantine of the same town. What authorities aren't saying yet is what was on board one of those planes. One of the aircraft was believed to be military-related, and some are speculating that a biological weapon was aboard. It is believed they were transporting the carrier of this weapon before the accident. Rumors are running rampant, but the government denies knowledge that they have created a zombie plague to destroy civilizations they don't agree with. It's just preposterous. . . . Well, so's taking a shit in the refrigerator, I say!"[3]

Was she insane? Talking like that on the news . . . And then he saw that tinted look in her eyes . . . and he knew . . . he had seen enough. He started forward to warn the customers, but his tongue caught in his throat. One of the patrons seated at a booth grabbed his arm and snarled that same rictus snarl that Jennifer had. Danny couldn't get his arm free when he tried to tug it away. And when he looked up he saw Charlene moaning toward him, all deformed-looking. He wanted to vomit.

"Charlene, no, please don't. I . . ."

He kicked the patron in the head. Twice. The patron still wouldn't let go, so he pushed with his foot against the creature's shoulder and tore himself free, pitching to the floor from the exertion. Naturally the hand came with him, detaching itself from the zombie's body. The zombie moaned. Danny jumped to his feet, took the hand, and stuffed it into the zombie's mouth. The zombie made a sound of incomprehension. He began to gnaw away at his own hand, chomping on it like tasty spare ribs. A finger fell to the ground. He stopped. Danny looked down at the finger. The zombie looked at Danny and then raced to pick up the finger in case Danny got hungry and thought to take it from him.

Charlene came down on top of Danny. He braced her with his arm, holding her off. He screamed when he saw her canine teeth flash in front of him, trying to bite and chomp through his face. He couldn't believe this. This was his boss. Yes, she was a bitch, but now she was a zombie bitch!

---

[3] A subsequent string of f-bombs were edited from the broadcast during the three-second delay.

With a strength he didn't know he had in him, he flung her off of him, then got up and charged through the others as they tried to stop him.

He ran out of the diner.

Groups of three and four zombies were on every street corner, moaning and walking at a snail's pace. Some were people who used to come into the diner occasionally. Now they lurched in Danny's direction, sensing fresh meat. There were others huddled in a semicircle, trying to make headway somewhere and snarling angrily as they were chased back. Danny wondered what it could be. When he got there he saw a fierce Chihuahua, fending off a horde of zombies, biting and growling. They kept trying to get their hands on it, but it barked and tore at their appendages, rending them apart.

It ran through legs and arms, stopped in front of Danny. When Danny started to run, the dog ran with him, first at his side, then running ahead, showing him where to go. A kinship was instantly formed.

Butt Muncher.

Cool nickname, Danny decided, and gave it to him. He had seen the dog bite one of them in the ass. Seemed apropos.

"He broke free of his harness!"

"What?"

"He broke free of his harness!"

"What?"

"He broke free—"

"Why do you keep repeating that?"

"Well, you said, 'What?'"

"Soldier, I heard you the first time. I was just expressing shock that it had happened! It's like saying 'What the fuck?'"

"But—"

"What now?"

"When did you say 'What the fuck'?"

"Fucking get it together, soldier! Tell me what happened!"

He swallowed. "He gnawed off part of his arm."

"Good God."

There was a bloodcurdling scream. General Deaconheinz looked over the soldier's shoulder and saw one of his men writhing on the floor, while the pocked and bubbling body of Dr. Parkingapp huddled over him, mouth thrust against his neck, chewing away.

The plane lurched to one side, going off course.

Military units were making their way down the streets, a combination of gear-saddled soldiers on Segways with mounted machine guns and military jeeps carrying personnel. Behind that was a slow-moving tank. Danny and Butt Muncher headed in their direction. Machine-gun fire went off around them, and flecks of flesh and blood soared through the air. Danny covered his ears, and the dog barked. The soldiers obliterated the zombies that were in front of them, leaving behind bricks of shredded flesh. It was impressive stuff, all that firepower, and after the initial shock of it wore off, it got Danny to thinking about Jennifer. The explosions reminded him of the Fourth of July, so many years ago, when they had shared their first kiss—with tongue. "Oh, God," he said. "She's everywhere."

The military didn't give him time to react. Danny and Butt Muncher were hustled off the streets and pushed into a makeshift medical tent. Danny was stripped naked and prodded with sharp poles by scientists in hazmat suits to make sure he did not have the infection. Every time he was poked, he thought of how Jennifer used to tickle him when they watched TV on the couch. So he broke out in hysterical laughter, which consternated the scientists. They set him straight by burning him in a sterilizing shower, prodding him in the rectum with a stick, and then smacking him in the face with a hot water sack. Butt Muncher was shaved bare and given the same treatment. When they were done, they allowed Danny to get dressed and reunited him with his new friend. They didn't tell him what was going on.

The soldiers were constantly running about, going this way and that. It was hard to get anyone to talk. Danny tried, but everyone ignored him. He finally grabbed one soldier by the arm and asked him what was happening.

The soldier shook his head. "You don't know?" He shouted instead of spoke, like he was always giving out orders or hard of hearing. "Moses! They tell nobody nothing around here! Always up to me. Well, gaddammit, we don't have anyone else to do it! Look, there aren't many of you that are okay. We passed up going back to Iraq to rectify this mess—that should tell you how bad it is. It's a plague that will turn you into the living dead. It will! The only way to stop 'em is to kill 'em, but they're already dead, so you got to kill 'em like you're sending 'em to Hell. There's no saving anyone. We've been instructed to use an abundance of brutal force. This is war!" He grabbed Danny's notebook from him and swatted it down on the table. "Now what the hell is this?"

Danny looked at his book, considering.

"Please don't do that," he said.

"Don't get upset. What's so special about it?"

"It's my poetry. I write poetry."

The soldier laughed. "Ah, the sensitive type. Is it epic poetry?"

Danny shook his head.

"How the fuck is poetry going to help us fight a war unless it's epic?"

"I don't know. It's a . . . lost art. And therapy."

"Therapy? For what?"

"My girlfriend, she broke up with me."

"You know what, I'd break up with you too if you showed me pussy shit like this." He tagged Danny's chest with the notebook, giving it back. "Bro, take your panties off. It doesn't matter what you do if you're not capable of changing the tide of battle."

He headed out of the tent, checking the clip on his gun. Immediately Danny was startled by a burst of machine-gun fire. He looked to the dog, and the dog whined.

> *"In death one must grin like a fish.*
> *That way you will look at home."*[4]

He ran through the street with Butt Muncher picking up the rear. The fighting had gone berserk. It was a war zone. Their camp had blown up, sending soldiers and Segways flying through the air like Popsicle

---

[4] From the collected notebooks of Danny McDanielson, poem entitled "War Smells of Fresh Meat."

sticks, and if Danny and the dog hadn't left when they did, they'd have been charred and then probably eaten. Zombies filled the streets, virtually every corner, sidewalk, and alleyway, moaning and groaning and in many cases on the ground on all fours, chewing tastily on unmoving soldiers and civilians. Machine guns blitzed and blazed; orders were shouted over the din, loud enough that they sounded as if they were coming over evacuation speakers. When Danny and the dog made it to the end of town, they were confronted with a roadblock. The soldiers didn't look like they were letting anyone through. One of them drew a rifle. He was also wearing a clown mask.

"Whoa!" said Danny. "Hold on! I just want to get out."

"Hoo-hah! Our orders are that no one, that includes you and me, is allowed to leave or enter this town."

"But—what am I supposed to do?"

"If it were my problem, I'd care. Now go on, get out of here."

"This is ridiculous. I'm okay. You can't shoot me."

"Hoo-hah! If you cross that there line I will, and unfortunately everyone in my battalion will too. There'll be nothing left of you or your dog. The government doesn't want to risk anything. This is a big country—ginormous, last time I checked the map—and we have to protect it. That's our duty. Yours as well as mine."

"Jesus. I'm just a poet."

"As I said, my orders are to shoot anyone that tries to get past. Alive or dead. Poet or not." He stopped and then asked, "You a good poet?"

"I guess. Why, you want to make an exception? National Endowment for the Arts and all that."

"Hoo-hah! No, just wanted to know if you were a fag." He laughed hysterically. "We don't like fags in the military. Incidentally the clown mask is to scare people off." He removed it. "I guess it's not working."

"Truthfully, you look ridiculous."

"That's what everyone's been telling me. I just don't believe them. But coming from a poet, now that's pretty hurtful." He flipped it back down like a ballplayer's shades. "Suck it, asshole!"

He fired into the air, and Danny fled.

* * *

Danny walked for blocks, the dog scurrying at his heels. In the streets, chaos reigned. Bullets flew. Corpses walked and then didn't. Guts spewed. Sewer drains were besieged with butchered limbs and tattered clothing. Danny's woe-is-me state held him oblivious to the danger around him. He sure missed holding Jennifer in his arms, feeling the small of her back, the sigh of her chest, the tickle of her hair against his cheek. It was unfortunate that this plague had come to town. The timing of it made the heartache of losing her that much worse. They were all suffering. At least he and this dog were okay . . . for now.

The plane was off course.

The general and the soldier didn't know it, but with the pandemonium breaking out, the pilots were nervous.

"Stand down, soldier. Put the gun down."

General Deaconheinz didn't like the idea that one of his men was attempting to fire a gun on a military aircraft. On one hand, it was damn stupid of him, on the other, it wasn't a bad idea to execute this creature.

The soldier nervously kept the gun aimed. "I have a shot," he whined.

"If you miss, we're dead."

"Tell me how it works."

"The plague, it's pretty bad. You ever been in love, soldier? It's a lot like being in love. It starts slowly, moves through the body quickly, and soon you are overcome. It becomes a part of you, transforms your body, your emotions—everything. Then it falls apart. It's not what you first thought it was. It changes you emotionally, physically, then it's never the same again. And like a lover leaving you, it moves on to someone else. Of course, the first one infected controls the rest of them."

"Depressing, sir."

"Of course it is, soldier. It's like the Ebola virus . . . after it's been kicked in the nuts."

"Sir . . ."

"What?"

"You're greatly upsetting me."

"You wanted the truth!"

"I changed my mind!"

"Oh, my God, you're going to do it, aren't you?"

He fired the gun.

The sight was more than he could handle. Jennifer was walking dead, ambling through the streets. He couldn't believe it. And yet he was relieved, because he hadn't killed her—she was already dead! The joy of that statement lasted only a short while, once he realized she was rallying the other zombies to eat his brains. He ran, and so did the dog, but they found another herd of zombies waiting. He was thinking the worst was to come . . . when two soldiers came to his rescue. He would learn their names afterward. With M-16s they pushed the zombies back, the sheer force and number of bullets astonishing even to themselves. They ran out of ammo when it came to Jennifer. Danny couldn't bring himself to allow her to be harmed. He got down on his knees and threw his hands in the air: "Hallelujah!" The soldiers stared. One of them took out a machete. "No," shouted Danny, "for the sweet love of all that is—leave her be!" He put the machete away. Danny watched as Jennifer, the eyeless zombie, staggered around. He felt so relieved, it brought tears to his own eyes.

The first body, the one that everyone knew about, was the one that fell from the sky. Corporal Brian Massa and Sergeant Marc D. Resnick were looking for it. Danny knew where it was. They set off toward city hall together. Corporal Massa and Sergeant Resnick blasted away zombies that got in the way, and Danny and the dog followed. Between bursts of machine-gun fire, Danny scribbled down words in his notebook, feeling inspired. *Darkness, fetid, yellow eyes . . .* He would make these words into a poem one day. He guided the two soldiers through town. When they got to city hall, Sergeant Resnick and Corporal Massa went berserk, using up entire clips of ammo. Danny cringed at the violence. There were piles of bodies in the street, the soup of blood and guts everywhere.

They banged through the front doors and started up the steps. They hurried, huffing. As they came out of the stairwell and onto the roof, a zombie smacked Danny in the face and he went down. The zombie was on top of him. He was Trevor Moses, or what used to be Trevor Moses before he became a walking corpse that smelled like pissed pants. The dog sprang on Dead-Trevor and bit his heel. Amidst this distraction, Danny landed a hard elbow across Dead-Trevor's face, and his jaw sank, leveling forward like a shovel. Dead-Trevor moaned. It seemed as if things were frozen in time. The zombie moved his mouth around, trying to bite, but it only slackened further. Danny grabbed hold of Dead-Trevor's lower jaw, pulled it off with a manly shriek, and then catapulted it across the roof. *For taking my girlfriend!* The zombie looked at him, confused, and then attacked. The dog landed mouth-first on the zombie's ass, living up to his name. Dead-Trevor reeled. Danny struggled to push him away, and in the process of doing so got hold of a BIC lighter that was in Dead-Trevor's pocket and ignited it. Dead-Trevor's crotch caught fire, and he fell to the ground twitching and moaning and squealing. "Jesus-shit-on-me, I'm sorry," said Danny, and he sprang to his feet and tried to put the fire out by repeatedly stomping on Dead-Trevor's zombie balls. Once the fire was out, Dead-Trevor was curled up with his hands between his legs.[5] The soldiers came through the door and quickly blew the zombie's head off. Face-painted with brain matter, Danny stood up like an American Indian at war. For the first time they looked across at the spire and registered shock. The zombie was still impaled, but he was moving sybaritically, not twitching as before, but dancing, waving his arms back and forth and bopping his feet up and down. He seemed to be rocking out, as if he had headphones on and was listening to music, "Born in the USA" playing in his head.

Corporal Massa was about to fire when Danny pushed the barrel of the gun down. The sergeant and the corporal looked at him as if he had gone out of his mind. Insanity seemed a logical response to what they were dealing with. Danny walked closer to the zombie, watching it gather speed through its motions. He drew closer. And closer. Fascinated. The zombie turned his head and his arms and legs stopped moving. He stared at Danny. Then he tried to look down, and Danny did the same. The zombie began to move animatedly once more, fresh guts vomiting from the hole in his body. When Danny looked

---

[5] Believed to be the inspiration for Danny McDanielson's poem, "Even Zombies Get the Blues!" from the collected notebooks.

into the street below, he saw the zombies had stopped and started moving again. It clicked for him, like rocket science.

"It's controlling them. He's the one."

"We know," said the corporal, raising his gun. "That's why we're here to kill it. He's a hive-ass motherfucker. Mission: Kill him so bad he remembers his death for the rest of his life. With honey and fucking flies on top. Cover your ears."

Cover your ears! Familiar words. Jennifer used to say just that before orgasm, warning him how loud she was going to scream. She knew it embarrassed him. What if this zombie were Jennifer, or someone else? It would have family, loved ones. . . .

"You can't."

"What? What am I supposed to do?"

"I don't know. I mean, he was probably like you or me at one time, and then . . . this happened. . . . He crashes to Earth, and finds himself stuck on this . . . this spire . . . and he can't get free. . . . So he calls in his minions to come together and free him from his suffering, but they're so stupid they can't figure out where he is. Plus, he may not be such a bad guy."

"You make him sound almost human," said the sergeant.

"He is kind of human."

"So. What's his name?"

"Does he have to have a name?"

"He's got to have a name."

"Maybe it's Dave."

"Dave? Fuck Dave."

"Roger?"

"Fuck him too."

"G?"

"Whaaat?"

"Just the letter, like a rapper."

"Stupid!"

Danny sighed. "No Dave, no Rogers, no G. Fine, you suggest."

"How about Syphilis? He looks like a disease, and he looks like a cock. It's perfect!"

The soldiers high-fived, laughed.

"Well. I still don't think you should kill it."

"What should we do with it, poet-boy? Hold its hand and say a prayer? They're killing the whole town. Everyone."

He socked the zombie in the face with the butt of his gun. The dead man stopped moving, blood gushing. Then he started moving again. His nose fell off. The dog set to it and swallowed. Better than the eye he ate earlier, but not as salty. He needed salt. And water. He was dehydrated.

"He just wants to get down. Can you blame him?"

"*Yeah?* I think you are being a sympathizer. That's a fucking zombie. You can't sympathize with something that doesn't have any brains. Everyone in this country wants to sympathize with something. They protest the environment, animal rights . . . but I'm in the army because I don't want to protest. I want to kill people, as many as I can. I consider it a privilege. Stand aside and let me do my job."

"Hold on. If you were impaled and were dead and still alive, you'd probably be angry about it. It's a Promethean dilemma. That's sad, don't you think?"

Corporal Massa thought on it, nodded.

"Guess . . . you have a point. I was a poor student in school and probably shouldn't be doing the thinking around here. Just from a human standpoint, I certainly wouldn't want no thing poking through my abdomen like that."

"Dude, it's like he got stabbed with a giant phallus. Not a fun way to go." This was Sergeant Resnick.

"What do we do when he gets off the spire?" asked Corporal Massa.

"Don't know," said Danny. "Let's work on getting it off first. Worry about the rest later."

"Sounds like a plan, Douche-Nuts."

Down in the stairwell, next to the fire extinguisher, there was an ax. The sergeant pulled it out of the glass and came back upstairs. He raised it above his head. Then he began chopping the bottom of the spire, below where the zombie was impaled. He chopped and chopped and chopped. He had to stop to wipe his brow, at which point Danny blurted out, "Sympathy!"

"What?" the two soldiers said together. And then, "What's he babbling about?"

"Beats me, dude."

"You said I was being sympathetic," said Danny, "so let's call him Sympathy."

The two soldiers looked at one another. Corporal Massa shrugged, took the ax from Sergeant Resnick, and then hefted it above his head. He muttered under his breath as he chopped. Finally the spire split, and with a size-fourteen boot to the pole, it tilted. The zombie flailed as the spire toppled. After a bit, he began to do his little dead dance, shimmying along the spire to release himself. When he wobbled to his feet, green gunk spewed from the hole in his midsection and his mouthless visage rocked up and down. Danny looked down to the street below. Zombie activity was slowing.

"You see, all he wanted was for someone to set him free."

The zombie danced.

"Now what's he doing, Douche-Nuts? Moonwalking?"

The zombie walked to the edge of the building, moving like he had ungainly hooves instead of feet. He fell off the roof. *Whiff.* The three of them stood over the edge looking down. The zombie was splayed in the street, arms and legs unmoving, brains seeping into a gutter. Danny wondered if zombies ever ran out of leaking brains. Seemed a reasonable curiosity.

After a while, an arm began to twitch and then a leg. The zombie began to move again. Shakily getting to his feet. Stumble-walking away.

The transformation was nearly complete. As his body fell through the sky, plummeting like a fallen angel, fragments of past memories drifted through his head at a rate commensurate with that of the diseased flesh peeling off his body during its rapid descent.[6] This memory had to do with General Deaconheinz—that man he had bit the ear and neck flesh off of and gargled down like mouthwash before something had propelled him out of the plane—coming to visit him in his laboratory. They were shoring up details about the project he was going to be working on for the government.

"If you do this, you'll be handsomely rewarded. The government will see to that. We will provide you with whatever you need."

---

[6] He de-beaked a passing bird while aerosolizing the sickness.

"Whatever?"

"Whatever you need. It is yours."

Dr. Parkingapp looked at his pinup calendar on the wall. Miss July was a sultry vixen from somewhere in small-town America.

"Well, sometimes, as a scientist, I get kind of lonely. Do you think you can get me Miss July?"

The general walked over to the calendar and flipped up a few pages and then let them fall. He looked at Dr. Parkingapp, sizing him up.

"I'm not dragging the United States military through the muck for something as silly as a pinup girl. You want to get one, use the money we pay you to make it happen. You can have all the whores you want. But somewhere along the way, we have to draw the line, and I'm drawing the line there. You geeky scientist types just don't know anything about women. And by the way, I've read your file, Dr. Parkingapp. I know about the underage girls you smuggled in from Taiwan."

"Okay, okay. I was just asking."

"Do you want the job or not?"

"Oh, I want it; I definitely want it."

He looked over at the calendar, down at the bottom where it had the facsimile signature: *XXO, Jennifer Bugles.*

Danny, the two soldiers, and the dog raced downstairs.

"Tell them not to shoot," said Danny to the soldiers.

They radioed ahead on their walkie-talkies. When the soldiers stopped firing, they noticed that the zombies were all collapsing to the ground. They looked around, confused. It was puzzling.

Sympathy stumbled his way through town, the same town, which he would soon leave, taking the population along with him, dragging his dead foot and heaving his aging-beyond-reason body forward. Others followed, but what bothered Danny most, though surely this didn't bother anyone else, was that he spotted Jennifer in the street going that way too. Zombie or not, she still upset him. He ran to intercept her. He knew that she couldn't think, that she wasn't herself. What if he offered himself to her? Just a nibble, that's all it'd take, and he could be a zombie along with her. But he pulled up, watching her shamble past.

With a heavy heart, he let her go, like dropping a caught fish back into the water. What choice did he have?

The zombie fell from the sky,
Bits and pieces,
Disintegrating upon descent.
Limbs shambling and pale,
Who knew what trouble he would cause?
Only some—a dog and a Danny.
And like Jesus upon the cross,
He found his disciples.

A town rent asunder,
A young man's heart crushed,
Like dying yellow embers,
A plague had come. . . .

Fetid and meat-hardy,
Promethean in disaster,
An unfeeling man's fate,
Government put-on,
And a poet with trace amounts of . . .
Sympathy . . .

For a zombie that fell from the sky.

MY DOLLY

BY DEREK NIKITAS

It was high time for me to fetch frozen Dolly from the butcher shop, but even in an ambulance the drive was rough, it being the Apocalypse out. This girl was too young to be called Dolly, just a teenager, but I named her Dolly because I liked the Golden Oldies, grassroots sheen of it. See, Dolly was dead, and along with the rest of her scrubbed memory, she lost whatever dull moniker her parents had imposed on her. It would be a new dawn for Dolly when I came to her rescue.

En route I kept the siren wailing. The sound bounced off the coastal pines, stripped bare of branches up to the top ten feet. The only cars left on this woodsy backroad were the few stalled in pine-straw beds, so it wasn't traffic but crickets and cicadas that impeded my progress.

Great hordes of them crackled in the air like static, kamikaze-bombing the windshield until it was framed with thick bug juice in the corners where the wipers couldn't reach. A million wings and limbs twitched in my sight line, and when the road curved, my back tires jackknifed across fresh slicks of crushed bugs on the pavement. There was no speed limit, since all the road signs were mucked with pestilence. I couldn't drive through these conditions without a permanent grimace, and my leather-gloved hands cramped from their grip on the steering wheel.

Milo's Specialty Meats was a clapboard roadside dive with gravel and dead bugs for a parking lot. This far out, the bug hordes receded a bit. I could even read the street signs, like the hurricane-evac-route marker, blue circle with white swirl icon, the eye of the storm. My coordinates were two miles inland, or thereabouts, as the Atlantic was lately taking bigger breaths, sucking back beaches and piers, blowing down boardwalks.

I parked and flicked off the siren and threw on my beekeeper's hat, tucking the netting into the collar of my shirt. I'd dressed for the occasion in a dark blue blazer, light blue shirt, and a nice silk necktie. I'd shaved for the first time in weeks.

The sign in Milo's entranceway read CLOSED, but I knew I was welcome anytime. Driver's door open, a few stray cicadas attached themselves to my lapel and stared at me with their fire eyes. The woods sang the chorus of a thousand one-note lovesongs, so I whistled along as I pulled open the ambulance hatch doors.

A cold white mist billowed inside. The open boxes stacked along the floor beside the stretcher were filled with hundreds of dry-ice blocks. I inhaled the chilled, thin air. I grabbed the stretcher, slid it out while the rails unfolded and the wheels touched ground. A half dozen cicadas and crickets instantly polluted the sheet's pristine whiteness with their dull armored bodies. That incessant insect buzz burrowed inside me, deep in my chest, and turned almost pleasant, the hum of anticipation.

I pulled the stretcher across the lot, and it jostled over the rugged rock. The store's glass entrance did not give way when I shoved my shoulder against it, so I bellowed, "Milo!" He had to be inside the shop because his pickup was parked in the side yard. I rapped both fists against the glass and called him out again.

A cartoon pig was sketched in wax pencil on the display window. "I'll huff and I'll puff," I muttered, looking for a softball-size rock to throw. I worried that Milo and his bearded Czech heifer of a wife had abandoned their only livelihood on account of a few rainstorms and some insects, but they had electricity and generators, enough dried meat and imported beers to last months. They had nowhere better to go.

Over by the gutter spout I found a nice granite chunk and reared back, hoisting it over my shoulder like a quarterback plotting a twenty-yard pass. My best hurl didn't penetrate the glass, but it burst a spiderweb of cracks across the topmost pane in the entrance door.

A small helicopter of a bug buzzed past my ear. I heard a lock slide open, and there was Milo's furious wife filling up the doorway, filling out an unflattering, sheer pink nightgown. She held one arm across her breasts to spare us both the shame.

"You break window, crazy fuckmother! Go away from here," she told me.

"I'm here to get Dolly," I said.

She eyeballed the stretcher, the ambulance. "Closed!" she grunted.

"Hold on—is Milo—"

"Closed!"

"My name is Renfroe. Milo told me to—"

"Closed for permanent! No meat!" She slammed the door shut to prove her point, and the top glass panel rained down in shards onto the cement slab below. After a moment, her face loomed in the horse door she'd created. Her hair was short on the sides, but six inches of tight black coils were piled on top, redolent of some particularly nasty wild mushroom. "Shit now!" she barked.

I reached into my pocket and pulled out a money clip, wagged it at her. I tore off my beekeeper getup, showed her my sincerest expression, and said, "There's a deceased girl in your meat locker, and I'm here to take her away from you. Milo and I arranged it, and I've got five hundred dollars right here for payment."

"Milos, he is dead from heart attack. One week past."

"By God, I'm sorry," I said. Then, after a solemn few seconds I added, "Can I talk to him anyway?"

"He has no remember."

The bugs were all over my face, in my hair. I squinted to keep them from landing in my eyes, but I held my ground and made a wide fan of that money so "Grunta" could get a good whiff of it. I forgot her name, but Grunta got the gist.

"You come help me fix hole," Grunta demanded.

"Can you tell me, is the girl still here?"

"Fix hole now, headshit!"

I tossed my beekeeper bonnet onto the cot and scrambled inside, lugging the stretcher behind me. Close up, Grunta smelled like pepperoni. She pointed to a stack of plywood boards atop the empty glass case that once enshrined the choicest meats.

"I get hammer," Grunta said. She waddled into the back room while I hoisted up a plywood slab large enough to cover the missing pane. I pressed it against the opening and waited. A calico cat appeared from some hiding spot and leaped up onto the glass case. It was stalking a beetle, bobbing its head to the rhythm of the beetle's stumbling buzz. I made kissing sounds at it, but the cat ignored me, as cats are wont to do.

Grunta hurried back into the storefront with the hammer raised in striking position, a dozen nails jutting head-outward from her pursed lips. She fastened the board I held to the doorframe with nails she plucked from her mouth. The loose flesh on her arm seemed to pucker up nicely as she worked. She had to be two feet shorter than me, twice as big around.

"No bugs!" she coughed, expelling the last couple nails. She hammered a cricket that had landed on the wall beside a tacked-up poster of Prague's Charles Bridge and its promenade of life-size saint statues. "You here for dead girl in freezer?" Her nostrils flared when she spoke.

"Yes, Milo and I agreed to a five-hundred-dollar fee for—"

"Milos is dead! He remembers nothing. I say seven-fifty."

"I'm not in any position to argue," I said.

"Come here," she demanded. The cat stepped gingerly from the meat case onto her shoulder and crouched there, tail switching. The room we entered was made for slicing things apart. Huge knives and saws lined the walls, an empty cutting-board table below them, stained with dark splotches. Drains in the floor would wash it all away.

A raw smell I thought was Grunta became stronger back here, sweetly rank. On the far end of the butcher shop stood the meat-locker door with a handle like a horizontal tavern tap. I almost reached for that handle, eager to break the vacuum seal, but instead Grunta led me into a meager office with an antique turn-dial television set, a few open TV trays with stacks of papers on them, and a human corpse seated upright in a rocking chair, slowly rocking. Milo was the source of the smell, and it was sharp enough to make my poor pointless epiglottis spasm.

The look of him made my heart pound hard enough to prove it was still in use. His ugliness was bearable, but what he evoked was not: negative spaces, black holes in human shape, maddening blurs to which your eyes refused focus, statues in flesh molded by some demon hand, oracles that announced with every twitch of their bones a vastness and darkness that no living brain could fathom. They could not be true but were. They attracted too many flies.

Grunta grabbed a plastic flyswatter from atop a paper pile and lashed at Milo's head with it. The cat on her shoulder rode out this violence like a rodeo cowboy.

I could hear the flies buzz, like in the poem by Dickinson, that creepy little Amherst goth who wrote a hundred hymnals to the Dead. The TV was muttering afternoon news: A California commune of three hundred souls had finally, after much preamble from their high priest, tossed themselves like lemmings into the deep molten canyon that, a few weeks earlier, an earthquake had ripped through downtown San Francisco. They'd leaped one by one screaming, each of them, "Mother Nature forgive us!" There had been no miracles to witness, no onset of the King.

Milo turned away from this broadcast and studied us both with the cool detachment that he must've reserved, in life, for fresh slabs of meat. His eyes were sunken and rheumy, and the skin on his face had tinted greenish, sagging so that his mouth arched downward like a Greek-tragedy mask. His hair, once a lush bloom of salt-and-pepper curls, was gone, and the flesh on his head seemed to have petrified into another layer of bone.

"Milos, this man come to see you," Grunta explained.

"Renfroe," I said. "We've talked a few times before," I said.

Milo winced and his mouth eased open, but he said nothing. Instead, he raised a liter bottle of vodka from between his legs and poured the last swill of it in the general direction of his mouth. Most of it trickled down his chin and seeped into the bib of moisture spreading downward from his undershirt collar. Beside the legs of his chair were other, empty liters of vodka, gin, Kentucky bourbon.

"Drunkard," Grunta complained, as her chin quivered.

"It kills some of their pain, the alcohol," I told her. "They crave it, I've noticed."

"Same as before dead for him, then."

"Does he speak to you?"

"At first," she said. "No more. He is quiet now."

In life, Milo would erupt with theatrical talk. He'd sweat and his face would grow ruddy. He despised his wife, harassed the young women who dared step into the store, wiggling sausages at them suggestively. There was always booze on his breath and a pistol under his cash register.

Made you wonder, but we'd all been musing lately on the Soul. You couldn't avoid wondering, in the presence of these walking, talking human shells. It was the reason I came back to Milo's Specialty Meats—for Dolly. Things were different. The universe had color and verve.

"Let me just pay you now—" I started, producing the chunk of money again.

Grunta snatched it out of my hands, the whole thousand bucks. She ran it under her nose to sniff it. It was real money and rather easily procured, though neither of us knew what it was worth anymore. Cash had become hardly more than memento. It was supposed to represent gold in a vault somewhere, sure, but gold was just a kind of rock.

"Uh, that's actually a thousand," I told her. "But I'll make you a deal."

Gunta pursed her lips. "What deal?"

"I'll give you the whole grand for Dolly and all the booze you have left."

"What is Dolly?"

"The dead girl."

Grunta shoved the money in her pocket. She scratched the cat under its chin, and the cat eased its eyes shut. I followed Grunta back into the butchery and watched her snap open the handle on the meat-locker door. The automatic light came on inside, a harsh medical white. Bags of anonymous meat cuts were stacked on plastic shelves; a half dozen long beef sides hung on a track like suits in a bedroom closet.

At the far end of the room was a packing crate made of cheap wood and nails, like a pauper's coffin. The girl inside it, I knew, was maybe nineteen or twenty, not more than a hundred pounds, barely five feet tall. She had less literal substance than the larger cuts of hooked meat around us, but this other flesh could not be revived like hers could.

The cat leaped down from her mistress's shoulder and skittered out through the open freezer door. I asked Grunta for the biggest flathead screwdriver she could find.

When she brought it back she said, "What are you doing with this girl?"

"Awakening," I explained. I slipped past her into the freezer, too eager now to batten down for questioning. When I leaned down beside the crate, both knees on the cold floor, Grunta jabbed her index finger into my shoulder to get my attention. Her breath misted as she said, "Tell me why you need this girl."

"I want to know what it's like . . . to be dead. I want to ask her."

Grunta snorted. "Ask Milos. It is nothing. No remembering."

I shimmied the screwdriver head into the crease between the crate and its nailed-down lid, slapped the handle with the palm of my hand to wedge it in deeper. "I want to take her on a trip," I said. I shoved down on the handle, and the crate nails screeched as they lifted out of place.

"She might not wish to be with you."

"She can do whatever she wants," I said, "but I can keep her safe."

"What is *safe* meaning for a dead person, eh?" Grunta asked.

I didn't answer. I was breathing aerobically now. When the lid was loose enough, I slid my fingers between the nails. The cheap balsa wood crackled and buckled. Dolly was there, zipped inside a clear plastic bag that hazed my view of her. She was laying in a bed of ice packs, piled around her and sprinkled atop her limbs and her abdomen. I brushed aside those that covered her face and tugged with both hands at the zipper until it gave way.

There was Dolly's face—white lips, cyanotic skin, paper-thin eyelids curved shut over the rounded half-moons of her eyes. A sleeping beauty, though frost had matted her dark hair in unseemly, petrified clumps. That luster would return, I knew.

"Jesu," Grunta sighed. "You are not going to bugger this carcass?"

I stood up again, and I outsized her, screwdriver tight in my fist. I let Grunta listen to the way my teeth chattered together. I could see her eyes darting. She was wondering how she'd gotten herself alone in a freezer with a strange man and a corpse in a crate.

Behind her, dead Milo shuffled into the freezer doorway, mouth agape. He raised a limp hand to waist level and waved lazily at us. I offered the screwdriver back to Grunta, handle first.

"There are some sick people in the world," I told her. "Especially now. See, before these troubles I was an emergency medical technician for the Port City area. When things began to go haywire, well, you can imagine the despair. People were afraid to die. People have always been afraid to die. But some people, they get so full of fear, so full of despair, they give up. Look at this."

I unzipped the plastic bag all the way down to Dolly's navel. She was naked as a newborn, modest breasts flattened almost boyish in her supine repose, but I paid only clinical attention. What I meant to show Grunta was to be found on both of Dolly's forearms, but I lifted only the left, raised it carefully and overturned it to expose the inside length of her arm. A single purplish groove ran from her wrist to the crook of her arm, a foot-long deliberate gash. It was puckered, though the wound itself was bloodless now. Dolly's fingers twitched as I held her hand. She was so utterly cold, my hands stung from the touch of her flesh.

I said, "Think of how lost she must have felt, to do this to herself. I don't understand that kind of despair, but the minute I found her, I knew she'd be back. Heck, she herself must've known she'd be back. I had to help her."

"You are the person who brings her here to my shop?"

I nodded. Milo stood now beside his wife, dumbstruck, but less than two weeks before he had agreed, for the price of a thousand dollars on deposit and five hundred on retrieval, to let me store the body of a suicide girl in his freezer. He was the only man I knew with cold storage large enough to keep her, the loose scruples to do it for cash, and the gusto to hold fort while everyone else in the county split the coast in fear of four horsemen.

I said, "She was one of the last emergency calls we got before they shut down local services. A security guard at the state university called it in. The school had been closed down for days, but somehow this girl sneaked herself into the library. They have private study carrels in the stacks, and he found her there with her sleeves rolled up and a razor blade. It was a mess when we arrived, though she'd only been dead for a few minutes. We were meant to bring her to the county morgue, but by then they'd already issued the incineration policy, and I couldn't do it, I couldn't let her be destroyed."

Grunta was scratching herself in the neck with the screwdriver, unamused.

I said, "Anyway, I think she wanted to come back. She took her own life in a place she thought was private, where she wouldn't be found before three hours lapsed."

Grunta gestured at Milo with her thumb. "He took only one hour for return."

"I've heard anywhere from one hour to a full day. Three hours is average."

"And this—this freezing is to keep her from walking dead?"

"It was an experiment," I said. "And I think it worked, mostly."

Grunta sneered at me. "Milos lets you keep her here? He agrees to this?"

I didn't know how to answer, but my silence told all. Grunta turned on her husband and shoved him one-handed. He croaked some awful sound and reeled backward against a suspended beef carcass. The meat swayed, and the hook to which it was impaled creaked from the strain, but it didn't drop.

"You are lucky you are dead already," she barked at him. "Villain!"

The freezer chill was making my nose run, so I headed back to the stretcher waiting in the entranceway. I enlisted Milo to help me lift Dolly out of the crate. He took her by the legs, and I got a grip on the plastic underneath her shoulders, hoping it wouldn't rip midtransit. We slid her onto the cot, bag and all, and I stuffed a dozen ice packs inside the bag alongside her legs and across her stomach. I didn't leer at where the gentle slope of her pubic bone was grazed by a soft chevron of manicured hair.

Grunta led me to a loading bay and heaved up the paneled door with one arm, swinging the other as a hint for me to get out quickly. "Hurry," she said. "The bugs." I rolled the stretcher back to the ambulance with relative ease, locked it into place. The bugs were in my hair, crawling along the length of my jugular. I'd lost my beekeeper's hat somewhere.

I worked quickly to load the alcohol I had also purchased—cases of imported Czech beer, five boxes of Russian vodka with the labels printed in Cyrillic. My coup was two entire cases stuffed with glass flasks of dark-green absinthe, wormwood infused, smuggled incognito in Heineken boxes. Myself, I didn't drink much more than a glass of wine on special occasions, but I knew that Dolly would need all this painkiller to get by when she awoke.

Back on the road, an FM station aired the soundtrack of our foreshortened lives—the Doors, REM, Blue Oyster Cult. Christian radio had gone shrill, of course, overtaken most of the airwaves not reserved for hard news—and it was always hard. For once I was thrilled to still be alive and scheming. I was like an expectant father on his way to the hospital. I blared the siren and the lights for nobody else as I floored it back into the pestilence cloud. The bugs came at me in a green hail and popped and crackled on the windshield like a celebration.

Toward the coast, the end of the line was abrupt. Orange barrels and wood crossbeams blocked the road, topped with blinking yellow lights. The inbound lane had been breached, barrels tossed into the marshy ditches now drowned out by seawater, caught and bobbing with other garbage in the rushes. The road, broken and sand-strewn, pressed onward into the waves. A sturdy wooden welcome plaque remained, though it read only WELCOME TO. The rest was submerged in the sea, out of which peeked the upper floors of restaurants and vacation homes, windows half-submerged like the looming eyes of crocodiles. The boat storage lofts still held an armada of compartmentalized pleasure crafts, though the units on the lowest visible floor were vacant, their boats most likely floating empty and silent miles beyond these washed-out barrier islands.

The flash storms came daily and savagely, pushing in like hurricane feeder bands from the east in twisted airstreams. Even now the sky brewed purple on the horizon, and I had to hurry.

I cut the siren and the engine, popped open the door. I pulled out the stretcher and the rails unfolded, wheels touching pavement. Dolly slept the same as I'd left her—but I unzipped the bag and took her hand and laid it out across my own open palm and saw that her eyelids spasmed while I watched.

I pushed the stretcher on past the broken barrier, decked out in my jacket and tie and slacks—not the suit of a pallbearer, but rather of a preacher, a baptist. I'd never known God, but I felt him there in the briny air pushing off the sea, the front guard of the coming storm.

His resistance was in the sand at my feet, mucking up the stretcher wheels. Dolly jostled as we moved over the rough ground, her small breasts quivering, and I looked away from them, out to sea.

A hundred yards out, five men stood on the balcony of a drowned-out restaurant. The place was four-star nautical kitsch—weathered wood siding and fishing nets and buoys. Its balcony had become a kind of dock on the raised waterline. The five shirtless men stood there in swim trunks and cutoff jeans, watching me.

I pushed Dolly to where the ocean undulated against the pavement. The road I walked had become like a boat launch angling down into the sea. The gulls circled and dived nearby, a few touching down on a massive gray hump. It was like a smooth boulder rising up from the shoals. It was, I realized, a dead beached whale. Truly dead. The baffling resurrections seemed a curse for humankind alone. Everything else that died was dead.

Thunder bashed on the horizon. The force of it seemed drawn up from the primordial deep that man had never conquered nor would. But here I was heedless, driving Dolly into the sea as the water drenched my shoes and soaked upward through my pant legs. It was lukewarm water, heated, so the hack radio scientist claimed, by the sudden spike in volcanic fuss along the midocean ridge, abyssal mountain ranges many leagues beyond the continental shelf.

After I waded waist-deep into the water, I moved alongside Dolly's body and unzipped the bag down to her toes, folded it behind her shoulders, and lifted her head into the crook of my arm. I wrapped my other arm around her hips. Her flesh was dimpled like plucked chicken skin, but I ignored the chill of her body and slipped her into the water. The ice packs scattered and bobbed around us.

The nimbostratus front line had begun to eclipse the sun and lay its shadows like an early dusk. I freed Dolly from her baggage and held her naked above the water, one arm beneath her shoulders and the other behind the backs of her knees. She was stiff at first, but every second her body relaxed itself into my grasp. Her loosened knee joints lowered her bare feet down into the water. I waded out farther, my necktie draped modestly over her breasts.

The water came up to lap at my elbows and then to ease the burden of her weight from my arms. Lightning sputtered through the clouds, gilding their purple masses. Traces of that electric rush drove into the sea current. It shivered up through my groin and fired into my throat and made me laugh like God had finally blurted the punchline.

My five-man Greek chorus had descended from their restaurant balcony onto a speedboat tied to the railings. One of them kept yanking the starter cord while the other four sat patiently in their seats. They were coming ashore ahead of the storm, skirting certain death. Or maybe they were already dead. Or they were live men coming for Dolly and me, eager to do whatever sick men do when laws no longer stifle their appetites.

I knelt into the oncoming waves and went under, kept my eyes open and felt that liquid-salt sting. I clenched her around the waist and pressed her chest against mine to keep her submerged where the amniotic warm could soften her chill. My lungs convulsed for air. My will dashed any whim I had to stay under and drown. My heart heaved blood through veins to remind me I was not yet together with the revenants.

I pressed my fingers to her face, wanting somehow to feel the moment of her consciousness, that current of thought trapped under ice, incubated. In my asphyxiating daze, I saw where two thousand miles north the frozen corpses of long-lost Arctic explorers now faced their eternal second consciousness without hope for motion, not until the ice caps melted off. I saw the bones of the decades-dead that hummed in their buried coffins but couldn't lift the lid, cursed instead to ruminate in that cramped and noiseless dark. I saw Ukrainian nuclear towns where cancers bred wild and where fetuses presumed to be stillborn were quickening again in their mothers' wombs. I saw African genocide fields of dead rising up like wheat at dawn, the burning pits spewing forth their charred offspring—

—and then I reared my head from the sea and breathed.

The five men had puttered their boat to within a few yards from us, two men at the fore peering down over the gunwale to catch sight of obstructions—street signs, the roofs of underwater houses. Behind them the dark skies brewed thicker shadow. The men were smoking cigarettes, so they were not among the dead. Unwelcome news for Dolly and me. One of them stood and pointed toward me and said "There!" A moment later, the boat veered more precisely toward us.

The waves rushed harder now. They slapped my face and worked to shove me off my feet and drag me away on a riptide. I stole more oxygen and dipped back underwater with Dolly. I brought her face within inches of mine to see her more clearly. All at once her body lurched and her legs scissored through the churning current.

I turned back toward shore. My shoes sought vainly for traction on the underwater pavement. Hardly five feet deep and the sea believed it could claim us. The backwash rushed against Dolly as I held her. She clutched at my jacket lapel. I didn't want to rise up and give those men a clear sign of my whereabouts.

I moved forward with each surge and held my ground as best I could. I kicked off one shoe and with a socked foot dug my toes into pavement cracks. When my lungs clenched for air again, I stood upright. My chin barely broke the surface, and panic hit. I was farther from shore than I'd been before.

An outward swell upended us. I was tumbling with her. Some impulse told my arms they had to fight, they had to let go, but even as she was sliding out of my grasp, I resisted.

Even Dolly kicked, flailed her arms. This was not the birth I had hoped for her. I screamed into the surf and got a windpipe full of saltwater for it. I coughed and gasped and thought, *Somebody's backyard pool, a hotel Jacuzzi, even a warm shower could've done the trick.* But like always, I'd overreached for the sake of the dramatic.

My arms clutched at nothing. Dolly gone. Lungs heaved. No breath. I spun and lost my sense of up as the storm dark draped down over.

Grips like fishhooks jammed under my armpits. I was caught and hoisted. I squeezed my fist with something inside it—flesh and bone that was, mercifully, Dolly's wrist. I had her, but someone else had me, lifting, a clamp along my gut so sudden I gagged away the water I had breathed. Hands pulling at my jacket, hands ushering me onto the speedboat deck. I sprawled across a thwart. The shirtless men dragged Dolly from the sea. She was onboard with the rest of us.

Above, spirals of gray churned inside the purple clouds like coiling, electric eels flashing their charges through the ether. The boat tossed and men bellowed, and the rain on my face brought stinging pain with its drive. I smelled smoke and gasoline and the acrid sweat of men who hadn't bathed in quite some time. One of them slapped my face around. "You all right, buddy? You with us?" His bearded face blotted out the sky.

"All right," I said, coughing. "The girl?"

The bearded man cringed at the rain bearing down on us. We were rushing toward shore, but the sea yet grabbed for us, crested over the hull, strived to capsize.

Someone said, "Jesus—"

And: "She's not—she's dead—she's one of the Dead—"

I tried to sit upright, but something held me down against the cushioned thwart.

"Leave her alone!" My voice.

"Look at her wrists. She ain't breathing. God, her eyes—"

Even with their shouting, the roar of the sea, and the boat engine, even with the constant thunder overhead—all that noise and still I heard something else coming on, like a lake of water coming to a boil.

"Aw, God," somebody said, "hail."

A surge of men's bodies hit the deck not wide enough to hold us all. I reached out to where I saw the knuckled curve of Dolly's spine. The wall of hail pummeled the boat and riddled the water surrounding us. It bashed into the wet naked flesh on the backs of these men. It punched rapid-fire against my shoulders, and the hardest hits were enough to knock my breath away. Each pellet was a hard-packed snowball bursting into slush against the pool of water on the floor of the boat. The men, hunched where they sat, laced their hands over the backs of their heads to guard their skulls from impact.

A wave crested white behind us as the boat scraped aground. The engine died with an electric snap. We lurched portward, aft end wrenched around toward the sea to catch the brunt of another raging wave and the slantwise barrage of frozen hail. The storm was bathed all in purple fog, and the lightning plunged its bright nervous membranes into the deep.

The boat upended and threw us all haphazard back into the surf. I was under, mouthful of water, someone's foot stomped into my gut. But my hands found solid ground, and I crawled and breathed and squeezed out the salt in my eyes. Dolly, naked, was already scrambling ahead of me out of the water. She was like a mermaid testing land with the legs she had wished for. There were no welts where the hail stones struck her, just the pale bluish cast of her back and rear and thighs. A tattoo was on her waistline, though I couldn't decipher it.

Our ambulance was ahead, but the tide had advanced in mere minutes to roil around the wheel wells. Hail pinged off the windshield and the hood and beat away the film of bug guts. Both my shoes were missing now. A hailstone grazed my cheek so sharply that I cried out, slapped my hand there, and found blood. Some of the other men were already crawling in the swash. They were lunging, desperate against the ice that would surely beat us all soon enough to death.

I rushed the land, howling like a beach-stormer off a landing craft. When I overcame Dolly, I grasped her by the elbow and yanked so abruptly that she almost collapsed on her uncertain legs.

One of the men ran beside us. He was wide open, unsuspecting. I swung my fist at his neck. He gagged and slapped his throat and buckled at the knees. I was feral, spittle at the mouth. Hail bashed my head, but it brought no pain. "Come on, come on, come on," I chanted.

We reached the ambulance, wrenched the passenger door open. Dolly's face—her bleached-out irises so dilated in surprise, so lively. The gape of her mouth was almost a smile.

No time left to circle around to the driver's door. The other men were upon us. I lunged through the cab and wrenched Dolly inside behind me. No strength left to pull her onto the seat, but she seemed to understand now, as she hoisted herself up from the wet ground. I was sprawled across the bench with Dolly on my legs, one hand to crank the starter key and the other to slap down the driver-door lock. The bearded man—he'd saved my life—was there at the window bashing with both fists, moaning God knows, blood slashed across his forehead.

I grabbed the gearshift underhanded and wrenched it into reverse. Still lying prone with Dolly's weight on me, I couldn't see through the windshield and my feet weren't within reach of the accelerator. So I slapped it with my palm instead. The ambulance revved backward out of the flood, a few more yards away from those desperate men, shirtless and bloody like biblical nomads.

I struggled into a proper driver's position, shifted back into forward.

The men were dark blurs behind a windshield fogged and slushed and bug strewn, but I kicked the gas and their shapes leaped aside from the onrushing headlight beams. The most dogged of their posse reached out and grazed the driver's-side mirror. He kept firm hold of it as I spun a wide U-turn away from the raging sea.

It was the bearded man again, the persistent prophet, furry face against the glass and feet skating along on the ground. I was fixing to unroll the window and congratulate him, but the side mirror broke loose and the stowaway disembarked with it.

There was clear road ahead, and when I turned to Dolly, I saw that she was as ashamed as Eve after tasting the fruit, legs dawn up against her nakedness. Her chin shuddered from cold or fear as she gazed on me. I'd be a liar if I claimed she looked anything else but horrified.

But this is how we're born, naked and afraid.

"Happy birthday, Dolly," I said.

SECOND WIND

BY MIKE CAREY

Here's my problem with dead people: They fall apart.

Okay, I grant you, the transition to being a stiff is a shock to the system. You wake up one morning, and you feel like shit—death warmed over, as they say, or rather death cooling rapidly toward background ambient. You feel for a pulse—not verifiably present. But is that because it's not there, or because you're a klutz and you can't take a pulse?

Okay, you can't feel a heartbeat, either. That's ominous, because you're so fucking scared by this time that your heart should be racing, not parked at the curb with the hand brake on.

You draw a ragged, stressy breath . . . and it just stays there. Nowhere to go. Your body isn't metabolizing oxygen anymore, and your formerly autonomic functions are all unplugged from the board. The pressure doesn't build. You could keep that breath pent up behind your teeth for a minute, an hour, a day and a half, and you're never going to feel the slightest need to let it out again.

The sign on the door just flipped, from OPEN to CLOSED. This is it. Grammatically, you can never start a sentence with "I am" again. It's "was/not-was," all the way.

But that's no reason to let up, is what I'm saying. Too many people use death as an excuse, and I'm sick of hearing it. The world's still out there, people. It's not going away. The rules of the game didn't change because you croaked, and like they say, if you don't get back in the saddle, you're gonna end up trampled and covered in horseshit. Your choice.

I used to be a stockbroker, which is probably what killed me. Or rather, being a *great* broker is what killed me—having the kind of obsessive edge that took me to the top of the NASDAQ while most of my respected peers were still flossing their teeth and picking out a tie that matched their hand-stitched braces.

It's a tough gig, don't mistake me. When you're playing a bunch of DAX-listed storm troopers off against a third-party boiler room, taking a trim on buy and sell at the same time, and cutting your T+3s so tight there's no skin left on your fingertips, it's a bit like riding a log flume must be. There are hundreds of millions of euros rolling under you, behind you, and you know damn well if you lose the flow and try to stop it before it's ready, you'll go down and never see daylight.

So, yeah, there's a certain level of stress that you live with. I won't say "thrive on," because that's macho bullshit: The adrenaline surge is pleasant for about a half an hour, tops. After that your body starts shaking itself to pieces and you're swallowing heartburn. A day in the dealing room is a day in the slaughterhouse: You come out of it with other people's blood and sweetmeats spattered on your shirt, and that's if you've done okay. If you've fucked up, it's your own.

I had my first heart attack when I was twenty-six. I usually tell the story so it happened on my actual birthday, but in fact it was the day after. I'd been out all night, flying high on wings of coke and frozen Stolichnaya, then I showered, popped a few dexies, and went back to work. The two guys I was with, they did the same thing, more or less, but they flaked out in the course of the morning—sneaked off to the room with the folding beds that the management lays on for quitters, to keep the crash at bay with a snatched half hour of sleep. I kept right on going, because I was on one of those flux-market rolls where nobody knows what's happening and you can squeeze the shit from one exchange to another to ride lag on a price you already know is falling. Too good to miss.

But like in a bad movie, I start to get a reverb on my hearing. Well, okay, what the fuck? I don't need to hear properly to see the numbers scrolling up the screen. I'm low-pointing, I'm settling, I'm re-staking dead buys, I'm making those Tokyo asswipes breathe my farts and think it's good fresh air.

And then I was on the ground with a couple of invisible sumo wrestlers sitting on my chest. Tokyo's revenge, I thought, as I blacked out.

Three days at the Portland Clinic on caviar and tenecteplase. Back in the saddle, clip-clop, clip-clop. Because the guys who stop never start again, and that's the gospel truth. I've seen it enough times to know that it's a natural law.

The second attack caught me by surprise, because this time I wasn't even working: I was with a woman—using *with* to denote the act of coitus. Normally I'm pretty good at sex; I can reach a plateau and stay there for as long as I like until my partner of choice is ready to join me for the final pull toward the summit. On this particular occasion, however, the lady had to struggle out from underneath my inert body and call the emergency services. I'd been wearing her panties as a party hat, and I still was when I woke up—not at the Portland but at the Royal Free. Fucking paramedics. They ripped off my diamond cufflinks, too, but how the hell do you prove it? When you're unconscious, people can take all the liberties they like.

So that was two, and the doctors said I should expect strike three to come over the plate pretty damn soon if I didn't change up and get myself some Zen-like calm. I didn't waste any time on that prescription: I am what I am, and I play to my strengths.

So I looked death square in his poker face, I saw what he was holding, and I implemented plan B.

Look, this isn't just me talking big, okay? I don't need to impress a Z-list shmuck like you, and in any case, it's basic. Basic stuff. Anyone with any sense can take the temperature and pack for the weather they know is rolling in.

The dead started coming back a few years ago now, around the turn of the new millennium. Actually, it probably started a whole lot earlier than that, but that was when the trickle turned into a flood. Some of them come back in the spirit, some in the body. An acquaintance of mine who makes what he humorously calls a living as an exorcist says it's all the same thing: Zombies are people whose ghosts cling to their own dead flesh out of fear or stubbornness or sheer habit, and they learn by trial and error how to get things moving again. You hear crazier stories, too—human ghosts ram-raiding animal bodies and doing a little forcible redecorating. "Formative causation," they call it, or some other bullshit periphrasis: You look like what you think you should look like, at least most of the time. But the animal soul is still in there with you, and when you're at your weakest, it will try and slip out from under. That, the so-called experts tell us, is what werewolves are.

Ghost, zombie, or loup-garou—those were the options I was looking at, assuming I didn't just "go gentle into that good night" like some passive-aggressive moron. So I planned accordingly, in between strike two and strike three. I had a shed-load of money put by already—salted away against a retirement I clearly wasn't going to live to enjoy. Now I put some of that cash to work, although first of all I set up a Celtic knot of offshore-registered shelf companies to handle my assets. Dead men can't legally own jackshit, but corporations are immortal. I bought a lot of real estate, because the property bubble had finally burst around about then, and you could pick up some really sweet deals. Partly I was just diversifying my holdings, but I was also looking for a place where I could set up postmortem. What I needed was a pied-à-terre that was both huge and invisible—standing on its own grounds, because nosy neighbors would be the last thing I needed.

I settled on a disused cinema in Walthamstow—the Gaumont. It was going for a song, despite having a Cecil Masey facade and most of the interior fixtures and fittings still intact. It was 1930s vintage and had never been either burned out or turned into a bingo hall. It had been a porno theater, briefly, but I wasn't too worried about sticky carpets. In fact, I wasn't worried about the auditorium at all. I stripped out the projection booth and fitted it with a bespoke arrangement of air-conditioning and freezer units. Temperature and humidity control were going to be key.

Somewhere around then was when my personal extinction event happened. RIP, Nicholas Heath—no flowers or known grasses, by request. But I'd been expecting it. It was, you know, a bump in the road. Nothing more. I'd already decided which kind of dead man I was going to be, and I'd made sure that the funeral parlor would hold off on the burial for at least a week, to give the other shoe a chance to drop.

To be honest with you, I don't like to talk about that part of it. Some people say they see tunnels, blinding white lights, heavenly messengers or moving stairways. I didn't see anything. But I did have the sense of not being completely in control, and that fucking scared me. I mean, for all I knew, it could be a lottery. Maybe you didn't get to choose which way the ball would bounce. I might find myself looking like Casper the friendly fuckwit, or Lassie, or in some other stupid, inconsequential, unworkable shape. Or nothing. Nothing at all. Not all the dead come back, even now.

But I did, and I came back as me. I sat up on the morgue slab, signed myself out, collected my effects, and hit the road. Forget about statutory notice, or packing up any of the stuff from my apartment. Dead men aren't covered by contract: My job was gone, my casa was someone else's casa, and the landlord had probably already changed the locks. I headed straight for the Gaumont, bolted the doors, and got on with the job.

It was good timing, in a way: I'd finally gotten the air-conditioning units working properly at two degrees Celsius, and I had the place all set up to move into. Which was just as well, because it was the last moving I did for a while: The fucking rigor mortis hits you soon after you sit up and look around, and for the next twenty-four hours, it's all you can do to roll your eyes to the heavens.

So I'm lying there, in the dark, because I didn't get a chance to turn the lights on before my muscles seized up, and I'm running through the list in my mind.

Rancidification.
Black putrefaction.
Butyric fermentation.
Dry decay.

These, collectively, were the joys now in store for me. And every second I wasted meant more hassle later, so as soon as the rigor passed, I spat on my hands—figuratively speaking—and started taking the appropriate measures.

Rancidification, the first stage, is far and away the most dangerous. That's when all the fluids in your body rot and go sour. The smell is fucking indescribable, but that's not what you've got to worry about. The souring releases huge quantities of gas, which builds up in your body cavity wherever there's a void for it to collect in. If you don't do something about it, the pressure of the gas can do huge damage to your soft tissues—rip you open from the inside out. But if you make incisions to let out the gas, every hole is a problem that has to be managed at the putrefaction stage.

I got a long way with some ordinary plastic tubing, which I shoved into a great many places I'm not keen to talk about. In the end I had to make some actual incisions, but I kept them to a minimum: I was also helped by an amazing substance called Lanobase 18, which is what undertakers use to soak up the fluid leaking from your internal organs and turn it into an inert, almost plasticized slurry.

As far as the putrefaction stage went, I was already ahead of the game just by having a cold, controlled space of my own. No insects to lay their eggs in my moldering flesh; no air- or ground-borne contaminants. I used that time to start the embalming process. I needed it because by now my stink had matured into something really scary. I kept having to pour cologne onto my tongue to blitz what was left of my airway and nasal passages, because even though I wasn't inhaling, the smell was still getting through to me somehow.

By the time I hit phase three, I was more than half pickled—and now it started to get easier. What was left of my flesh changed its consistency, over the space of a couple of weeks, into something hard and waxy. Adipocere, they call it. It's kind of unsettling at first, because it doesn't feel like anything even slightly organic, but it has the huge upside that it doesn't smell of anything much. I could live with myself now.

Dry decay mainly affects your bones, through a leeching of organic compounds called diagenesis, so I just let it happen and turned my attention to other things.

Unfortunately, I'd missed a trick or two while all this was going on. I had the projection booth itself and the adjacent generator room armored up like the fucking führer-bunker, but I hadn't bothered with all the ground-floor doors and windows. I didn't think I'd need to: The Gaumont had stood empty and undisturbed for so many years, who was going to pay it any attention now?

But the key word there is *undisturbed*. I'd had a whole lot of kit delivered when I was setting up my freezer and air-conditioning arrays, and I'd had some guys in to reinforce the upstairs walls and doors. I might as well have put out a fucking welcome mat: I was telling all the neighborhood deadbeats that the cinema was now inhabited and that it might contain something worth stealing.

In point of fact, it didn't: Everything that was valuable was locked away behind steel bulkhead doors up on the first floor. But that didn't stop a variegated collection of scumbags from breaking in downstairs, smashing the windows, and ransacking what was left of the old furniture, looking for something they could purloin, pawn, or piss into. Some of them had even moved in and were now squatting in the auditorium or the storerooms behind it.

First things first. I made some calls, using one of the false names and e-mail addresses I'd set up for my offshore holding company, and hired some guys from a private security firm to come in and clear out the squatters' little rat nest. They threw everything out into the street; then they maintained a presence while I got the builders to come back in and make the place secure.

They put steel shutters on the ground-floor windows, and steel bulkhead doors over the old wooden doors, attached to I beams sunk two feet into freeway-mix concrete. I had the work team coat the windowsills and door frames with green antivandal paint, too: The losers could still sleep in the fucking doorway if they wanted to, but I wasn't going to make it comfortable for them, and that was as far as they were going to get. As a dead man walking, I was too vulnerable: I wanted to have the freedom of the building without worrying about who I might run into. In any case, this was my retirement home now: Why the hell should anyone else get the benefit of it? That's not how life works; take it from a dead man.

Relaxing isn't something I do all that well, but now I felt like I could finally slow down and take stock. I'd ridden out the roller coaster of physical decomposition, at least to the point where I could maintain a steady state. I had my place secured and my lines of communication laid down so that I could get what I needed from the outside world without dealing with it directly.

I took a day off. Watched some movies on cable. Opened a bottle of Pauillac and sniffed the wine-breath, since drinking it without any digestive enzymes was an idiot's game.

It was half a day, actually. Half a day off. By the afternoon I was restless, worried about what I might be missing. I fired up the computers—three of them, each registered with a different ISP and apparently logged on in a different time zone—and put some of my money back into play on the New York Exchange.

That was a good afternoon and an even better evening. Stress couldn't touch me now—look, Ma, no glands—I couldn't get tired, and I didn't need to take bathroom breaks, so I kept going steadily through a fourteen-hour session, not logging off until the exchange closed.

Then I switched to the Nikkei Dow and did the same for another five hours.

Man, I thought, *this is . . . you know . . . liberating*. Death means never having to wipe your ass again, never getting pulled out of the zone by your body's needs or by someone else blabbing in your ear like they've got something to say. It means you can keep going forever, if you want to.

Of course, forever is a long time. A long, long, *long* fucking time.

On day three, the deadbeats broke in again. They'd actually sneaked back while the concrete was still setting and pushed one of the steel plates up out of line so they could work it loose later with a crowbar. I could hear them doing the same thing with the door of the projection room—my fucking holy of holies.

Yeah, dream on, you verminous little bastards. That door and the wall it was set in were about as porous as a bank vault: Not needing to breathe meant not having to cut corners where personal security was concerned. All the same, I couldn't stop thinking about what would have happened if the door had been open—if I'd been down on the ground floor picking up my mail or something. I couldn't take that risk again.

This time I thought it through properly: Defense in depth was what I needed, not one big-ass door with one big-ass bolt on it. I had the builders—none of whom ever met me in person, of course—completely redesign the ground floor, replacing all the existing walls with steel bulkheads and at the same time putting in a whole lot of new ones. I took my inspiration from the crusader forts of the late Middle Ages, turning the Gaumont into three separate keeps, one inside the other. Only a single vault door connected the outer keep with the middle one, and the middle keep with the inner one. Other doors were devoid of bolts, locks, or handles: They were all independently lockable via a computer-controlled system, and the first thing I did was to slave the whole damn thing to the main server up in the projection booth. I put the closed-circuit (CCTV) cameras in, too—dozens of them, set up so there were no dead angles. I could check out any given stretch of corridor, any given room, and make sure it was clear before I opened the doors and cleared myself a route.

What? This sounds like overkill? No, genius, it wasn't. I was thinking things through, that's all. Every fortress can turn into a trap, so every fortress needs a back door. And this particular fortress needed a mail slot too, because for some of the things I was doing online I still needed physical documents, physical certification, actual rather than digital signatures. It's stupid, but it's true: Some parts of the world haven't started surfing the electron tide yet, and they only believe in what they can hold in their hands. Hah. Maybe not so stupid, when you think about it.

So now I could swing back into top gear, stop watching my back. And I did. Believe me, I did.

To tell you the truth, I got lost in it. I must have spent a week or more at a time just bouncing from one exchange to another in an endless, breakneck rhythm. You know those velodromes, where the racers ride their bikes almost horizontally on the canted walls? Well, that's what I was like. The only thing that kept me touching the ground at all was my unthinkable velocity. Which is fine, so long as you never slow down.

But I did.

It was subtle at first, subtle enough that I didn't even realize it was happening. I missed a spike here, came in slow on a deal there—not big things and not connected. I was still coming out ahead and still in control. It took me a couple of days to realize that I was too much in control, that I was going through the motions without feeling them and making conscious decisions instead of letting instinct play through me.

I tied down, cashed in, and logged off. Sat there in silence for a while, staring at the screens. A wave of grief swept through me, and I don't care if that sounds stupid—a sense of bereavement. Nicky Heath was dead. I hadn't really gotten that fact into my head until then.

If you stop, you never start again—my own golden rule. But I didn't feel like I could touch the keyboard right then. I was afraid of screwing up, afraid of hitting some rock I would have seen a mile off back when I had a functioning endocrine system. *Look, Ma, no glands.*

I think I must have been hearing the noises in the walls for a while before that—bangs and scrapes and scuffles, muffled not by distance but by the thickness of the brickwork and the layers of steel plating. But now I let myself listen to them. Jumbled, discontinuous, slightly different each time. It wasn't the freezer unit or the big electrical generator downstairs. The only things that made noises like that were living things. People. Animals. Members of the big but still exclusive club of entities-with-a-pulse.

I turned on the CCTV monitors and did the rounds of the cameras. She wasn't hard to find, once I started looking: She was in the outer keep, way down on the ground floor, in a blind stretch of corridor between two of my self-locking doors—nowhere near the big steel portal that led through into the middle zone.

It was still a nasty shock, though. Sort of like scratching your balls and coming up with a louse.

From what I could see, she had to be one of the homeless people—probably in her early twenties but looking a damn sight older, huddled in way too many layers of clothes in a corner made by the angle of wall and door. She had dirty blond hair and a sullen, hangdog face. Hard to tell anything else, because she was folded down into herself, knees hugged to her chest and head down. It was probably cold down there, in spite of all the layers.

Where the hell had she come from? She couldn't have been in there since the last invasion, because I wouldn't have missed her, and in any case, she'd be dead by now. There wasn't anything to eat or drink, and she clearly hadn't brought anything in with her that she couldn't carry in her pockets.

I backtracked with the cameras until I found the smoking gun—a large vent pipe for one of the freezer units that had been run through the outer wall of the building. She'd just hit it with something—a hammer or a rock—again and again until the flimsy metal bent back on itself far enough for her to squeeze through. That had let her into a part of the building that was on the route I used when I went down to collect the mail. She must have scooted through a door or two that was unlocked when I came through, and then got caught in the dead-end stretch of corridor when I made the return journey and locked up again.

She'd tried to get out: Those were the sounds I'd heard. She'd hammered and clawed at the door and probably screamed for help, but only faint echoes had come up to the projection room, and I'd been too absorbed in what I was doing to decipher them.

Now she looked to be in a bad way. The monitor only resolved in black and white, but there were dark patches on her hands, which I assumed were probably blood—her fingernails damaged from trying to pull on the edge of the doorjamb—and when she briefly came out of her huddle to grab a gulp of air, I saw that her lips were swollen in a way that suggested dehydration.

I got up and paced around the room, trying to think it through. I wasn't capable of panic, but I felt a dull, blunt volume of unhappiness expand inside me, like the intestinal gases back in the first stage of decay.

I could just let her die was the first thought that came to mind.

I could open up the doors to let her back out the way she'd come, but she might be too weak to move. She might die anyway.

If I opened the doors, someone else could get in. Safer just to leave her.

But someone could have seen her climbing inside and not come out again. Someone might be looking for her right now or calling the police or crawling through that hole with torches and crowbars and . . .

No, nobody else had found the hole. The CCTV cameras didn't show anyone else, either in the room where the vent let out or anywhere else in the outer keep. *I should have put more sophisticated alarms in*, I thought irrelevantly—movement sensors, or infrared scanners, or something. I shouldn't have let this happen. Now here I was, already guilty of false imprisonment or some such bullshit, with the police probably searching the goddamned neighborhood and Christ only knows what kind of trouble to look forward to if she was found here, alive or dead or anywhere in between.

I stopped pacing because I'd come up hard against a wall. I wanted to punch it, but that would have been a really stupid thing to do—no blood flow, so no scabbing, no skin repair. Any wound I opened in my own flesh would stay open unless I sewed it shut.

I stared at the wall for maybe five minutes, galloping through the same rat-runs inside my head. When I'd done it enough times to be sure they always ended up in the same place, I got moving again.

I had no choice. I had to bring the dumb bitch up to good-as-new spec before I cut her loose. I had to make sure there was no harm and no foul, whatever that took.

I found a bucket the builders had left behind and a washbasin in what had once been a cleaner's cupboard behind the projection booth. I cleaned the bucket out as far as I could, then filled it with cold water. I flicked some switches on the main board, releasing the locks on all but one of the doors between me and the woman—leaving just the door that she was leaning against.

Then I went down, let myself out through the inner and middle keeps, and made my way around to her stretch of corridor. She must have heard me coming, because when I turned the last bend, I caught the sound of her fists banging on the other side of the door, and her voice, muffled through the thick wood, telling me she was stuck.

I left the bucket of water right in front of the door and went back up to the projection booth. I watched the woman on the CCTV hook-up: She was still hammering and shouting, pushing at the door, thinking or at least hoping that someone could hear her.

I relocked all the other doors before opening just that one. Since she was leaning her weight against it, she just tumbled through when it opened. She saw the bucket, stared at it with big incredulous eyes, and finally cupped her hands and drank from it. She coughed up a storm and vomited a little, too, but she was alive at least. That was a good start.

Food was more of a problem, because unless there were a few hardy rats down in the basement somewhere, there was nothing edible in the entire building. I got around that by going to the Ocado Web site, whose online order form allows you to specify exactly where you want the food to be dropped off. I specified the mailbox, which was actually a double-doored receptacle like the ones post offices use—big enough to take thick bundles of legal papers, and, as it turned out, big enough for a bag of groceries too.

I ordered stuff she could eat cold, to keep things simple—turkey breast, bread and rolls, a bag of ready-cut carrot slices, some apples. I added some fun-size cartons of orange juice, and then on an impulse, a bar of Cadbury's dairy milk.

This time I had to approach her from the opposite direction, since she'd gone through the door to get to the water bucket and was now on the other side of the door. It didn't matter: From the master board up in the projection booth, I could open up any route I liked and make absolutely sure of where she was before I moved in, did the drop-off, and retreated again to the booth and the CCTV monitors.

At the sound of the lock clicking, she went scooting back through the door like one of Pavlov's dogs.

She wolfed the food down like she hadn't seen bread since the Thatcher years. It was a fucking unedifying sight, so I turned off the CCTV and left her to it for a while.

The next time I checked, she was done. The floor was strewn with wrappers, apple cores, a crumpled juice carton. The woman had spotted the camera and was staring at it as though she expected it to start talking to her. Actually, it could do that if I wanted it to: The cameras each came with a speaker as standard. But I didn't have anything I wanted to say to her: I just wanted her to eat, drink, wash, fix herself up, and fuck off out of there.

Wash. Okay. I ordered some more groceries and added soap and shampoo to the list, not to mention another bucket. The next time I fed her, I left both drinking water and wash water, but she didn't take the hint, maybe because the water was cold. Too bad. I didn't have any way of heating it up, and I wasn't running a fucking guesthouse.

I spent about three days plumping her up. On the second day I left her some bandages and antiseptic for her fingers, which she ignored, just like the wash water. On the third day I made a similarly useless gesture with some clean clothes, ordered online in the same way from the ASDA superstore at Brentwood.

Okay, so my reluctant houseguest wasn't interested in personal hygiene, even on a theoretical level. I don't know, maybe the dirt acts like insulation out on the street, and maybe after the first month or so your panties get welded to your privates past the point where you can take them off. Maybe not, though, since she had to be managing to piss somehow. Following that thought through, I realized it was probably a good thing that the cameras had such crappy resolution. I could see the corner she was using as a latrine, now that I looked for it, and I sure as hell didn't want to see it any clearer.

Well, the bottom line was that she had to go out looking no worse than when she came in: I wasn't under any obligation to make her look better.

On day four I drew her a map, showing her how to get back to the vent pipe, and left it with the food. Then I threw the lock on the door behind her and all the other locks leading back to the outer wall and her exit point.

She examined the map as she ate her breakfast, which was croissant and apricot jam. She'd shown a real taste for pastries by this time and none at all for fresh fruit or cereal.

But after she'd finished, she didn't make a move to step over the threshold. She just wiped her mouth on the napkin provided, dropped it into the water bucket—which always drove me crazy because I had to fish the fucking thing out again—and settled back down against the wall.

What was she playing at? She had to realize I was allowing her to leave.

"Come on!" I shouted at the monitor. "Get out of there. You're free as a bird. Go!"

She settled into her characteristic, head-bowed huddle.

Impulsively, I flicked the microphone switch on the CCTV board. I'd never used it before, so I had no idea if it even worked, but a light flashed on the board and the woman jerked her head up as though she'd just heard something—a click, maybe, or else a little feedback flutter from the speaker.

"Hey," I said. "What do you think you're doing? Time to go, lady."

She blinked twice, her face full of comical wonder. She took her time about answering, though, and when she did it was kind of a non sequitur.

"Who are you?" she demanded.

"The owner," I said, and then, not to be put off, I repeated, "Time for you to get out of here."

She shook her head.

I blinked. "What do you mean, no?" I asked, too incredulous even to be pissed off. "This is my place, sweetheart. Not yours. You're not wanted here."

The woman just shrugged. "But I like it here."

The way she said it made me want to go down there and up-end the water bucket on her head. She sounded like a little kid asking if she could stay a bit longer at the beach.

"How can you like it?" I demanded, really annoyed now. "It's a fucking corridor. You like sleeping on concrete?"

"That's what I was doing outside," she said, calmly enough. "And at least here I don't have homeless guys wanting to charge me a blow job for a place by the fire."

"Because there is no fire."

"But there is food."

"Food's off," I said bluntly. "That was the last of it."

She put her head between her folded arms again, as a way of telling me the conversation was over.

"I mean it," I said. "Food's off. You stay here, you starve to death."

She didn't answer. Fine, so she wanted to be alone. I turned off the sound and left her to it.

"Dumb bitch," I said to the monitor, even though she couldn't hear me now.

That was going to be the first item in a varied agenda of invectives, but I realized suddenly what had just happened, what was *still* happening. I was angry. I'd managed to get angry, somehow, even though on the face of it I didn't have the necessary equipment anymore.

If I could do anger, then presumably I could do other flashy emotional maneuvers too. Quickly I fired up my computers and logged on to my U.S. trading board. I didn't surface for five hours, and by that time I was three hundred thousand up on the day.

Saint Nicholas was back, with gifts of ass-kickings for all.

After I closed out on the day, I checked in with the woman. She seemed to be asleep, but she stirred when I clicked the mike back on.

"What's your name, darling?" I asked her.

"Janine," she muttered, looking muzzily to camera.

"I'm Nick."

"Hi, Nick."

"You can stay here tonight," I said. "Tomorrow we'll talk."

But we didn't. Not much, anyway. I made a food drop at 6:00 A.M., before she was even awake, then came back upstairs and logged on. I had another good day on the markets, and the day went by in a blur. I did order a folding bed, though, and some blankets and pillows to go on it. I picked a local store that could deliver immediately, had them leave it round by the back door, and lugged it in myself after they'd gone. It made my skin prickle just a little to be in the outside air again, even though it wasn't a warm day or anything. Just psychosomatic, I guess.

Over the next few days, I furnished Janine's corridor pretty lavishly. She arranged it: All I did was buy the stuff and bring it to the door then let her choose for herself where to put it. I'd started to leave the mike on by this time so she could tell me what she wanted—a chair and a table, a kettle for making tea, a chemical toilet, even a little portable DVD player and a few movies for her to watch while I was busy on the trading boards.

The weirdest thing of all, though, was that I actually started talking to her while I was dealing. It seemed to help me concentrate, in some way I couldn't quite define. Most of the things she liked to talk about were stupid and irritating—her favorite celebrities, previous seasons of *Big Brother*, her hatred for supermodels. I just made "I'm still listening" noises whenever they seemed to be called for and channeled the aggravation into some world-class short-selling.

It got so that if she actually shut up for a while, I'd throw in a question or two to get her talking again. Questions about herself she didn't like to answer, except to say that she was living on the street because of something that had happened between her and her stepfather back when she turned eighteen. I got the impression that it had been a violent and dramatic kind of something, and that the stepfather had gotten the worst of the deal.

"He came on to you?" I asked, genuinely, if slightly, curious.

"I suppose. He came into the bathroom when I was showering one morning and tried to get in with me."

"That's pretty unequivocal," I allowed.

"Pretty what?"

"Clear-cut. Hard to misinterpret."

"Yeah, right. So I smacked him in the mouth with the showerhead really hard, and then I ran out."

"Naked?"

"No, Nick. Not naked."

"Then you were showering in your street clothes?"

A pause. "I didn't run out straightaway. He fell down and hit his head. I had time to grab some stuff."

This was in Birmingham, Janine told me, as if I could possibly have mistaken her accent. She'd taken a bus down to London the same day, hoping to stay with a friend who was studying hairdressing and beauty at Barnet College. But the friend had acquired a boyfriend and wasn't keen on that arrangement. She passed Janine off to another girl, whose floor she occupied for a while. Not a very long while, though: There was an argument about the rules for the use of the bathroom, and she was out on her ear again before the end of the week.

I was starting to see why Janine wasn't big on washing.

"So what about you, Nick?" she asked me, when we'd been doing this for maybe a week or so. "What do you do for a living?"

"Well," I said, "when you put it like that, Janine, the answer has to be nothing."

"I can hear you typing away up there," she said. "Are you writing a book?"

"Yeah," I lied. "I'm writing a book. But it's not to earn a living."

"How come? You're already rich?"

"I'm already dead," I said.

That remark led to a very long silence. The next time I checked on her, she was asleep.

In the morning, she asked me if she could see me.

"The cameras only work one-way," I pointed out.

"I don't mean on the cameras. I mean, you know, face-to-face."

"I'll think about it," I lied.

But she wouldn't leave the idea alone: She kept bringing it up last thing at night, when I was logging off and cashing in. I kept being evasive, and she kept going quiet on me, which was fucking annoying. I'd say good night, get nothing back: She went to sleep each night surrounded by a miasma of hurt silence.

In the end, I did it by accident—almost by accident, I should say. When I unlocked the doors one morning so I could drop off a food delivery, I flicked one switch too many. She was waiting for me as I turned the corner, leaning against the open door with her arms folded in a stubborn, take-no-prisoners kind of pose. The crazy thing is, I sort of knew on some level that I'd done it, that I'd opened the final door and removed that last degree of prophylaxis between us. I just didn't let myself think about it until we were face-to-face and it was too late to back out.

She stared at me for a long time in silence. Then her face wrinkled up in a sort of slo-mo wince. "You look horrible," she said.

"Thanks," I answered inadequately. "You say the sweetest fucking things."

That made her laugh just a little, the sound pulled out of her almost against her will. She took a few steps toward me, then stopped again and sniffed the air cautiously.

"What's that smell?" she wanted to know.

"Which one? I have a complex bouquet."

"It's like . . . antiseptic or something."

"Formaldehyde, probably. I'm pickled inside and out, Janine. It's why I don't smell of rotten meat."

"You smell of that too."

I bridled at that, like some living guy accused of having bad body odor. "I don't," I said. "I went to a lot of fucking effort to—"

She made a gesture that shut me up, kind of a pantomime of throwing up her hands in surrender, except that she only threw them up about an inch or so. "I'm sorry," she said. "You're right. You don't smell rotten. You just *look* like you should smell rotten. Your skin is all waxy and sweaty, and I can see stitches in your neck."

My carotid was one of the places where I'd inserted a trocar to draw off some of my bodily fluids way back when I was fighting the war on rot. "Don't get me started," I advised her.

So she didn't.

"Show me where you live," she suggested instead.

She stayed upstairs with me for an hour or so, wrapped in three coats against the cold. Then she retired back to her little dead-end corridor, home sweet home, and spent the rest of the day watching movies. Musicals, mostly: I think she was plugging herself back into the world of the living to make sure it was still there.

The next day I bought her a couple of hot-water bottles, and she was able to stay longer. I didn't mind the bottles, so long as she kept them under the coats so the heat stayed right against her skin. The thermostats were still set at the same level, so the room didn't warm up at all, and she didn't come close enough to me for the heat to be a problem.

I think that was the first day I forgot to lock her in, and after I'd forgotten once, it kind of felt like going back to that state of affairs would be a slap in the face to her—a way of saying that I thought I could trust her; but then decided I didn't, after all.

That thought raised all kinds of other thoughts, because it suggested that I *did* trust her. There was no reason why I should. Back when I was alive, I'd never felt more for people like her than a kind of queasy contempt, mixed with the unpleasant sensation that usually translates—by some spectacular whitewashing process—as "There but for the grace of God . . ."

But God doesn't have any grace, and I don't have the time or the temperament for helping lame ducks over stiles. If I meet a lame duck, generally speaking, I make *duck a l'orange*.

So what the fuck was going on here, anyway?

At first, I justified it to myself by counting up my market winnings. Janine could make me feel things again, as though my endocrine system was pumping away like it did in the old days—and that gave me a lot of my wonted edge back. But plausible as that explanation was, it was ultimately bullshit. After a week or so, I was spending more time talking to her than I was in managing my portfolios. A week after that, I wasn't even bothering to log on.

At this point I was even making a loss on the deal, because I kept buying her stuff. It wasn't even stuff she needed to live anymore: It was chocolates and beer and donuts and even—I swear to God—a fucking hat.

You're probably thinking that there was some kind of a sexual dynamic going on. Janine certainly thought so. When I presented her with the final little chachka—the straw that broke the camel's neck, so to speak—she stared at it for a long time without reaching out to take it. She looked unhappy.

"What?" I demanded. "What's the matter? It's just a necklace. See, it's got a *J* on it, for Janine. Those are diamonds, you realize. Little ones, but still . . ."

She looked me squarely in the eye—no coyness, no pissing around. "Do I have to blow you to sit at the fire?" she asked.

I thought about that. I wasn't insulted: It was a fair question, I assumed, given the way she lived outside on the streets. I also wondered for a split second if she might be offended if she realized how far I was from being attracted to her. She was dirty, she was as skinny as a stick, and she had bad skin. Back when I had a pulse, I would have sooner fucked a greased oven glove.

"There is no fire," I reminded her.

She nodded slowly. "Okay, then," she said, and took the necklace.

But the writing was on the wall, because once I figured out what it wasn't, I couldn't hide anymore from what it was.

That shitty old poem: It's not "lame ducks over stiles." It's "lame *dogs*."

I watched her sleep that night, and I knew. I let myself see it instead of hiding from it. Fuck, it was nice, you know—watching ghost expressions chase themselves across her face. Hearing her breathe.

The next morning I gave her a roll of notes—maybe twenty grand, maybe a little more—and told her to get lost.

She cried and she asked me what she'd done to hurt me. I told her she'd figure it out if she thought about it long enough. When she asked about the money, I said it was a one-time payment: She should use it to get the hell away from here, and not talk about me to anyone she knew on the street, or else I'd have all the homeless schmucks in Walthamstow climbing up my drainpipes.

She cried some more, and I knew she didn't buy it. It didn't matter, though: That was all the explanation I was prepared to give her. I walked her down the stairs, through the maze, all the way to the door. I unlocked it for her. She stepped across the threshold then turned to stare at me.

Neither of us said anything for the space of three heartbeats. Maybe four: My memory isn't reliable in that respect.

"Imagine if the necklace had been a collar," I said.

She nodded. "I get it," she said.

"And if I fitted a little leash to it. Took you out for walkies."

"I said I get it, Nicky. I don't think it was like that."

But I knew she was wrong. Old ladies have their cushion dogs, their ugly little pugs and Pekes and Chihuahuas. Dead guys have homeless women.

"Thanks," Janine said, "for the money. It's more than I ever had in my life."

"You're welcome," I said. "Rent a flat. With a bath or a shower or something."

She refused to be insulted: She just gave me a slow, sad smile.

"It's not good for you here," she said.

"It's great for me here. Two above freezing. Low humidity. A perfectly controlled environment."

"Stay in the world, Nicky," she murmured, her eyes still brimming in a really unsettling, organic way.

"Is that the same as the street?" I countered. "I'll pass, thanks."

She made like she was going to hug me, but I raised a hand to ward her off, and she got the point: No body heat or radiated thermic energy, by request.

"Bye, then," she said, with a slight tremor in her voice.

"Bye, Janine," I said.

"Is it okay if I write to you?"

"Why not? So long as you make sure there's adequate postage."

She turned and ran, pretty much, across the parking lot and out of sight around the corner of the building. That was the last I saw of her.

I waited to see if she'd come back: It seemed quite likely that she might do that, think of one last thing to say or ask if she could stay one more night or something. I gave her ten minutes, in the end, despite getting that prickly feeling again from having real, unfiltered air flow across my flesh. Finally I shut the front door, did a quick round of the outer circle to make sure I hadn't taken on any more unwanted passengers, then went back upstairs and locked myself in again.

It was really quiet. Quiet as the tomb, like they say, except for the freezer units humming away behind the far wall. I thought about going down and grabbing one of her DVDs, but they were all feel-good shit that would make me want to hawk.

I didn't really feel like going online: The vibe was wrong, which meant the best I could hope for was adequate. But finally, around about midnight, I fired up my digital engines of destruction and got back in the hot seat for a few hours of Far-Eastern mayhem. Because, it's still true, you know? Still gospel, in my book:

The guys who stop never start again.

CLOSURE, LIMITED

A Story of World War Z

BY MAX BROOKS

BERUFJORDHUR, ICELAND

Thomas Kiersted looks exactly like his prewar picture. His frame may have thinned considerably, and his salt-and-pepper hair may have lost all its pepper, but his eyes show no trace of "survivors' stare." He waves to me from the deck of The African Queen. *The three-hundred-foot former sailing yacht is still a magnificent vessel, despite her patched sails and naval gray paintwork. This former plaything of the Saudi royal family now flies the flag of the European Union and is the mobile headquarters of "Closure Limited."*

Welcome aboard! *Doctor Kiersted holds out a hand as the supply launch pulls alongside.* Quite a party, eh? *He refers to the collection of warships and troop transports anchored in the fjord.* Good thing for us this is only a recce expedition. It's getting harder and harder to secure our subjects. South and East Asia are secure, Africa's drying up. Russia used to be our best exporter, unofficially, of course, but now . . . They really mean it, closing their borders. No more "flexible negotiations," not even on the individual level. What's this world coming to when you can't bribe a Russian?

He chuckles as we head below to B deck. A loud commotion roars down the passageway from a lit hatchway.

No, it's not that. *Kiersted gestures over his shoulder.* Cricket season, Sri Lanka versus the West Indies. We get the BBC live feed directly from Trinidad. No, our subjects are all kept below in specially modified cabins. Not cheap, but nothing we do here is.

We descend to C deck, past crew cabins and various equipment lockers. Officially our funding comes from the EU Ministry of Health. They provide the ship, the crew, a military liaison to help collect subjects, or, if no troops are available, enough money to pay for private contractors like "the Impisi," you know, the "Hyenas." They don't come cheap either.

None of our public funding comes from America. I watched the debates your Congress had on C-SPAN. I cringed when that one senator tried to support it openly. He is now, what, working as an underling in your Department of National Graves Registration?

The irony is most of our money comes from America, from private individuals or charities. Your (*Name Removed for Legal Reasons*) set up the fund that's given dozens of your countrymen a chance to use our services. We need every dollar, or Cuban peso, I should say, the only money that really means anything now.

It's difficult and dangerous to collect subjects, very dangerous, but that part of the process is relatively inexpensive. The preparation—that is where the real money goes. It's not enough to just find a subject with the right height, build, gender, and reasonably close facial features. Once we have them—*he shakes his head*—then the real work begins.

Hair has to be cleaned, cut, possibly dyed. Most of the time facial features have to be reconstructed or else actually sculpted from scratch. We have some of the best specialists in Europe . . . and America. Most of them work for standard wages, or even "pro bono," but some know exactly how much their talent is worth and charge for every second of their time. Talented bastards.

We come to E deck, now closed off by an armored hatch guarded by two large armed men. Kiersted speaks to them in Danish. They nod, then look at me. My apologies, *he says,* I don't make the rules. *I show my ID, both U.S. and UN, a signed copy of my legal disclaimer, and my letter of consent, stamped with the seal of the European Union's Minister of Mental Health. The guards examine them closely, even using prewar ultraviolet lights, then nod to me and open the door. Kiersted and I pass into an artificially lit passageway. The air is still, odorless, and extremely dry. I hear the thrum of either several small or one extremely large and powerful dehumidifier. The hatches on either side of us are solid steel, opened only by electronic key, and warning in several languages for unauthorized personnel to stay out. Kiersted lowers his voice slightly.* This is where it happens. Preparation. I am sorry we can't enter; a safety issue for the workers, you understand.

We continue down the passageway. Kiersted gestures to the doors without touching them. Face and hair are only part of the preparation. "Wardrobe personalization"—*that* is a challenge. The process simply won't work if the subjects are, say, wearing the wrong clothes or missing some kind of personal item. Here, at least, we can thank globalization. The same T-shirt, say, made in China, could be found in Europe, America, anywhere. The same for electronic items, or jewelry; we have a jeweler on contract for specialty items, but you'd be surprised how many times we've found clones for so-called "one-of-a-kind" pieces. We also have a specialist for children's toys, you see, not to make them, but to modify them. Children specialize their toys like no one else. A certain teddy bear is missing an eye, or an action figure has one black boot and one brown. Our specialist, she has a warehouse in Lund. I've even seen it, a massive old airplane hangar, with nothing but specialty piles of exact toy pieces: dolls' hairbrushes and Action Man guns—hundreds of piles, thousands. Reminds me of when I visited Auschwitz as a student—the hills of eyeglasses and little children's shoes. I don't know how she does it, Ingvilde. She is driven.

I remember once we needed a "special penny." The client was specific. He used to be some kind of "entertainment agent" in Hollywood, managed (*Name Withheld for Legal Reasons*) and a lot of other dead stars. In his letter he said that he once took his son to a place called "Travel Town," some sort of train museum in Los Angeles. He said it was the only time he'd ever spent a full afternoon with his son. Travel Town had one of those machines where you put a penny in, and cranking the handle presses it into a special medallion. The client had said that on the day they fled, his son had refused to leave it behind. He even made his father punch a hole through it so he could wear it around his neck on a shoelace. Half the client's letter was devoted to describing that special penny. Not just the design, but the color, aging, thickness, even the spot on it where he'd punched the hole. I knew we'd never find anything close to that. So did Ingvilde, but you know what she did? She made another one, completely identical. She found the company's records online and gave a copy of the design to a local machinist. She aged it like a master chemist—the right combination of salt, oxygen, and artificial sunlight. Most importantly, she made sure that the penny was made before the 1980s, before the American government removed most of the copper. You see, when you squeeze it flat and the inside metal shows . . . Sorry . . . "too much information" as you Americans say. I only mention it to illustrate the kind of dedication we have to our work here. Ingvilde, incidentally, works on a subsistence salary. She's like me—"rich person's guilt."

We reach F deck, the deepest level aboard The African Queen. *Although artificially lit like the deck above, these bulbs are as bright as the prewar sun.* We try to simulate sunlight, *Kiersted explains,* and each compartment is specially equipped with sounds and smells tailored to the client. Most of the time it's peaceful—the smell of pine and the chirp of birds—but it really depends on the individual. We once had a man from mainland China, a test case, to see if it was worth their government setting up their own operation. He was from Chongqing, and he needed the sounds of traffic and the smells of industrial pollution. Our team actually had to mix up an audio file of specific Chinese cars and trucks, as well as this noxious brew of coal and sulfur and lead-filled gasoline.

It succeeded. Just like the special penny. It had to. Otherwise why the hell would we do it? Not just spend all the time and money, but the sanity of our workers. Why are we constantly reliving something the whole bleeding world is trying to forget? Because it works. Because we help people, we give them exactly what the company name says. We have a seventy-four-percent success rate. Most of our clients are able to rebuild some semblance of a life, to move beyond their tragedy, obtain some semblance of "closure." That's the only reason you'd find someone like me here. This is the best place to work through "rich person's guilt."

We come to the last compartment. Kiersted reaches for his key, then turns to face me. You know, before the war, "rich" used to mean material possessions—money, things. My parents didn't have either, even in a socialist country like Denmark. One of my friends was rich, always paid for everything, even though I never asked him to. He always felt guilty about his wealth, even admitted it to me once, about how "unfair" it was that he had so much. "Unfair." *For the first time since our meeting, his smile fades.* I didn't lose one family member. I mean it. We *all* survived. I could figure out what was coming, as Americans say, "put two and two together." I knew enough to sell my house, buy the tools to survive, and get my family to Svalbard six months before the panic. My wife, our son, our two daughters, my brother, and his whole family—they're all still alive—with three grandchildren and five great nieces and nephews. My friend who had "so much," I treated him last month. They call it "rich person's guilt," because life is the new wealth. Maybe they should call it "rich person's shame," because, for some reason, people like us almost never talk about it. Not even to each other. One time I met with Ingvilde at her shop. She had a picture on her desk, facing away from me when I entered. I didn't knock, so I surprised her a little bit. She snapped that frame down on her desk before she even knew it was me. Instinct. Guilt. Shame. I didn't ask who was in the picture.

We stop at the final compartment. A clipboard rests on the bulkhead next to the hatch, a clipboard holding another legal disclaimer. Kiersted looks at it, then me, uncomfortably.

I apologize. I know you've already signed one, but because you're not an EU citizen, regulations demand that you reread and re-sign another form. The rereading part is a pain in the arse, and if it were up to me, I'd allow you to just sign it, but . . . *His eyes flick to the surveillance camera on the overhead.*

I pretend to read. Kiersted sighs.

I know that a lot of people don't agree with what we do here. They think it's immoral, or at least wasteful. I understand. For a lot of them, not knowing is a gift. It protects them and drives them. They use it to push their lives forward, rebuild both physically and mentally, because they want to be ready for the day when that missing person suddenly walks through the door. For them, limbo is hope, and sometimes, closure is the death of hope.

But what about the other type of survivors, the ones who're paralyzed by limbo? These are the ones who search endlessly through ruins and mass graves and endless, endless lists. These are the survivors who've chosen truth over hope but can't move forward without some physical *proof* of that truth. Of course, what we provide isn't the truth, and they know it, deep down. But they believe it because they want to believe it, just like the ones who look into the void and see hope.

I finish filling out the last page of the form. Kiersted reaches for his key card.

Incidentally we've managed to assemble a basic psychological profile of those who seek our help. They tend to be of an aggressive nature—active, decisive, used to making their own destiny. *His eyes dart sideways to me.* This is a broad generalization, naturally, but for many of them, losing control was the worst part of that time, and this process is as much about regaining that control as it is about saying good-bye.

Kiersted slides his card, the lock flashes from red to green, and the door opens. The compartment I step into smells like sage and eucalyptus, and the sound of waves crashing echoes through bulkhead-mounted speakers. I stare at the subject in front of me. It stares back. It pulls at the restraints, trying to get to me. Its jaw drops open. It moans.

I am not sure how long I stare at the "subject" in front of me. Eventually I turn to Kierstad, nod my approval, and notice the smile return to his face.

The Danish psychiatrist walks to a small locked cabinet on the rear bulkhead. "I see you didn't bring your own."

I shake my head.

Kiersted returns from the cabinet and places a small automatic pistol into my hand. He checks to make sure there is only one round in the chamber, then he steps back, exits the compartment, and closes the hatch behind me.

I center the laser sight on the subject's forehead. It lunges at me, rasping and snapping. I pull the trigger.

AMONG US

BY AIMEE BENDER

I

One zombie met another zombie on the road.

One zombie said to the other zombie: How do you do? Shall we go eat some people?

The second zombie did not answer. They stood for a second, swaying. Then the second zombie leaned forward and took a big bite out of the first zombie's head.

He ate the first zombie over the course of a sunny July afternoon. In a minipark, by a wooden bench. Only one zombie, this second zombie, was at all interested in eating his fellow zombies. Most found that bad-tasting. The idea was to go after live blood, live humans, the zombies like vampires, preying on that which they did not have—the life force of a living being. Dead people eating live, as opposed to live people eating dead. Even plants, one might think, would have greater culinary appeal to a zombie than another rotting zombie corpse. But this was the latest zombie, the newest re-reincarnation of zombie, an evolutionary glitch in the reanimation process, and the eating of his fellow zombies just made him crazier and hungrier. He grew. He roared in the dappled light of the minipark. He doubled into himself.

After all, he had been dead, and then wasn't dead, so he was already being overused as a commodity. Let the poor guy decompose in peace.

II

The salmon farm in Ketchikan, Alaska, ran out of funds. They could not keep feeding their salmon brand-new fish food just made for salmons. So they stirred leftover salmon bits into the salmon food. It seemed like a good idea at the time: The salmon bits were free, because they were taken from the leftover dead salmon guts that had not been good enough to package in tins and send to the humans. But the salmon, when fed salmon, became poisonous to eat. Toxic. People got sick. When investigated, the farm was slapped with a giant lawsuit and has since gone under.

In England, the cows, when fed cow bits, became mad: Cows like to eat grass, not the bonemeal of their cousins. The people who ate the mad cow got sick and died. A sickness in the brain.

III

My friend's mother came over for dinner. She lived across town. She didn't get out much.

My friend's mother usually cooked for herself, but he was worried about her, so all three of us were going out to a restaurant together. She sat on the couch. She was one of those people who did not lean back on couch cushions but sat up perched on the very edge. In another life, she was surely a small bird. She watched out the window at an old man walking down the sidewalk using a silver walker. Then she turned to us, bright-eyed, in her scarf with what looked like hard-boiled eggs on it.

So, she said. What do we want for dinner?

My friend thought about it, tapping his fingers on the table. But I couldn't help cringing, over by the bookshelves. A kind of thick, sludgy rage gargled through me.

My friend was listing restaurants. After ten, he trailed off.

I don't know, I said slowly, when they turned their heads to me. Where do *you* want to go?

We might like Italian, she said cheerfully.

But do *you*? I said. Do *you* want Italian?

She looked at me, quizzical.

Or are you, perhaps, a queen? I asked. My friend shot me a look. She extended her neck, higher.

A queen? she said. I don't understand. If we don't want Italian, what might we like instead? Are we hungry? Do we prefer French?

I ran out of the apartment. I ran screaming down the street. I called her later to apologize. I never asked what they ate.

I V

There is a movie written by an unusual screenwriter from the final year of the previous millennium in which a portal opens in the city and people can slide down it and enter the brain of a famous actor. It is a world unto itself. Later in the movie, the famous actor himself finds the portal and slides down it and enters his own brain. This causes such disruption in the system that while he's in there, everyone forgets how to talk and they can only say his name, over and over again. It is all they know how to say.

V

Usury, says the man on the radio, is money that makes money.

It is money that climbs on top of other money to make more money, but there is no service rendered. The interest rate is exorbitant. Most world religions outlaw it; it is a bad sign of greed, of the avaricious nature of a financial situation gone awry. What people need are services or products: Now those are a worthy exchange. It is, they say, one of the foundations of the current economic crisis, because we are living off debt, off credit-card offers from banks so eager they mail applications addressed to pets, off mortgage-loan mismatching, off corporate loan errors and sketchy pricing for risk, off all these questions about regulation, off mountains of promises made based on air.

V I

The big zombie who ate zombies?

He ate and ate and ate.

But more decay cannot reverse decay, and eventually he grew sick. He was large and used to be strong, and he lay in a park, breathing hard. The other zombies feared him, but when they saw he was ill, they surrounded him in a circle.

They grunted. They shambled. They swayed. After a while, they grew bored and lumbered off. Alone, Big Zombie died, again. He was reanimated shortly after. This time, worse. He was too hungry to look for another zombie, so this time he ate his own arm. His own leg. His own head, all eating, until he started to digest himself, until all that was left was a mouth and a GI tract. A mouth, an esophagus, a stomach, intestines.

VII

And, finally—a true story.

I was at the house of a man who had recently gotten divorced. He was sixty years old, and his wife had kept the household together for forty years, and then all of a sudden decided she was done with him. She left him, all at once. He did not know how to boil an egg. He did not know where to buy toothpaste.

A friend recommended he have people over, since he was dying of loneliness, of the sounds in the new house that felt like the clanging of death bells. At sixty, the rest of his life was a vacancy. He'd met one woman online who seemed like she might be willing to take over his life for him, but the woman moved in after two days and he found her rifling through his wallet and looking too closely at his stock statements, and about money he was clear, so he threw her out. He put her piles of shoes in rows in the hallway. She yelled at him from outside. She forgot his correct name and called him the name of her ex-lover, by accident.

He had five of us over to watch TV together, a show. I knew him from work; others knew him from church. We ate pizza and drank beer and watched TV and talked.

At the end of the show, he looked around the room.

Thank everyone for coming, he said.

We all nodded and smiled.

You're welcome, we said, filing out. Thank you for having us.

But it stuck in my head, a little, walking down the stairs to my car. What had he said?

The show was a series, so we were back again the next week. Each of us needing somewhere to go on Wednesday nights.

Thank everyone for coming, he said again, at the end.

I waited a week, to be sure. The following week, the same.

I drove home. The traffic lights were green. The city, black silhouettes. Golden lights in front windows.

Thanks, I thought. It should have been *thanks*.

Thanks, everyone, for coming.

But he had said: Thank everyone for coming.

Why?

The bugs, inside. The jittery bugs. The lurch, the shamble, the arms, the groan.

Two miles from my apartment, stalled at a red light, I had an idea.

He was a smart man, and English was his first language. He surely knew the correct verb and grammar. He spoke fluidly at all other times. The only explanation I could find was that this is what he had been told to say to guests. Most likely, they had had people over for years. She had invited the people. She had made the food. She had picked out his clothes. At the end, she told him, John, go thank everyone for coming.

And he had so fully stepped out of his own point of view that he simply echoed her words, exactly. He was so far gone from himself that he did not do the natural act of conjugation that would make the words fit his point of view.

They say it's all fantasy—zombies? It's all made-up goofiness? It's all silliness we create for our own delightful fear?

GHOST TRAP

BY RICK HAUTALA

Although it was often part of his job, Jeff Stewart hadn't been expecting to find a body today. It was Saturday morning, and he was doing some diving for his friend and drinking buddy, Mel "Biz" Potter. A storm had passed through the night before, and they were looking for some of Biz's lobster pots that had broken off their buoy ropes in the rough seas. Locals called such lost traps "ghost traps" when they lay on the bottom of the ocean, where a lobster could still scuttle inside. If more than one lobster ended up in a trap, the bigger, stronger one would kill and eat the others, but that only prolonged its captivity until, eventually, it died of starvation.

Even on the sunniest day, there was no light down as deep as Jeff was. Today, following the storm, the sky was as gray as soot, the seas choppy. Even at six or seven fathoms, Jeff could feel the powerful tug of the tide. He'd agreed to help Biz out—like he did once or twice a summer—for the comradeship and the simple pleasure that diving gave him. No matter how much Marcie, his girlfriend, bitched about him screwing around on the one day of the week they had to spend together, Jeff took advantage of any and all excuses to dive. He relished the freedom, the sense of weightlessness and total isolation.

His day job was working search, rescue, and recovery for the U.S. Coast Guard, so Jeff had seen more than his fair share of drowned bodies—"sinkers," as he and his coworkers called them. When this one came into view, illuminated by the diffused beam of Jeff's underwater light, he couldn't help but be startled.

Most drowning victims, if you found them soon enough—say, within twenty-four to forty-eight hours, before the lobsters, crabs, and other scavengers scurrying around on the bottom of the ocean started to consume the dead meat—ended up the same way. Once they were dead, the blood pooled in their rumps and lower legs, weighing them down so they were sitting on the ocean floor with their legs splayed out in front of them. Their arms invariably would be raised and extended, like they were reaching for something to cling to, something solid so they could hoist themselves back up to the surface.

In all his years of diving, the one thing Jeff had never been able to get over—the single most fascinating thing—was the dead person's face . . . especially the eyes. Once the blood drained out of the head and upper body and settled into the lower trunk, the puckered skin turned as white and translucent as marble. Winding traces of veins stood out like faded tattoos just beneath the skin. Of course, someone with darker skin wouldn't be as white as alabaster, but the effect—at least on every body Jeff had ever recovered—was as fascinating as it was gruesome. The eyes—if some sea creatures hadn't gotten at them yet—would be wide open and staring with an expression of stunned surprise. It was as if the victim still couldn't believe he or she had actually drowned.

But it was one thing when Jeff was fifty or more feet below the surface of the ocean looking for a drowning victim. Finding one when he wasn't ready for it sent a startled rush through him, like an electric jolt to the groin. He drew back involuntarily, waving his arms and kicking his legs to keep his orientation. His heart was pounding like a drop-forge hammer, and a thick, salty pressure throbbed behind his eyes. The flashlight almost slipped from his hand, but he clutched it tightly. After the initial shock began to subside, he trained the beam back onto the drowned man. Kicking easily and still trying to force himself to calm down, he approached slowly.

Judging by the clothes on the corpse, he looked like he'd been down here quite a while. Tattered remnants of a plaid work shirt and protective yellow rubber coveralls—something all lobstermen wore when working—were covered with thick strands of green slime and were rotting away. The man was sitting with his legs out in front of him, his toes pointing upward. Jagged black shreds of rubber boots still clung to his feet and lower legs. His arms were extended and swaying from side to side like thick fronds of kelp moved by the deep-sea currents. The man's hands were extended, his fingers hooked. Long yellowed fingernails looking like chipped old porcelain stuck out from the ends of the withered, bone-white hands.

Jeff couldn't help but think the man looked like he had been waiting patiently for him . . . or *someone* . . . to come along and find him in the darkness seven fathoms below the surface.

Tiny pinpricks of light squiggled across Jeff's vision. He realized he was still breathing too fast for safety and consciously slowed his breathing. He willed his racing pulse to slow down while he considered who this might be . . . what might have happened . . . and how long he'd been underwater. To the best of his knowledge, no one had gone missing at sea recently. This man might have been swept overboard during the recent storm and not been reported missing yet, but the condition of his clothes and skin seemed to eliminate that as a possibility. The only people who'd been lost at sea so far this summer season had been a couple of lobstermen out of Vinalhaven, whose bodies had washed up on the Nephews, an island due east of the Cove. Jeff didn't know of anyone else who'd gone missing.

As he drew nearer, Jeff noticed something peculiar. There was something wrapped around the man's waist. It was difficult to tell what, lost as it was in the dark folds of slime and the man's rotting clothes, but it looked like the heavy links of a chain. Following it outward, Jeff found one end of the chain tied to a cement block. Barnacles encrusted the corroded iron and cement block, further evidence that whoever this was, he had been down here for a long, long time.

It finally dawned on him that what was bothering him was something about the man's eyes.

They shouldn't still be there in his head.

No matter how long or short a time someone had been underwater, the eyes were the first to go. Fish and crabs and other ocean scavengers went after the softest, juiciest parts first. After a few days or weeks, the eyeballs would be gone, leaving nothing but empty sockets.

But this man's eyes were still intact, even though he had clearly been underwater long enough for barnacles to attach to the chain and the cement block holding him down.

After swimming around the corpse, taking a last good look at it, Jeff tilted his head back, gave a few powerful kicks, and started back to the surface. He made sure he rose slowly, keeping pace with the bubbles of his exhaled breath. When he broke the surface, he swept his mask back and tore the regulator from his mouth. Biz's boat was less than fifty feet away from where Jeff's diving marker bobbed up and down in the steep swells. He raised a hand and waved while shouting until Biz saw him and started up his engine. Jeff clung to his diving marker until Biz pulled up alongside him and cut the engine.

"Toss me a rope," Jeff said, gasping so hard it hurt his throat. He took in a mouthful of seawater and spit it out. "I gotta go back down."

Biz regarded him quizzically for a moment or two, but he didn't say a word before darting to the cabin and returning with a coil of rope.

"You find a ghost trap?" Biz asked, as he leaned over the side rails and handed the rope to Jeff.

"Worse 'n that," Jeff said. He took in another mouthful of water and couldn't help but swallow some.

Biz's frown deepened.

"There's someone down there," Jeff said.

At first, Biz reacted like he wasn't sure what Jeff meant. Then his eyes widened and he said, "You mean you found a person?"

Jeff nodded grimly.

"I wanna mark him so's we can come back out 'n' find 'im easily. We gotta report this to the state."

"For fuck's sake," Biz said. He didn't look at all pleased to be involved in anything like this, but Jeff ignored him as he fumbled to get the regulator back into his mouth and pulled his mask down. After adjusting everything, he tied one end of the rope to his diving marker and uncoiled the rope. With one last look at Biz, he did a quick surface dive. As he dropped back down into the depths, his heart felt like a cold, tight fist in his chest.

"I'll betcha I know *exactly* who it is."

Like most nights, Jeff was drinking with his buddies down at the Local. He had a glass of beer—his fifth so far tonight—raised halfway to his mouth when Jim "Pappy" Sullivan spoke up. He hadn't even realized Pappy was listening as he told three of his drinking buddies—Ralph, Johnny, and Flip—about what he'd found this morning. Lowering the glass to the bar, Jeff nudged his Red Sox baseball cap back on his head and turned on his barstool to look directly at Pappy.

"You do, do yah?"

"Ay-yuh. Sure as shit."

A wide smile of satisfaction spread across the old man's face. Pappy relished being the center of attention, even though he had a reputation for being full of shit as often as not. Now that he had Jeff and everyone else's attention, he seemed to wait for a cue to continue. When the wait got too long to bear, Jeff said, "So . . . you wanna tell me?"

Pappy grinned from ear to ear, exposing the row of missing teeth on his bottom jaw.

"I'll bet my left nut-sack you found Old Man Crowther."

"I don't want your fuckin' left nut-sack," Jeff said, smirking, "but what makes you so goddamned sure it's Old Man Crowther?"

"How long's he been missing?" Pappy said.

"Damned if I know," Jeff said. "I don't even know who the fuck he is."

An unlit cigarette was stuck behind Pappy's right ear, held in place by a snarl of wiry gray hair. He'd probably bummed it from the barmaid, Shantelle. He reached up and took it, rolling it between his grease-stained fingers as he nodded toward the barroom's back door.

"Step on outside with me whilst I have a smoke," he said, sliding off his barstool, " 'n' I'll tell yah." He paused, cocking his hips to one side as he fished in his jeans pocket for his lighter. "Goddamned fucking law that won't let me smoke in a bar. Like I come here for my goddamned health!"

While this was going on, Jeff glanced back and forth between his friends. They seemed to have no opinion as to what he should do, so he picked up his beer and followed Pappy out the back door. Out behind the Local was a deck that looked out over the harbor. The screen door slammed shut behind them, sounding like a gunshot in the night. The sound made Jeff jump, and he wondered why he was so keyed up. He had enough beer in him to feel convivial, but he was still a little freaked out by what he had found this morning.

By the light of the moon, which was almost full and shining brightly, and the streetlights lining the road leading down to the wharf, Jeff could see the lobster boats at their moorings. Pappy lit up his cigarette and, leaning forward with both elbows resting on the railing, clasped his hands in front of him as though in prayer. The cigarette dangled from his lower lip, sending up a thin curl of smoke, which made him squint. Moths and June bugs buzzed around the single light by the back door, snapping and popping against the screen.

"So tell me," Jeff said, "who the fuck is Old Man Crowther, and why're you so sure it's him?"

Pappy inhaled and blew a billow of smoke from his nostrils without taking the cigarette from his mouth.

"Got to be 'im," he said, the glowing tip of the cigarette bobbing up and down like a firefly in the darkness.

"This sinker I found—he had a length of chain wrapped around his waist. You're saying somebody killed Old Man Crowther and tossed him overboard?"

"Either that or he did it to himself." Pappy puffed some more on his cigarette as though lost in thought.

"Maybe they'll be able to tell when we bring 'im up. How long's this Old Man Crowther been missing?"

Pappy tilted his head to one side and scratched the white beard stubble on his jowls. His fingernails made a loud rasping sound.

"Oh, I'd say it must'a been . . . maybe thirty years or more since he disappeared."

"Thirty years ago . . . I was still in high school," Jeff said. "A body can't last that long down under."

"May've been even longer 'n that, now that I think of it." Pappy turned to Jeff, scowling as threads of smoke rose into his face. " 'Twas back in the early seventies, as I recall."

Jeff considered for a long, silent moment. Pappy finally took the cigarette from his mouth after taking another deep drag and exhaling.

Jeff pursed his lips and shook his head. "No way," he said. "Can't be him. Someone been down there that long, their body'd be long gone. He'd'a been et by scavengers long ago."

Pappy smiled and shook his head as he took one last drag of the cigarette and then snapped the butt out into the darkness. Jeff watched it fly, spinning end over end until it hit the ground in a small shower of sparks.

"I saw the body that's down there," Jeff said, "'n' there's no fuckin' way anyone'd be in that good a condition after thirty years."

"You never knew Old Man Crowther. That old cocker had a hide on him's tough as nails."

"Sorry, Pappy, but it's gotta be someone else. . . ."

Jeff finally noticed how dry his throat was and realized he was still holding on to his beer. When he raised it and took a swallow, his throat made a funny little gulping sound.

"You was a kid back when it happened," Pappy said, "so's probably you don't remember."

There was something in the old man's tone of voice that caught Jeff's attention.

"Remember what?"

"It."

"What do you mean . . . 'it'?"

Pappy sniffed and shook his head from side to side as though amused by some private joke or deeply saddened. He reached up to his ear as if to grab another cigarette, then started scratching his head.

"How old are you?" he asked.

"I was born in sixty-eight," Jeff said.

"Okay, so you would'a been . . ." Pappy did some quick calculations on his fingers. "You'd'a been maybe four or five when it happened."

Jeff was starting to lose his patience. Pappy had a reputation for being full of shit, and he cursed himself for letting himself be suckered in. He was positive the old man was bullshitting him now just to have someone to talk to. There was no way it had been Old Man Crowther's body he'd found today.

From behind him, he could hear the faint strains of laughter from inside the Local. Even though the evening was warm and pleasant, Jeff wanted to go back inside, where there were people and laughter and aimless conversation. But as his gaze drifted down to the harbor and out to sea, he couldn't stop thinking about the corpse he had found this morning. A shiver ran up his spine, like invisible fingers.

"So you don't remember anythin' 'bout the plague we had back then?" Pappy asked.

Jeff almost asked *What plague?* but a faint childhood memory stirred within him.

He'd only been a kid at the time, maybe six or seven years old, but there had been a period of time—it might have been a few months, but it could have been longer or shorter, memory being the tricky thing it is—when his mother wouldn't let him play outside after dark with his friends like he usually did. As big a deal as it had been at the time, it was only a faint memory now, but Jeff recalled hearing talk about how there was something wrong . . . something weird going on in the town. He remembered his parents and maybe some other adults using words like *disease* and *infection* to describe what was going on. He had always assumed there was some type of flu bug going around they wanted to protect him from.

Against his better judgment, instead of going back into the bar, Jeff said, "You gonna tell me about it, or are you gonna just flap your gums?"

Pappy looked at him with a long, vacant stare. His brow wrinkled. One white eyebrow was cocked so high it looked like an albino caterpillar had curled up on his forehead.

"Far's we know, Old Man Crowther was the last one to be infected," Pappy said. His voice was edged with tension. It sounded hollow in the night. "Them was bad times . . . bad times, but you know what folks is like 'round these parts. We ain't gonna talk about it much, and we sure as shit don't want any outsiders talkin' about it."

"But you said Old Man Crowther was infected," Jeff said, surprised at the impatience in his voice. "Infected with *what?*"

He couldn't put out of his mind how much finding that corpse today was bothering him. It was unlike any other body he had ever found.

"You're saying Old Man Crowther got sick with . . . with somethin' so bad he wrapped a length of chain around his waist, tied it to a cement block, and heaved himself overboard?"

"We figure he did it to spare the town more misery . . . to end the situation."

Pappy sighed and then was silent for a long moment as he stared down at the harbor. Finally, he nodded.

"Ay-yuh. That's 'bout the size of it. They found his dory washed up on Black Horse Beach, so everyone figured he must'a done somethin' like that." He turned and looked directly at Jeff with intensity in his eyes that bordered on crazy.

"But you don't know for sure."

Pappy snorted and said, "If'n I was you, I'd do the smart thing and leave 'im down there. We don't need to have that whole fuckin' situation startin' up again. 'Twas hard enough containin' it back in the day. Nowadays—Key-*rist!*" Pappy hocked up a wad of mucus and spit it into the darkness. "With cell phones 'n' the Internet 'n' all, the whole friggin' world'll get involved. Who knows what'll happen then?"

Jeff was struggling to phrase a question from the cascade of thoughts that filled his head, but he drew a blank. He wanted to believe that Pappy, as always, was talking out of his ass, but thinking about that corpse's eyes made him wonder if there might not be something to what the old man was saying.

Before he could get out his first question, Pappy straightened up and said, "Well, I'll be damned, but a powerful thirst has taken hold'a me. Nice chattin' wi'cha, boy-o."

Without another word, he turned and walked back into the Local, the screen door slamming shut behind him. Jeff realized Pappy didn't really know if that's what Old Man Crowther had done. The old man had just been speculating.

Jeff stayed on the back deck a while longer, staring down at the harbor and trying not to let his gaze shift farther out to sea. Moonlight glittered on the dark water like splinters of silver. It was a beautiful view, but he couldn't stop picturing the dead man—whoever the hell he was—sitting on the ocean floor down there in the pitch darkness.

The moment he opened his eyes and saw the sunlight streaming through the bedroom window, Jeff winced. A hot, needle-sharp pain slipped behind his eyes as he rolled over in bed. Disengaging himself from Marcie, he moaned softly, bringing both hands to his forehead as he swung his feet from under the covers and onto the floor. Marcie's eyelids fluttered open for a moment, but then she rolled over onto her side away from him and heaved a sigh.

"Do you *really* have to go this early?" she said, addressing the wall.

"Gotta. I have to work."

"On a freakin' Sunday?"

"Uh-huh, even on a Sunday."

Marcie was silent for a long stretch as Jeff leveraged himself off the bed and scooped up the jeans and socks he'd worn the day before, which were lying in a crumpled heap on the floor by the foot of the bed. After he'd finished getting dressed without a shower—he'd need one for sure after today's dive—he leaned over Marcie and kissed her on the shoulder. She didn't respond. He knew she couldn't have fallen back asleep that fast, but he wasn't going to stir things up just now. She could be mad at him all she wanted. It wasn't just that he had to dive today. He *had* to go back down there to find out exactly who that man was at the bottom of the sea.

By the time he arrived at the dock, the place was already a media circus. Reporters, TV camera crews, and assorted rubberneckers lined the stone wharf and dock, making it next to impossible for Jeff to make his way down the gangplank with his diving equipment to the waiting patrol boat. A couple of reporters shouted out questions to him, but he pushed past them, ignoring them.

"Word got out quick," Jeff said, as he heaved his air tanks onto the boat.

Mark Curtis, one of the Coast Guardsmen, frowned and shook his head.

"Wouldn't be so bad," he said, "if someone had kept his goddamned mouth shut at the Local last night."

Chastened, Jeff climbed aboard. The captain, a guy from Belfast named Harvey Rollins, gunned the engine. Mark and the other crewmen cast off, and the boat started out, leaving behind a heavy, curling wake that rocked the dock.

After they got to the diver's marker Jeff had left yesterday, he made one final check of his equipment in preparation for going overboard. His diving partner today, as usual, was Wesley Evans, who was married and lived in Tenants Harbor. They had dived together for more than ten years. Perhaps because they were so used to communicating with each other by hand gestures below water, they hardly ever spoke above water. But they trusted that each of them knew intuitively what the other was thinking or going to do underwater. They were a good team, even though it struck Jeff as rather peculiar that they didn't hang out together when they were off duty.

Once he and Wes were ready, after nodding to each other they plunged overboard. Even in June, the ocean water was chilly, but Jeff's dry suit protected him from the initial cold shock. A wave splashed him full in the face, sending a bracing chill through him. After making sure his regulator was working properly, he swam out to the diver's marker and grasped the rope he'd tied off yesterday. Running it through one rubber-gloved hand, he kicked and went under, sinking into the embracing darkness with Wes a short distance behind. The daylight shimmering above them quickly collapsed, plunging them into a preternatural gloom, which gradually blended into an inky darkness below. Jeff and Wes switched on their flashlights, illuminating the water below with a diffused glow.

Down . . . down they went, and the deeper they went, the more a nameless apprehension filled Jeff. He knew what he was going to see when he got to the end of the rope, and he was dreading it. He was wondering if he could handle seeing the dead man's empty gaze again. Overnight, especially after talking to Pappy, his memory of what he had found got magnified by his imagination. He tried to prepare himself mentally for what he was about to see, but he still wasn't ready for it when the drowned man's figure came into view.

Jeff hesitated, treading water several feet above the ocean floor. Wes stopped swimming, too, and they looked at each other for a lengthening moment, neither one of them indicating what they should do next. Jeff thought he saw a cloud of confusion in his diving partner's eyes, and he experienced a sudden, urgent desire to go back to the surface and talk to Wes before they proceeded. He felt he needed to prepare him for what he was about to see.

But the moment passed without any communication between them, and they continued on down to the ocean floor. Their movements raised silt from the seabed, causing swirls of sand to rise like dark, billowing clouds that shimmered with flakes of silica in the beams of their flashlights.

Jeff willed his pulse to slow down as he swept his light over the drowned man until it came to rest on the chain wrapped around the man's waist. He couldn't bring himself to look at the man's eyes.

Not yet. With a nod and a quick hand gesture, Jeff indicated to Wes that removing the chain from the block should be their first order of business, but for some reason, Jeff couldn't force himself to move any closer to the corpse. He couldn't shake the eerie feeling that the man was staring at him through the darkness.

Jeff jerked back when he swung his flashlight around to illuminate the man's face. He told himself it *had* to be a trick of the light and shadow . . . or the way the man's head was moving ever so slightly in the deep currents . . . or . . . or *something*. Whatever it was, Jeff was convinced that as he moved, so too the dead man's eyes moved, tracking him with a dull, blank stare.

Wes had swum away from the body and was leaning over, inspecting the cement block tied to one end of the chain. It was sunk deep in the sand and draped with seaweed and slime. As he lifted the chain and shook it, the dull clanking sounds the links made was transmitted through the water. Jeff glanced at his diving partner but then looked back at the drowned man.

His fear was steadily winding up into a feeling of outright dread bordering on panic. He reminded himself that losing focus underwater was *always* dangerous. He had to get his shit together—*now*—or else both he and Wes could end up in real trouble. It didn't help to remind himself that he had a simple job to do. All he had to do was release this drowned man from the chain holding him down and bring him up to the surface. Let the authorities handle it from there. He had done this too many times to count, but never, *never* had he experienced such unnerving feelings as he was having now.

He was still desperate to talk to Wes, if only to calm his own irrational fears. Should he motion to his partner that they had to surface so they could plan what their next steps would be?

Jeff knew that would be foolish.

This was a simple dive and recovery. Wes and everyone on the Coast Guard boat might think he was losing his nerve. He had to get a grip on himself.

Wes's back was turned to the corpse as he fiddled with the chain, trying to release it from the cement block. The dead man's arms were still extended, waving gently from side to side in the tidal surge, but it looked for all the world like he was straining forward against his restraints, reaching out to catch hold of Wes from behind while he wasn't looking.

Jesus, stop it! Jeff cautioned himself.

He should have been helping Wes unloosen the chain, not hanging back like this, letting his imagination get carried away with such foolish fears. Once that end of the chain was free, it would be a simple matter to unwind it from the corpse's waist and then, slowly, carefully, bring him up to the surface.

It was easy, a simple, clean job a rookie could do blindfolded, but Jeff was ashamed that—for whatever reason—he was allowing his fear to take such firm hold of him. With a new determination, he moved over to Wes, who had just about worked the chain free. With Jeff's help, it was only a matter of a few more seconds before they finished untying the cement block.

While they worked together, though, Jeff hadn't been able to shake the feeling that the whole time their backs were turned to the corpse, the dead man was staring at them, watching, studying their every move. And Jeff couldn't stop wondering if the drowned man, who-ever he was—whether he was Old Man Crowther or some other luckless fool who had been murdered or decided to end it all because of a broken heart or trouble with the IRS—might be angry at them for disturbing his final resting place. The chain and cement block certainly indicated how much he wanted to stay on the bottom of the ocean.

What Pappy had told him last night about the strange plague that had afflicted the town years ago came back to Jeff. He wondered if it was possible that this man had been infected by whatever the disease was and had drowned himself to end it all—for himself and, possibly, for the entire town.

Like a mummy's curse, Jeff thought, *some things are best left un-disturbed.*

But he couldn't leave now, not once the government was involved.

He never should have told anyone—not even Biz—what he had found.

He should have left well enough alone.

If he hadn't been so startled and, yes, even scared yesterday, he might have thought it through and kept his goddamned mouth shut.

But now, no matter what else happened, he and Wes had to bring this guy back to the surface so the state medical examiner could determine what had happened to him.

With apprehension winding up in his gut like a steel spring, Jeff turned back to the body. Wes approached it as if there was nothing unusual going on, but Jeff stayed back, determined to be cautious.

The drowned man's upraised arms swung around to the left side, toward Wes. They moved like dual needles of a compass being drawn to true north. Wes seemed not to notice. He was bending down, unwinding the length of chain from around the corpse's waist. Silt swirled in thick clouds, mixing with the bubbles coming from his respirator. The heavy chain clinked as the links, long rusted into place, shifted free. Jeff could see that Wes was struggling with it, but he didn't move to help.

He couldn't.

The beam of his flashlight was trained on the dead man's face, and he gazed steadily into the drowned man's eyes.

They were moving.

They jerked spastically from side to side, glaring with a cold, glassy stare that suddenly fixed on the back of Wes's bowed head.

"Look out!" Jeff yelled, but all that came out was an explosion of bubbles spewing out from around his regulator. As the corpse's hands reached out and grabbed Wes by the back of the neck, hooked fingers dug like hawk's talons into Wes's shoulders. They dimpled the material of the dry suit for a second or two and then ripped into it.

Wes reacted instantly, but Jeff knew it was already too late. The yellowed fingernails raked across Wes's back, shredding the dry suit and cutting it into ragged black ribbons. Bright red billows of blood spewed forth, looking like the sudden eruption of a volcano. Wes started thrashing around, flipping over as he tried to fight back. One hand went to the back of his neck, as if checking the damage; the other hand waved in front of his face as he fended off his attacker.

But Wes couldn't break free of the dead man's grasping hands. Yellowed fingernails raked across his face, sweeping away his mask and regulator. A blast of bubbles exploded from Wes's mouth, and Jeff could faintly hear the terrified screams. With another sweep of the dead man's hands, Wes's face was transformed into a tangle of shredded pink meat and exposed bone. Blood oozed from the wounds in thick, spiraling red ribbons that drifted away on the current.

Finally finding his courage, Jeff propelled himself forward. Making sure to keep a safe distance from the dead man, he grabbed Wes around the waist and yanked him back. The bubbles of escaping air mixed with swirling silt and clouds of blood, making it all but impossible for Jeff to see, but he knew which way was up. Without air, he knew he had to get Wes up to the surface as fast and as safely as he could.

Otherwise, he would die.

They would both die.

Struggling to contain his panic, Jeff clasped Wes to his chest and started swimming. He hardly noticed it when something caught hold of his left leg and held it for just a second or two. When he pulled away, a stinging sensation like a bee sting pinched his left calf muscle, but he ignored it as he swam toward the surface holding Wes.

It took effort not to surface too fast. There was no sense risking either him or Wes getting the bends. Taking the regulator from his mouth, he forced it into Wes's mouth, but Wes was either unconscious or already dead. His motionless lips were as pale as snow. They didn't move. His eyes were glazed over with a dull, milky stare.

The swim to the surface seemed to last forever, but the water gradually lightened, and before long, shimmering blue sky and a burning dot of sunlight sparkled above. Jeff could see the dark, hulking wedge of the underside of the Coast Guard boat, and he made his way toward it. When his head broke the surface, he let go a roar as he inhaled a lungful of air. It took a near superhuman effort to swim over to the side of the boat and the diving platform. Several crewmen leaned over to help him get Wes onboard.

"What the fuck?" the captain shouted, as Jeff heaved himself up out of the water and climbed over the gunwales and onto the deck. Several crewmen were already tending to Wes, but Jeff feared the worst.

"You guys run into a shark down there?" one of the crewmen asked.

"Jesus!" another crewman said. "Looks like someone went at him with a chainsaw."

Kneeling down on the deck, Jeff and the men rolled Wes over onto his back. Blood was flowing from the wounds on his neck and face, dripping in large splashes onto the deck.

The captain went back to the cabin and started the engine and revved it. Within seconds, the cutter was speeding across the water, heading back to harbor. Looking down at Wes's pale, motionless face, Jeff shivered and shook his head.

"No need to hurry," he said to Mark Curtis, who was still kneeling beside Wes's motionless form. "He's gone."

"Christ on a crutch," Curtis said, lowering his gaze and shaking his head from side to side. Then he turned to Jeff and pointed at Jeff's left leg.

Jeff looked and saw, through the gap in his dry suit, the flap of water-puckered skin, already looking an angry red with infection. Blood ran in a thick, single stream down to his ankle and onto the deck.

"Looks like you got cut, too," Curtis said, frowning as he looked at Jeff's wound. "What the fuck happened down there?"

Shock hit Jeff when a cold sting reached deep into him, striking all the way to the bone. Within seconds, the coldness radiated up his leg and into his groin and chest, where it started to squeeze his heart. His hands and feel were already growing numb.

Jeff stared blankly at the wound, barely aware, as Curtis knelt down beside him and inspected it more closely.

"Jesus," Curtis said. "I'll get the medical kit so we can get some antiseptic on that and bandage you up. You don't want it getting infected."

"Infected," Jeff said, his voice an empty echo.

"That's a helluva gash you got there. We should get you to the hospital and have someone throw a few stitches into that to close it up."

Jeff was shaking his head from side to side as a terrible, sad knowledge filled him.

"It's already too late," he said, as the dull heaviness spread through his body, dulling his mind.

"Huh? What do you mean, 'too late'?" Curtis asked. "It ain't nothing but a scratch."

But Jeff lowered his head and stared at the blood running in a ruby red stream down the slick black surface of his dry suit. Already, it felt like his guts were filled with an iciness that was eating him from the inside out. His vision was getting cloudy, and the buzzing of the boat's engine was unbearably loud.

"It's the plague," Jeff said in a low, hollow tone. "It's back."

As the boat sped back to the dock, he gazed across the expanse of blue water at the approaching town. The glaring white steeple of the Congregational church stood out against the sky. The scene was gorgeous, but an immense sadness filled him. He was tormented by a question: Would he be able to do what Old Man Crowther had done?

Would he have the balls to do what was necessary to protect the town?

As soon as the boat got back to the dock, he would have to find a cement block and a length of chain and head right back out to sea.

THE STORM DOOR

BY TAD WILLIAMS

Nightingale did not take the first cab he saw when he stepped out into the rainy San Francisco streets. He never did. Some might call it superstition, but in his profession the line between superstitions and rules of survival was rather slender. He stepped back onto the curb to avoid the spray of water as the second cab pulled up in response to his wave. Paranormal investigators didn't make enough money to ruin a pair of good shoes for no reason.

Somebody should have warned me that saving the world from unspeakable horrors is like being a teacher—lots of job satisfaction, but the money's crap.

"Thirty-three Gilman Street," he told the driver, an ex-hippie on the edge of retirement age, with shoulder-length gray hair straggling out from under his Kangol hat and several silver rings on the fingers holding the wheel. "It's off Jones."

"You got it." The driver pulled back into traffic, wipers squeaking as city lights smeared and dribbled across the glass beside Nightingale's head. "Helluva night," he said. "I know we need the rain and everything, but . . . shit, man."

Nathan Nightingale had spent so much of the past week in a small overheated and nearly airless room that he would have happily run through this downpour naked, but he only nodded and said, "Yeah. Helluva night."

"Gonna be a lot more before it's over, too. That's what they said. The storm door's open." The driver turned down the music a notch. "Kind of a weird expression, huh? Makes it sound like they're"—he lifted his fingers in twitching monster-movie talons—"*coming to get us*. Whooo! I mean, it's just clouds, right? It's nature."

"This? Yeah, it's just nature," agreed Nightingale, his thoughts already drawn back to that small room, those clear, calm, terrifying eyes. "But sometimes even nature can be unnatural."

"Huh? Oh, yeah, I guess so. Good one." But it was clear by his tone that the driver feared he'd missed the point.

"That's it—the tall house there."

The driver peered out the window. "Whoa, that's a spooky one, man. You sure you gonna be okay? This is kind of a tough neighborhood."

"I'll be fine, thanks," said Nightingale. "I've been here before; it was kind of my second home."

"If you say so." The driver called just before Nightingale slammed the door, "Hey, remember about that storm door. Better get an umbrella!"

Nightingale raised his hand as the man drove off. *An umbrella.* He almost smiled, but the wet night was getting to him. *If only all problems were that easy to solve.*

As he pressed the button beside the mailbox, lightning blazed overhead, making it seem as though one had caused the other. A moment later the thunder crashed down so near that he did not hear the sound of the door being buzzed open but felt the handle vibrating under his hand.

The light was out in the first-floor stairwell, and no lights were on at all on the second floor, what Uncle Edward called "the showroom," although no one ever saw it but a few old, trusted collector friends. Enough of the streetlight's glow leaked in that Nightingale could see the strange silhouettes of some of the old man's prize possessions—fetish dolls and funerary votives and terra-cotta tomb statuettes, a vast audience of silent, wide-eyed shapes watching Nightingale climb the stairs. It was an excellent collection, but what made it truly astounding were the stories behind the pieces, most of them dark, many of them horrifying. In fact, it had been his godfather's arcane tales and bizarre trophies that had first lured Nightingale onto his odd career path: At an age when most boys wanted to be football players or firemen, young Nate had decided he wanted to hunt ghosts and fight demons. Later, when others were celebrating their first college beer-busts, Nightingale had already attended strange ceremonies on high English moors and deep in Thai jungles and Louisiana bayous. He had heard languages never shaped for the use of human tongues, had seen men die for no reason and others live when they should have been dead. But through the years, when the unnatural things he saw and felt and learned overwhelmed him, he always came back here for his godfather's advice and support. This was one of those times. In fact, this was probably the worst time he could remember.

Strangely, the third floor of the house was dark, too.

"Edward? Uncle Edward? It's me, Nathan. Are you here?" Had the old man forgotten he was coming and gone out with his care-taker Jenkins somewhere? God forbid, a medical emergency . . . Nightingale stopped to listen. Was that the quiet murmuring of the old man's breathing machine?

Something stirred on the far side of the room, and his hackles rose; his hand strayed to his inside coat pocket. A moment later the desk lamp clicked on, revealing the thin, lined face of his godfather squint-ing against the sudden light. "Oh," Edward said, taking a moment to find the air to speak. "Guh-goodness! Nate, is that you? I must have dozed off. When did it get so dark?"

Relieved, Nightingale went to the old man and gave him a quick hug, being careful not to disturb the tracheotomy cannula or the ven-tilator tubes. As always, Edward Arvedson felt like little more than a suit full of bones, but somehow he had survived in this failing condi-tion for almost a decade. "Where's Jenkins?" Nightingale asked. "It gave me a start when I came up and the whole house was dark."

"Oh, I had him take the night off, poor fellow. Working himself to death. Pour me a small sherry, will you?—there's a good man—and sit down and tell me what you've learned. There should be a bottle of Manzanilla already open. No, don't turn all those other lights on. I find I'm very sensitive at the moment. This is enough light for you to find your way to the wet bar, isn't it?"

Nightingale smiled. "I could find it without any light at all, Uncle Edward."

When he'd poured a half glass for the old man and a little for him-self as well, Nightingale settled into the chair facing the desk and looked his mentor up and down. "How are you feeling?"

Arvedson waved a dismissive hand. "Fine, fine. Never felt better.

And now that we're done with that nonsense, tell me your news, Nate. What happened? I've been worrying ever since you told me what you thought was going on."

"Well, it took me a while to find a volunteer. Mostly because I was trying to avoid publicity, you know, all that 'Nightingale, Exorcist to the Stars' nonsense."

"You shouldn't have changed your name: It sounds like a Hollywood actor now. Your parents wouldn't have approved, anyway. What was wrong with Natan Näktergal? It was good enough for your father."

He smiled. "Too old country, Uncle Edward. Remember, being well-known gets me into a lot of places. It also leads people to misjudge me."

Arvedson made a face. He still hadn't touched his sherry. "Fine. I'm also old country, I suppose. I should be grateful you even visit. Tell me what happened."

"I'm trying to. As I said, it wouldn't have done to recruit just anyone. Ideally, I needed someone with special training, but who gets trained for something like this? I figured that my best bet was through my Tibetan contacts. Tibetan Buddhists spend years studying the Bardo Thodol, preparing to take the journey of dying, which gave me a much larger group to choose from. I finally settled on a man in Seattle named Geshe, who had pancreatic cancer. He'd refused pain relief, and the doctors felt certain he only had a few days left when I met him, but he was remarkably calm and thoughtful. I told him what I wanted and why, and he said yes."

"So you had found your . . . what was your word? Your 'necronaut.' "

Nightingale nodded. "That's what I called it before I met Geshe—it sounded better than 'mineshaft canary.' After I got to know him it, it seemed a little glib. But he was precisely the sort of person I was looking for—a man trained almost since childhood to die with his eyes and mind open."

Lightning flashed and a peal of thunder shivered the windows. In the wake, another wash of rain splattered against the glass. "Filthy weather," said Arvedson. "Do you want another drink before you start? You'll have to get it yourself, of course, since we don't have Jenkins."

"No, I'm fine." Nightingale stared at his glass. "I'm just thinking." Lightning flashed again, and so he waited for the thunder before continuing. "You remember how this started, of course. Those earliest reports of spontaneous recovery by dying patients. Well, it didn't seem like anything I needed to pay attention to. But then that one family whose daughter went into sudden remission from leukemia after the last rites had already been said—"

"I remember. Very young, wasn't she? Nine?"

"Yes, a few weeks before her tenth birthday. But of course what caught my attention was when the parents started claiming it wasn't their daughter at all, that she'd changed in ways that no illness could explain. But when I got in to see the child, she was asleep, and although she looked surprisingly healthy compared to my general experience with possession cases, I couldn't get any kind of feeling from her one way or another. When I tried to contact the family a few days later, they'd moved and no one could find them.

"There were others also, too many to be coincidence, most of them unknown to the general public. The greatest hindrance in these situations is the gutter press, of course: Any real study, let alone any chance to help the victims and their families, is destroyed by the sort of circus they create. These days, with television and the Internet, it's even worse. If I don't strenuously keep my comings and goings a secret, I wind up with cameras in my face following me everywhere and looking over my shoulder."

"They are vermin," said Edward Arvedson with feeling.

"In any case, when I talked to you, I had just learned of an accident victim in Minnesota who had recovered from a coma and, like the girl in Southern California, seemed to have undergone a complete personality shift. He had been a mild and soft-spoken churchgoer, but now he was a violent, alcoholic bully. His wife of twenty-four years had divorced him; his children no longer saw him. The front yard of his house in Bloomington was a wreck, and when he opened the door, the stink of rot and filth just rolled out. I only saw him for a few seconds through the chain on his front door, but what I witnessed was definitely madness, a sort of . . . emotionless focus that I've only seen in the criminally insane. That doesn't prove anything, of course. Brain damage can do that, and he'd certainly been badly injured. But he *recognized* me."

"You told me when you called," said Arvedson. "I could tell it upset you."

"Because it wasn't like he'd seen my picture in the *Enquirer*, but like he *knew* me. Knew me and hated me. I didn't stay there long, but it wasn't just seeing the Minnesota victim that threw me. I'd never heard of possessions happening at this rate, or to people so close to death. It didn't make sense!"

"It has my attention, too," Edward said. "But what I want to hear now is what happened with your Buddhist gentleman."

Nightingale let out a breath. He swallowed the last of his sherry. "Right. Well, Geshe was a very interesting man, an artist and a teacher. I wish I could have met him at a different time, but even in our short acquaintance he impressed me and I liked him. That's why what happened was so disturbing.

"He had checked out of the hospital to die at home. He'd lost his wife a few years earlier and they'd had no children, so although some of his students and colleagues came by to sit with him from time to time, at the end there was only his friend Joseph, an American Buddhist, and the hospice nurse who checked in on him once a day. And me, of course. Geshe and I didn't speak much—he had to work too hard to manage the pain—but as I said, he impressed me. During the long days in his apartment, I spent a great deal of time looking at his books and other possessions, which is as good a way to get to know someone as talking with them. Also, I saw many of his own works of art, which may be an even better way to learn about another human being. He made beautiful Buddhist thangkas, meditation paintings.

"As Geshe began to slip away, Joseph read the Bardo Thodol to him. I've never spent much time studying it, myself. I think that hippie-ish Tibetan Book of the Dead reputation put me off when I was younger, and these days I don't really need to know the nuts and bolts of any particular religious dogma to work with the universal truths behind them all. But I have to say that hearing it and living with it, even as Geshe was *dying* with it, opened my eyes."

"There is great truth at the heart of all the great faiths," Arvedson said solemnly.

"Yes, but what I truly came to admire was the calmness of the people who wrote the bardos—the practicality, I suppose, is the best word. It's a very practical book, the Bardo Thodol. A road map. A set of travel tips. 'Here's what's going to happen now that you're dead. Do this. Don't do that. Everything will be okay.' Except that this time it wasn't.

"The famous teacher Chögyam Trungpa Rinpoche said the best thing we can do for the dying and the newly dead is maintain an atmosphere of calmness, and that's certainly what Geshe seemed to have around him at the end. It was raining outside most of that week, but quietly. Joseph read the bardos over and over while he and I took turns holding Geshe's hand. With my special sensitivities, I was beginning to sense something of what he was sensing—the approach of the Great Mystery, the crossing, whatever you want to call it—and of course it troubled me deep down in my bones and guts. But Geshe wasn't frightened in the least. All those years of training and meditation had prepared him.

"It was fascinating to see how the dying soul colors the experience, Uncle Edward. As I said, I have never delved too deeply into Tibetan Buddhism, yet the version of dying I experienced through Geshe was shaped so strongly by that tradition that I could not feel it any other way. It was as real as you and I sitting here in the dark, listening to the wind and the rain." Nightingale paused for a moment while the storm rattled the windows of the old house. "The thousands of gods, which are one god, which is the light of the universe . . . I can't explain. But touching Geshe's thoughts as he began his journey—although I felt only the barest hint of what he felt—was like riding a roller coaster through a kaleidoscope, but simultaneously falling through an endless, dark, silent void."

"'When your body and mind separate, the *dharmata* will appear, pure and clear yet hard to discern, luminous and brilliant, with terrifying brightness, shimmering like a mirage on a plain,'" Arvedson quoted. "At least, that's what the bardo says."

"Yes." Nightingale nodded. "I remember hearing it then and understanding it clearly, even though the words I heard were Tibetan. Joseph had begun the Chikkhai bardo, you see—the bardo of dying. In the real world, as we sometimes think of it, Geshe had sunk so far into himself he was no longer visibly breathing. But I was not really beside him in that little room in Seattle, although I could still hear Joseph's voice. Most of me was *inside*—deep in the experience of death with Geshe.

"I could feel him, Uncle Edward, and in a way I could see what he saw, hear what he heard, although those aren't quite the right words. As the voices of people I did not know echoed around us—mostly Geshe's friends and relations and loved ones, I suspect, for I do not think he had many enemies—he and I traveled together through a misty forest. It seemed to me a bit like some of the wild lands of the Pacific Northwest, but more mountainous, as if some of Geshe's Tibetan heritage was seeping through as well."

"Climbing," said Edward Arvedson quietly.

"Yes, the part of the afterlife journey the Egyptians called "the Ladder" and the Aztecs thought of as the beginning of the soul's four-year journey to Mictlan. I've never dared hold a connection with a dying soul as long as I did with Geshe, and going so deep frightened me, but his calm strength made it possible. We did not speak, of course—his journey, his encounters, were his alone, as each of ours will be someday—but I felt him there beside me as the dark drew in.

"I won't tell you everything I experienced now, but I will tell you someday soon, because it was a researcher's dream come true—the death experience almost firsthand. To make the story short, we passed through the first darkness and saw the first light, which the bardos call the soft light of the gods and which they counsel the dead soul to avoid. It was very attractive, like a warm fire to someone lost in the night, and I was feeling very cold, very far from comfort and familiar things—and remember, *I* had a body to go back to! I can only imagine what it seemed like to Geshe, who was on a one-way journey, but he resisted it. The same with what the bardo calls the 'soft light of the hell-beings.' I could feel him yearning toward it, and even to me it seemed soothing, alluring. In the oldest Tibetan tradition, the hot hells are full of terrors—forests of razor-leaved trees, swamps bobbing with decomposing corpses—but these aspects are never seen until it's too late, until the attractions of one's own greed and anger have pulled the dying soul off the path.

"But Geshe overcame these temptations and kept on moving toward the harsher light of truth. He was brave, Edward, so brave! But then we reached the smoky yellow light, the realm of what the bardo calls *pretas*—"

"The hungry ghosts."

"Yes, the hungry ghosts. Found in almost every human tradition. Those who did not go on. Those who can't let go of anger, hatred, obsession . . ."

"Perhaps simply those who want more life," Arvedson suggested.

Nightingale shook his head. "That makes them sound innocent, but they're far from that. Corpse-eating *jikininki*, ancient Rome's lemures, the *grigori* of the Book of Enoch—almost every human tradition has them. Hell, I've *met* them, although never in their own backyard like this. You remember that thing that almost killed me in Freiberg?"

"I certainly do."

"That was one of them, hitchhiking a ride in a living body. Nearly ripped my head off before I got away. I still have the scars."

The nighttime city waited now between waves of the storm. For a moment it was quiet enough in the room for Nightingale to hear the fan of his godfather's ventilator.

"In any case, that smoky yellow light terrified me. The bardo says it's temptation itself, that light, but maybe it didn't tempt me because I wasn't dying. Instead it just made me feel frightened and sick, if you can be sick without a body. I could barely sense Geshe, but I knew he was there and experiencing something very different. Instead of continuing toward the brilliant white light of compassion, as the bardo instructed, this very compassionate man seemed to hesitate. The yellow light was spreading around us like something toxic diffusing through water. Geshe seemed confused, stuck, as though he fought against a call much stronger than anything I could sense. I could feel something else too, something alien to both of us, cold and strong and . . . yes, and *hungry*. God, I've never sensed hunger like that, a bottomless need like the empty chill of space sucking away all living warmth."

Nightingale sat quietly for a long moment before he spoke again. "But then, just when I was fighting hardest to hang on to my connection to Geshe, it dissolved and he was gone. I'd lost touch with him. The yellow light was all around me, strange and greasy . . . repulsive, but also overwhelming.

"I fell out. No, it was more like I was shoved. I tumbled back into the real world, back into my body. I couldn't feel Geshe anymore. Joseph had stopped reading the Chikkhai bardo and was staring in alarm. Geshe's body, which hadn't moved or showed any signs of life in some time, was suddenly in full-on Cheyne-Stokes respiration, chest hitching, body jerking: He almost looked like he was convulsing. But Joseph swore to me later on that Geshe had stopped breathing half an hour earlier, and I believe him.

"A moment later Geshe's eyes popped open. I've seen stranger things, but it still startled me. He had been dead, Uncle Edward, really dead, I swear he had. Now he was looking at me—but it wasn't Geshe anymore. I couldn't prove it, of course, but I had touched this man's soul, traveled with him as he passed over, the most intimate thing imaginable, and this just wasn't him.

"'No, I will not die yet,' he said. The voice sounded like his, but strong, far too strong for someone who had been in periodic breathing only a minute earlier. 'There are still things for me to do on this earth,' he said. It was the eyes, though. That same cold, flat stare that I'd seen through the doorway in Minnesota, the one I've seen before in other possession cases, but there was none of the struggle I'd seen in classic possession, no sense of the soul and body fighting against an interloper. One moment it was Geshe, a spiritual man, an artist; the next moment it was . . . someone else. Someone as cold and detached as a textbook sociopath.

"He closed his eyes then and slept, or pretended to, but already he looked healthier than he had since I met him. I couldn't tell Joseph that I thought his friend was possessed—what a horrible thing to say to someone already dealing with several kinds of trauma!—and I didn't know what else to do, what to think. I sat there for most of an hour, unable to think of anything to do. At last, when the nurse came and began dealing with this incredible turn of medical events, I went out to get a drink. All right, I had a few, then went home and slept like a dead man myself.

"I should never have left them, Edward. When I went back the next day, the apartment was empty. A few weeks later I received an e-mail from Joseph—or at least from Joseph's address—saying that after his miraculous recovery, Geshe wanted to travel to Tibet, the place of his heritage. I've never heard from either of them since."

The lightning, absent for almost a quarter of an hour, suddenly flared, turning the room into a flat tableau of black-and-white shapes. The thunder that followed seemed to rock the entire building. The light on Edward Arvedson's desk flickered once, then went out, as did the lights on his ventilator. Through the windows Nightingale could see the houses across the street had gone black as well. He jumped up, suddenly cold all over. His father's oldest friend and his own most trusted advisor was about to die of asphyxiation while he watched helplessly.

"Good God, Edward, the electricity . . . !"

"Don't . . . worry . . ." Arvedson wheezed. "I have a . . . standby . . . generator."

A moment later Nightingale felt rather than heard something begin to rumble somewhere in the house below, and the desk light flickered back on, although the houses across the street remained dark. "There," said his godfather. "You see, young Natan? Not such an old-fashioned fool after all, eh? I am prepared for things like this. Power for the street will be back on soon; it happens a lot in this ancient neighborhood. Now, tell me what you think is happening."

Nightingale sat back, trying to regain his train of thought. If only the old man wasn't so stubborn about living on his own with only Jenkins—no spring lamb himself—for company.

"Right," he said at last. "Well, I'm sure you're thinking the same thing as me, Uncle Edward. Somehow these predatory souls or spirits have found a way to possess the bodies of the dying. Which would be bad enough, but it's the incredible frequency with which it seems to be happening. I can't possibly investigate them all, of course, but if even half the reports that reach me are real, it's happening all over the world, several times a day."

The rain was back now, lashing the windows and tattooing the roof of Edward's Victorian house. When the old man spoke, there was an unfamiliar tone in his voice. "You are . . . frightened, my dear Natan."

"Yes, Uncle Edward, I am. I've never been this frightened, and I've seen a lot. It's as if something fundamental has broken down, some wall between us and the other side, and now the living are under attack. What did the cab driver say to me on the way over, babbling about the weather—'the storm door is open' . . . ? And I'm afraid the storms are just going to keep coming thicker and faster until all our houses are blown down."

"But why? And why now?"

"Why? Because they've always been there—the hungry ones, the envious things that hate us because we can still breathe and sing and love. Do they want that back, or do they just want to keep us from having it? I don't know. And why now? I don't know that either. Perhaps some universal safeguard has stopped working, or these entities have learned something they didn't know before."

"Then here is the most important question, Nate. What are you going to do about it, now that you know? What can one person do?"

"Well, make sure it isn't just one person trying to deal with it, to begin with. You and I know lots of people who don't think I'm a charlatan—brave people who study this sort of thing, who fight the good fight and know the true danger. More than a few of us have dedicated our lives to keeping the rest of humanity safe, without reward or thanks. Now I have to alert them all, if they haven't discovered this already." He stood and began to pace back and forth before the desk. "And to make sure the word gets out, I'll use the very same tabloid vultures that you and I despise so much. They'll do good without knowing it. Because for every thousand people who'll read headlines that say things like 'So-Called Demon Hunter Claims Dead Are Invading the Living World' and laugh at it as nonsense, one or two will understand . . . and will heed the warning." He moved to the window, looked out into the darkness. "We can only hope to hold these hungry ghosts at bay if every real paranormal researcher, exorcist, and sympathetic priest we can reach will join us—every collector you know, every student of the arcane, every adventurer behind the occult lines, all of those soldiers of the light that the rest of society dismiss as crazy. This will be our great war."

Nightingale turned and walked back to his chair. "So there you have it, Uncle Edward. I'll spread the word. You spread the word, too. Call in old favors. If enough of us hear the truth, we may still be able to get the storm door shut again."

The old man was silent for a long time as thunder rolled away into the distance.

"You're a brave young man, Nate," he said at last. "Your parents would be proud of you. I'm going to have to think for a while about the best way to help you, and though it embarrasses me to admit it, I also need some rest. You'll forgive me—I get tired so quickly. I'll be all right until Jenkins comes back in a few hours. You can let yourself out, can't you?"

"Of course, Uncle Edward." He went to the old man and gave him a quick hug, then kissed his cool, dry cheek. He carried his empty sherry glass to the sideboard. "Now that I'm back in town, I'll be by to see you again tomorrow. Good night." On his way to the door, Nightingale stopped and held his fingers up to catch the light from the desk lamp and saw that the darkness on the tips of them was dust.

"Tell Jenkins he's getting sloppy," he said. "I can't imagine you giving him a night off in the old days without finishing the cleaning. Looks like he hasn't dusted in weeks."

"I'll tell him," said his godfather. "Go on, go on. I'll see you very soon."

But Nightingale did not go through the doorway. Instead, he turned and slowly walked back into the room. "Uncle Edward," he said. "Are you certain you're going to be all right? I mean, the power's still off. You can't breathe without your ventilator."

"The generator can run for hours and hours. It'll shut itself off when the regular power comes back." He waved his hand testily. "Go on, Nate. I'm fine."

"But the strange thing," said Nightingale, "is that when the generator came on half an hour ago, the ventilator didn't. There must be something wrong with it."

Arvedson went very still. "What . . . what are you talking about?"

"Here. Look, the little lights on it never came back on, either. Your ventilator's off."

The room suddenly seemed very quiet, nothing but the distant sound of cars splashing along out on Jones Street, distant as the moon.

"What happened to Edward?"

The old man looked surprised. "I don't . . . Nate, what are you saying . . . ?"

The gun was out of Nightingale's coat and into his hand so quickly it might have simply appeared there. He leveled it at a spot between the old man's two bushy white eyebrows. "I asked you what happened to Edward—the real Edward Arvedson. I'm only going to ask this once more. I swear I'll kill him before I let you have his body, and I'm betting you can't pull your little possession trick again on a full-grown, healthy man like me—especially not before I can pull the trigger."

Even in the half-light of the desk lamp, the change was a fearful one: Edward Arvedson's wrinkled features did not alter in any great way, but something moved beneath the muscles and skin like a light-shunning creature burrowing through the dark earth. The eyes fixed on his. Although the face was still Edward's, somehow it no longer looked much like him. "You're a clever boy, Nightingale," said the stranger in his godfather's body. "I should have noticed the ventilator never came back on, but as you've guessed, this sack of meat no longer has a breathing problem. In fact, it no longer needs to breathe at all."

"What's happened to him?" The gun stayed trained on the spot between the old man's eyes. "Talk fast."

A slow, cold smile stretched the lips. "That is not for me to say, but rather it is between him and his god. Perhaps he is strumming a harp with the other angels now . . . or writhing and shrieking in the deepest pits. . . ."

"Bastard!" Nightingale pulled back the trigger with his thumb. "You lie! He's in there with you. And I know a dozen people who can make you jump right the hell back out."

The thing shook its head. "Oh, Mr. Nightingale, you've been playing the occult detective so long, you've come to believe you're really in a story—and that it will have a happy ending. We didn't learn new ways to possess the living." The smile returned, mocking and triumphant. "We have learned how to move into the bodies of the recently dead. Quite a breakthrough. It's much, much easier than possession, and we cannot be evicted, because the prior tenant . . . is gone. Your Uncle Edward had a stroke, you see. We waited all around him as he died. Oh, and believe me, we told him over and over what we would do, including this moment. Like you, he caused us a great deal of trouble over the years—and as you know, we dead have long memories. And when he was beyond our torments at last, well, this body was ours. Already my essence has strengthened it. It does not need to breathe, and as you can see . . ." The thing rose from the wheelchair with imperial calm and stood without wavering. Nightingale backed off a few steps, keeping the gun high. ". . . it no longer needs assistance to get around, either," the thing finished. "I feel certain I'll get years of use out of it before I have to seek another—time enough to contact and betray all of the rest of Edward Arvedson's old friends."

"Who are you?" Nightingale fought against a despair that buffeted him like a cold wind. "Oh, for the love of God, what do you monsters want?"

"Who am I? Just one of the hungry ones. One of the unforgiving." It sat down again, making the wheelchair creak. "What do we want? Not to go quietly, as you would have us go—to disappear into the shadows of nonexistence and leave the rest of you to enjoy the light and warmth." The thing lifted its knotted hands—Edward's hands, as they had seemed such a short time ago—in a greedy gesture of seizure. "As you said, this is a war. We want what you have." It laughed, and for the first time the voice sounded nothing at all like his godfather's familiar tones. "And we are going take it from you. All of you."

"I don't think so. Because if you need bodies to survive here, then those bodies can be taken back from you." And even as Nightingale spoke, his gun flashed and roared, and the thing in his godfather's shape staggered and fell back against the wheelchair cushions, chin on chest. A moment later the so-familiar face came up again. Smiling.

"Jenkins," it said. "If you would be so kind . . ."

Something knocked the gun from Nightingale's hand, and then an arm like an iron bar slammed against his neck. He fought, but it was like being held by a full-grown gorilla. His struggles only allowed him to slide around enough in his captor's grip to see Jenkins's blank eyes and the huge hole in the side of the caretaker's head crusted with bits of bone and dried tissue.

"I lied about giving him the night off," said the pseudo-Edward. "The living get impatient, but my colleague who inhabits him now was perfectly willing to stand in the dark until I needed him." Now Arvedson's body stood again, brushing at its clothes; the hole Nightingale's gunshot had made in its shirt was bloodless. "Bullets are a poor weapon against the risen dead, Nightingale," it pointed out with no little satisfaction. "You could burn the body, I suppose, or literally pulverize it, and there would be nothing left for us to inhabit. But of course, you will not get the chance to tell anyone about that."

"Bastards!" He struggled helplessly against the Jenkins-thing's grip. "Even if you kill me, there are hundreds more like me out there. They'll stop you!"

"We will meet them all, I'm sure," said his godfather's body. "You will introduce us—or at least the new resident of your corpse will. And one by one, we will remove them. The dead will live, with all the power of age and riches and secrecy, and the rest of your kind will be our uncomprehending cattle, left alive only to breed more bodies for us. Your driver was right, Mr. Nightingale: The storm door really is open now. And no power on this Earth can shut it."

Nightingale tried to say something else then, shout some last words of defiance, but the pressure on his neck was crushingly strong, and the lights of the world—the lamp, the headlights passing in the street below, even the storm-shrouded stars beyond the window— had begun leaching away into utter darkness.

His last sight was of the cold, hungry things that had been hiding behind that darkness, hiding and waiting and hating the living for so long, as they hurried toward him to feed.

KIDS AND THEIR TOYS

BY JAMES A. MOORE

Of course they poked it with a stick. What else would twelve-year-olds do with a freshly discovered corpse? Later, when the fascination was fading, they would do what they were supposed to do and tell the police about the body, but then, at that first moment of discovery, they had a new toy and it had to be carefully examined before it could be given away.

They probably would have called the police, too. Certainly that was part of the unspoken agreement between them, but then their new toy moved and all of the rules changed.

"Fuck me Freddie, are you serious?" Tom's voice broke as the dead man moaned and turned its head in the summer heat. They were all so shocked that no one called him on dropping the f-bomb.

Every last one of them saw the motion and heard the noise. They were all watching when the neck muscles shifted and the head rolled unevenly. The face of the dead man was revealed. He was no one they had ever seen before, and maybe that fact helped add to the madness of the moment, or maybe it was simply that at twelve years of age they had so little in the world that could truly be called theirs.

Jack glanced about, checking to see if there were any grown-ups around. He couldn't decide if the lack of them made him happy or worried him sick. They were near the old quarry at the edge of his granddad's property. None of them were supposed to go swimming at the quarry, but that had never stopped anyone before. You leave a perfectly good lake's worth of water in a convenient spot and add in the summer heat, and the next thing you know, there's a new swimming hole. The big bonus was that Grandpa Murphy was too old to come check on them much.

None of them knew why a man was lying dead on the ground, but it didn't look like he'd been murdered or anything. He was just lying there, gray and a little bloated, and there they were and there he was, and of course there were sticks nearby. Charlie had learned for them that you should always use a stick to poke dead things. A couple of years earlier, when he'd found a dead pigeon on the ground, he'd scooped it up and run all the way to the fort before anyone else got there. Charlie had allergies something fierce, and he hadn't even smelled the bird's rot. The others sure did though, which was why he still had to deal with the nickname Skunk. No amount of washing would get rid of the stink on him until he went home and took a real bath, and none of them saw any reason not to pick on him about it. You do stupid things and you have to pay the price. That was one of the simple rules that dictated their lives.

The thing tried to sit up, and Tom jabbed the stick into its shoulder and pushed as hard as he could. It let out another bleating noise and fell back, struggling feebly as its milky eyes rolled in its leaking head. The halo of flies around it buzzed harder for a moment and then settled down onto their latest meal again.

Tom laughed. "That's sick, dude."

Charlie nodded his head and licked his thick lips. Charlie had a sister two years older than any of them, and it was agreed that the features that made him look like a fish made her look like a pinup girl. It was weird how that sort of thing worked. Jack cleared his throat and looked around again. "Should we call someone?" He hated to ask, of course, because he knew everyone would look at him funny.

Tom sneered. Tom liked to sneer. He was a dick sometimes. "You crazy? We have to see what this is all about."

"Well, I mean, is he really dead? Or is he just sick?" He pointed at the dead thing, which seemed to be getting stronger. "Cuz if he's just sick, we could get in some deep shit." He knew about that sort of thing, of course. His brother Steve was over in Iraq, and there were all sorts of stories about what happened to prisoners over there. Sometimes when they weren't treated right, the soldiers who were watching them got in deep trouble. Sometimes they wound up in jail. It hadn't happened to Steve, of course, because Steve was one of the good guys, but a few of the guys he knew over in Iraq had gotten into some serious shit.

"Dude, he's a zombie." Tom scowled and poked hard enough with the stick to tear the fabric of the shirt over the dead man's chest. The skin under that was soft, and something wet and black leaked out and stained the shirt's light blue threads a dark gray. Tom shook his head. "If he's alive, I'll kiss Skunk on the mouth."

"Zombies are real?" That was José, who was only eleven, but cool enough that he got to hang out with them anyway.

Jack looked from the dead man to José. "Guess they have to be. I mean, we got one right here, right?"

They all looked again, trying to make sure it really was a zombie. There were stories, of course. They had as much use for the nightly news as they did for instruction manuals, but you sort of had to hear things, even if you weren't trying. There were places in California and in Mexico that had supposedly been overrun by the dead. Most everyone thought the whole thing was some kind of joke, or maybe a publicity stunt for a new Hollywood monster movie. You had enough money, you could probably convince the news stations to play along. At least that was what his daddy said.

The dead man swung a wild arm at the stick Tom had pushed into its chest and knocked the thick branch back, taking a chunk of wet rot along for the ride.

Skunk gagged a little. Seemed his allergies didn't suck so bad that day.

"What are we gonna do with it, guys?" Jack again. He had to ask. He had to know. They couldn't just leave a thing like that lying on the ground. Some of the stories said the dead people ate other people, and that would be sort of like leaving a rabid dog on the side of the road, wouldn't it?

Tom had a solution. Tom always had a solution. That was why he was the boss so much of the time. "Let's tie it up and hide it somewhere." Tom's blue eyes looked from under his thick, dark bangs, and he flipped the too-long hair from his broad, tanned face. "Let's play with it."

Jack wasn't sure if that was the best idea ever, but there was that thrill, that secret shiver that danced across his skin as he thought of all the things they could learn about zombies if they experimented a bit.

"Where are we gonna hide a zombie?" José's voice rose half an octave as he spoke. "How are we gonna get it where no one's gonna take it from us?" His Mexican accent was faint: He'd lived in the area as long as any of them could remember, but that accent never quite left him.

"I know where." Jack licked his lips and tasted sweat on his tongue. The heat was hammering down on them as the summer day grew older. They needed someplace where the roasting weather wouldn't ruin their new plaything. "I got the perfect place."

Some secrets are too big not to share, and in this case the secret also needed to be moved as quickly as possible, because the dead man was definitely getting more active. Billy Chambers and Ben Deveraux were recruited to join them on their quest. Billy worked on his dad's farm, and that meant he worked with horses. He was perfect, really, because he knew how to throw a lasso. Maybe he'd come in fourth in the junior rodeo the year before, but he was fast enough for their needs, and he was one of them. Ben too, even if he didn't get to come out and play as often.

Billy threw the lasso around the dead man's shoulders—extra wide so they wouldn't accidentally pull his head off or something— and they passed the rope around in a circle until they'd looped the heavy cable around the monster's chest and arms half a dozen times.

It fought back, thrashing and croaking incoherently. Its teeth—big and white in the gray receding gums—clashed together loudly again and again as it tried to bite at them, but they were smarter; they never got that close. After the arms were bound to the waist, Billy pulled it backward and Tom and Jack caught and held the legs, while Skunk and José tied them together with more rope. Most of their parents would have been shocked to see how well they could work together when they had to. Their folks would have been surprised by a lot of things that their little ones were capable of, but isn't that always the case?

Once they had their new toy properly bound and gagged—not for silence, but to keep those teeth of his from getting ahold of them—

the group half carried and half dragged him across the field to the storm shelter Jack's grandfather had built into the property. A wallet, thin and black, fell from the thing's pants, and Tom snapped it up so fast that almost no one noticed as they struggled with their burden. Almost no one. Jack saw, but he kept it to himself. Tom's family was poor—Jack's dad called them "dirt farmers" when he thought Jack wasn't around to hear—and if anyone needed the cash, it was Tom. Besides, Tom always thought of cool things to do whenever they came across a few dollars.

The part of Texas where the boys lived was known for many things, including tornadoes. The storm season wasn't quite ready to come around, and that meant that there was no reason for anyone to disturb them or their experiments. The area was far enough away from the house and deep enough under the ground that there was no reason to worry about anyone hearing them, especially since Grandpa Murphy was at least half deaf.

The air in the storm shelter was nearly cold after they'd been in the blasting heat of the day. It brought sweet relief and a rush of gooseflesh across Jack's skin. Still, he wouldn't even consider bitching about the weather. From what he understood, they had it a lot worse where Steve was. All desert heat and crazy people with bombs who wanted to kill Americans whenever they saw them. He'd never met anyone from the Middle East, and he planned to keep it that way if all they wanted to do was bomb people. What sort of animals killed and killed without any good reason? Besides, they didn't even believe in Jesus.

"So what are we gonna do with him, guys?" Ben held his hand in front of his face and tried to wave away the smell of dead man. Like that was even possible.

"Don't do too much until I get back, okay?" Jack ran to the top of the creaking wooden stairs.

"Where are you going?" Tom asked.

Jack smiled. "Grampa Murphy has air fresheners in the house. He likes to hide his farts."

Tom smiled and nodded his approval. "Sweet." Jack started to close one of the doors to the shelter but stopped when Tom called out. "Hey."

"Yeah?"

Tom jerked his chin toward their new toy. "Think you can get a knife or two?" Jack licked his lips and thought about it. "Maybe."

"Cool."

He managed to confiscate two cans of air freshener, a box of matches, a bar of soap, and a small jar of peanut butter.

He got the knives the next day.

That night Steve called from Baghdad. He sounded very tired but glad to hear their voices. There were only two phones in the house, so Jack only got to listen in for a couple of minutes and talked to his big brother for even less time.

"Hey, Steve?" He waited to ask his questions until Mom had run to the kitchen to get the hamburgers off the stove and into the oven to stay warm, and until he knew his Dad had run to the bathroom.

"Yeah, bud?" His brother's voice sounded forever away, tinny and static and still so very wonderful.

"Are the dead people moving out where you are?"

There was a pause for a few seconds, and he could almost see Steve looking around to make sure no one heard him. "Yeah. Some of them are. But we don't talk about that, okay? Not ever."

"Are they different than prisoners of war?"

"Of course."

"How come?"

"Prisoners of war are still alive, Jack. They're still people."

Before he could respond any further, his mom was back on the line, and so he just listened and basked in the voice of his older brother, the hero.

He was glad zombies weren't people anymore. He'd been a little worried about that.

"Where do they come from?" That was José, who was always asking a billion questions.

Charlie just shrugged. Jack didn't know either, but just lately he'd taken to watching the news a lot more closely. "Maybe it's a virus. I hear if they bite you, you become a zombie, too."

Tom snorted. "My dad says they aren't zombies. He says they're the undead."

"Doesn't that mean the same thing?" José again.

Jack shook his head. "No. Undead is vampires. I saw it on that Dracula movie."

"The movie's wrong." Tom shook his head and practically dared Jack to contradict him again. "My dad knows better than Hollywood."

"Whatever." Jack dismissed the attitude. You had to make exceptions when you were with Tom. He could really be a dick. But mostly he was cool.

Ben had managed to get out of the house again. Sometimes you had to break the rules, and a zombie was worth the risks. "I heard it was the water in Mexico. It's so full of shit that it kills you and makes you a zombie."

That made a little sense. Mexico was a big place, and both California and Texas were connected to it. "No. My brother Steve says they've got zombies over there too."

Ben frowned and shook his head, genuinely puzzled. "Maybe the zombies over there are Mexican?"

"Do they have Mexican soldiers?" Charlie sniffed. His allergies were back with a vengeance. Maybe he was allergic to zombies too. He was allergic to almost everything else.

Billy nodded. "Yeah. José could join the army if he wanted. You know, when he's old enough."

"I'm an American. I was born here."

"Yeah, but your folks are Mexican, right?"

"Well, yeah, of course."

"See? You could be a soldier." Billy had a good head on his shoulders, as Dad liked to say.

"I think it's demons." That was Tom, who had walked back over to their pet zombie. The thing snarled and thrashed. Jack didn't know how smart it really was, but the zombie always got more active when Tom got near it. Tom used the knives and sticks the most while the others watched. Maybe it knew how to tell them apart, even though Tom had poked out one of the eyes.

"Demons? Like in the movies?"

"Like in the Bible. Jesus fought demons."

"It didn't react when you put a cross around its neck." Billy again, who was normally the only other person who would stand up to Tom.

Tom looked at the zombie for a minute and then backed away as it tried to lunge for him.

"So. Maybe it's a Jewish zombie and doesn't know any better." Jack didn't know enough about Jews and all the other religions, so he kept his opinions to himself.

Tom stepped away from the zombie, and Ben took that as a sign that he could play. He picked up a long steel post he'd found and poked it into the dead man's thigh. The meaty spot squelched, and the point drove a good inch and a half into the cold dead meat.

Jack frowned as the zombie hissed and dislodged a maggot from its upper lip.

"Do you think he can feel anything, guys?"

No one had a definitive answer.

Tom stared hard at the thing on the ground and got that look on his face, the one that said he'd come up with a really cool idea and he wanted to be the one to do something first. He grabbed the carving knife Jack had snuck from the old set that was half buried in his grandfather's kitchen cabinets, and slipped past Ben.

Tom made sure everyone was looking at him. "Let's find out. Let's see if this fucker feels anything." He drove the tip of the knife through the dead man's wrist and held on as it jumped and tried to snap at him.

Tom took the time to look each of the boys in the eye before he started sawing at the mutilated wrist, straining and grunting as he fought the blade between the small bones. The thing's arms were still tied in place around the chest, but the rope was fraying now, soggy with the black nastiness that passed for blood. The zombie let out a warbling noise and struggled, thrashed, its teeth snapping again and again as it tried to reach Tom.

Tom was smarter than that. He stayed away from the head of the thing.

Long after the hand had been cut away, the zombie struggled against its bonds and let out low keening noises.

Jack couldn't be sure. He thought maybe the zombie felt something, but whether or not it really qualified as pain, he couldn't say.

After a while Tom got tired of chopping digits away from the fingers that curled and uncurled like spider legs. The stump of the wrist didn't bleed anymore, but Jack could see the muscles and bones left there trying to move the hand that was no longer where it had always been. The motion was almost hypnotic.

Jack watched the news after dinner and heard the rumors that the dead were coming back in greater numbers. According to somebody in the governor's office, the problem was getting so big in Dallas and Houston that people were rioting and trying to get out of the cities before the situation could get any worse. The only pictures they showed were of traffic jams, cars trying to move and going nowhere fast on the roads away from the cities. Police had to work longer hours, and the National Guard was coming in to help.

They were just rumors, of course. There was no proof. No real evidence, as his dad said. There'd been pictures a couple of times, but no one wanted to show them anymore. Or maybe they weren't allowed to. That was what Ben said. His dad worked for the local paper, and Ben said the government wasn't allowing anyone to take pictures and show them on the TV or even put them in newspapers. His mom and dad didn't let him go online except when they were in the room, and they wouldn't even talk about the zombies in front of him. He was too young, as far as they were concerned. If they knew he'd seen one, touched one, poked holes in one, they'd have tanned his hide for him.

When the news anchor started talking about the possibility of mandatory cremation—he thought that was when they burned the bodies, but he wasn't completely sure—Mom screamed at Dad and made him change the channel to *Wheel of Fortune*.

After that the atmosphere in the house grew cold and awkward. Later, after he'd been sent to bed even though he wasn't tired, he heard his parents talking in their bedroom. Mom was worried. Dad tried to calm her down and swore he wouldn't let any of them come back from the dead if something bad happened.

Ben was happy about that. He didn't know how his dad would stop them from being zombies, but he had faith in the man. His dad was young and could still do pretty much anything. Ben knew it in his heart.

He drifted to sleep, only vaguely aware of his mom crying through the wall.

His dad would make it right. That was all that mattered, wasn't it?

"What? You going pussy on us?" Tom's voice held more than the usual menace. He looked at the bigger boy and felt his brow pull lower over his eyes. Maybe Skunk was scared of Tom, but Jack never had been.

"I'm not going pussy. I just don't want to touch that thing." Tom had taken his carving skills to the next level. He hadn't actually cut the left leg off the zombie, but it wasn't for lack of trying. The pants had been cut away, and a length of rope had been used to tie the leg in place. Two tent posts from Tom's old tent had been hammered into the ground and anchored the ankle firmly. The rope had already cut deep into rotting flesh, and even in the permanent semidarkness of the storm cellar he could see the bone under the rope. Tom had peeled off most of the skin, and the muscles—gray and black and rotting in the summer heat—shifted and twitched every time the dead man tried to get away from the, well, from whatever passed for pain in its ruined head. Tom still wasn't sure about that part.

Ben wasn't there, but everyone else was. Half of them were looking away, finding something else to stare at as the confrontation started, but Billy and José were looking on with expressions that held an edge of anticipation. The zombie was starting to grow old, as toys go, and the heat was taking a toll on the rotting flesh. Most of the experiments that could be done at this point were the sort that made a bigger mess, and it was harder to get that crap off their clothes. Tom had come up with the idea of garbage bags, and he'd used two of them to make himself a sort of raincoat against the foul substances he'd spilled as he carved and hacked at the ruined leg.

Now he held the knife that Jack himself had confiscated for them and waved the bloodied, slicked mess in front of him. "Everyone else did it, Jack. What makes you so special?" There was an edge to his voice, an implied threat: *Either you're one of us or you aren't.*

"You were supposed to wait for everyone, Tom. What makes *you* so special?" He crossed his arms over his chest and stared hard.

Tom blinked and shook his head, barely believing that anyone would speak out against him. And Jack allowed himself a small smile as the heads of their mutual friends turned to look at Tom with unspoken accusation.

Tom still didn't understand well enough: Yes, he was bigger; he might even be a better fighter than any of the others—well, except for Billy—but he wasn't as smart as he thought he was.

The zombie leaned forward and let out a series of grunting noises as it lunged for Tom's leg. Tom moved out of the way and swung the knife angrily, opening a slash across the monster's cheek and nose. It recoiled and barked furiously.

Sometimes Jack worried about Tom. Not often, of course, but every now and then.

Billy broke the tension. "It's too hot for this. Let's go swimming."

That seemed like a fine idea to Jack. In no time they were back at the scene of the crime, and he glanced over at the spot where they'd found the dead man again and again as they goofed around and cooled off their bodies and their tempers.

Tom knew the man's name. He was the only one who knew. He had to know. He had the wallet, didn't he?

Jack watched Tom do a cannonball from the side of the quarry, splashing them all. He rose back up and looked toward Jack as he treaded water.

Looking at him made Jack feel strange in the pit of his stomach, the same way the idea of cutting into the dead man made him feel. There was something wrong with Tom. Or maybe there was something wrong with him. He didn't know for sure which it was.

Later that same day, after he'd cleaned up and everyone had gone their own ways, the phone call came in for Jack's family. Steve had caught shrapnel in his leg. He would be all right, but there was a chance he'd be coming home sooner than expected.

And Jack got that feeling in his stomach again. He'd been praying for Steve to come home early, and now maybe he would be, but if he had to get hurt to come home, was that really a good answer to his prayers?

The question was too big for him to wrap his head around easily.

The next day he got down to the storm cellar later than he'd planned. He had to take care of some chores around the house, and then his mom wanted him to drop off the casserole she'd baked over to his grandpa's place. It wasn't like he had to go out of his way, but the man was in a talkative mood, and it was almost an hour before he could get out of the house and head for the storm cellar. He loved his grandfather, but he wasn't always exciting to talk to.

The smell was the first thing that caught him. The zombie hadn't been pleasant to smell anyway, but now the odor was enough to stagger him. He descended the steps and listened to the sounds of the guys laughing.

When he reached the bottom of the steps, he stopped and stared, barely believing what he saw.

The zombie was opened up like a grisly flower, his abdomen cut wide and the skin spread open like petals. Loops of ropy intestines fell in piles, and the ribs had been cut open. His legs had been stripped of everything but gristle and bone, and his arms had been freed but lacked enough remaining muscle to make them a threat.

It wasn't just Tom this time. All of the guys were there, and all of them had plastic bags wrapped over their clothes and shoes alike.

"What the hell?" He could barely recognize his own voice.

Tom grinned. His smile held an edge, and his eyes were a blatant challenge. Tom had called him on not joining in the day before, and now he'd drawn a line in the sand. Either Jack crossed the line and joined them, or maybe he proved he was chickenshit.

Tom spoke softly, confidently. "We got tired of waiting." He pointed to the zombie. "But we saved you the head."

Jack's face felt like it would catch fire. His stomach had congealed like a frozen lump, and there was a strange ringing in his ears. What they'd done . . . well, it wasn't right.

The dead man wriggled, and its chest moved up and down as it strained to make a noise.

Jack stared hard at Tom. "What was his name?"

"What?" Tom had no idea what Jack meant.

Jack's hand shook just a little as he pointed at the struggling heap of ruined meat and hacked pieces. "I saw you pick up his wallet. It fell from his pocket when we were carrying him here, and you grabbed it. What was his name?"

Tom shook his head. His broad face worked as he tried to find the right expression for answering the unexpected question and accusation. "Who cares?"

"I do!" Jack moved closer to him, his body shaking. His blood seemed too thick, pushed too hard to move through his body. "I do. Maybe he has a family that wants to know he's dead. Maybe he has a little brother or a big sister and they miss him, Tom. Maybe he has a wife or a mom who doesn't know why he disappeared."

It was Steve, of course, that he was thinking about. He'd heard about people getting so ruined that no one could identify the bodies. What if Steve had been that badly hurt instead of just getting his leg messed up? What if they'd never known what happened to him?

"Well, you're the only one." It was Tom's turn to cross his arms over his chest.

"Am I?" Jack looked at each of them, his ears still ringing. "Don't any of you care about what he was before we found him?"

Skunk looked at him with a puzzled frown on his round face. "He's dead, Jack. What does it matter?"

"He was alive once!" Jack's eyes stung as he took a step toward Charlie, and the boy flinched like he'd swatted at him.

"Well, he's dead now!" That from Billy, who stepped closer himself, looking ready to take a swing—Billy, who had always been ready to defend someone if something got out of hand. Only now he was standing in front of Charlie as if he needed defending from Jack. "He's dead, and no one cares who he was."

Tom put down his knife and reached for the sharpened stick he'd used from the first. "Is it the knife, Jack? Are you afraid to cut yourself?" He spun the length of wood between his fingers like a baton. When he stopped, the unsharpened edge was held toward Jack. "Come on. This is safer. You can't cut yourself. You can maybe get a splinter."

Jack looked at him and shook his head. They didn't get it. They didn't want to or they couldn't—he didn't know which. He wasn't afraid of the dead man. He was afraid of what they were doing. How could they be the good guys if they hurt things just because they could? He shook his head again, because even that didn't seem to quite cover it. What if there was still a person stuck inside that wasted, rotted thing?

Caution is made for grown-ups. Kids tend to leave caution in the dust. Despite his recent epiphanies, Jack was still just twelve. He reached for the stick, fully meaning to push it aside, and his left foot caught the viscera that had spilled around the dead thing. He couldn't have pulled a better slapstick moment if he'd had a banana peel. Jack's heel went up and he went down, his ass slapping against the wet ground and his head bouncing lightly. He could feel the filth and decay soaking his jeans and the hair on the back of his head. The dead man next to him on the ground struggled to reach him, but its limbs no longer worked and it could only wiggle closer. Jack had time enough to push away, his adrenaline kicking in at the thought of how close he was to the vile thing.

All of the boys laughed, except for Jack. There was nothing funny about the situation—well, okay, the fall was worthy of a chuckle, maybe—and his confusion and frustration were as deep as ever. Instead, Jack braced his hands and pushed himself into a sitting position then onto his knees before he tried to stand up. And he slipped a second time, falling across the dead man, his hand slapping the corpse's face as he struggled to save himself.

Jack felt a sudden pain spike deep into his left palm and across the little finger.

"Ow! Fuck!" he looked toward the pain as he pulled his hand back and froze. The zombie had bitten down good and hard. He looked at the blood welling from his hand and skittered back, his eyes flying wide. There was a tooth sticking out of the ridge of his hand. He'd pulled it from the corpse's mouth when he yanked his hand away.

The zombie lunged as best it could and snapped at him again. Without even thinking, Jack kicked at the face and knocked the jaw aside with ease. The muscles had atrophied to the point where even its ability to stay together was more luck than nature.

"Jack. You're bit." Billy's voice was distant; it sounded like a whisper.

"I gotta get to Grampy's house. He can fix it," Jack said through lips that felt numb. The ringing was back in his ears, only now there was a different source to it.

Skunk spoke up next, shaking his head. "It's been in the news, Jack. Ain't no cure. You get bit, you become one of those things. It's all over."

"That's shit!" Jack blinked his eyes and shook his head, denying what he had heard himself. "That's shit! No way!"

He looked at the dead thing again. It was barely even capable of moving. His desire to give it comfort was dead, torn away like the flesh on his bleeding hand. He lashed out again and again, kicking at the broken face, until his tears completely obscured his vision and he had to stop and wipe them away.

All around him his friends stared at him in sickened fascination.

Billy shook his head. "It ain't shit, and you know it. You been watching the news, too. Those things, they're spreading. You can't even go home, Jack. You might try to hurt your own family."

"It isn't that fast." He shook his head again. "It takes time."

Tom shook his head, too, but his face was unreadable. "Not much time. Maybe a couple of hours."

"Well, I have to try and get it fixed."

"Too late." Tom stepped to the side and took two more steps. It took Jack only a second to realize he was blocking the way past the dead thing.

"You need to get the hell out of my way. I'm sick of you, Tom."

Charlie was wheezing; his breaths sounded wrong. José leaned over and shook his head, whispering something in the other boy's ear.

Tom didn't answer. Instead he jabbed out with the stick in his hand and drove the point into Jack's left shoulder.

"Ow! What the hell, dude?" Jack covered the spot quickly, not even thinking as he used his wounded hand. The good news was that the bite barely even hurt now. The spot where he was poked felt worse. It flared with a little extra pain as the blood from his hand fell across the small area where the stick had broken skin. Jack pulled his hand back quickly. He could make the infection worse that way, couldn't he? He wasn't really sure.

He was about to say something else to Tom, when the boy poked him a second time, on his other arm. This time the point put a hole in his shirt and the blood was more obvious.

"Tom! Stop it!" He stared hard as Tom's smile spread.

"Skunk, cover the door."

Jack knew that tone in Tom's voice. It was the cool and level voice of the expedition leader. The same tone used to gather the troops and offer instructions when they were hunting for crawfish or trying to sneak up on someone they were about to pull a stunt on.

"Billy, get your rope."

Jack looked around quickly as both Skunk and José headed for the narrow staircase, and Billy reached down, his eyes never leaving Jack, and grabbed his lasso.

"What are you doing, guys? Come on, this isn't funny." He could barely breathe.

The look in their eyes said otherwise. The look they cast his way said the fun was only about to begin.

José reached up and closed the storm doors firmly, leaving them lost in the near darkness. To his left, the rope in Billy's hands snapped in the air twice and then grew silent.

SHOOTING POOL

BY JOE R. LANSDALE

My daddy told me it wasn't a place I ought to be, because the owner, who had once been a good friend of his, and the owner's friends were troublesome, which was his way of saying they were no-accounts or hoods. My mother didn't want me there, either, but after high school, about twice a week, sometimes three times a week, me and my friends Donald and Lee would go over to the pool hall to shoot a few runs of Solids and Stripes, which was the only pool game we knew.

I think what we liked about going there was that pool was thought of as a tough guy's game, a game played in bars with lots of cigarette and cigar smoke and some rough-looking characters hanging around. And that's just the way Rugger's Pool Hall was. I saw Jack Rugger and his friends at my father's garage from time to time, where my daddy kept their cars running. My daddy was no shrinking violet, either, but his strength and anger were generally of a positive sort and not directed at my person. Rugger and his pals were a mystery to me, because they talked about drinking and whoring and fighting and about how bad they were, and the thing was, I knew they weren't just bragging.

I figured I was pretty bad myself, and so did Donald and Lee. They were my fan club. In school, with my six-three, two-hundred-pound frame, and the bulk of it weight-lifting muscles, I was respected. I had even, on occasion, gotten into fights outside of school with older, bigger college boys and whipped them. I had a few moves. I was always waiting for a chance to prove it.

So, this time I'm talking about, we walked over there from school to buy a couple of soda pops and shoot some pool and slip a cigarette and talk about girls and tail, like we'd had any, and when we got there, Rugger's cousin, Ray Martin Winston, was there along with Rugger and a retarded kid who cleaned up and kept sodas in the soda machine. The kid always wore a red baseball cap and over-alls, lived in the back, and Rugger usually referred to him as "the re-tard." The kid went along with this without any kickback. He was as dedicated to Rugger as a seeing-eye dog, and about as concerned with day-to-day activities as a pig was about algebra.

Ray Martin was older than we were, but not by much. Maybe three years. He had dropped out of school as soon as he could, and I had no idea what he did for a living, though it was rumored he stole and sold and ran a few whores, one of which was said to be his sister, though any of it could have been talk. He was a peculiar-looking fella, one of those who seem as if their lives will be about trouble, and that was Ray Martin. He was lean but not too tall, had a shock of blond hair, which he took great care to lightly oil and comb. It was his best feature. It was thick and fell down on his forehead in a Beach Boy kind of wave. His face always made me think of a hammerhead shark. It had to do with his beady black eyes and the way his nose dropped straight down from his thick forehead and along the length of his face until it stopped just above lips as thin as razor cuts. His chin looked like a block of stone. He had chunky white teeth, all them about the size of sugar cubes. He would have made a great Dick Tracy villain. He had a reptilian way of moving, or at least that's how it seemed to me, as if he undulated and squirmed. I guess in the back of my head there was a piece of me itching to find out just how dangerous he really was.

We shot a game at our table, while Ray Martin shot alone at one of the other three, knocking the cue ball around, racking and break-ing and taking shots. Free time had given him good aim and a good arm for the table.

I was feeling my oats that day, and I looked over and said, "You're pretty good playin' yourself."

Ray Martin raised his head and twisted it, cracked his neck as he did, and gave me a look that I had never seen before. Rugger came over quickly with a beer from the cooler, handed it to him, and said, "Ought to be someone comin' in pretty soon. Maybe you can get a game up."

Ray Martin nodded, took the wet beer bottle, sipped it, and examined me with the precision of a sniper about to pop off a shot. "Sure," he said. "That could happen."

He went over and sat in a chair by the wall and drank his beer and kept his eye on me, one hand in his baggy pants pocket. I turned back to the game, and Donald leaned over close and said, "He didn't take that well. He thought it was some kind of crack."

"I meant it as a crack," I said.

"I know. And he took it as a crack."

"You think I'm worried?"

Donald's face changed a little. He licked his lips. I thought his lower jaw shook. "No. I'm not worried about you. I know you can take care of yourself."

I didn't believe him altogether. I had seen that spark of doubt in his eyes, and it annoyed me. I didn't like him thinking I might not be as bad and tough as I thought I was. I saw the retarded kid glaring at me, his mouth hanging open, and it somehow hit me that the kid thought the same thing, though truth was, if that kid had two thoughts, they probably canceled each other out.

I gave Ray Martin a glance, just to show him my ball sack hadn't shrunk, and his stare was still locked on me. I won't lie to you, I was feeling brave, but there was something about the way he looked at me that clawed its way down inside of me. I had never seen anyone with that kind of look, and I wrote it off to the way his face was and that no matter what he was thinking and no matter where he was looking, he'd look like that. Hell, his old mother probably looked like that; she probably had to tie a pork chop around her neck to get fucked.

I peeked at Rugger. He was looking at me, too, but with a different kind of look, like someone watching a dog darting across the highway in front of an eighteen-wheeler, wondering how it was going to turn out. I thought maybe he was hoping I'd make it. When he and my father were kids, my daddy had been on his side in an oil-field fight that had become a kind of Marvel Creek legend. Him and dad against six others, and they had won, and in style, sending two of their foes to the hospital. I guess, through my dad, that gave me and the old man a kind of connection, though now that I look back on it, he wasn't that old. Probably in his forties then, balding, with a hard potbelly, arms that looked as if they had been pumped full of air, legs too short and thin for the bulk of his upper body—a barrel supported by reeds.

This concern and Donald's doubt didn't set well with me, and it made me feel all the more feisty. I was about to say something smart to Ray Martin, when the front door opened and a man about thirty came in. He was wearing khaki pants and a plaid shirt and a blue-jean jacket and tie-up boots. He was as dark as Ray Martin was blond and pale. "How're y'all?" he said. He sounded like someone who had just that day stepped off the farm for the first time and had left his turnips outside. I looked out through the front door, which was glass with a roll-down curtain curled above it, and parked next to the curb I could see a shiny new Impala. It wasn't a car that looked like it went with the fella, but it was his.

Rugger nodded at him, and the fella said, "I was wonderin' you could tell me how to get to Tyler?" Rugger told him, and then the hick asked, "You got any food to sell here?"

"Some potato chips, peanuts," Rugger said. "Got a Coke machine. We don't fry no hamburgers or nothin'."

"I guess I'll just have some peanuts then."

Rugger went over and pulled a package off the rack, and the hick paid for them. He went to the Coke machine and lifted the lid and reached down in the cold water and threaded a cola through the little metal maze that led to where you pulled it out after putting in your money. You don't see those kinds of machines anymore, but for a while, back in the sixties, they were pretty popular.

He pulled the cap off with the opener on the side of the box and turned around and said, "Ain't nothin' like a store-bought Co-Cola," as if there were any other kind. He swigged about half the drink in one gulp, pulled it down and wiped his mouth with his sleeve, and tore open his bag of peanuts with his teeth and poured them into the Coke bottle. The salt made the soda foam a little. He swigged that and chewed on the wet peanuts and came over and watched us play for a moment.

"I've played this game," he said, showing me some crunched peanuts on his teeth.

"Yeah," I said. "Well, we got a full table."

"I see that. I do. I'm just sayin' I know how. My old pappy taught me how to play. I like it. I'm pretty good too."

"Well, good for you," I said. "Did your old pappy teach you not to bother folks when they're playin'?"

He smiled, looked a little wounded. "Yes, he did. I apologize."

"Hey, you," Ray Martin called.

We all looked.

"You want to play some pool?" he said to the hayseed. "I'll play you."

"Sure, I'll play," the hayseed said, shrugging his shoulders. "But I warn you, sometimes I like to play for nickels and such."

Ray Martin stretched his razor-thin lips and grinned those sugar-cube teeth. "That's all right, yokel. We'll play for such, as you call it."

"I reckon I am a bit of a yokel," said the fella, "but I prefer to be called Ross. That's what my old mama named me."

"Say she did?" Ray Martin said. "All right, then, Ross, I'll ask you somethin'. You know how to play anything other than Stripes and Solids? You shoot straight pool?"

"I know how it's done," Ross said.

"Good. Let's you and me knock 'em around."

It wasn't a very exciting game. Ross got to break on the flip of a coin, and he managed to knock the cue ball in the hole right off, without so much as sending the ball's shadow in the direction of any of his targets.

Ray Martin took his shoot, and he cleared about four balls before he missed. Ross shot one in with what looked like mostly a lucky shot, and then he missed, and then Ray Martin ran what was left. They had bet a dollar on the game, and Ross paid up.

"You're good," Ross said.

"I've heard that," Ray Martin said. "You want to go again?"

"I don't know."

"Sure you do. You want to get that dollar back, don't you?"

Ross scratched the side of his nose then shifted his testicles with one hand, as if that would help him make a decision, and said, "I reckon. . . . Hell, all right. I'll bet you that dollar and two more."

"A high roller."

"I got paid; I can spare a little."

Ray Martin grinned at him as if he were a wolf that had just found an injured rabbit caught up in the briars.

By now we weren't shooting anymore, just leaning against the wall watching them, not really knowing how to play straight pool but pretending we did, acting like we knew what was going on.

The game results were similar to the first. Ray Martin chalked his cue while Ross dug a few bucks out of his wallet and paid up. Ray Martin called out, "Hey, Retard, get over here and rack these balls. You keep them racked, I'll give you a quarter. You don't, I'll give you a kick in the ass."

The retard racked the balls. Ross said, "I don't know I want to play anymore."

"Scared?" Ray Martin asked.

"Well, I know a better pool player when I see one."

"How about one more?" Ray Martin said. "Just one more game and we'll throw in the towel."

Ross pursed his lips and looked like he wished he were back on the farm, maybe fucking a calf.

"Hell, you can spare another two or three dollars, can't you?" Ray Martin said.

"I guess," Ross said, and did that lip-pursing thing again. "But I tell you what: You want to go another game, let's go ahead and play it bigger. I ain't been winnin', but I'm gonna bet you can't do three in a row. My pappy always said bet on the third in a row 'cause that's your winner."

"He rich?" Ray Martin asked.

"Well, no," Ross said.

Ray Martin laughed a little, a sharp little laugh like a dog barking. "That's all right; even someone mostly wrong has got to be right now and again."

"Very well, then," Ross said, "I'm gonna trust my old pappy. I'll bet you . . . say, ten dollars."

"That's bold."

"Yeah, and I'm about to change my mind, now that I think about it."

"Oh, no," Ray Martin said. "You made the offer."

"Now that I think about it, it was stupid of me," Ross said. "I guess I was feelin' kind of full of piss and vinegar. How about we drop it? My old pappy ain't even right when he says it's gonna rain."

"No. You're on. Retard's got 'em racked. Come on, country boy, let's shoot."

Of course, when it got right down to it, we were all country boys, just some of us lived in town, as if in disguise, but this Ross, he was a regular turd knocker. He tried to get out of it, said, "Heck, I'll pay you a dollar to forget it. I shouldn't have bet anything. I ain't really no bettin' kind of man. I'm actin' bigger than my goldarn britches."

"You welchin' on a bet, mister?" Ray Martin said, and when he said it, he laid the pool cue on the table and stepped close to Ross. "You welchin'?"

"No. I'm not welchin'. I'm just tryin' to pay my way out so as I can get out cheaper."

Ray Martin shook his head. "Pick up your cue, farmer. You're in."

Ross lost the coin toss on the break, and Ray Martin started out good, went for several shots before he missed. Ray Martin leaned on his pool cue then and looked smug. Ross picked up his cue, studied the table, shook his head, said, "I'll give it a try."

His first shot was a doozy. He busted two balls, and both of them went into pockets. He said, "Now that's somethin'. Even a blind hog finds an acorn now and then." And then he started to shoot again. He didn't miss. Not one shot. When he finished, he looked up, surprised. "Maybe my old pappy was right."

Ray Martin paid Ross the money as if the bills he was peeling out of his wallet were strips of his own skin, and then he insisted on another game. Ross said he'd had enough, that he'd had a lucky run, but Ray Martin jumped the price up to fifty dollars, and after a bit of haggling, they went at it. Ross got the flip, and he started shooting. He didn't miss a shot, and once he even jumped the cue ball over another ball to make a shot. I'd never seen anything like it. The way he moved then was different. There was a fluid sort of way he had of going around the table, nothing like the gangly moves he'd shown before, and his face had changed as well: It was dark with concentration, and there was a sparkle in his eye, as if he were actually powered by electricity.

When he was finished, he said, "I'm gettin' better."

"You sure are," Ray Martin said.

"I guess I could play another game, you want," Ross said.

Ray Martin shook his head and said, "You don't get that much better that quick, and seems to me you ain't talkin' slow as you were before. You sound a little uptown to me."

"Well, a Co-Cola and a good game perks me," Ross said. "I guess it's the sugar."

Ray Martin's eyes narrowed and his forehead wrinkled. "You're a hustler. You hustled me."

Ross looked as if he had just received a blow. "I can't believe you're talkin' like that. You wanted to play. I tried to quit. I tried to pay out on you."

"You were playin' me," Ray Martin said. "You and that car. That ain't no car like a cracker would have. I should have known. You ain't from around here. You're a pool-hall hustler. You're makin' the towns, ain't you?"

"I'm just a man likes a good contest now and again," Ross said, "and I've had a lucky day."

"Tell you somethin'," Ray Martin said, "your goddamned luck just run out." And then Ray Martin's hand dipped into his pocket. We saw a flash of silver, and Ross made a face, and Ray Martin's little cheap Saturday-night special coughed, and we all jumped, and then Ross, who was still holding the pool cue, dropped it, fanned his right knee out to the side, then collapsed as if someone had opened a trapdoor beneath him. The way he fell, the way he crumpled, there wasn't any doubt he was dead. A little hole in his forehead began to ooze blood. The air filled with the stench of what Ross had left in his pants.

Rugger said, "Oh, hell."

The retard said, "You hit him right 'tween the eyes, and he done shit on himself."

Ray Martin turned and looked at me and my friends. We were as quiet as the walls around us. He pointed the gun in my direction. "You," he said, "you look in his pockets, see you can find his keys."

I hesitated only a moment, and Rugger said, "I got it."

Rugger went over and pushed the guy around on the floor so that he could get to his pockets easy, found the keys, held them up, shook them.

"Now my money, and his too," Ray Martin said. "I'm claimin' some interest."

Rugger got the man's money and gave it to Ray Martin, who folded it up and shoved it in the front pocket of his jeans. He tossed the keys on the pool table.

"All right," Ray Martin said, turning back to me. "I want you, tough guy, you and no one else to take those keys and go outside and unlock the trunk of his car, and then I want you back in here faster than a bunny fucks, you understand? Otherwise, you go in the trunk with him after I shoot your balls off. You got me, dry fuck?"

"Yeah," I said, and when I spoke, my mouth was dust-dry. The word came out more like a cough. This wasn't some scuffle in the halls at school, some after-school fistfight at the Dairy Queen. This was the real thing. This was the world where real tough guys lived, and I wasn't one of them.

I took the keys and went outside and unlocked the trunk of the Impala and lifted it up and went back inside. "Give me them keys," Ray Martin said. I gave them to him. He said, "I don't like nobody likes to cheat me. I got rules. Don't cheat me, don't hang with niggers, and don't let women tell you what to do. Keep your hands away from my wallet. And don't never back down. Them's my rules. He broke one of them."

"You didn't have to shoot him," Rugger said. "We could have just beat his ass and got your money back."

"You got him right 'tween the eyes," the retard said, suddenly overcome again with Ray Martin's marksmanship.

"Shut up, Retard," Rugger said. "Now we got a mess."

"Mess can get cleaned up," Ray Martin said. He looked at Donny. "You, nickel dick, go over there and lock the door and pull the blind down. Now."

Donald pulled the blind down over the glass and locked the door. Ray Martin waved the gun at Donald and said, "When I tell you, you look out there see ain't no one comin'. Someone's comin', you close the door and lock it. Ain't no one comin', you say so, and don't be wrong. Got me?"

"Yes, sir," Donald said, as if he were speaking to a teacher.

"You, tough guy," he said to me, "you acted like you wanted some of my action. You still wantin' it?"

"No," I said.

"No, huh. That the way you talk to me? You heard how your friend spoke to me. Let me hear some of that."

"No, sir," I said.

"Now you're talkin'. Stay sharp, I might need you to wipe my butt with your tongue. But right now, you get hold of this fucker's legs, and you," he said to Lee, "you get his head, and you boys take him out and put him in the trunk of his car and close the lid and come back in, and don't screw around."

We picked up the body, and a hair-covered fragment from the back of his skull fell against the tile with a sound like pottery being dropped. As we lifted him, I found myself drawn to his face. Ross's eyes were wide open, and I saw then that everything he had been or might have been, all of his plans and memories, dreams and schemes, they had fled out through the hole in the back of his skull, across the floor in a puddle of blood and brain fragments, a piece of his skull. The body was empty. It was in that moment I knew something I had never really known before. Oh, I knew it on an intellectual basis. I knew we all died. But this wasn't like on TV. This guy didn't just look like a guy lying down. He was truly dead. Looking at him, in that moment, I knew there was nothing beyond the moment, nothing beyond our time on Earth, that dead was dead, and I had never wanted to live more than I did in that moment with my eyes locked on Ross's face. Hell, he wasn't Ross anymore. He was just meat. Dead meat.

I got ahold of Ross's feet. The mess in his pants smelled strong. Lee got his shoulders, and we lifted him and carried him toward the door. When we were about there, Donald unlocked and opened the door and looked out, then pushed the door wide open. Me and Lee put Ross in the trunk of the Impala, curled him around his spare tire, and closed the lid. We went back inside. It was all like a dream.

"All right, now," Ray Martin said, "lock the door."

"What now?" Rugger said, lighting a cigar. The smell of it wafted over the stink Ross had left.

"Get the retard to wipe the floor up . . . but not yet. The backseat of that Impala, it's still got room." Ray Martin looked at us.

I said, "Wait a minute."

"We ain't gonna tell nobody," Donald said.

"Nobody," Lee said, just in case Donald hadn't stated our case firmly enough.

"Hell," Ray Martin said, "I know that. Dead men, they don't talk."

I didn't realize it, but I had backed up against the pool table. I remember it crossing my mind to grab a pool cue, a pool ball, anything. But I knew I wouldn't. I wouldn't do anything. I couldn't move. It was like I was glued to the floor. I thought maybe I was about to do in my pants what Ross had done in his.

"I know these boys," Rugger said softly. "They'd be missed. Their folks know they're here."

That was a lie, but it was a beautiful lie, and I clung to it, hoping.

"You can tell them they was here but they left," Ray Martin said. "I don't want to take chances. And this one," he said, pointing the Saturday-night special at me. "I don't like him. I didn't like him soon as I saw him."

"I know that," Rugger said, and I saw that when he pulled his cigar out of his mouth his hand was shaking. Even he, a man who had fought a mess of oil-field guys with my daddy, he knew Ray Martin was beyond just trouble. Guys like him had invented trouble; they had given it its name. "This boy here," Rugger said, "his daddy and me once fought a bunch of oil-field workers together."

"What's that mean to me?" Ray Martin said.

"It means you and me is kin," Rugger said, "and I'm asking a favor. It's not like you didn't get your money back."

Ray Martin went quiet. You could almost see his brain working behind his skull. "All right," he said. "I wasn't gonna do nothin'. Not really. Well, maybe with the tough guy here." He waved the gun at me. "But here's the thing, and you little turds listen tight as a nun's ass, 'cause you don't, you'll be seein' me and this here gun, maybe a knife or a tire tool . . . : You didn't see a fuckin' thing."

"No. Nothin'," I said.

"What you gonna do with the hayseed?" Rugger asked.

"He wasn't no hayseed. He was a goddamned pool shark. I'm gonna drive him out to the river bottoms. I know a place you can drive that car off, and it'll go deep. And you, Rugger, you're gonna follow me. Maybe we ought to pop the retard too, put him in the backseat."

Rugger shook his head. "He's all right. He won't remember nothin' come tomorrow mornin'. Hell, I got to tell him when to shit."

"You got him right 'tween the eyes," the retard said.

"Shut up," Rugger said. "You go on and sit down on that stool and shut up."

The retard hung his head and went and sat on the stool.

"You can get you a Co-Cola," Rugger said, and the retard got a soda and popped it and went and sat back on the stool and sipped it.

Ray Martin said, "I don't know, man. I'm thinking on it some more, and I don't know I should let these ass-wipes go."

"They ain't gonna say nothin'," Rugger said. "You boys . . . you ain't gonna say nothin', are you?"

"About what?" Donny said.

"There you go," Rugger said.

Ray Martin put the gun in his pocket and said, "Maybe."

"The retard finishes his Coke," Rugger said, "we'll have him wipe up that blood, spray some air freshner around. You drive the fella's car to the bottoms, Ray Martin, and I'll follow. We'll get rid of him. You boys, you go on out the back way. And don't you never say nothin'. Nothin'. Not a fuckin' word."

"No, sir," I said, "we won't," and then I looked at Ray Martin and said, "We won't say anything, sir. I promise."

Ray Martin grinned at me. His teeth reminded me of an animal trap. "Go on then, punks, before I bend you over this pool table and fuck you in the ass, one at a time."

We went quickly out the back door and didn't say a word, just split and went three different ways.

Of course, I saw Donny and Lee after that, in school, in the halls. We waved or smiled, but we didn't hang. I don't think they thought I was so tough anymore. We went our own ways after that. I never went back to the pool hall. I doubt they did. I thought about telling someone about what happened, but didn't, and to the best of my knowledge, neither did Donny or Lee. I had nightmares. I still have nightmares.

I saw Rugger around town a few times and nodded at him. He always looked at me like he'd never seen me before, and he never came back to the garage. Ray Martin I never saw again, and I'm not bothered by that. I never even asked anyone about him, and I think I heard he was in prison somewhere for something or another. I think about Ross a lot, that face, that empty face, all the life there was and ever would be gone from it, leaving the rest of us aware and alone, waiting.

WEAPONIZED

BY DAVID WELLINGTON

For a while it looked like the robots were going to win our wars for us.

I believed it. After what I saw in Syria, back in 2012, sure. I was embedded with a Stryker group tasked with locking down the Blue Zone there. We were rolling in a lead vehicle that was six kilometers outside Damascus when its brakes locked up. The driver looked as surprised as I was. A canned voice from the dashboard told us the vehicle had been halted automatically because an IED had been de-tected. I've been doing this long enough that those three little letters made my flesh crawl. Up ahead in the road an old man with a long white beard and a skullcap was driving a flock of overheated sheep across the dusty road, urging them on, out of the way of the hundred tons of olive-drab depleted-uranium armor bearing down on them. He had been carrying a plastic carrier bag, and he'd dropped it in the middle of the road, as if he was too distracted by the sheep to worry about his lunch.

They still get you like that, sometimes. If you're not paying atten-tion.

"Don't worry, Ms. Flores. We're all good." The driver gave me the grin that soldiers always give to journalists, that practiced, cockeyed smile they think is going to get them five seconds on the evening news.

"What do you do now?" I asked the driver. "Call in a sweeper team?" I sighed, having been through this routine before. It could be an hour before the IED was disabled and the road cleared for travel again, and I had a deadline to meet.

"Naw," he said, lacing his fingers behind his head. He was a kid, like all the soldiers I met that summer, barely out of high school. He had bad acne on his cheeks, and his first tattoo, on the back of his hand, was still bright enough to look like a cartoon. "The Silverhawk'll get it."

The Silverhawk Unmanned Aerial-Weapon Platform was a sort of mini-zeppelin with solar-panel wings and an MTHEL slung under its gondola. It was designed to operate above the cloud layer, loitering for months at a time, soaking up sunlight and not doing much of anything. When an alarm went off in some distant monitoring station, the Silverhawk slowly came to life, picking out its target some three hundred meters below using satellite imagery to find traces of plastic explosive in the plastic bag we were all watching so intently. I never saw the Silverhawk, nor the officer who confirmed the strike, nor even the pencil-thin beam of the MTHEL, a deuterium fluoride laser weapon that heated up the plastic bag to a couple of thousand degrees for a split second—long enough to make the IED inside go *pop*. There was a fizzing noise I could hear through the Stryker's up-armored windows, and then a bright plume of smoke jumped into the air.

"Jesus," I said. "That's it? That was so easy."

"Hold on," the driver told me. "Silverhawk's a two-shot platform." He nodded at the old shepherd, who was staring at us with a look of dawning realization. The old man tried to run. He made it maybe a dozen meters before his head burst open in a cloud of superheated blood. I tried not to react. I'd seen people die before, after all.

Eventually the suddenly unsupervised sheep started heading one by one for a line of distant hills.

"Our CO tells us," the driver let me know, "if we could get about a hundred and twenty of 'em airborne over Damascus, we could have another Green Zone here before the year's out. Then we can get rotated out, go home." Building on the success of the famous Predator drone, the Pentagon had staked the future of warfare on the robots, and for good reason. They were inhumanly good at their job. They didn't have to be fed or killed, and their operators could run them from safe observation bases half a world away. They could be sent into places no human being should ever have to go. If they did get killed, nobody shed a tear. My driver loved them. "This is good for everybody, right? Except you, maybe. No more body bags for you to take pictures of."

But of course there was another market adjustment that year. A bad one. The robots that were supposed to win our wars were too expensive. Only three Silverhawk UAWPs were built before the project ran out of money.

We didn't come close to running out of wars we needed to fight. The Damascus Blue Zone started turning red again, even though back-home approval ratings were dropping and the protests were getting bigger every time a plane full of human remains came back from the Middle East. So another way had to be found. A cheaper way—and when it comes to killing people, there's always a cheaper way.

As long as you have a strong-enough stomach.

The first time I saw the new breed of soldiers, I thought they were engineers in hazmat suits. They were at the far side of a Forward Operating Base in backcountry Muzhikistan, far enough away I didn't notice anything strange about their bright yellow outfits. They were off-loading a cargo helicopter, stacking crates in a warehouse and then going back for more. They moved with almost painful slowness and methodical care, which I assumed meant that the cargo was dangerous or unstable.

It was the kind of thing I would file away for later, something to build a hunch on. If there was a story there, though, I figured it could wait. I was done with my time at that particular FOB. I'd already worked up the story I'd come for: The field medical kits issued to our soldiers in Muzhikistan were full of expired medicines. It was the kind of thing that was happening with depressing regularity in 2019, when the new Green Party Congress was slashing every part of the defense budget they could get their hands on. I was sitting at an outdoor officers' mess, waiting for one last interview with the colonel who had approved shipping out the substandard kits. I was ready to file, but I figured I'd give him one last chance to rebut before I fired my copy off to New York. After all, as soon as this came out, it was going to be his head on the chopping block.

He was twenty minutes late. I was beginning to think I'd been stood up. I'd long since finished off my last bottle of purified water, and I was getting overheated, even in the shade of a picnic umbrella. I could have spent the time tightening up my copy, but instead my eyes kept drifting back to the men dressed all in yellow over by the helipads. They moved so strangely, at first I'd thought they were just being careful with their cargo, but it wasn't just that. There was a certain sameness to their movements. Each of them bent exactly so from the knees before they lifted a crate, and they all lifted at exactly the same moment, as if they'd been choreographed. As if they weren't individual people at all, but some kind of machine—

"Ms. Flores. I apologize but I was held up in a briefing." The colonel loomed over me, blocking out some of the central Asian sun. I blinked a couple of times and smiled up at him. "I'm afraid I'll need to make this quick."

"No problem," I said. "I just wanted to know if you had anything else to say."

He grunted. "Anything more to damn myself with, you mean." He knew about my story, of course. You can't keep anything secret for long in an environment as prone to gossip and boredom as a military base. He knew I had the goods on him. He was looking at a court-martial if not a full congressional hearing. As soon as my story went in, his career was over. He'd be lucky if he avoided jail time. "I'm not sure why you've decided to destroy me," he said, chewing on each word, "when everything I've done was well in line with the orders I received from—"

There was a rattling crash from over by the helipads. I darted my head around to see what had happened. The yellow-suited men there were all frozen, standing around one of the crates that had fallen on the tarmac and broken open. The men in yellow didn't seem to know what to do next. They just stood in place, not even looking at the mess.

Then I had a glimpse of what was inside the crate.

"Ms. Flores, please, I must insist you stay back," the colonel shouted at me.

Too late. I was halfway across the parade ground already. I was trying to fasten my video camera to the epaulet on my left shoulder at the same time as I pressed my bone-conduction microphone to the bottom of my chin. He came up fast behind me and grabbed my arm, but I yanked it free again.

"This is a restricted area, Ms. Flores."

I didn't care.

A human arm had slid out of the cracked-open side of the fallen crate. An arm wrapped in bright yellow plastic, exactly the same shade as the hazmat suits the handlers wore. As I took another step closer, the crate sagged and one end popped open, and three bodies in yellow suits slid out onto the blazing concrete of the helipad.

The handlers, the ones standing around, didn't look surprised to learn they'd been carrying coffins. They didn't make any move to put the bodies back in the crate, either.

I reached up to my shoulder to switch on the camera. Before I could reach it the colonel ripped it off my shirt and smashed it on the ground.

"Sorry. Vital national-security interests at stake."

I gave him my best hard-boiled journalist stare, but it didn't faze him one bit.

"Jesus, get back. Get these fuckers back, will you?" someone called.

Turning again toward the scene of the accident, I saw a soldier in sergeant's stripes pushing his way through the crowd of yellow suits. He wasn't wearing so much as a gas mask. In his hands he was carrying what looked like the controller for a very elaborate video-game console. He tapped out a simple command on the buttons and stared at the yellow suits around him.

Three of them stepped forward and grabbed the bodies under their shoulders. They dragged them fully out of the crate and laid them out on the concrete in a row. The sergeant tapped some more buttons, and the yellow suits stepped back and away.

Then the bodies started to twitch. A hand lifted here. A leg kicked out there. One by one they sat up, slowly, stiffly. One by one they got carefully up on their feet.

Then the three of them—three men who I had been certain were just corpses a minute before—bent and picked up the pieces of the crate they'd been shipped in. Without a word or any kind of spoken order, they carried the pieces into the warehouse, then went back to the helicopter to get another, unbroken crate.

The sergeant headed back into the warehouse as if nothing strange had happened at all. The yellow suits went back to work without a word.

It was about that time I really took a hard look at those hazmat suits, and realized they weren't what I thought. For one thing there were no hoses sticking out of the hoods, no air supplies hanging off of belts, no Velcro flaps up the back for easy access. Most startlingly, there were no faceplates. The yellow suits covered the workers from head to foot, every inch of them, without a seam. The yellow plastic covered their faces without a break. Not even any eyeholes. There was no way the people inside the suits could see out. No way they could see what they were doing.

I turned to look at the colonel.

"You going to tell me what I just saw?" I asked.

The army trains its officers very well to keep their secrets.

But then again, I was trained to figure them out anyway.

"Come on," I said. "You know I'll find out eventually." We had retired to the icy darkness of his office, a modular unit built into a shipping container. It had a table that folded down from one wall, a bunch of folding chairs, and a very noisy air-conditioning unit that I wanted to sit on all day. "My agency will file a Freedom of Information Act suit. My editor will call the senator he plays golf with every Saturday. If none of that works, I'll just flood the blogs with rumors until every UFO nut and survivalist from Oklahoma to Ohio demands to know what's going on."

The colonel poured himself a glass of mineral water that fizzed noisily, and then he sipped at it. He didn't offer me a drink.

"I don't know what you think you saw, Ms. Flores," he told me. "That was just a very minor accident during the off-loading of a helicopter. No one was hurt, and no equipment was damaged. That hardly seems like the kind of thing you would bother putting your byline over. What could you possibly want with this?"

I folded my arms across my chest. "Someone," I said, "is going to get this story. It might as well be me. You've got some kind of secret weapon here. Something brand new. I want a full explanation. You go ahead and clear it with the Pentagon, whatever you need to do. But I want facts, I want figures and names and dates. And if those . . .

those things are going out in the field, I want to go with them. I want to see what you're doing with them. I don't believe for a second that you've invented some new kind of human-shaped robot just to unload cargo."

"I suppose you're right," he admitted finally, sitting back in his chair. "Someone will get to tell this story. Eventually. But it won't be you."

"Uh-huh." I knew what that meant.

And then I knew what it was going to take to change his mind.

"The story I've been working on," I said, "the one I spent six weeks here for—it's going to go badly for certain people when it gets out. I can't just bury it, of course: I have my journalist ethics to consider."

He gave me a chilly smile. There was no doubt in my mind what he thought my professional sensibilities were worth.

"But it doesn't have to go out right away. I could call my editor, tell him that some of my facts didn't line up. That I needed more time to get them straight."

The smile on his face was frozen solid.

"He'd be willing to wait a while. Maybe even thirty days. Which would give certain people a little more time to cover their asses."

The smile cracked. You didn't get to his rank in the army without knowing how to make decisions in a hurry, and he didn't waste time arguing with me. He knew I had him over a barrel. "I'm personally taking out a detail to run counterinsurgency operations tomorrow. You can go with us. Under certain conditions."

"Like?"

"No cameras."

"You already destroyed mine."

He sneered at my ruse. "I mean no cameras at all. Not even the one in your cell phone. I won't interfere with what you write. But there will be no pictures of what you see. Furthermore, I'll accompany you at all times. If I decide that your . . . safety is in jeopardy at any time, I'll put you on the first transport back to base."

"You expect me to agree to this? What's to keep you from sending me back as soon as I start finding out something interesting?"

"The fact that no matter what you see or don't see, you'll be getting access to the biggest story of your career," he said. I noticed for the first time that his eyes were a deep, glacial blue. "Just the briefing I give you before we leave will probably net you a Pulitzer."

I laughed. "Come on. Just because you're field-testing a new kind of robot—"

"Those aren't robots, Ms. Flores. Those are American citizens. Or rather, they were. Before they died."

It was eighty degrees out when I woke up the next morning, just before dawn. It would creep over a hundred by lunchtime. I dressed, packed a few things, and slipped down to the motor pool, where I found the colonel waiting for me. He had an MP frisk me for illicit cameras, but I was clean. I had only brought along a couple bottles of water, a notebook, a pen, and a tube of sunblock. I wasn't about to blow this scoop by failing to meet his conditions.

Once he was sure I was properly defanged, he started loading up a troop transport—an unarmored truck with an open flatbed, not even a canopy to protect the soldiers onboard from the sun.

They didn't need that kind of protection. They didn't feel the heat, I knew now. They didn't feel anything.

The yellow suits they wore had their own acronym, of course, like everything the Army owns—IPWs, Insect-Proof Wrappers. They were made of very tough Mylar and designed to keep bugs from getting at the troops inside. The army couldn't stop their animated corpses from rotting away, but they could slow the process down a little. The colonel estimated that the average member of his new battalion would last six months before its performance was degraded by decomposition.

The wrappers served another purpose, of course, which was to keep me—and the Muzhiki population—from seeing what our new soldiers looked like.

The new soldiers were dead. I still had a hard time accepting it, but the colonel wasn't just pulling my leg. They were dead bodies, most of them the bodies of soldiers who died in other conflicts. The army had approached their families, very quietly, and gotten their permission to use the bodies for any purpose required. The families, in exchange, got enough money to send the decedent's children to community college, or maybe enough for a down payment on a house, if they could afford the mortgage. They had not been told what the bodies would be used for but had signed waivers saying they didn't require further information.

Considering how bad the economy was back home, I didn't imagine they had a lot of trouble getting those waivers.

The army picked up the bodies in unmarked trucks and took them to a special facility in Baghdad. Within a week they were up and moving about again, new soldiers for a new era of warfare.

"The current nomenclature for them is PMCs. As in PostMortem Combatants," the colonel told me.

"So they're . . . undead," I said, staring into the back of the truck. Fifty blank yellow faces looked back at me. "Zombies."

The colonel winced at the word. "They're not going to eat your brains, if that's what you mean. They don't eat. They don't think or feel any pain. Their brains are completely shut down. We control them by sequential electrical stimulation of nerve fibers."

In high school biology class I'd seen that at work. The teacher had a pair of severed frog's legs attached to a dry-cell battery. When she flipped a switch, the legs kicked. This was the same principle. Just a little more advanced.

"We insert a microchip in the top of the spinal column," the colonel said, reaching over to touch my neck just below my hairline. I flinched as if his fingers were icy cold. "The chip is programmed with a number of algorithms. If we want the PMC to walk, the chip activates the leg muscles in the correct sequence to lift one foot and put it in front of the other. If we want them to pick up a crate, the chip has a subroutine for that. This generation of chip has some fifty basic programs, any of which can be chosen by the controller."

The controller—meaning anyone, like the sergeant I'd seen at the FOB—had the right equipment to send the right signals to those chips. The controller could give a general order, and the PMCs would act as a group, or he could choose a certain PMC, identified by serial number, and give it specific commands.

"And this is cheaper than robots?" I asked.

The colonel favored me with one of his chilly smiles. "The chips are made in China for under ten dollars. They can be inserted without surgical equipment: All it takes is a syringe and a strong, wide-bore needle. The Mylar for the wrappers costs us pennies for the square yard. Ms. Flores, it will cost us more to feed and house you on this trip than it did to activate my new troops."

He looked especially proud of that fact.

"But they're not . . . intelligent on their own. They can't make decisions for themselves," I said. "They can't be the equivalent of real troops."

"Let's find out together, shall we?" He helped me up into the back of the truck. In a few minutes we were rolling deep into disputed territory.

We passed through scattered villages as the truck bumped and bounced over smoothed-out stretches of desert that could barely be called roads. The Muzhiks came out of their houses to watch us pass by, shepherds and store owners in wool vests despite the heat, old women draped from head to toe in modest garments that looked dusty and uncomfortable even first thing in the morning. They were Asian Muslims, almost uniformly belonging to a very old, very quiet Sufi sect, though their genes had been passed down from Genghis Khan and his many wives. They did not wave or smile. They stared at the yellow men in the truck and hurried back to their business.

Muzhikistan is a very old country and one of the poorest on Earth. The people there have nothing to offer the world that it can't get more cheaply or more efficiently somewhere else. The only thing even vaguely important about the country is that if you want to get oil from Russia down to Baghdad, or vice versa, you have to go through Muzhikistan. Russia and the U.S. had joined forces in the early 2010s to build a super-high-tech and strategically vital pipeline that managed to cut Muzhikistan in half.

And of course some of the locals had taken exception to that.

They claimed that the pipeline infringed on ancestral nomadic herding grounds that had been passed down from father to son since before the fall of the Roman Empire. They claimed that the foreign workers who came in to install and then service the pipeline were stealing Muzhiki jobs, corrupting Muzhiki youth with their outsider culture, and wrecking the Muzhiki environment with spills and industrial waste products. In all of these things they were 100 percent correct. The Muzhikis took their case to the UN. The Western world, which these days doesn't even bother pretending we're here for anything but the oil, gave a collective shrug.

So some Muzhikis—the young, the bored, the inevitable dead-enders—started blowing up sections of pipeline and killing oil workers at lonely, isolated maintenance stations. That's when the army came in.

It was police work that was needed. But in the last fifteen years, the army has gotten very good at a certain kind of brutal police work. I'd seen it in Syria, in Palestine, in Afghanistan (against the Taliban, the anti-Taliban militias, and the resurgent Taliban in 2014, when I had to wear a burka in public or risk being picked off by snipers). It worked. A small group of soldiers would identify the village where a suspected terrorist lived. They would go door-to-door, demanding to know where the perp was hiding. Some old men would get beaten up. A lot of women would run into the street screaming. And then a soldier from Missouri wearing a hundred thousand dollars worth of body armor and electronics would haul a shriveled old farmer in a tattered robe out of a spider hole, and nobody would ever see the old guy again.

While no one was watching me, I took the tube of sunscreen out of my bag and smeared the thick goo all over my cheeks and throat. No one noticed that it was my first application of the day. The living men around me were in their zone, ready for a confrontation. The PMCs couldn't see what I was doing.

When our truck pulled into the main square of a village about seventy kilometers from the FOB, I knew what to expect. Of course, I wasn't prepared for how the new soldiers—the PMCs—would be different.

The colonel raised one hand in the air, and the sergeant controlling the PMCs started pressing buttons. In perfect synchrony the yellow suits clambered up from where they'd been sitting totally motionless for the whole ride and leaped down into the dusty square. They brushed past me one after the other, and I had a chance to realize they didn't smell like anything but plastic before they were deployed.

The colonel stood up on the roof of the truck's cab with a bullhorn and a poster-sized photograph of a kid with crazy eyes. It didn't look like a class picture or a formal portrait—more like a grainy blowup of a satellite photo, maybe taken while the kid was enrolled in a terrorist training camp over in Waziristan. The colonel started shouting through the bullhorn in the local dialect of Arabic. I understood maybe one word in five, but I had heard such announcements often enough before: "We are looking for this person. He is wanted for insurgency and is an enemy of all freedom-loving people. If he is surrendered immediately we will leave you in peace. You have five minutes to comply."

Except this time they didn't get the five minutes. That had always been a problem, that waiting period: In five minutes a trained insurgent could be halfway across town, halfway up into the hills that loomed over the village like the sheltering arms of Allah Himself. Or he could be arming himself, his family, his neighbors—getting ready for a draw down with the U.S. military.

This time he wasn't given the chance. The sergeant bent over his controller and tapped a few keys, pulled a few trigger buttons. And the PMCs went to work.

They didn't canvass the village, knocking on doors, asking questions. They couldn't talk, and I guess maybe knocking wasn't one of their fifty programmed behaviors. They didn't move through the village like police at all. They dismantled it.

The little houses were made out of corrugated tin or of wood so rare and so old and dry it snapped when they pulled at it. Some of the houses were little more than tents with one cinder-block wall, and those came down with almost comical ease.

The women of the village started screaming on cue. Old men and young boys came rushing out of their collapsing homes, shouting in Arabic and grabbing up stones to throw or brandishing long traditional knives. It was enough to make me sick—although I did notice one thing in favor of the colonel's new troops. They weren't killing anyone. They weren't beating anybody who showed a sign of resistance, they weren't humiliating people in their own homes. They weren't even armed, because apparently shooting a gun was not one of their fifty programmed actions.

They were destroying with their bare hands everything the Muzhiki owned, and they could not be stopped.

It was enough to get the reaction the colonel wanted. There was a sudden horrible wail from a woman just old enough to be the wanted man's mother. And then the target of the raid, the guy from the poster, came rushing out of where he'd been hidden behind some sheep in a makeshift pen. He was armed, as was to be expected, with an AK-47 assault rifle, and he came out shooting.

I ducked reflexively as the bullets chattered out of the gun's barrel, tearing into the yellow-covered flesh of one of the PMCs. The dead soldier stopped what he had been doing—which was pulling down the roof of a granary shed—and turned to face his attacker. The insurgent fired again and again into the yellow target before him, and suddenly I understood why the army had chosen that preposterous color for the PMCs' uniforms.

It didn't matter if they got shot. In fact, it was better if they got shot, because then somebody in a camouflage uniform, somebody living, wouldn't.

The PMC didn't fall down. It staggered a little as each bullet tore into its body. It didn't move to counterattack or raise its arms to shield its face. The insurgent kept shooting, even as the expression on his face went from furious hatred to total incomprehension to blank shock. Eventually his weapon ran dry.

Then the PMCs moved in, crowding him with their bodies. Jumping on top of him, holding him down with their . . . uh . . . dead weight. The insurgent tried to free the bayonet from the end of his rifle and stab at his subduers, but they didn't care if they got stabbed, any more than they cared about being shot. Eventually they disarmed him and dragged him back to the truck. He was pushed, bleeding a little but not seriously injured, up into the flatbed, where he stared at me with mad eyes. He kept licking his lips as if his mouth had gone bone dry. The colonel had a set of plastic restraints ready and secured him without any further fuss.

The PMCs filed back onto the truck without so much as waving good-bye to the people they'd so effectively terrorized. We were back on the road before the dust had even begun to settle.

We were out on mission for ten days, during which time I saw the PMCs take apart half a dozen villages. Every time we actually caught an insurgent, he was whisked away in a helicopter before I had a chance to talk to him, and we would move on to the next destination before I knew we were done. At the end of the day the truck would take us to some dry riverbed or natural cave, where we would bunk for the night—the sergeant and a couple of corporals in one tent, the colonel and I sleeping in another. The PMCs didn't need shelter, even when a dust storm kept us pinned down for most of one day. At a button-press from their controller, they would sit down with their heads between their knees and just . . . go limp. Occasionally one of them would fall over, but no one bothered to prop it back up again.

They didn't eat. They could be woken up at any time of day or night as needed. They didn't get bored; they didn't trade scuttlebutt; they didn't need to dig latrines every time they dug in at a new position. And they required very little in the way of medical attention.

That was what the corporals were for. They had a big crate mounted on the side of the truck, which was full of patch kits and a big heat laminator they used to fix holes in the IPWs. They would cut off a length of yellow Mylar from a big roll and then lay it in place over any cuts or tears in the wrappers. Then using what were for all intents and purposes extremely powerful hair dryers, they fused the patches into the PMC's wrapper to repair the airtight seal. The Mylar would get hot enough to bubble and give off fumes, so the corporals wore surgical masks when they worked, but the PMCs never complained or even flinched.

"What happens," I asked the colonel one night while we were watching this process, "if one of them breaks a leg or gets hit by a mortar round or—"

"If they fall below a certain threshold of functionality, we remove them from service."

"What does that entail?" I asked. "Last rites? A military funeral?"

"They've already had those honors. We give them command number fifty, the last one they'll ever perform. They dig a grave for themselves and then climb in and fill it back up. What are you doing with that sunscreen?" he asked suddenly.

I had been rubbing it into my forehead and eyelids. I stopped and had to think of an appropriate lie. It was well after dark, and even the moon was a bare sliver of white in the sky. "It's got moisturizers in it," I said as calmly as I could. "And my skin gets pretty dry and flaky in this desert air."

He looked a lot more suspicious than I liked, so I changed the subject quickly.

"So how do you think the public is going to react when people read my report?" I asked.

The colonel rubbed at his face for a moment. It had been a long deployment for someone who really ought have been working a desk job. "They'll probably be up in arms for a while," he sighed, "until they start seeing the results. Imagine if we could replace all of our land forces with PMCs. Imagine what that would mean: No more casualties; the defense budget could be cut in half overnight. The thing your kind don't appreciate—" he said, but I had to stop him.

"'My kind'? What's that supposed to mean?"

He gave me a cold stare. "Reporters." He pulled a crate over by the front of our tent and sat down on it. He did not offer me one. "The thing you can't seem to understand is that we don't want to be doing this. We don't want to be doing any of this." He waved expansively, taking in the rocks around us, the hills off to our left, all of Muzhikistan. "We would like very much to just go home. Soldiers don't like being shot at. Officers don't like filling up body bags. Nobody likes paying for us to do this. If we could end war as we know it, don't you think everyone would agree it's worth getting over a little squeamishness?"

"Some people will say you're desecrating the dead," I told him. "No matter how cheap your secret weapon is. Anyway—if we replace all our ground troops with dead people, won't you be out of a job?"

I could see his teeth gleam even in the darkness. "What job? You've already sabotaged my career."

It was true, but I didn't think gloating would be useful, and I couldn't bring myself to sympathize. "Listen, I think I'll turn in for the night."

Another nonspecific wave. He didn't seem to care much what I did, as long as I stayed out of trouble.

Inside the tent I took out my tube of sunblock and, with the cap on, gave it a good squeeze. It was mostly empty now, but I could feel the thickness of the concealed circuitry in the bottom of the tube. It vibrated silently in my hand, telling me it was working properly.

It wasn't, of course, sunscreen in the tube. Instead it was a very special goop designed by a Dutch television network—a kind of liquid camera. Each tiny droplet of the cream was a photosensitive cell, a charged bubble that held a positive charge when it was smeared on but which flipped over to a negative charge when it was exposed to light. The droplets on their own were only capable of recording a single pixel worth of information, but when you spread enough of them on any given surface, they added up. The circuitry hidden in the tube could read the charge states of the bubbles and build a coherent picture out of what they were seeing—a black-and-white image with a resolution in the low megapixels. The pictures were then stored in solid-state memory for download at any wireless node. Everything I'd seen on our tour of the Muzhikistan countryside was being recorded in that tube—and would be until I ran out of goo.

I had promised the colonel I wouldn't bring any cameras. Instead I'd brought a couple million of them. I was hardly the first journalist, though, to tell a little lie to get to a big truth.

It looked like I had one more day's worth of cream left, which should have been more than enough. We were supposed to be heading back to the FOB the next morning, and I already had enough footage to shock the world.

I wasn't counting on the counter-counterinsurgency.

The colonel didn't wake me in the night to let me know the PMCs had been sent out on assignment. Even when I woke on my own and found them gone from the camp, he refused to tell me where they'd gone or why. "We received some troubling intelligence last night," was all he would say, "so I sent them to investigate."

"You promised me full access," I said.

"No. If there was any chance of you coming to harm, I said I would send you back to base immediately. That's what I'm doing now."

"Danger? What kind of danger?"

But clearly we'd moved beyond the realm of things I needed to know. He refused to say another word; instead, he gave one of the corporals orders to call for my immediate evacuation.

I was still waiting for the chopper that would take me back to base when the PMCs started marching back into our camp. Apparently the colonel hadn't been lying about the danger. There were only forty-one of them—nine must have been damaged to the point where they couldn't even crawl home—and twelve of the ones that made it back were so badly hurt they had to be given command fifty, the order to bury themselves for good. Their arms hung loose inside their IPWs. Their heads swayed limply on crooked necks. Some of their IPWs were torn open, and I got my first glimpse of what a six-month-old dead body looks like: Imagine a mummy with its wrappings torn off. Their eyes were sewn shut, their faces mummified, lips desiccated and drawn back over yellow, protruding teeth. I'd seen dead bodies before, but still I was shocked, perhaps because I'd gotten so used to the sanitized, cheery yellow version of their faces.

I also got to smell them up close for the first time. The IPWs had been hermetically sealed for a reason that had nothing to do with keeping bugs out. I'd been covering war zones long enough that I knew the smell of death, of course—that curiously foul stench you can't really describe in words. I had expected that the rankness of a torn-open PMC would be unbearable, toxic. Actually, this wasn't so bad. But it was different. The PMCs smelled musty. Ancient. Like something pulled out of a pyramid that hadn't been mummified properly.

The colonel took one look at them and started bellowing orders. "Get these things ready to go back out. We're not letting them win this one. You—" he shouted at the sergeant, "find out what the satellites are saying. I need intel, intel, intel!"

I've been in triage centers when a squad of injured soldiers comes in, and it's a horror show. Blood everywhere, limbs hanging by scraps of skin, soldiers who are badly disfigured holding on against the pain to make sure their less-fortunate buddies don't die before they arrive. This was nothing like that. The PMCs didn't scream, and they didn't smell like shit and blood. But there was a similar level of tense energy in the air, a familiar sense of the wrongness of it. The PMCs were nearly invulnerable; the insurgents we'd captured hadn't so much as slowed them down. So what the hell had happened last night?

The colonel was busy giving orders. Every other living person in the camp was busy carrying them out. It was my big chance to ask the PostMortem Combatants what was going on—and I had one shot at doing it before I was shipped back to the FOB, out of harm's way and miles from the biggest story in my career.

So I took my chances. I didn't know I was walking into a trap.

"Sorry about this, guy. I hope he's right and that you're not even a little bit aware of what's going on," I said. The PMC in front of me, one of the few not even scuffed by whatever had happened to the rest, didn't respond, of course. It couldn't. There might be a human body inside its yellow Insect-Proof Wrapper, but for all intents and purposes it was just another, cheaper kind of robot.

I knew that. I understood it, with my brain. My heart still jumped in my chest when I spread the last of my liquid-camera goo on my hand, then wiped it across the dead guy's face mask.

I needed to know what the PMCs were being sent into—what had damaged so many of them, and what the colonel expected them to do about it. The colonel wasn't going to let me tag along for their mission so I would have to get the next best thing—a POV shot of the fighting.

For the circuitry in the tube to record properly, it had to be within three meters of the liquid camera. I cut a little hole in the PMC's wrapper with a multitool and shoved the tube inside, against his chest. I had no idea how I was going to retrieve it later when it had recorded the video I wanted, but I figured I could worry about that when the time came. Once I was safely back at the base, I would have all the time in the world to figure it out. First, though, I had to get back to my tent without being seen. If the colonel knew what I was doing—well, I didn't want to think about it. I turned around and figured in the chaos of the corporals' fixing up the PMCs, I could avoid detection just a little longer, if I kept my head down, if I moved quietly behind that pile of crates—

"Interesting," the colonel said, behind me. He tapped me on the back with a combat baton.

It felt like he was holding an icicle and running it up and down my spine. I tried to think of a good excuse why I was skulking around the PMCs, but my brain absolutely refused to help me.

"I could have you up on charges for tampering with army material," he said, smiling. I'd never seen him look so happy. "I could have you charged with treason. Giving aid to the enemy."

"Maybe," I said, because it was the best I could think of, "I could just drop that story altogether. You know, the one about the medical supplies, I mean, after all—"

"I have a better idea," he said, and tapped me again with his baton.

It was one of the new models that has a military-grade taser built into the business end. It felt like I was a light switch, and someone had just flipped me to OFF.

I woke up with yellow Mylar pressed against my face.

I've spent my career describing other peoples' pain and torment. I've seen things I will never, never write about, smelled things no normal girl from New Jersey should ever have had to smell.

I've never been more scared than at that moment. I have nightmares about it still.

I tried to gasp for breath, but Mylar filled my mouth and my nose. I clawed and tore at my face, trying to clear my airway, and found my hands were swathed in the yellow plastic as well, so that I couldn't even get a good grip on the IPW covering my face. My heart raced and threatened to burst. My sweat glands went into overdrive, and every muscle in my body started to tense with a flood of adrenaline.

I couldn't see, smell, or hear anything. I was in total darkness. I felt my body start to shut down.

Then a trickle of oxygen found its way to my mouth. I breathed in sweet air and realized I might live through the next thirty seconds. It helped a little to cut the fear.

As it transpired, when I'd been sealed into my own personal IPW, the hood hadn't been completely fused shut. Otherwise I would have asphyxiated long before I woke up. With hands like useless paws, I somehow managed to tear the hood open some more, enough to get my nose and mouth clear, then my eyes.

I was lying on my back in the desert looking up at a trillion stars. They've never looked brighter or more beautiful.

Eventually I started to think again. To think about what had happened to me. The colonel had decided to get rid of me. That much I already knew. I would have assumed that after he stunned me, he would have just shot me and had me buried somewhere far away from any sign of habitation. But no, I should have known better. He knew all about covering his ass, about always giving himself a believable excuse.

I sat up and looked around me and saw twenty-nine PMCs sitting near me in their rest postures—heads between their knees, arms folded behind their necks. A couple of them had fallen over.

I got up, still wearing my IPW, and scanned the horizon, looking for any sign of civilization. There was none. I had no idea where I was and no way to figure it out. Underneath the wrapper my pockets felt empty. I was unarmed, with no food or water, and the only people in the world who knew where I was were trying to kill me. It looked like they might succeed.

I could see the cover story the colonel had worked up for my death. Ever-so-curious journalist demands to be sent into the danger zone. When the army says no, fearing for her safety, she disguises herself as one of the new anonymous soldiers and goes anyway. Tragically, she does not make it back.

It was a pretty good plan, I had to admit. My editor might ask some uncomfortable questions when he heard the cover story, but he would have no leads, no witnesses who weren't 100 percent loyal to the colonel. There would be nothing anyone could do.

Without a sound or any kind of warning, the PMCs around me started to wake up. With a horrible uniformity they rose stiffly to their feet. I couldn't see the sergeant with the controller, but I knew that he didn't need to be anywhere nearby: He could control them via satellite from anywhere in the world. What mattered was that they were here and ready. Whatever it was they'd come to fight, it was on its way.

The enemies came over the nearest hilltop a few minutes later, picking their way very carefully down the loose rocky slope. I had no idea what kind of armaments they might be packing—enough to smash PMCs to bits, I knew. That meant they'd be carrying heavier stuff than just AK-47s. Maybe they were insurgents with RPGs and hand grenades, maybe just a mortar team. I braced myself for the first explosions.

There were no explosions. Instead, the enemy just kept coming, one step at a time, with a slowness that made me want to scream. It wasn't the only strange thing about them. For one thing they were mostly naked. Each of them had no more than a blanket to cover himself. And they all wore them the same strange way—draped over their heads, obscuring their faces completely.

As completely as the hoods of the IPWs around me.

The problem with waging warfare on the cheap is that anybody can do it. The chips that transformed our dead soldiers into PMCs cost less than ten dollars and required no special equipment to implant—the colonel had been quite clear on this. The thing is, in the more urbanized parts of Muzhikistan, an AK-47 would cost fifteen dollars. For the insurgents, making their own zombified troops would actually save them money.

They did not carry weapons any more than our PMCs did. Poking out from under their blankets, their fingers were withered and spindly and looked like claws. Very quickly I realized that that was exactly what they'd become.

When the two groups of undead soldiers met in battle, they slammed into each other with all the strength they possessed. There was no concern for taking cover, for flanking the enemy, for any of the small-unit tactics modern soldiers have had drilled into them. This was like a war of chimpanzees, with brute strength the only thing that mattered. PMCs grappled and slapped at the insurgent dead. The insurgents tore and pulled at the IPWs our troops wore. Bones snapped. Limbs were torn free and cast aside without thought.

It was a massacre—for both sides. The colonel had said he wouldn't let his PMCs lose this struggle, and it looked like he intended to expend every last one of his troops if he needed to. I saw them being trampled by the insurgents, sometimes a dozen or more insurgents piling on top of a PMC, holding it down until they could tear it to shreds. Others were clawed at and beaten until they were tangled up in the shreds of their own IPWs, too constricted to move or fight.

For a while I just stood there watching, struck immobile by the horror of what I saw. It couldn't last, though. I'd been sent here to die, after all, and I was still wearing most of an IPW.

An insurgent caught me unaware, grabbing at my legs with emaciated arms. Its—his—blanket had fallen away in the melee, and his mummified face stared up at me unseeing. I shrieked and tried to kick him off, but his undead strength was far too much for me, and I began to fall. The only thing that kept me from being dragged down and torn to bits was that another insurgent came up by my side and grabbed my arm. Then he started to pull, until I felt my bones twisting in my shoulder.

The pain was intense. I clamped my eyes shut and started to pray, something I hadn't done since I was a schoolgirl. I don't think it was God who saved me, though.

It was a PMC.

I don't know if they are programmed to come to each other's aid. Maybe the one who saved me was just looking for fresh targets and saw the two insurgents who were pulling me in opposite directions. But a figure in bright yellow came out of nowhere then and smashed into the insurgent holding my arm, knocking him loose. Somehow I managed to slip out of the grasp of the one holding my legs. My IPW slid off of me as I struggled free, and I think the dead insurgent may have wanted to kill the wrapper more than it wanted to kill me.

Once I was free I just ran. Ran as far and as fast as I could. A couple of the insurgents pursued me, but I had one distinct advantage over them—my desperation. I still had something to lose.

I didn't go back until hours later. Even then I took my time about it, hiding in the rocky debris of a hillside until I was sure, absolutely sure, that all of the insurgent dead were gone. It took all my courage to approach the place again, but I had to do it.

On the battlefield only one figure was moving, and it didn't look very dangerous. It had only one functioning arm and was using it to try to dig its own grave. To carry out command fifty. It wasn't making much progress.

I helped it as best I could, digging at the loose earth with my bare fingers. I didn't know—I'll never know—if it was the PMC that saved me when I should have died. I owed that dead man at least as much.

I hadn't come back to bury the unquiet dead but for a task almost as grisly. It took me a long time to search all the bodies that lay motionless on that field. The whole time I was convinced that the colonel was going to come rolling over the hill in his troop transport, that he knew I was still alive and was coming to finish the job himself if he had to. But I had one last thing I had to do. Then I could flee once more. I could head over the hill, up toward higher ground, where maybe I could see some sign of the pipeline. I could follow it to some compound full of friendly engineers and maintenance crews, or maybe just to the nearest Muzhik village. Anywhere I could get some water, and after that, start my long journey home.

But not quite yet. First, I studied the bodies and pieces of bodies all around me, looking for one particular corpse. There was no distinguishing mark on any of the IPWs, nothing to tell me I'd found the right one. Nothing—until—there.

I bent over one dismembered PMC and saw a slightly greasy sheen on the front of its featureless hood. It had to be the one, the one I'd slathered with my liquid camera. I tore open its IPW with shaky fingers and found the tube of fake sunblock still pressed against its chest.

The world had to see the images it held.

TWITTERING FROM THE CIRCUS OF THE DEAD

BY JOE HILL

WHAT IS TWITTER?

"Twitter is a service for friends, family, and co-workers to communicate and stay connected through the exchange of quick, frequent answers to one simple question: *What are you doing?* . . . Answers must be under 140 characters in length and can be sent via mobile texting, instant message, or the Web."

—from *twitter.com*

 TYME2WASTE

> **TYME2WASTE** I'm only trying this because I'm so bored I wish I was dead. Hi Twitter. Want to know what I'm doing? Screaming inside.
> 8:17 PM February 28th from Tweetie
>
> ---
>
> **TYME2WASTE** My didn't that sound melodramatic.
> 8:19 PM February 28th from Tweetie
>
> ---
>
> **TYME2WASTE** Lets try this again. Hello Twitterverse. I am Blake and Blake is me. What am I doing? Counting seconds.
> 8:23 PM February 28th from Tweetie
>
> ---
>
> more

TYME2WASTE Only about 50,000 more until we pack up and finish what is hopefully the last family trip of my life.
8:25 PM February 28th from Tweetie

TYME2WASTE It's been all downhill since we got to Colorado. And I don't mean on my snowboard.
8:27 PM February 28th from Tweetie

TYME2WASTE We were supposed to spend the break boarding and skiing but it's too cold and won't stop snowing so we had to go to plan B.
8:29 PM February 28th from Tweetie

TYME2WASTE Plan B is Mom and I face off in a contest to see who can make the other cry hot tears of rage and hate first.
8:33 PM February 28th from Tweetie

TYME2WASTE I'm winning. All I have to do to make Mom leave the room at this point is walk into it. Wait, I'm walking into room where she is now . . .
8:35 PM February 28th from Tweetie

TYME2WASTE She's such a mean bitch.
10:11 PM February 28th from Tweetie

TYME2WASTE @caseinSD, @bevsez, @harmlesspervo yay my real friends! I miss San Diego. Home soon.
10:41 PM February 28th from Tweetie

TYME2WASTE @caseinSD Hell no I'm not afraid Mom is going to read any of this. She's never going to know about it.
10:46 PM February 28th from Tweetie

more

TYME2WASTE After she made me take down my blog, it's not like I'm ever going to tell her.
10:48 PM February 28th from Tweetie

TYME2WASTE You know what bitchy thing she said to me a couple hours ago? She said the reason I don't like Colorado is because I can't blog about it.
10:53 PM February 28th from Tweetie

TYME2WASTE She's always saying the net is more real for me and my friends than the world. For us, nothing really happens till someone blogs about it.
10:55 PM February 28th from Tweetie

TYME2WASTE Or writes about it on their Facebook page. Or at least sends an instant message about it. She says the internet is "life-validation."
10:55 PM February 28th from Tweetie

TYME2WASTE Oh and we don't go online because it's fun. She has this attitude that people socially network 'cause they're scared to die. It's deep.
10:58 PM February 28th from Tweetie

TYME2WASTE She sez no one ever blogs their own death. No one instant messages about it. No one's Facebook status ever says "dead."
10:59 PM February 28th from Tweetie

TYME2WASTE So for online people, death doesn't happen. People go online to hide from death and wind up hiding from life. Words right from her lips.
11:01 PM February 28th from Tweetie

more

TYME2WASTE Shit like that, she ought to write fortune cookies for a living. You see why I want to strangle her. With an Ethernet cable.

11:02 PM February 28th from Tweetie

TYME2WASTE Little bro asked if I could blog about him having sex with a certain goth girl from school to make it real but no one laughed.

11:06 PM February 28th from Tweetie

TYME2WASTE I told Mom, no, the reason I hate Colorado is 'cause I'm stuck with her and it's all waaaaay too real.

11:09 PM February 28th from Tweetie

TYME2WASTE And she said that was progress and got this smug bitch look on her face and then Dad threw down his book & left the room.

11:11 PM February 28th from Tweetie

TYME2WASTE I feel worst for him. A few more months and I'm gone forever but he's stuck with her for life and all her anger and the rest of it.

11:13 PM February 28th from Tweetie

TYME2WASTE I'm sure he wishes he just got us plane tickets now. Suddenly our van is looking like the setting for a cage match duel to the death.

11:15 PM February 28th from Tweetie

TYME2WASTE All of us jammed in together for 3 days. Who will emerge alive? Place your bets ladies and germs. Personally I predict no survivors.

11:19 PM February 28th from Tweetie

---

more

TYME2WASTE Arrr. Fuck. Shit. It was dark when I went to bed and it is dark now and Dad says it's time to leave. This is so terribly wrong.

6:21 AM March 1st from Tweetie

TYME2WASTE We're going. Mom gave the condo a careful search to make sure nothing got left behind, which is how she found me.

7:01 AM March 1st from Tweetie

TYME2WASTE Damn knew I needed a better hiding place.

7:02 AM March 1st from Tweetie

TYME2WASTE Dad just said the whole trip ought to take between thirty-five and forty hours. I offer this as conclusive proof there is no God.

7:11 AM March 1st from Tweetie

TYME2WASTE Writing something on Twitter just to piss Mom off. She knows if I'm typing something on my phone I'm obviously engaged in a sinful act.

7:23 AM March 1st from Tweetie

TYME2WASTE I'm expressing myself and staying in touch with my friends and she hates it. Whereas if I was knitting and unpopular . . .

7:25 AM March 1st from Tweetie

TYME2WASTE . . . then I'd be just like her when she was 17. And I'd also marry the first guy who came along and get knocked up by 19.

7:25 AM March 1st from Tweetie

----

more

TYME2WASTE Coming down the mountain in the snow. Coming down the mountain in the snow. 1 more hairpin turn and my stomach's gonna blow . . .

7:30 AM March 1st from Tweetie

TYME2WASTE My contribution to this glorious family moment is going to come when I barf on my little brother's head.

7:49 AM March 1st from Tweetie

TYME2WASTE If we wind up in a snowbank and have a Donner Party, I know whose ass they'll be chewing on first. Mine.

7:52 AM March 1st from Tweetie

TYME2WASTE Of course my survival skilz would amount to Twittering madly for someone to rescue us.

7:54 AM March 1st from Tweetie

TYME2WASTE Mom would make a slingshot out of rubber from the tires, kill squirrels with it, stitch a fur bikini out of 'em and be sad when we got saved.

7:56 AM March 1st from Tweetie

TYME2WASTE Dad would go out of his mind because we'd have to burn his books to stay warm.

8:00 AM March 1st from Tweetie

TYME2WASTE Eric would put on a pair of my pantyhose. Not to stay warm. Just cause my little brother wants to wear my pantyhose.

8:00 AM March 1st from Tweetie

TYME2WASTE I wrote that last bit cause Eric was looking over my shoulder.

8:02 AM March 1st from Tweetie

----

more

TYME2WASTE But the sick bastard said wearing my pantyhose is the closest he'll probably come to getting laid in high school.
8:06 AM March 1st from Tweetie

TYME2WASTE He's completely gross but I love him.
8:06 AM March 1st from Tweetie

TYME2WASTE Mom taught him to knit while we were snowed in here in happy CO and he knitted himself a cocksock and then she was sorry.
8:11 AM March 1st from Tweetie

TYME2WASTE I miss my blog which she had no right to make me take down.
8:13 AM March 1st from Tweetie

TYME2WASTE But Twittering is better than blogging because my blog always made me feel like I should have interesting ideas to blog about.
8:14 AM March 1st from Tweetie

TYME2WASTE But on Twitter every post can only be 140 letters long. Which is enough room to cover every interesting thing to ever happen to me.
8:15 AM March 1st from Tweetie

TYME2WASTE True. Check it out.
8:15 AM March 1st from Tweetie

TYME2WASTE Born. School. Mall. Cell phone. Driver's permit. Broke my nose playing trapeze at 8—there goes the modeling career. Need to lose 10 lbs.
8:19 AM March 1st from Tweetie

more

TYME2WASTE Think that covers it.

8:20 AM March 1st from Tweetie

TYME2WASTE It's snowing in the mountains but not down here snow falling in the sunlight in a storm of gold. Goodbye beautiful mountains.

9:17 AM March 1st from Tweetie

TYME2WASTE Hello not so beautiful Utah desert. Utah is brown and puckered like Judy Kennedy's weird nipples.

9:51 AM March 1st from Tweetie

TYME2WASTE @caseinSD Yes she does have weird nipples. And it doesn't make me a lesbo for noticing. Everyone notices.

10:02 AM March 1st from Tweetie

TYME2WASTE Sagebrush!!!!!! W00t!

11:09 AM March 1st from Tweetie

TYME2WASTE Now Eric is trying on my pantyhose. He's bored. Mom thinks its funny but Dad is stressed.

12:20 PM March 1st from Tweetie

TYME2WASTE I dared Eric to wear a skirt in the diner to get our takeout. Dad says no. Mom is still laughing.

12:36 PM March 1st from Tweetie

TYME2WASTE I promised him if he does it I'll invite a certain hot goth to the pool party in April so he can see her in her tacky bikini.

12:39 PM March 1st from Tweetie

TYME2WASTE Theres no way he'll do it.

12:42 PM March 1st from Tweetie

---

more

TYME2WASTE ZOMG hes doing it. Dad is going into the diner with him to make sure he isn't killed by offended Mormons.
12:44 PM March 1st from Tweetie

TYME2WASTE Eric came back alive. Eric saves the day. I'm actually glad to be in the van right now.
12:59 PM March 1st from Tweetie

TYME2WASTE Dad says Eric sat at the bar and talked football with this big trucker guy. Trucker guy was fine with the skirt and pantyhose.
1:03 PM March 1st from Tweetie

TYME2WASTE He's still wearing it. The skirt. He's probably a total closet tranny. Sicko. Course that would be fun. We could shop together.
1:45 PM March 1st from Tweetie

TYME2WASTE @caseinSD Yes we do have to invite a certain goth to the pool party now. She probably won't even come. I think sunlight burns her.
2:09 PM March 1st from Tweetie

TYME2WASTE Every time I start to fall asleep the van hits a bump and my head falls off the seat.
11:01 PM March 1st from Tweetie

TYME2WASTE Trying to sleep.
11:31 PM March 1st from Tweetie

TYME2WASTE I give up trying to sleep.
1:01 AM March 2nd from Tweetie

more

TYME2WASTE Oh fuck Eric. He's asleep and he looks like he's having a wet dream about a certain goth chick.

1:07 AM March 2nd from Tweetie

TYME2WASTE Meanwhile I'd have a better chance of sleeping if there were only steel pins inserted under my eyelids.

1:09 AM March 2nd from Tweetie

TYME2WASTE I'm so happy right now. I just want to hold this moment for as long as I can.

6:11 AM March 2nd from Tweetie

TYME2WASTE I just want to be home. I hate Mom. I hate everyone in the van. Including myself.

8:13 AM March 2nd from Tweetie

TYME2WASTE Okay. This is why I was happy earlier. It was 4 in the morning and Mom pulled into a rest area and then she came and got me.

10:21 AM March 2nd from Tweetie

TYME2WASTE She said it was my turn to drive. I said my permit is only for driving in Cali and she just said get behind the wheel.

10:22 AM March 2nd from Tweetie

TYME2WASTE She told me if I got pulled over to wake her up and we'd switch and everything would be all right.

10:23 AM March 2nd from Tweetie

TYME2WASTE So she went to sleep in the passenger seat and I drove. We were down in the desert and the sun came up behind us.

10:25 AM March 2nd from Tweetie

---

more

TYME2WASTE And then there were coyotes in the road. In the red sunlight. They were all over the interstate and I stopped so I wouldn't hit them.

10:26 AM March 2nd from Tweetie

TYME2WASTE Their eyes were gold and the sun was in their fur and there were so many, this huge pack. Just standing there like they were waiting for me.

10:28 AM March 2nd from Tweetie

TYME2WASTE I wanted to take a picture with my cell phone, but I couldn't figure out where I left it. While I was looking for it they disappeared.

10:31 AM March 2nd from Tweetie

TYME2WASTE When Mom woke up I told her all about them. And then I thought she'd be mad I didn't shake her awake to see them so I said I was sorry.

10:34 AM March 2nd from Tweetie

TYME2WASTE And she said she was glad I didn't wake her up, because that moment was just for me. And for like three seconds I liked her again.

10:35 AM March 2nd from Tweetie

TYME2WASTE But then in the place we ate breakfast I was looking at my e-mail for a sec. & I heard Mom saying to the waitress, we apologize for her.

10:37 AM March 2nd from Tweetie

TYME2WASTE I guess the waitress was standing there waiting for my order and I didn't notice.

10:40 AM March 2nd from Tweetie

----

more

TYME2WASTE But I didn't sleep all night and I was tired and zoned out and that's why I didn't notice, not 'cause I was looking at the phone.

10:42 AM March 2nd from Tweetie

TYME2WASTE And Mom had to trot out her stories about being a waitress herself and that it was demeaning not to be acknowledged.

10:45 AM March 2nd from Tweetie

TYME2WASTE Just to rub it in. And she can be completely right and I can still hate the way she makes me feel like shit at every opportunity.

10:46 AM March 2nd from Tweetie

TYME2WASTE I napped but I don't feel better.

4:55 PM March 2nd from Tweetie

TYME2WASTE Dad of course has to go the slowest possible route by way of every back road. Mom says he missed a turn and added 100 miles to the trip.

6:30 PM March 2nd from Tweetie

TYME2WASTE Now Mom and Dad are fighting. OMG I want out of this van.

6:37 PM March 2nd from Tweetie

TYME2WASTE Eric I am psychically willing you to find some reason for us to get off the road. Put on the pantyhose again. Say you have to pee.

6:49 PM March 2nd from Tweetie

TYME2WASTE Anything. Please.

6:49 PM March 2nd from Tweetie

---

more

TYME2WASTE No no NO Eric, no. When I was sending you psychic signals, I was not signaling to you to pull over for this.
6:57 PM March 2nd from Tweetie

TYME2WASTE Mom doesn't want to pull over either. Write it down, kids, first time in two years we've agreed on anything.
7:00 PM March 2nd from Tweetie

TYME2WASTE Oh Dad is being a prick now. He says there was no point in taking backroads if we weren't going to find some culture.
7:02 PM March 2nd from Tweetie

TYME2WASTE We are driving up to something called the Circus of the Dead. The ticket guy looks really REALLY sick. Not funny sick. SICK sick.
7:06 PM March 2nd from Tweetie

TYME2WASTE Sores around his mouth and few teeth and I can smell him. He's got a pet rat. His pet rat dived in his pocket and came out with the tickets.
7:08 PM March 2nd from Tweetie

TYME2WASTE No it wasn't cute. None of us want to touch the tickets.
7:10 PM March 2nd from Tweetie

TYME2WASTE Boy, they're really packing them in. Show starts in 15min. but the parking lot is 1/2 empty. The big top is a black tent with holes in it.
7:13 PM March 2nd from Tweetie

more

363

TYME2WASTE Mom says to be sure to keep doing whatever I'm doing on my phone. She wouldn't want me to look up and see something happening.
7:17 PM March 2nd from Tweetie

TYME2WASTE Oh that was shitty. She just said to Dad that I'll love the circus because it'll be just like the internet.
7:18 PM March 2nd from Tweetie

TYME2WASTE Youtube is full of clowns, message boards are full of fire-breathers and blogs are for people who can't live without a spotlight on them.
7:20 PM March 2nd from Tweetie

TYME2WASTE I'm going to tweet like 5 times a minute and make her insane.
7:21 PM March 2nd from Tweetie

TYME2WASTE The usher is a funny old Mickey Rooney type with a bowler and a cigar. He also has on a hazmat suit. He says so he can't get bitten.
7:25 PM March 2nd from Tweetie

TYME2WASTE I almost fell twice on the walk to our seats. Guess they're saving $ on lights. I'm using my iPhone as a flash-light. Hope there isn't a fire
7:28 PM March 2nd from Tweetie

TYME2WASTE God this is the stinkiest circus ever. I don't know what I'm smelling. Are those the animals? Call PETA.
7:30 PM March 2nd from Tweetie

more

TYME2WASTE I can't believe how many people there are. Every seat is taken. Don't know where this crowd came from.

7:31 PM March 2nd from Tweetie

TYME2WASTE They must've had us park in a secondary parking lot. Oh, wait, they just flipped on a spotlight. Showtime. Beating heart, restrain yourself.

7:34 PM March 2nd from Tweetie

TYME2WASTE Well that got Eric and Dad's attention. The ringmistress came out on stilts and she's practically naked. Fishnets and top hat.

7:38 PM March 2nd from Tweetie

TYME2WASTE She's weird. She talks like she's stoned. Did I mention there are zombies in clown outfits chasing her around?

7:40 PM March 2nd from Tweetie

TYME2WASTE The zombies are waaay gross. They have on big clown shoes, and polka dot outfits, and clown makeup.

7:43 PM March 2nd from Tweetie

TYME2WASTE But the makeup is flaking off, and beneath it they're all rotted and black. Yow! They almost grabbed her. She's quick.

7:44 PM March 2nd from Tweetie

TYME2WASTE She says she's been a prisoner of the circus for six weeks and that she survived because she learned the stilts fast.

7:47 PM March 2nd from Tweetie

---

more

TYME2WASTE She said her boyfriend couldn't walk on them and fell down and was eaten his first night. She said her best friend was eaten the 2nd night.

7:49 PM March 2nd from Tweetie

TYME2WASTE She walked right up to the wall under us and begged someone to pull her over and rescue her, but the guy in the front row just laughed.

7:50 PM March 2nd from Tweetie

TYME2WASTE Then she had to run away in a hurry before Zippo the Zombie knocked her off her stilts. It's all very well choreographed.

7:50 PM March 2nd from Tweetie

TYME2WASTE You can totally believe they're trying to get her.

7:51 PM March 2nd from Tweetie

TYME2WASTE They rolled a cannon out. She said here at the Circus of the Dead we always begin things with a bang. She read it off a card.

7:54 PM March 2nd from Tweetie

TYME2WASTE She walked up to a tall door and banged on it and for a minute I didn't think they were going to let her out of the ring, but then they did.

7:55 PM March 2nd from Tweetie

TYME2WASTE Two men in hazmat suits just led a zombie out. He's got a metal collar around his neck with a black stick attached.

7:56 PM March 2nd from Tweetie

---

more

TYME2WASTE They're using the stick to hold him at a distance so he can't grab them.

7:57 PM March 2nd from Tweetie

TYME2WASTE Eric says he has fantasies about a certain goth girl putting him in a rig like that.

7:58 PM March 2nd from Tweetie

TYME2WASTE This show would be a great date for the two of them. It's got a hint of sex, a whiff of bondage, and it's really really morbid.

7:59 PM March 2nd from Tweetie

TYME2WASTE They put the zombie in the cannon.

8:00 PM March 2nd from Tweetie

TYME2WASTE Auuuughhh! They pointed the cannon at the crowd and fired it and fucking pieces of zombie went everywhere.

8:03 PM March 2nd from Tweetie

TYME2WASTE The guy in the row in front of us got smashed in the mouth with a flying shoe. He's bleeding and everything.

8:05 PM March 2nd from Tweetie

TYME2WASTE Fucking yuck! There's still a foot inside the shoe! It's totally realistic looking.

8:08 PM March 2nd from Tweetie

TYME2WASTE The guy sitting in front of us just walked off w/his wife to complain. Same dude who laffed at the ringmistress when she asked for help.

8:11 PM March 2nd from Tweetie

-----

more

TYME2WASTE Dad had a zombie lip in his hair. I am so glad I didn't eat lunch. Looks like a gummy worm and it smells like ass.

8:13 PM March 2nd from Tweetie

TYME2WASTE Naturally Eric wants to keep it.

8:13 PM March 2nd from Tweetie

TYME2WASTE Here comes the ringmistress again. She says the next act is the cat's meo

8:14 PM March 2nd from Tweetie

TYME2WASTE OMG OMG that was not funny. She almost fell down and the way they were snarling

8:16 PM March 2nd from Tweetie

TYME2WASTE The men in hazmat suits just wheeled in a lion in a cage. Yay, a lion! I am still girl enough to like a big cat.

8:17 PM March 2nd from Tweetie

TYME2WASTE Oh that's a really sad sick looking lion. Not fun. They're opening the cage and sending in zombies and he's hissing like a housecat.

8:19 PM March 2nd from Tweetie

TYME2WASTE Roawwwwr! Lion power. He's swatting them down and shredding them apart. He's got an arm in his mouth. Everyone cheering.

8:21 PM March 2nd from Tweetie

TYME2WASTE Eeeuuuw. Not so much cheering now. He's got one and he's tugging out its guts like he's pulling on one end of a tug rope.

8:22 PM March 2nd from Tweetie

---

more

TYME2WASTE They're sending in more zombies. No one laughing or cheering now. It's really crowded in there.
8:24 PM March 2nd from Tweetie

TYME2WASTE I can't even see the lion anymore. Lots of angry snarling and flying fur and walking corpses getting knocked around.
8:24 PM March 2nd from Tweetie

TYME2WASTE OH GROSS. The lion made a sound, like this scared whine, and now the zombies are passing around organ meat and hunks of fur.
8:25 PM March 2nd from Tweetie

TYME2WASTE They're eating. That's awful. I feel sick.
8:26 PM March 2nd from Tweetie

TYME2WASTE Dad saw I was getting upset and told me how they did it. The cage has a false bottom. They pulled the lion out through the floor.
8:30 PM March 2nd from Tweetie

TYME2WASTE You really get swept up in this thing.
8:30 PM March 2nd from Tweetie

TYME2WASTE The Mickey Rooney guy who led us back to the seats just showed up with a flashlight. He says we left the headlights on in the van.
8:31 PM March 2nd from Tweetie

TYME2WASTE Eric went to turn them off. He has to pee anyway.
8:32 PM March 2nd from Tweetie

more

TYME2WASTE The fireswallower just came out. He has no eyes and there's some kind of steel contraption forcing his head back and his mouth open.

8:34 PM March 2nd from Tweetie

TYME2WASTE One of the men in the hazmat suits isFUCK ME.

8:35 PM March 2nd from Tweetie

TYME2WASTE They shoved a torch down his throat and now he's burning! He's running around with smoke coming out of his mouth and

8:36 PM March 2nd from Tweetie

TYME2WASTE fire in his head coming out his eyes like a jack o lante

8:36 PM March 2nd from Tweetie

TYME2WASTE They just let him burn to death from the inside out. Realest thing I've ever seen.

8:39 PM March 2nd from Tweetie

TYME2WASTE What's even realer is the corpse after the hazmat guys sprayed it down with the fire extinguishers. It looks so sad and shriveled and black.

8:39 PM March 2nd from Tweetie

TYME2WASTE The ringmistress is back. She's really weaving around. I think something is wrong with her ankle.

8:40 PM March 2nd from Tweetie

TYME2WASTE She says someone from the audience has agreed to be tonight's sacrifice. She says he will be the lucky one.

8:41 PM March 2nd from Tweetie

more

TYME2WASTE He? I thought the sacrifice was usually a girl in this sort of situation.

8:41 PM March 2nd from Tweetie

TYME2WASTE Oh no he did not. They just wheeled Eric out, cuffed to a big wooden wheel. He winked on the way past. Psycho. Go Eric!

8:42 PM March 2nd from Tweetie

TYME2WASTE They hauled out a zombie and chained him to a stake in the dirt. There's a box of hatchets in front of him. Don't like where this is going.

8:43 PM March 2nd from Tweetie

TYME2WASTE Everyone's laughing now. The lion scene was a little grim, but we're back to funny again. The zombie threw the first hatchet into the crowd.

8:45 PM March 2nd from Tweetie

TYME2WASTE There was a thunk, and someone screamed like they got it in the head. Obvious plant.

8:45 PM March 2nd from Tweetie

TYME2WASTE Eric is spinning around and around on the wheel. He's telling the zombie to kill him before he throws up.

8:46 PM March 2nd from Tweetie

TYME2WASTE Eeeks! I'm not as brave as Eric. A knife just banged into the wheel next to his head. Like: INCHES. Eric screamed too. Bet he wishes now

8:47 PM March 2nd from Tweetie

TYME2WASTE OMGOMGO

8:47 PM March 2nd from Tweetie

---

more

TYME2WASTE Okay. He must be okay. He was still smiling when they wheeled him out of the ring. The hatchet went right in the side of his neck.

8:50 PM March 2nd from Tweetie

TYME2WASTE Dad says it's a trick. Dad says he's fine. He says later Eric will come out as a zombie. That it's part of the show.

8:51 PM March 2nd from Tweetie

TYME2WASTE Yep, looks like Dad's right. They've promised Eric will reemerge shortly.

8:53 PM March 2nd from Tweetie

TYME2WASTE Mom is wigging. She wants Dad to check on Eric.

8:54 PM March 2nd from Tweetie

TYME2WASTE She's being kind of crazy. She's talking about how the guy who sat in front of us never came back after he got hit by the shoe.

8:55 PM March 2nd from Tweetie

TYME2WASTE I don't really see what that has to do with Eric. And besides, if I got hit by a flying shoe . . .

8:55 PM March 2nd from Tweetie

TYME2WASTE Okay, Dad is going to check on Eric. Sanity restored.

8:56 PM March 2nd from Tweetie

TYME2WASTE Here comes the ringmistress again. This is why Eric agreed to go backstage. With the fishnets and black panties she's very goth-hot.

8:56 PM March 2nd from Tweetie

---

more

TYME2WASTE She's being weird. She isn't saying anything about the next act. She says if she goes off script they don't let her out of the ring.
8:57 PM March 2nd from Tweetie

TYME2WASTE But she doesn't care. She says she twisted her ankle and she knows tonight is her last night.
8:58 PM March 2nd from Tweetie

TYME2WASTE She says her name is Gail Ross and she went to high school in Plano.
8:59 PM March 2nd from Tweetie

TYME2WASTE She says she was going to marry her boyfriend after college. She says his name was Craig and he wanted to teach.
9:00 PM March 2nd from Tweetie

TYME2WASTE She says she's sorry for all of us. She says they take our cars and dispose of them while we're in the tent.
9:01 PM March 2nd from Tweetie

TYME2WASTE She says 12,000 people vanish every year on the roads with no explanation, their cars turn up empty or not at all and no one will miss us.
9:02 PM March 2nd from Tweetie

TYME2WASTE Creepy stuff. Here's Eric. His zombie makeup is really good. Most of the zombies are black and rotted but he looks like fresh kill.
9:03 PM March 2nd from Tweetie

more

TYME2WASTE Still got the hatchet in the neck. That looks totally fake.
9:03 PM March 2nd from Tweetie

TYME2WASTE He's not very good at being a zombie. He isn't even trying to walk slow. He's really going after her.
9:04 PM March 2nd from Tweetie

TYME2WASTE oh shit I hope that's part of the show. He just knocked her down. Oh Eric Eric Eric. She hit the dirt really, really hard.
9:05 PM March 2nd from Tweetie

TYME2WASTE They're eating her like they ate the lion. Eric is playing with guts. He's so gross. He's going totally method.
9:07 PM March 2nd from Tweetie

TYME2WASTE Gymnastics now. They're making a human pyramid. Or maybe I should say an INhuman pyramid. They're surprisingly good at it. For zombies.
9:10 PM March 2nd from Tweetie

TYME2WASTE Eric is climbing the pyramid like he knows what he's doing. I wonder if they gave him backstage training or
9:11 PM March 2nd from Tweetie

TYME2WASTE He's up high enough to grab the wall around the ring. He's snarling at someone in the front row, just a couple feet from here. Wait
9:13 PM March 2nd from Tweetie

TYME2WASTE no lights fuck thta was stupid whyd they put out the
9:14 PM March 2nd from Tweetie

---

more

TYME2WASTE someones screaming
9:15 PM March 2nd from Tweetie

TYME2WASTE this is really dangerous its so dark and lots of people are screaming and getting up. im mad now you don't do this to people you don't
9:18 PM March 2nd from Tweetie

TYME2WASTE we need help we areacv
9:32 PM March 2nd from Tweetie

TYME2WASTE gtttttgggtttggttttttttgggbbbnnnfrfffgt
9:32 PM March 2nd from Tweetie

TYME2WASTE I cant say anything theyll hear. were beinb ver y qiuet wevegot a plas
10:17 PM March 2nd from Tweetie

TYME2WASTE were off i70 mom says it was exit 331 but we drove a long way the last town we saw was called ucmba
10:19 PM March 2nd from Tweetie

TYME2WASTE cumba
10:19 PM March 2nd from Tweetie

TYME2WASTE the people in the stands were all dead except for us and a few others and they were roped together tethered
10:20 PM March 2nd from Tweetie

TYME2WASTE please someone send help call UT state police not making this up
10:22 PM March 2nd from Tweetie

----

more

TYME2WASTE @caseinSD lease help you know me you know I wouldnt isnta joke
10:23 PM March 2nd from Tweetie

TYME2WASTE have to be quiet so I can't call got the ringer is turned off
10:24 PM March 2nd from Tweetie

TYME2WASTE AZ state police mom says its arizona not UT our van is a white econlein
10:27 PM March 2nd from Tweetie

TYME2WASTE its quiet less screaming now less growling
10:50 PM March 2nd from Tweetie

TYME2WASTE theyre dragging people into piles
10:56 PM March 2nd from Tweetie

TYME2WASTE eating theyre eating them
11:09 PM March 2nd from Tweetie

TYME2WASTE the man who got hit by the shoe earlier walked by but he isn't like he was he hes dead now
11:11 PM March 2nd from Tweetie

TYME2WASTE just mom and me i love my mom shes so brave i love her so much so much i never ment it none of the bad things not one i am with her i am
11:37 PM March 2nd from Tweetie

TYME2WASTE imso csared
11:39 PM March 2nd from Tweetie

more

TYME2WASTE theyresearching to see if anyone is left with flashlights the men in hazmat soups i say go out mom says no
11:41 PM March 2nd from Tweetie

TYME2WASTE were here were waiting for help please forward this to everyone on twitter this is true not an internet prank believe believe believe pleves
12:03 AM March 3rd from Tweetie

TYME2WASTE ohgod it was dad went by mom sat up and said his name and mom and dad and mom and dad
12:09 AM March 3rd from Tweetie

TYME2WASTE notdad oh my oh bnb nnnb ;;/'/.,/;'././/
12:13 AM March 3rd from Tweetie

TYME2WASTE /'/.
12:13 AM March 3rd from Tweetie

TYME2WASTE Were you SCARED by this TWITTER FEED???!?!?
9:17 AM March 3rd from Tweetie

TYME2WASTE The FEAR—and THE FUN—is only just BEGINNING!
9:20 AM March 3rd from Tweetie

TYME2WASTE "THE CIRCUS OF THE DEAD" featuring our newest RINGMISTRESS the SEXY & DARING BLAKE THE BLACK-HEARTED.
9:22 AM March 3rd from Tweetie

TYME2WASTE Watch as our newest QUEEN OF THE TRAPEZE introduces our PERVERSE & PERNICIOUS performers . . .
9:23 AM March 3rd from Tweetie

---

more

TYME2WASTE . . . while DANGLING FROM A ROPE ABOVE THE RAVENOUS DEAD!

9:23 AM March 3rd from Tweetie

TYME2WASTE A CIRCUS so SHOCKING it makes the JIM ROSE CIRCUS look like THE MUPPET SHOW!

9:25 AM March 3rd from Tweetie

TYME2WASTE Now touring with stops in ALL CORNERS OF THE COUNTRY!

9:26 AM March 3rd from Tweetie

TYME2WASTE Visit our Facebook page and join our E-MAIL LIST to find out when we'll be in YOUR AREA.

9:28 AM March 3rd from Tweetie

TYME2WASTE STAY CONNECTED OR YOU DON'T KNOW WHAT YOU'LL MISS!

9:30 AM March 3rd from Tweetie

TYME2WASTE "THE CIRCUS OF THE DEAD" . . . Where YOU are the concessions! Other circuses promise DEATH-DEFYING THRILLS!

9:31 AM March 3rd from Tweetie

TYME2WASTE BUT ONLY WE DELIVER! (Tix to be purchased at box office day of show. No refunds. Cash only. Minors must be accompanied by adult.)

9:31 AM March 3rd from Tweetie

THE CONTRIBUTORS

KELLEY ARMSTRONG is the author of the Women of the Otherworld paranormal suspense series, the Darkest Powers YA urban fantasy trilogy, and the Nadia Stafford crime series. She grew up in Ontario, Canada, where she still lives with her family.

AIMEE BENDER is the author of three books; the most recent is the story collection *Willful Creatures*. Her short fiction has been published in *Granta, Harper's Magazine, The Paris Review, Tin House*, and more, as well as heard on PRI's *This American Life*. She lives in L.A. and teaches creative writing at USC.

STEPHEN R. BISSETTE has won many industry awards as a cartoonist, writer, editor, and publisher. A pioneer graduate of the Joe Kubert School of Cartoon and Graphic Art, he currently teaches at the Center for Cartoon Studies and is renowned for *Saga of the Swamp Thing, Taboo* (in which *From Hell* and *Lost Girls* were originally published), *1963, S. R. Bissette's Tyrant®*, and cocreating the character John Constantine. He illustrates books and has authored fiction (including the Bram Stoker Award–winning *Aliens: Tribes*) and nonfiction (*Comic Book Rebels, Buffy the Vampire Slayer: The Monster Book*, and more). His papers reside in Huie Library's Special Collections at Henderson State University in Arkadelphia, Arkansas. He most recently coauthored *Prince of Stories: The Many Worlds of Neil Gaiman* and illustrated *The Vermont Monster Guide* (by Joseph A. Citro). Visit his Web site at www.srbissette.com.

MAX BROOKS's *The Zombie Survival Guide* formed the core of the world's civilian survival manuals during the Zombie War. Mr. Brooks subsequently spent years traveling to every part of the globe in order to conduct the face-to-face interviews that have been incorporated into *World War Z*, which was a *New York Times* bestseller.

MIKE CAREY is the author of the Felix Castor novels, published in the U.S. by Orbit, and of a great many comic book series. He is probably best known for his unbroken run on Lucifer, a sequel of sorts to Neil Gaiman's The Sandman, but he has also written the Fantastic Four, Daredevil, Hellblazer, Vampirella, and Red Sonja. He is currently writing X-Men Legacy for Marvel and The Unwritten for DC's Vertigo Comics, as well as doing game design for Electronic Arts and working on the sixth Castor novel.

JOHN CONNOLLY was born in Dublin in 1968. He is the author of twelve books, the latest of which, *The Lovers* and *The Gates*, will be published in 2009. For further information, visit his Web site at www.johnconnollybooks.com.

CHRISTOPHER GOLDEN previously edited three volumes of Hellboy short stories and coedited the anthology *British Invasion*. He is the author of such novels as *The Myth Hunters, The Boys Are Back in Town, Of Saints and Shadows,* and (with Tim Lebbon) *The Map of Moments*. Golden cowrote the lavishly illustrated novel *Baltimore, or, The Steadfast Tin Soldier and the Vampire* with Mike Mignola. He has also written books for teens and young adults, including the zombie novel *Soulless* and the thriller series Body of Evidence. He has also written short stories, novellas, articles, video games, nonfiction books, and scripts for film and television. Golden was born and raised in Massachusetts, where he still lives with his family. His original novels have been published in more than fourteen languages in countries around the world. Please visit his Web site at www.christophergolden.com.

RICK HAUTALA, under his own name and the pseudonym A. J. Matthews, has published more than thirty novels and story collections, including the million-copy bestseller *Nightstone*, and more than fifty short stories in a variety of national and international magazines and anthologies. He is currently cowriting *Graffito*, a Web series, with Mark Steensland, who has also directed award-winning films based on his scripts, including *Peekers*, *Lovecraft's Pillow*, and *The Ugly File*. He lives in Maine. You can visit his Web site at www.rickhautala.com.

JOE HILL's first book was the Bram Stoker Award–winning story collection *20th Century Ghosts* (PS Publishing). He followed it with the *New York Times* best-selling novel *Heart-Shaped Box* and an Eisner Award–nominated comic, *Locke & Key*. You can find him on Twitter under the name joe_hill.

M. B. HOMLER is a writer and editor living in New York City. He works with many terrific authors and is working on a novel.

BRIAN KEENE is the author of more than twenty books, including *Urban Gothic*, *Castaways*, *Ghost Walk*, *Dark Hollow*, *Kill Whitey*, *Unhappy Endings*, *Dead Sea,* and many more. He also writes comic books for Marvel Comics and others. Several of his novels and stories have been optioned for film, one of which, *The Ties That Bind*, premiered in 2009, and another of which, *Dark Hollow*, is in postproduction. The winner of two Bram Stoker Awards, Keene's work has been praised in such diverse places as the *New York Times*, the History Channel, the *Howard Stern Show*, CNN.com, *Publishers Weekly,* *Fangoria* magazine, and *Rue Morgue* magazine. Keene lives in Pennsylvania with his wife, son, dog, and cat. You can communicate with him online at www.briankeene.com.

JOE R. LANSDALE is the author of more than thirty novels and two hundred short stories and articles. His work has received the Edgar Award, seven Bram Stoker Awards, the British Fantasy Award, the Herodotus Award, two *New York Times* Notable Book Awards, and many others. His novella *Bubba Ho-Tep* was made into a film of the same name, and his story "Incident On and Off a Mountain Road" was made into a film for Showtime's *Masters of Horror*. His most recent releases are the novel *Vanilla Ride*, a Hap and Leonard adventure, and *The Portable Lansdale: Sanctified and Chicken Fried*. He lives in Nacogdoches, Texas.

TIM LEBBON is a *New York Times* bestselling writer from South Wales. He's had almost twenty novels published to date, including *The Island, The Map of Moments* (with Christopher Golden), *Fallen, Hellboy: The Fire Wolves, Dusk,* and *Bar None,* as well as scores of novellas and short stories. He has won three British Fantasy Awards, a Bram Stoker Award, and a Scribe Award, and has also been a finalist for International Horror Guild and World Fantasy Awards. Several of his novels and novellas are currently in development for the screen in the U.S. and UK. Find out more about Tim at his Web site www.timlebbon.net.

DAVID LISS is the author of six novels, most recently *The Devil's Company.* He has five previous best-selling novels: *A Conspiracy of Paper,* winner of the 2000 Edgar Award for Best First Novel by an American Author, *The Coffee Trader, A Spectacle of Corruption, The Ethical Assassin,* and *The Whiskey Rebels.* In 2008, at the United Nations Convention against Corruption in Bali, Indonesia, he was named an Artist for Integrity by the United Nations Office on Drugs and Crime. No one is really sure why he should receive this honor or what it means, but it very possibly makes him the Bono of historical fiction. David Liss's novels have been translated into more than two dozen languages. He lives in San Antonio with his wife and children, and can be reached via his Web site, www.davidliss.com.

JONATHAN MABERRY is the multiple Bram Stoker Award–winning author of *Patient Zero, Ghost Road Blues, Zombie CSU, They Bite!* and *The Wolfman,* among others. He is the regular writer for Marvel Comics Black Panther and has written stories for Wolverine, Spider-Man, Punisher, and Marvel Zombies. Jonathan has sold more than twelve hundred feature articles, numerous short stories, plays, video scripts, song lyrics, twenty nonfiction books, and several novels. He is president of the Pennsylvania/New Jersey chapter of the Horror Writers Association and a contributing editor for *The Big Thrill,* the monthly newsletter of the International Thriller Writers. He is also the cocreator of *On the Slab,* a horror entertainment news show in development for Disney/ABC. Jonathan is an eighth-degree black belt in jujutsu and in 2004 was inducted into the International Martial Arts Hall of Fame. Find his Web site at www.jonathanmaberry.com.

JAMES A. MOORE is the author of more than twenty novels, including the critically acclaimed *Fireworks, Under The Overtree, Blood Red*, the Serenity Falls trilogy (featuring his recurring antihero, Jonathan Crowley), and *Deeper*. He has twice been nominated for the Bram Stoker Award and spent three years as an officer in the Horror Writers Association, first as secretary and later as vice president. Moore's first short story collection, *Slices,* sold out before ever seeing print. He recently finished his latest novel, *Smile No More*, a story of Rufo the Clown. His latest Jonathan Crowley novel, *Cherry Hill*, is slated for release in 2009. He lives in the suburbs of Atlanta, Georgia, with his wife, Bonnie, and their menagerie, which includes one dog, four cats, eight ducks, many fish, and a parrot named Dos. Please drop by his Web site at www.jimshorror.com or leave him a note on his bulletin board at www.horrorworld.org.

HOLLY NEWSTEIN's short fiction has appeared in *Cemetery Dance* magazine and *Borderlands 5* anthology. She is the coauthor of the novels *Ashes* and *The Epicure*, published by Berkley Books under the pen name H. R. Howland. She lives in Maine with the author Rick Hautala.

DEREK NIKITAS is the author of the novel *Pyres* (St. Martin's Minotaur, 2007) nominated for a Best First Novel Edgar Allan Poe Award. His second novel with St. Martin's Minotaur, *The Long Division,* will be published in October 2009. His short stories have appeared in *Ontario Review, Chelsea, Ellery Queen Mystery Magazine, New South*, and *The Pedestal Magazine*, among other publications. He has received a nomination for a Pushcart Prize and a 2007 fellowship to the Sewanee Writers' Conference. He received his MFA in creative writing from the University of North Carolina at Wilmington and is currently teaching creative writing in the brief-residency MFA program at Eastern Kentucky University.

DAVID WELLINGTON is the author of seven novels. His zombie novels *Monster Island, Monster Nation*, and *Monster Planet* (Thunder's Mouth Press) form a complete trilogy. He has also written a series of vampire novels, including (so far) *13 Bullets, 99 Coffins, Vampire Zero*, and *23 Hours* (Three Rivers Press). As an undergraduate he